The Paris Contagion

By

C A Farlow

FARALLON GROUP

Other Books by the CA Farlow

The Nexus Series – ARC 1, Books 1-3

Published by Spectrum Books, London

A Quantum Convergence

A Quantum Uncertainty

A Quantum Singularity

<u>Forthcoming</u>

Quantum Time, Nexus Series ARC 2, Book 1

GeoPolitical Thrillers

Published by Farallon Group, US

<u>Forthcoming</u>

Deflection

A Farallon Group Trade Paperback

DEDICATION

For all the women and men who fight to preserve our democracy
and our freedoms,
who protect the safety of our country and the world,
who strive for world peace,
whether in active duty on the front lines or
beneath the cloak of secrecy.

To JP for your support and encouragement
through another long project.

FOREWORD

This book deals with the here and now, with fact and a little bit of fiction, with a story which could be taken from tomorrow's headlines published in the world's news services.

Future conflicts will arise over resources: food, potable water, energy reserves, arable land, or class disparities. They will be fought from a distance with drones or up close by terrorists (whether domestic or foreign). Terrorists will become a threat to world safety.

Biological, chemical, and nuclear weapons will be deployed by the unrecognized or power hungry to gain control, suppress ideologies, or gain world recognition. These weapons and their precursors will be available to anyone who can pay.

Those working within research facilities around the globe, may be tempted to steal, use and/or sell bio-agents, weapon designs, and other technical advances to the highest bidders.

Despots, dictators, and autocratic leaders will rise and buy these weapons or technical advances for their own gain. They will have no moral objection using them against countries they deem "enemies of the state" or their own citizenry.

AUTHOR'S NOTE REGARDING TIME

As events occur simultaneously around the globe, a twenty-four hour military clock in Coordinated Universal Time (UTC) provides event correlation. Readers can compare local time to UTC and to the time in other locales as the story unfolds.

UTC is the world's time standard and the modern equivalent of Greenwich Mean Time (GMT). It begins and ends in Greenwich, England (UTC=0). UTC adds one hour per time zone moving east from Greenwich. One hour is subtracted moving west. The International Dateline is twelve hours away from Greenwich on the opposite side of the globe.

For the reader, the following time key is provided to quickly correlate time zones:

- If it is Midnight in Greenwich, England (UTC=00:00) UTC+0
- Moving east, it's one hour later in London, England (01:00) UTC+1
- Moving east, it's two hours later in Paris, France (02:00) UTC+2
- Continuing east, it's nine hours later in Seoul, South Korea (09:00) UTC+9
- The International Dateline is twelve hours east of Greenwich, England (12:00) UTC+12
- Amundsen-Scott Base, Antarctica, is one hour east of the International Dateline, or thirteen hours east of Greenwich, England (13:00) UTC+13
- Moving west from Greenwich, England, it's four hours earlier in Washington, DC (20:00 - evening before) UTC-4

A Time Zone Chart is provided on the next page to correlate events happening, concurrently, around the world.

Hrs+/-	TimeZone																								
UTC	UTC	Day1 12AM	1	2	3	4	5	6	7	8	9	10	11	12PM	1	2	3	4	5	6	7	8	9	10	11
0	Greenwich, UK	Day1 12AM	1	2	3	4	5	6	7	8	9	10	11	12PM	1	2	3	4	5	6	7	8	9	10	11
+1	London, UK	1AM	2	3	4	5	6	7	8	9	10	11	12PM	1	2	3	4	5	6	7	8	9	10	11	Day2 12AM
+2	Paris, FR	2AM	3	4	5	6	7	8	9	10	11	12PM	1	2	3	4	5	6	7	8	9	10	11	Day2 12AM	1
+9	Seoul, ROK	9AM	10	11	12PM	1	2	3	4	5	6	7	8	9	10	11	Day2 12AM	1	2	3	4	5	6	7	8
+13	Amundsen-Scott	1PM	2	3	4	5	6	7	8	9	10	11	Day2 12AM	1	2	3	4	5	6	7	8	9	10	11	12PM
-4	Washington DC	Day0 8PM	9	10	11	Day1 12AM	1	2	3	4	5	6	7	8	9	10	11	12PM	1	2	3	4	5	6	7
-6	Denver, CO	Day0 6PM	7	8	9	10	11	Day1 12AM	1	2	3	4	5	6	7	8	9	10	11	12PM	1	2	3	4	5

NOTE: The shaded areas indicate nighttime hours.

MAPS

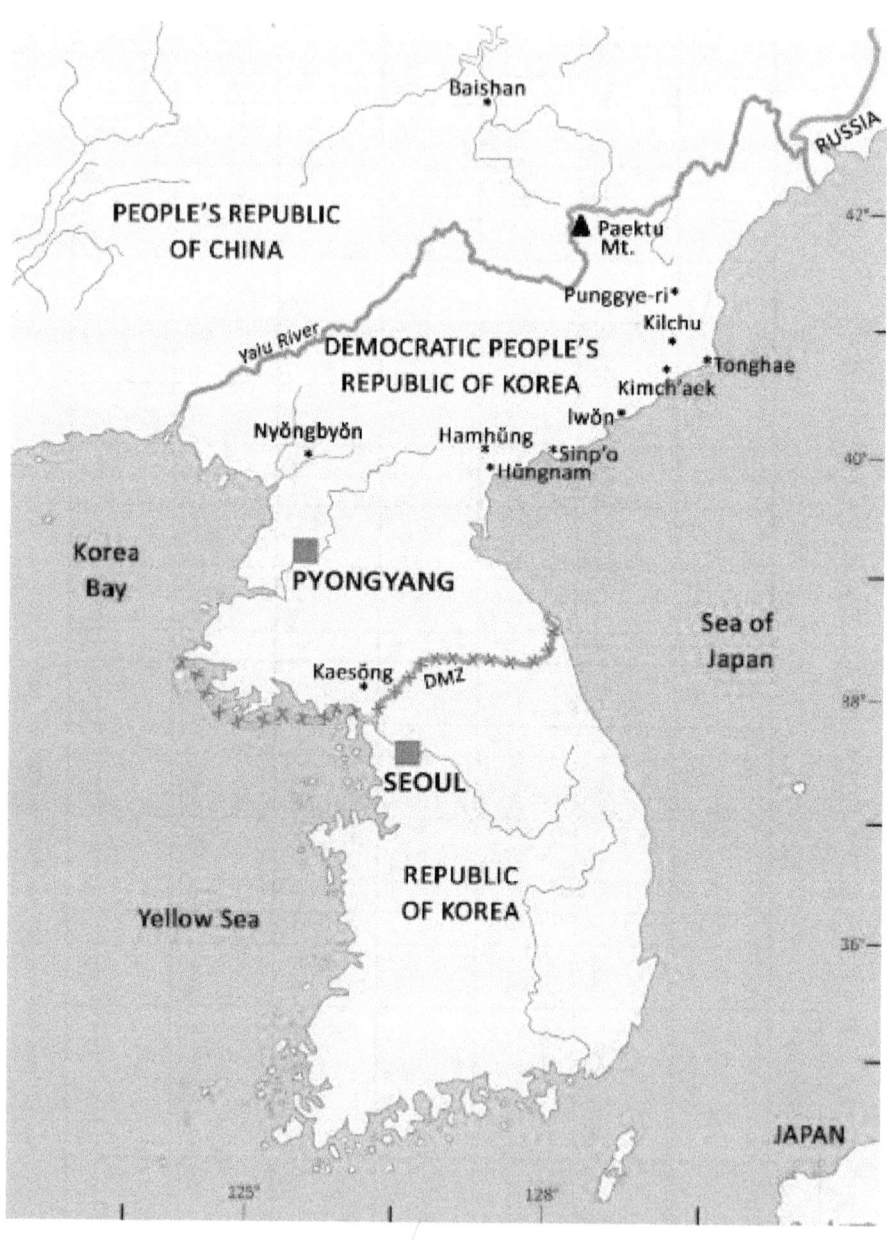

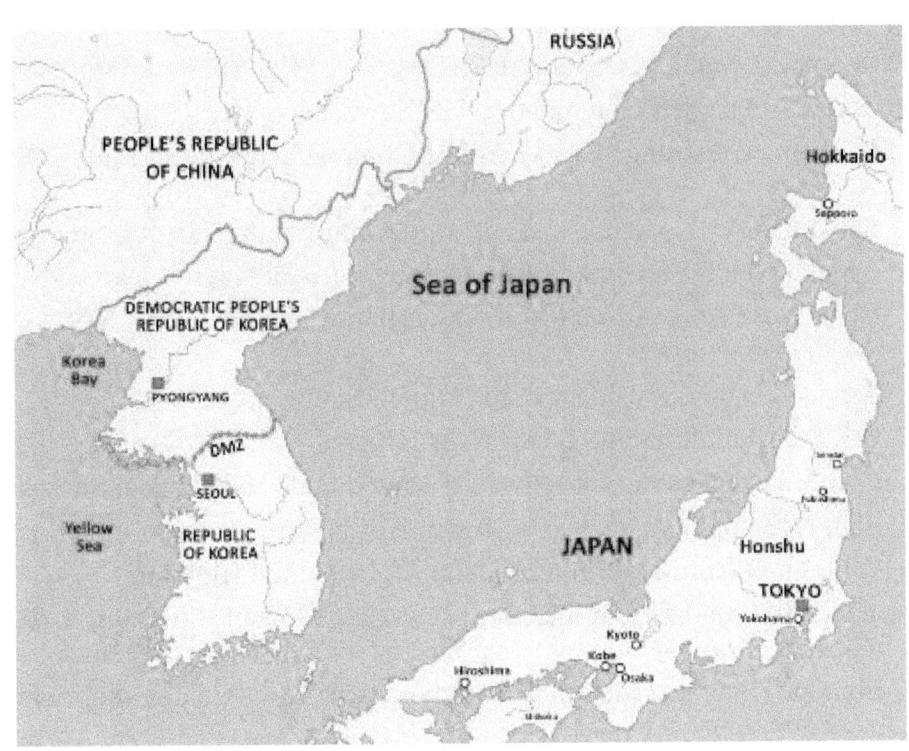

ENSEMBLE CAST
In Order of Appearance

Cassandra Stanley, Captain, US Navy

James Alexander, Commander, US Navy

William Armstrong, Vice Admiral-Commander, Pacific Fleet, US Navy

Samantha A. S. Michaels, Analyst, Central Intelligence Agency

Amelia Grant, Lieutenant, Her Majesty's Royal Navy

Charles Benson, Admiral-US Navy, then Chair of Joint Chiefs of the US Military

Amanda Haley, President of the United States

Pak Sung-un, Supreme Leader North Korea

Cynthia Brockstone, Geophysicist United States Geological Survey

Kim Hye-su, Lead nuclear scientist, North Korea

William O'Rourke, Prime Minister of the United Kingdom

Tabitha Aronoff, Commander, US Navy, Chief Surgeon, *USS Arlington*

Francis Douglas, Metallurgic Laboratory, Los Alamos National Laboratory

Julia Alexander, MD, Commander James Alexander's mother

Bong Sok-mun, North Korean Assembly

Stephen Nelson, Commander, US Navy Pilot

Choi Myung-yong, President of South Korea

Ri Ae-Cha, MD, North Korea

Beatrice Taylor, US Presidential Private Secretary

Deidre Williams, MD Epidemiologist

René Auberguist, MD, Ph.D., Epidemiologist

Jason McAllister, Chief, Amundsen-Scott Base, Antarctica

Pak Jong-nam, elder brother of North Korea's Supreme Leader Pak

Sung-un

Liu Qishan, President of the People's Republic of China

Walter Jackson, Chief-Presidential Security Detail, US Secret Service

Melissa Hirsch, Captain, US Navy

George Talley, MD, General, US Army Medical Corps

Andrew Ratcliffe, MD, DARPA

Jackson Montgomery, US Navy Drone Pilot

Steven Carlson, Lieutenant Commander, US Navy

Michael Harston, Captain, US Navy *USS Princeton*

Isaac Gordon, Commander, Her Majesty's Royal Navy, *HMS Unicorn*

Felicity Barker, Chief-Presidential Security Detail, US Secret Service

Maggie Gee, Pembrook Welsh Corgi

Halsey, Pembrook Welsh Corgi

Nimitz, Pembrook Welsh Corgi

Elizabeth, Pembrook Welsh Corgi

PLEASE NOTE: A glossary of military terms and abbreviations is included at the back of the book.

SECTION ONE

2 November, 07:04 Hours Local (UTC 22:04, 1 November)
The Sea of Japan (East Sea)
Combined Wargames—Japan, South Korea, US Fleets
Command Deck, *USS Arlington*
CGN-47, Ticonderoga-class Guided Missile Cruiser

"BATTLE STATIONS. ALL HANDS—BATTLE STATIONS. THIS IS NOT A DRILL." The automated warning repeated as Captain Cassandra Stanley burst onto the command deck of her boat. Passive sensor systems within the Command Information Center (CIC) four decks below detected a missile launch.

"Report!" she barked swinging into her command chair and activating the armrest displays.

"Captain, CIC reports the launch of a long-range, ballistic missile. Trajectory is south, southeast. It should pass directly over our heads in approximately two-point-one minutes. Early estimated launch coordinates are 41°17'50" N, 129°0'50" E," her chief petty officer of the watch summarized.

Stanley rubbed her chin, wondering what was happening. Data began to fill her small screen. Green blips for friendlies and red flashing icons for hostiles. The *Arlington* was a hidden asset in the wargames the US fleet was assigned to. Her ship was ordered to remain within a large low-pressure system building over the northern Sea of Japan. The sea-level cloud deck visually masked the cruiser from satellite surveillance. They were running in complete passive mode, no active transmissions, all anti-radar stealth systems operating at maximum, creating an electronic-blackout zone around her ship—a proverbial hole in the ocean. No one but Admiral Armstrong, commander of the US Pacific Fleet (USPACFLT), knew their deployment orders: stay north of latitude 40° north and west of longitude 131° east, stay dark, passively monitor the wargames, only intercede if Japan utilizes its new cruise missile system. If a Japanese launch is detected, the *Arlington* was to go active and test their AEGIS Ballistic Missile Defense Systems (ABMD) against Japan's new toys. The *Arlington* was a rogue, acting as an ace up the admiral's sleeve.

The Japanese fleet was over five hundred miles south-southeast of the *Arlington* being chased northeast by a pack of US nuclear attack submarines. The Japanese fleet hadn't so much as sneezed, let alone launched any new weapons. It was all they could do to evade the sub-surface hunters and survive to continue the games.

"Plot the launch coordinates and missile trajectory on the board, and bring up the birds. But quietly, James. Let's not flare our position yet."

"Aye, ma'am." Commander James Alexander, her tall, blonde executive officer, turned and spoke into his mic. "CIC bring the birds online, take over control of satellites alpha one through four. Zero alignment with the coastline and our plotted course."

He nodded as an acknowledgement was relayed from the CIC. "Birds are tracking now. We should have an active plot."

Captain Stanley turned to the large plexiglass board bisecting her command deck. The board contained a combination of digital and analog data: digital plots of all military and commercial maritime ships, including their courses, and analog grease-pencil notations of miscellaneous data. The petty officer of the deck was currently sketching an extension of the missile's trajectory across the Sea of Japan. Her dashed line crossed directly over the *Arlington* and continued south over Tokyo and on, toward Indonesia and Australia. This missile was a threat and presented a clear and present danger to allies of the United States.

Stanley sat up straight, as her mind sorted various scenarios, discarding some, keeping others, combining the ones with the highest probability of success. The entire time, she never took her eyes off the flashing crimson circle which enclosed the launch site. The coastal town of Iwŏn, Democratic People's Republic of Korea, lay in its center. What were the North Koreans up to now?

"Bring AEGIS online, take systems out of standby, actively track that missile. Prepare to fire tubes one and three as the missile passes onto our port side." She turned her chair to the helmsman. "Bring us about to heading two-seven-zero. Put us into the waves."

Commander Alexander looked at her with a frown, but a small shake of her head stopped his questions. He never hesitated as he passed on the appropriate orders to activate their AEGIS Ballistic Missile Defense Systems. "Going hot, I repeat, we will be hot in twenty seconds."

"Course on two-seven-zero, Skip. Speed two-two knots," the helmsman reported.

"Thank you." She felt the deck lurch under her as the 560 foot cruiser rolled through the troughs of thirty-foot seas, kicked up by the weather system they were headed farther into. Waves began to crash over the bow of the *Arlington* as she turned into the teeth of the oncoming storm. Cassie faced back to the navigation board as the *Arlington* settled into her new heading.

The petty officer of the deck acknowledged the orders from missile control. "CIC is switching to active tracking. We have a plot." The digital data on the large plexiglass board wavered for a second and resolved into a detailed picture of their position and the flightpath of the overarching missile. The analog data was erased with a swipe of a cloth, and the petty officer stepped back from the board as the *Arlington's* active systems took over the plotting duties. A stream of data on the velocity, altitude, trajectory, and attitude of the missile scrolled down the left side of the board. All this information was used by the captain and her executive officer to visually differentiate a commercial aircraft from a true ballistic missile. This check and balance system was added after a US Guided Missile Cruiser shot down an Iranian commercial airliner when it was mistaken for an attacking Iranian F-14 Tomcat in 1988.

Commander Alexander stepped up to Captain Stanley's chair and leaned over the broad arm. Although he made it look as if he was checking the plot data on one of her active displays, he was hiding his discussion with the captain. He whispered, "What the hell, Skip? What's going on?"

She replied with barely a twitch of her lips as she crossed her legs and leaned back into her chair. "Looks like the North Koreans are testing their mettle in protest of the fleet's wargames cruising in 'their' sea." Stanley ran a hand through her close-cropped chestnut hair and over her mouth as she elaborated. "That missile is headed to Tokyo Did you see gunny's plot?" Out of the corner of her eye, she saw him nod slightly, her focus on the board.

She noticed his frown, "We don't have a choice, James. We're in line with the flightpath, and we can bring it down out here—safely, away from landfall and any civilian population. The rest of the fleet is too close to Japan to successfully intercept."

"We'll light up like a flare if we fire."

"Already have, as soon as we went active."

He nodded again and stepped back. Tilting his head to the side, she knew he was listening to status reports coming in over his earbud. Stanley hated the clutter of background noise created by overlapping information, orders, and acknowledgements going back and forth between command deck personnel, and CIC. So, she kept all her deck hands, officers included, in communication by using earbuds and throat mics. That way there was no possibility that one of her orders would not be heard or misunderstood.

Captain Cassandra Stanley commanded one of the most powerful multifunctional warships in the US Navy with enough firepower to wipe out a small city or fleet. The *Arlington* carried a full complement of Tomahawk cruise missiles and long-range antiaircraft missiles, in addition to her AEGIS Combat System, and, unknown to most, several nuclear-tipped warheads which could be loaded on the Tomahawks.

The AEGIS system was capable of detecting and destroying intercontinental ballistic missiles as they reentered the earth's atmosphere. First designed as part of the Strategic Defense Initiative or Star Wars program during the Reagan-era, this system used passive as well as active integrated radar systems to track and launch satellite-guided intercepting missiles. Her ship also carried a sonar system with a full complement of depth charges and torpedoes—conventional and nuclear—which allowed them to track and disable submarines. Threats from above or below could be neutralized. The *Arlington* was one strong lady.

"Ten seconds to overflight," her CPO reported.

"Prepare to fire on my mark."

"Aye, Skip," her firing officer, a newly minted ensign, replied as she flipped open a clear cover and held her finger above the underlying button. Stanley ignored the slight quiver in the officer's voice. First time anyone pushes the big red button in an active conflict situation always brought out the nerves.

"In five, four, three, two, one, the bird is overhead." The CPO said. The captain began to count in her head. *Four, three, two.*

"Fire One." She paused for two heartbeats to allow the first of her AEGIS missiles to clear the below-deck launch tube. "Fire Three!" her voice commanded as the exterior windows darkened automatically to block out the brilliance of her missiles' flaming contrails.

Stanley sat rigid. Her ice blue eyes never left the active plot on the navigation board. Now two white lines were streaking toward the red arc in hopes of intercepting the ICBM headed southeast toward Tokyo.

"Ma'am communication from Admiral Armstrong, priority one, your eyes only."

"Hold one, comm," Stanley said. Under her breath, she urged, "Come on. I know you can do it."

When the white lines intersected the red, the red arc vanished. Only one white line continued south. "Self-destruct on bird three. I repeat, self-destruct on bird three," the executive officer ordered. Several seconds later, the remaining white line terminated as bird three winked out of existence.

The captain stood from her chair and surveyed the bridge of her beloved cruiser. "Well done, everyone. Resume prior course. I'll have a new one shortly." She strode from the deck and entered her day cabin, aft of the command dais. The ship rolled beneath her feet as the *Arlington* turned back across the waves again.

Dropping into her chair, Stanley entered her code into the desktop display and pulled up the communique from Admiral Armstrong: *Report to carrier immediately.* Short and sweet as always. She punched a stud on her desk. "James?"

"Aye, ma'am."

"Prep one of the helicopters for a hop to the carrier."

There was a pause before he acknowledged her command. "Ten minutes. It will be a rough ride, Captain. And a full survival suit is recommended, given the water temperature is thirty-three degrees."

"I understand. I'll pack a change of clothes." Stanley released the comm stud and whispered to herself, "Rough trip indeed." She didn't know what she was going to face, but launching her AEGIS missles without permission was going to be trouble.

1 November, 18:14 Hours Local (22:14 UTC)
Sublevel 4, CIA Headquarters
Langley, Virginia, United States

Colonel Samantha A. S. Michaels, US Marine Corps (retired) sat at her oaken desk in her office. Dark shadows lurked in the corners of this subterranean space. A halo of incandescent light from a single gooseneck lamp illuminated the desk's marred surface. She sat tilted back in a matching oak office chair, eyes rapidly scanning the material in her lap. Her feet rested on the corner of her desk, ankles crossed. Her highly polished black leather loafers reflected the warm yellow light from her lamp.

Colonel Michaels was dressed in black and blended into the shadows. Sharply creased Armani trousers covered her long legs. A high-collared, black silk shirt draped over her strong shoulders, tucked neatly into the trousers. A narrow black belt, a perfect match to her loafers, wrapped around her waist, its silver buckle winking in the light with each breath. Peeking from the hem of her trousers, red socks, traced with silver web-pattern designs, added a spot of color to her black-on-black ensemble.

On the desk, sitting within the circle of soft yellow light, was a haphazard stack of black and white satellite images. An old-fashioned silver and gray stereoscopic viewer stood open on its wire bipod legs. A yellow legal pad, divided into a hand-drawn grid of columns and rows, was partially filled with numbers and object descriptors. A cerulean-enameled Monte Blanc fountain pen rested on the pad. The sapphire embedded in the clip sparkled in the yellow light.

Without warning her office door was thrown open. Harsh white light from the hall's overhead fluorescent fixtures flooded the room. Sam squinted at the intruder as her reading was interrupted. Her eyebrow rose as she recognized her lieutenant haloed in the glowing doorway.

"Colonel, excuse me for interrupting your reading," an upper-class, Oxford-educated British voice said. "We have a priority request." The young lieutenant seemed to be struggling to contain her amusement. Lieutenant Amelia Grant was on loan to Sam from the Royal Navy and their Office of Naval Intelligence.

"Problems, Lieutenant?" the colonel's rich contralto questioned.

The dark-haired lieutenant snapped to attention, her five-foot-five-inch frame rigid. "Ma'am, no ma'am."

"At ease, Grant." Colonel Michaels rocked forward and lowered her feet slowly to the floor, placing her reading on the desk. Illuminated in the circle of light was the cover of a vintage October 1956 DC Comic book, volume #233. She placed her hand reverently on its protective plastic cover. This issue was the first appearance of Katherine (Kate to her friends) Kane, aka Batwoman, from their Batman series. The authors originally conceived her character to dispel rumors of Batman's homosexuality. She looked down at the comic and chuckled to herself at the absurdity of such a creation. Batwoman came out as a lesbian when she reappeared in her own series in 2014. The comic book, like the other items on the desk, were relics of times past—antiques, seen mostly in galleries, museums, or private collections. Outdated and out of time, but useful when the need arose.

Sam placed herself in that category as well. She too was a relic of times past. Not one piece of modern technology was ever found within the confines of her office. She was methodical and worked alone. She visually-inspected every image before drawing any conclusions, as she was taught to do by the World War II veterans of Operation Crossbow, who trained Sam in stereoscopic image analysis. These men and women, working at Bletchley Park, identified and targeted the launch sites of Germany's deadly V2 rockets. Their stereoscopic analyses saved thousands during the later years of the war.

Looking up at the young woman still hovering in the doorway, Colonel Michaels invited her in. "Come on in, Grant. Let's see what has the director's knickers in a wad this time." Her voice filled the small cold space.

The lieutenant entered as the door swung shut on its self-closing hinges, plunging the room back into darkness. Her aide stepped up to the desk and placed a manila folder on top of the comic. Written on the outside of the folder in bold red print were the words:

TOP SECRET-EYES ONLY
SITE: 41°17'52.8" N, 129°0'54" E

The colonel's eyebrows rose to her hairline as she read the geolocation on the cover of the file. She reached out a hand and opened the folder, exposing a pair of black and white satellite images clipped to the left cover and a one-page, single-spaced report on the right. A newspaper clipping sat loose in the folder. "Have you had a look, Grant?"

"No, ma'am. I just received the file. I was up in the AD's office filing your last study when the director's assistant handed me this. She said the director needed your analysis yesterday." The young lieutenant pointed at the file. "Seems this is a priority request from the National Security Council. So, I headed back down here, double quick."

"Of course she did, of course he does, of course they do." Sam laughed to herself. Everyone wanted something yesterday. She pulled the images out and reached for her viewer.

The phone on Colonel Michael's desk rang, interrupting her review of the satellite images. Without looking up from the stereoscopic viewer, she reached out and punched the speaker button. "Yes?"

"Ma'am, we have a missile launch detected. NORAD (North American Aerospace Defense Command Headquarters, under Cheyenne Mountain, Colorado) has reported a ballistic missile launch at 22:04 UTC from a mobile platform outside the city of Iwŏn, DPRK."

Lieutenant Grant inhaled sharply. The colonel looked up. Grant settled into one of the chairs facing Sam's desk.

"Trajectory?" Sam asked.

The response was immediate. "South-southeast on a flightpath to Tokyo." Sam rocked back in her chair as if sucker punched. "Hold one," the caller stated.

Again, looking at Grant, Sam raised an eyebrow in question. The lieutenant shrugged. The caller came back on the line. "We have reports of an AEGIS system going active. I repeat, an AEGIS system is active and has launched its guided missiles. Two birds are away."

"Which ship?" Sam mentally called up a map of the area and the ongoing US wargames. She couldn't understand why anyone would fire a ballistic missile in that region. She had just been looking at the satellite images of the nuclear test facility in Punggye-ri, North Korea. Is this launch a coincidence? Is the United States being suckered into an active conflict situation? The caller didn't immediately answer, probably still receiving telemetry from the satellites.

"Looks like the *Arlington*."

Sam looked at Grant again and cocked her head in question.

Grant answered, "The wargames are still active in the area, ma'am. The *Arlington* is Captain Stanley's boat."

Sam knew whose boat it was. She tilted her chair back and placed her feet on the corner of her desk. One slim finger tapped her bottom lip as she waited for more information from the secure monitor room.

Moments later, an excited voice burst from Sam's telephone speaker: "ICBM down. I repeat, splash one missile."

"Thank NORAD for me and send down any satellite images you have of the launch site and destruction zone." Sam disconnected the call.

What was Cassie playing at? Sam wondered. Activating the AEGIS system without authorization in a time of peace would create hell up and down the chain of command. AEGIS had never been fired in a combat situation before. Did this constitute a combat situation? Sam rapidly put the pieces together—a hostile missile was fired at an ally's country—yes, Cassie did the right thing regardless of the ramifications of the launch.

Sitting up again, Sam asked, "Grant, what assets do we have in the area for search and recovery of any debris?"

Her aide pulled a small handheld unit from her rear pocket and thumbed the device to life. Sam raised an eyebrow at this blatant use of technology. Technology which could be hacked even within the Faraday cage of her office. Her aide held up the small pad. "Fully stand alone, manual data entry only. It's nothing more than a digital notepad, ma'am."

"Be that as it may, no more tech in this office, lieutenant."

"Yes, ma'am." Grant scrolled on her device. "Two hunter-killer Victoria-class submarines, both of the Royal Navy." Grant cleared her throat. Sam thought she was hiding a smirk. Obviously, the Brits wanted to keep an eye on the wargames as well. "The *HMS Windsor* and *Unicorn*."

"Get a request to Her Majesty's Naval Command in Whitehall. Please ask for their assistance in recovering any missile fragments which might remain at or near the surface." Grant stood, snapped to attention, pivoted, and exited the darkened office.

Sam rubbed her temples. Obviously, her evaluation of the Punggye-ri nuclear test site needed to be expanded. The director's file was limited in scope and incomplete. She lifted the receiver on her analog telephone and dialed the sat-recon room to hurry up her request for any images of the North Korean area from the last thirty minutes.

2 November, 07:19 Hours Local (UTC 22:19)
Standing Committee Room, Mansudae Assembly Hall
Pyongyang, Democratic People's Republic of Korea

Five men sat around the end of the long teak table. A sixth sat at the head. The current president of the Presidium (Head of the Current Standing Committee of the Democratic People's Assembly) nervously rubbed his hands together beneath the table out of sight. He felt the others seated next to him were equally fearful. They were the chairmen of the other four ruling governmental committees—Foreign Affairs, Budget, Legislation, and Credentials. But the man at the head of the table was the one frightening them.

Pak Sung-un, supreme leader of the country and dictator of the Democratic People's Republic of Korea, leaned back in a plush leather chair and eyed each man. "Gentlemen, I have good news." He rocked forward, folding his pudgy hands on the tabletop. "Fifteen minutes ago, we successfully launched an Intercontinental Ballistic Missile."

The four chairmen were stunned, as shocked expressions crossed their faces. The president fell back in his chair as if physically struck. This was an overt show of aggression which threatened the tenuous truce his country was maintaining with the South Koreans and Americans. The supreme leader continued. "Our missile exited the atmosphere and is traveling toward the Pacific Ocean.

"This success indicates we are moving forward with all haste to meet my grandfather's wish of *juche*. National self-sufficiency was his primary focus." He paused. "And with my goal for reunification of the peninsula, we will need to establish military dominance." Pak's smile stretched into a wide grin.

As the weight of this news settled in the room, the president stuttered nervously, "S-sir, with all due respect, is now a good time for such a display?" He always knew Pak would bring destruction to his beloved Korea. But stopping the leader was all but impossible.

Pak slowly turned his chair to face the president squarely. "You dare question the timing of our demonstration?" He stood and leaned menacingly toward him, hands flattened on the tabletop. "You dare question my wisdom to show our military might? I will not allow the archenemy or the fools from the South to take over this country.

"The minds of our people are being ruined. Our people are inundated with their television, their music, and filth from their internet." He paused. "We will take all actions to stop this. Going forward, those caught accessing the western internet or listening to K-Pop will face a capital offense—punishable by death."

The four committee chairs slowly pushed away from the table, isolating the president. "No, no, sir. I would never question your decisions. But we are at a critical point in the negotiations with the South. This military action may be seen as a threat to the peace and destroy the talks."

"I don't care about—" The door to the committee room opened and a head appeared around the edge. Pak turned to the young officer and barked at the man, "What?"

"Apologies, sir." He entered the room and bowed low. "We have received a communique from Iwŏn." With a shaking hand, the officer held out a yellow envelope.

Pak grabbed the envelope and ripped it open. He pulled out the flimsy and read the message. His face darkened. His scowl was an indication of the news within the message. His anger escalated. He spoke in a barely controlled whisper, and his low growl reverberated off the walls of the committee room. "Call the Supreme People's Assembly together immediately."

"There are talks scheduled on the next scheduled assembly day, sir. May we call the meeting for the following day?"

"There will be no more talks." Pak's shout exploded in the room. The five men cringed. "It is time for this nation to stand up. Fight for what is ours. We will take back what the archenemies took from us."

"Sir, we cannot stand against the might of the South and their allies. It would be suicide for us to take overt military action against them."

"Do you truly believe that?" Pak shouted. The president sat frozen. "If you do, you are a traitor to this country. If you believe talks will lead us to peace and unification, you are delusional. The continuing presence of the Americans in the South is the root-cause of the growing instability on the peninsula. It is the cause of our continuing tit-for-tat weapons race with their South Korean puppets.

"We must take command of this situation. Drive the Americans out. It is time to take back the missing piece of our country." He looked each man in the eye. "We will continue our show of military strength. We will continue working toward *juche* with the expansion of our agricultural programs." He sneered. "But we will hide our real intentions from the South and their supposed allies." The supreme leader's face was flushed a sickening purple. He took a calming breath. "My third decade of rule is coming, and we will celebrate with unification."

Pak rounded the table. The five men stood, stepping back to bow formally. He stopped nose to nose with the president of the People's Assembly. Leaning forward, the supreme leader whispered in the man's ear. "I will deal with you, later."

Pak's personal aide moved to the door, opening it as Pak approached. "Call the car to take me to Hamhŭng."

Exiting the room, Pak Sung-un mumbled to himself as his anger roiled just beneath the surface. "I will not be ignored by the world. I will force the west and their South Korean puppets to pay attention to North Korea. Pay attention to ME! We will move on all fronts to grab their attention. One way or another." He paused to think and then muttered, "And the best way to do that is when the world is challenged by instability. I will *create* that instability," the Supreme Leader of the

Democratic Republic of Korea vowed as he climbed into his Mercedes. "Then, I will cut them down one at a time."

3 November, 00:07 Hours Local (UTC 15:07 2 November)
Hŭngnam Fertilizer Complex
Hamhŭng, South Hamgyŏng Province
Democratic People's Republic of Korea

It was after midnight in Hamhŭng. The faculty of the University of Chemistry and Medicine stood in a series of rows on the steps to the university's central laboratory complex. Their starched white lab coats flapped in the brisk wind. They were waiting on the arrival of the supreme leader. He was traveling from Pyongyang to see the progress of their various chemical and biological projects. This facility produced North Korea's primary chemical export. Now production was shut down due to mechanical failure at their bulk processing plant. Everyone standing on the steps knew telling Supreme Leader Pak they were no longer able to produce their monthly allotment of *Ice Drug* was a death sentence. Methamphetamine was one of the country's major exports. The director hoped to redirect the supreme leader's focus away from *Ice Drug* to several promising projects within the bio-enhancement department.

A mud-splattered Mercedes finally pulled to the base of the steps. The director of the university stepped down to open the rear door before the driver could exit the vehicle. Pak levered himself from the plush backseat. The scientists held their collective breath for what was coming next.

"Director Kwan, my incompetent driver is responsible for the delay in my arrival. He could not find a shorter route from Pyongyang."

Director Kwan bowed. "No need to worry, Supreme Leader. We are pleased to have you visit our facility and see our new discoveries and advances." He stood to his full height and continued. "What may we show you first?"

"I want to see your progress in the biological projects and the status for integration into our military objectives."

"Of course, sir. If you would." Director Kwan swept his arm up the set of stairs toward the large concrete building. "We will tour through the biology section. Our seven years of building and development have produced some interesting results. Our feedstock cultures are ready to be shipped to the Pyongyang Bio-Technical Institute. Their large-scale pesticide production facility will produce our agents easily."

Pak smiled coldly. "Very good, director. I am most pleased. Continue."

As the pair entered the secured facility, the rest of the faculty melted away into the dark, relieved *Ice Drug* was forgotten this night.

"Supreme Leader, allow me to introduce to you our key researchers—Doctors Hwang and Ri. They will lead you through their research ideas as well as give you a status report on the projects."

Numerous workers in utilitarian gray jumpsuits shuffled past as they entered the main laboratory building. Kwan tried to divert Pak's attention. "If you will look here, sir." He pointed to an observation window overlooking a large laminar-flow clean room. "This is our Level II safety containment area. Most of our initial cultures are grown here. Once a pure strain is identified, we move the cultures to our Level III laboratory for testing viability of bulk production."

However, Pak was not distracted from the high level of activity bustling down the hall. He asked the director, "What are all these people doing moving about your facility? I would not expect this much activity at midnight."

Kwan struggled to answer, but Doctor Ri stepped in, her soft voice requiring them to listen carefully. This drew Pak's attention to her. "Supreme Leader, we have successfully isolated and grown an optimal strain in our laboratory. To ensure viability and efficacy we are required to perform…" she paused as if searching for the proper words, "various tests." She pointed to the line of workers, heads hanging low. "These individuals are volunteers from Kyo-hwa-so Number Nine. They will be participating in our tests."

"I see. This is very brave of them." The supreme leader nodded and said, "If additional volunteers are needed, I nominate my incompetent driver."

Doctor Ri continued. "For volunteering, they may receive additional rations or early release from the re-education program."

As Pak smiled, Director Kwan pointed down the hall. "This way, Supreme Leader. Let us show you our incubators and ability to exploit dual usage at the Bio-Technical Institute."

The tour continued for several hours, ending outside the Level III containment rooms. "Due to the accident and shut down at the Number Twenty-Five production plant in Chŏngju, we have absorbed their work. Now we are working to produce the carrier and agent. Our colleagues from the Research Institute of the Armed Forces Ministry have begun their search for a deployment method."

"How soon?"

Kwan was taken aback. Was the supreme leader planning on using their work? He didn't know how he felt about that. But not answering truthfully would be a dangerous action. "Within the next six months."

Pak rounded on the slightly built director. "You have one month, director. I expect your feedstock to be delivered to the Bio-Technical Institute immediately." Pak seemed to consider his orders. He leaned close to the director, asking quietly, "Why six months?"

"As you've seen, we have a viable carrier and an active agent.

However, we do not have a means of distribution."

"Ah, something that can be easily managed. I appreciate your candor, director. One month. Let me worry about distribution."

Doctor Ri allowed her colleagues to stride ahead. She cleared her throat. Pak glanced at her. Smiling thinly, she said, "Sir, we are ready now."

3 November, 03:17 Hours Local (UTC 07:17)
Situation Room, White House
Washington, DC, United States

Sam sat in one of the leather chairs along the wall of the large rectangular room. The wall to her left was covered in high-definition monitors all focused on various views of the Korean peninsula and the Sea of Japan. The monitors could function individually—each showing a different image, or be blended into a single large image. Members of the National Security Council staff were moving around the dais beneath the wall of monitors focused on secure computer workstations. Looking down at her notes, she reviewed her findings of the last thirteen hours. "The president is on her way," a communications officer stated from the secure booth in the rear of the room.

Several members of the Joint Chiefs—heads of each of the five United States military branches—entered the room, and Sam stood at attention. "Samantha, good to see you, although, it could be under better circumstances," Admiral Benson said as he walked up to her. Sam had served under then three-star Vice Admiral Benson when he was commander of the US Navy Fifth Fleet in the Middle East. Now, he was head of the US Navy.

"Sir, a pleasure." Sam tilted her head to acknowledge the second part of his statement. "I don't know that I'll have much to add at this time. Things are fluid, and with the North Koreans you never know if they're rattling swords or making an offensive move."

"Too true I'm afraid." He looked her over with a critical eye. She stiffened her spine just a fraction more. Even though she was technically a civilian, old habits die hard. "How's the back?" His question was a whisper.

Sam smiled. "Fine, sir. I've completed—"

Her response was interrupted by a flurry of activity as the president of the United States with her cadre of security advisors entered the room.

"Seats everyone." President Amanda Haley dropped into the chair at the head of the table to face the wall of hi-def monitors. The others in the room quickly took their seats and looked expectantly at Admiral Benson. He nodded and folded his hands on the walnut tabletop. "Situation, please, Admiral."

"At this time, Madam President, we know the following: approximately thirteen hours ago, the Democratic People's Republic of Korea launched an intercontinental ballistic missile from a mobile platform outside the hamlet of Iwŏn on the eastern coast of the country. The missile's flight was on a trajectory to Tokyo, potentially with enough range to pass beyond Japan to Darwin, Australia. As you know, the US Pacific Fleet—in conjunction with our allied navies from South Korea and Japan—is conducting wargames in the Sea of Japan. As part of the operations, Admiral Armstrong stationed one of his Ticonderoga-class guided missile cruisers—the *USS Arlington*—within a gathering stormfront north of the gaming area." A map of the Sea of Japan popped up on the main wall monitor. The *Arlington* was noted with a flashing US flag. "The North Korean missile flew directly over this vessel. The captain deployed her AEGIS missiles to remove the threat to Japan and others. The North Korean missile was eliminated by one of two missiles fired in defense of our allies."

Sam smiled to herself. *If Admiral Benson is presenting the situation this way, maybe Cassie won't be in as much trouble as I expected.* Sam knew "in defense" was only used when an action was deemed required to prevent loss of assets or personnel in a combat situation. Interesting how wargames suddenly became a defensive combat situation.

"This is the first active-combat use of our AEGIS system. The system was deployed and did successfully intercept the ICBM." As the admiral concluded his remarks, the situational map highlighted the east coast of North Korea which had the town of Iwŏn circled in red. The projected flight path of the ICBM was noted by a red line with the AEGIS missile tracks shown in white.

The president rocked back in her chair and tapped the fingers of her right hand on the leather desk pad. Her gaze never left the central monitor. Sam looked at the president. Amanda Haley was the first woman to be elected to the office. She was one year into her second term, an election she won with a landslide victory after a successful first term. Her dark brown hair was showing more streaks of gray than she had when she first ran five years ago, and tonight it was pulled back in a ponytail, not her usual French braid. She wore dark running pants with a University of California, Berkeley Bears sweatshirt. The collar of her pale gray polo shirt was popped. The light-colored shirt accentuated her gray-blue eyes. Sam understood this was her first international military conflict situation.

"Right. What's the background here? North Korea has been silent these last few years." All eyes pivoted to Sam.

Admiral Benson rose. "Madam President, allow me to introduce Colonel Samantha Michaels." Sam stood from her chair. "The colonel served with me in the Gulf, completing three tours of carrier-based combat missions in support of our ground troops in the region. She retired from the Marine Corps following the crash landing of her F-14 Tomcat in Iraq. She received the Medal of Honor for her heroic rescue of her injured navigator, as well as the crew of the downed search and rescue helicopter sent to bring the pair back. She led this group of injured personnel across sixty miles of desert, commandeered a boat on the coast of Iraq, and successfully rejoined the carrier group at sea. She kept all seven of her crew alive, though significantly injured herself." Sam hated to be introduced like this. She felt her jaw tighten. She wasn't a hero. She did what any flight officer would do to keep her people alive.

"Following the completion of a Ph.D. in nuclear weapons development and deployment strategy from the Kennedy School of International Policy at Harvard, she was hired as an analyst by the CIA with a specialty in Asia and the surrounds. She specializes in photo-analysis and evaluation of NBC—nuclear, biological, and chemical threats—across the world. Colonel Michaels..." The admiral sat back down.

President Haley swung around to face Sam. "Well, Colonel, I'll repeat my question. What's going on here?"

Sam moved to an open place along the side of the elongated oval table and placed her notes on one of the leather desk pads. Turning to one of the NSC staff, she nodded at the officer. "Captain, may I have the first slide, please." The lights in the room dimmed.

The monitor melded into one display as a map of the Democratic People's Republic of Korea appeared. "This is the DPRK, also known as North Korea. The country is slightly larger than the state of Mississippi with a population of approximately 25.8-million souls. It is bordered on the west by mainland China, the north by Russia, the east by the Sea of Japan, and to the south across the Demilitarized Zone is South Korea. The North Korean state is a totalitarian, Stalinist-dictatorship. It was established in 1948, prior to the Korean Conflict. And since, it has been led by three generations of the Pak dynasty. It is a hermit kingdom shrouded in mystery, rumor, and innuendo. As the most isolated country in the world, little is known about their inner workings. Next slide please." A photo of the current dictator Pak Sung-un filled the screen.

"Broadly, Pak's objective is three-fold: first, to drive out the aggressive forces of the United States; second, terminate the dominance and interference of foreign forces; and third, fight for the unification of the motherland. All this is to be accomplished through a strategy of self-reliance.

"The country has negligible population growth with a median age of thirty-five-point-three years." The sound of several small breaths exhaling rose from the seated advisors at this fact. The median age of the United States was more than forty years. "The country has minimal arable land and is dependent on trade with China and Russia to feed their population a basic subsistence diet of one-thousand calories per day. Though rich in coal, limestone, some rare earth elements, and some naturally occurring uranium deposits, the country has no petroleum reserves and uses Magnox-style nuclear reactors, augmented by several coal-fired thermal plants and a few hydroelectric dams, to produce electricity. The Magnox reactors are an antiquated and unsafe nuclear technology acquired from the British in the late 1970s by Pak's grandfather.

"Overall, the DPRK is hard-pressed to achieve their goal of *juche*." Sam pronounced the Korean word for "self-sufficiency" with no western accent. "The North Korean ideology of *juche* is true socialism and can only exist when the state is independent through the creation of a national economy which emphasizes self-defense." She saw the president tip her head slightly. "This ideology drove the creation of an industrial base, 90 percent of which is dedicated to the further development of their military capabilities. The average North Korean citizen suffers and bears the hardship of this militarization. North Korea will not gain *juche* without the resources of the south. Therefore, reunification is their endgame."

Without prompting, the next slide flashed up. Sam smiled a thank you at the young officer. "This is a nighttime satellite image of the middle Sino-Japan region." After a moment for the group to view the image, Sam continued. "Seoul, South Korea, is here." She highlighted a brilliant splash of white light. "The Sea of Japan and the Yellow Sea are here and here." The darker blotches of open ocean contained a multitude of light specks. "Large ocean-going vessels, various supertankers, and sea-tainer vessels are the small light sources." Sam zeroed in on the absolutely black-blank area in the center of the photo. "This is North Korea." The president leaned closer, searching the image for any light. "State-mandated black out occurs at every sunset to minimize wasting their limited energy resources. As I said, 90 percent of the country's industry is focused on creating a military capable of forcing the world to pay attention to them."

Sam nodded, and the next slide showed an image of a large missile atop a multi-wheeled carrier moving along a parade route. "This image was smuggled to South Korean television from within the DPRK. On every fifteen April, known as the Day of the Sun, a military parade is held in honor of the birth of Pak Sung-un's grandfather Pak Il-jong. This is an Intercontinental ballistic missile on top of a mobile rocket launcher. It was not reported whether this was a cardboard mockup or a real missile. But given the depression of the launcher's tires, I believe it is a launchable bird." Sam was trained to notice the tiniest of details others would miss. "I believe this is the type of missile launched from Iwŏn toward Tokyo yesterday. A single-stage Pukkuksong-1."

The next slide was a small fishing village along a rocky coast. "This is Iwŏn. North Korea is highly skilled at camouflaging their military installations and concealing their strategic assets. I reviewed the last six months' sequential satellite imagery and found no military activity within this area. Therefore, I believe the missile was delivered and deployed from a mobile launcher as seen in the previous slide." The captain flipped back to the last image.

"Please bring the lights up." Sam turned to the table at large but focused her gaze on the president. "Four things are needed to successfully launch and control an ICBM in flight and deliver its warhead payload to a distant target: a miniaturized guidance system, a propulsion system which fits within a rocket's housing, a payload or deliverable warhead, and fuel. Until this launch, we knew North Korea had developed the guidance technology and successfully miniaturized it, though it was never tested. Several rocket engine test burns were broadcast on the state-controlled television station, so propulsion had been achieved. We know through surveillance, and the firsthand reports of defectors, North Korean military controls various nuclear, biological, and chemical agents which could be loaded into a long-range missile's payload. Therefore, it has developed viable warheads. Up until now, what we thought they lacked was a reliable source of a safe, stable rocket fuel. After this launch we learned our belief they lacked such fuel is incorrect."

"And that means?" The president sat forward again, her gaze boring into Sam.

Sam pushed her silvered braid over her shoulder. "The North Koreans may now be capable of delivering a warhead anywhere within the Pacific basin." Gasps rose from the table.

"Now see here." The National Security Advisor half rose from his chair. "You can't go around making those kinds of assessments without proof. There is no way a fifth-world country can be a threat to us."

"Country status aside, sir, that's exactly what I am saying. We currently have several assets scouring the impact area for missile fragments. If and when they recover any pieces, I will be able to give you a range estimate for this launch. However, from the information we do have—rate of acceleration, trajectory, altitude attained—I estimate a 1,500 to 2,000-kilometer range with 60 percent probability."

One of the Army generals interrupted Sam. "That puts a missile on the roof of several of our southeast Asian bases and covers most of our allies in the region." The discussion devolved into an argument between the joint chiefs and various security advisors.

"Enough." The president's quiet voice cut through the room. "Colonel, I appreciate your evaluation and expertise. Thank you." Her gaze swept across those at the table. Sam sat back down along the wall. "What we need now is a plan. What are we going to do in response?"

Admiral Benson gave Sam a "well, now's your chance" look. "If I may, Madam President." A nod had Sam standing again. "I recommend caution." The room again erupted into a cacophony of overlapping voices. Sam spoke over the noise. "We need to be careful and not box Pak in. If he feels threatened, he will strike back more forcefully than before. Perhaps a report to the UN Security Council with a recommendation of various sanctions may be in order. Targeted sanctions, excluding those on food or heating oil, might slow Pak down and allow us time to refine our understanding of what precipitated this action." When the president frowned, Sam continued, "It may have been a reaction to our wargames off their coast or them flexing their muscles, showing they can play in the big boys' sandbox. Or…" Sam paused to gather her thoughts. "It may be more serious." Sam felt the weight of all eyes shift onto her. "It may be a false-flag operation to distract us from his real objective. A precursor of an all-out offensive to reunite the Korean Peninsula under the Pak regime. Whatever it is, Pak is testing integrated weapons systems in preparation for their use. An increase in situational readiness at the Demilitarized Zone to level two would also be warranted." Sam swallowed. "Shooting down their bird will anger Pak and cause him to react in some manner."

The room went silent as Sam's words sank in. The president stood, which brought everyone to their feet. "I expect a recommended course of action on my desk within the next two hours." She turned to her Secretary of State. "Call the UN Ambassador down from New York. That's all, people." Sam began to gather her notes and moved to the communications officer to retrieve her flash drive. When she turned around the president was standing at her shoulder. "A word, Colonel?"

"Of course, Madam President."

4 November, 10:25 Hours Local (UTC 01:25)
The Sea of Japan (East Sea)
Combined War-games-Japan, S. Korea, US Fleets
Command Deck, *USS Arlington*
CGN-47, Ticonderoga-class Guided Missile Cruiser

Cassie Stanley sat in her command chair and surveyed her crew. The *Arlington* had been recalled, and they were cruising south to rejoin the main body of the US fleet. Her meeting with Admiral Armstrong hadn't taken long, and she was miffed she had to risk her helicopter crew and equipment to ferry her to the carrier in such dodgy weather. She frowned as she thought about the white-knuckled trip. When her helicopter landed, the carrier deck crew immediately began procedures to remove the two inches of rime-ice which accumulated on the helicopter during the short flight. Only after deicing could her crew open the side door of the helicopter. If the flight had been five minutes longer, the helicopter would have dropped from the sky due to the added weight. They had just made it.

Now she was being recalled to the Pentagon to personally give her action report to the head of the Navy. And probably reassigned to a desk in that same building. Or demoted out of hand and discharged for failure to obey orders. "James, my office, please." Her tall blonde executive officer nodded and began removing his throat mic and earbud. "Clancy, you have the conn." The young ensign jumped off her seat at weapons control. "I have the conn. Aye, ma'am."

Her office door was five steps behind her command chair. Cassie stood and turned to leave the bridge, passing the chair. She paused and lovingly caressed the leather back. Sighing, she resumed her steps aft to her office. "Have a seat, James."

"Ma'am?"

Cassie laughed. "We're in private. Cut the ma'am crap." James didn't join in her laughter.

"I'm being recalled to Washington." Cassie didn't mince any words. "I'll depart on a Super Hornet in the next hour." James cringed. Both officers knew a Super Hornet flight from southeast Asia was as non-stop as possible. It meant multiple in-flight refuelings, no bathroom breaks, and no meal service. At Mach-plus speed it was an arduous journey for the pilot as well as the passenger. "You will take temporary command of the *Arlington*."

"Ma'am?" When she frowned, James relented. "Cassie, what's this all about? It's the AEGIS launch, isn't it?"

"Perhaps." Cassie rocked back in her ergonomic chair. "Seems Admiral Armstrong is not happy we gave ourselves away and compromised his winning the wargames. Moreover, we didn't get to see the new Japanese tech deployed."

"And the AEGIS launch?"

Cassie leaned forward and folded her hands on the desktop. "Didn't say a word about that. I imagine the big boys in DC want their pound of flesh. He's allowing them the fun of dressing me down for an unauthorized launch." She shrugged her shoulders. "It's a done deal, James. And we got the missile over open water before it could do any harm. Regardless of the outcome, we did the right thing."

James didn't look happy. "You know what I think?" Cassie raised an eyebrow. "I think they're pissed they didn't get to be front and center to stop the missile."

"You may be right, but nonetheless I'm off and you're in command. Don't hurt my boat, James. And no retaliation against Admiral Armstrong."

"Of course, ma'am. No retaliation."

James' answer was too quick, and Cassie could almost see the wheels turning in his head. "I mean it, James. You will follow all orders to the letter." Cassie gave him her best command glare, and he flinched.

She knew what was coming for the *Arlington* and her crew. The admiral would give them the worst tasks, leave them steaming in the worst positions—probably at the rear of the fleet where the cross-wakes of all the boats ahead of them tore the sea into a mess. The *Arlington* would be tossed about like they were on spin cycle. It wasn't called the Maytag™ position for nothing. "I expect to be back, and I want my crew and boat in one piece." She glared at him again.

"Aye, ma'am."

"Fine, now get out of my office and make yourself useful. Oh, and I'll need another helicopter prepped to ferry me back to the carrier."

5 November, 01:13 Hours Local (UTC 5:13)
Michaels/Stanley Residence
Georgetown, Virginia
Suburb of Washington, DC, United States

Sam was exhausted. It was two days since her middle of the night presentation to the president, and she hadn't left her office at Langley since. She couldn't remember how many satellite images she had reviewed, how many cups of coffee she had drunk, or when her last meal was. Now, she had six hours to eat, bathe, and sleep to recharge before her next presentation to the president. Sam was given one order—determine the real objective of Pak and the DPRK.

"Easy for her to ask," Sam grumbled, as she dug for her keys in the bottom of her messenger bag. Pushing the door open with her hip, she moved to place her takeaway bag on the counter when she heard it. The bag hit the floor with her messenger bag as Sam pulled her Glock from the holster at the small of her back. She dropped behind the counter and stilled her rapid heartbeat to determine where the sound originated.

There it was again. A floorboard flexed. Someone was moving around on an upper floor. Sam stood slowly. She crept to the base of the back stairs. No, the sound was from the front of the house. She flowed along the wall of the hall toward the front stairs. The house was dark when she entered the garage. Sam glanced at the security pad by the front door. Four green lights and one red winked at her. The alarm was silenced. That required a fifteen-digit code. Sam almost laughed out loud. Who used a fifteen-digit code anyway? Only paranoid CIA analysts with a love for all things analog.

Another creak. The front bedroom on the third floor. *Gotcha*, she mouthed.

Sam crept up the stairs, moving from one side of the stairwell to the other to keep her field of view open above—Glock held in front of her chest in a two-handed grip. Rounding the newel post on the top floor, Sam crouched beside the half-open bedroom door. The plush carpet dampened her footfalls, though she left her shoes at the base of the stairs. She pushed the door open slowly just as water began to run in the shower. "What the…"

Crossing the room in three long strides, Sam crashed through the bathroom door, gun aimed ahead. "STOP! Hands Up!" Sam shouted just as the naked woman in the room spun around and screamed.

"Fuck!" Sam dropped her weapon to her side and slumped against the door. "God, Cassie, I could've killed you."

Sam's back chose that moment to seize, and she slowly crumpled to the floor in agony.

Cassie moved to her partner's side and dropped to her knees. "Let me help you into the shower. Looks like you need the hot water more than I do." They both ignored the Glock lying on the bathroom floor.

After a long mutual shower, Sam reclined flat in bed, resting on a heating pad set to toast. Cassie bustled around the master bedroom, pulling her pajamas from the dresser. "I'm going down for a glass of wine. Do you need anything?" Sam stared at the ceiling, adrenalin still coursing through her veins. She could barely breathe. Sam realized she could've killed Cassie.

"No, I'm good." Her stomach decided to contradict and growled loudly. They shared a snicker. Sam groaned as her back spasmed again. Laughing was not a good thing.

"I'll take that as a 'feed-me' request. But I didn't see anything in the fridge when I got home. I was going to call for takeaway after my shower. Any requests?"

"You may want to check out the bag in the kitchen. It's Thai. You could nuke it and we could share."

Cassie returned to the bedroom with a tray ten minutes later. "If we need more, I'll call for another order." Sam raised her head and lifted an eyebrow in question. "Good thing you ordered Pad Thai, and you can't tell I had to scrape it off the floor."

They laughed and Sam groaned as her back tightened again. "Sorry, I didn't mean to make you laugh." Placing the tray on the nightstand, Cassie leaned over Sam. "Do you think you can sit up to eat?"

"I've got to. I don't want Pad Thai in bed with us tonight." Sam wiggled her eyebrows.

"No way. Not going to happen, Ace." Sam pouted. "You're going to eat, take some pain medication, and sleep."

Sam tried to push herself upright and failed, sliding back down on the bed with a stifled gasp of pain. Cassie leaned over and grasped her shoulders. "Easy now. I've got you." Though half a foot shorter and more than fifty pounds lighter than Sam, Cassie was whippet-strong and easily pulled her partner into a partial sitting position. Several pillows allowed Sam to remain semi-upright.

Finishing their shared meal, Cassie snuggled along her side.

Sam asked, "Why are you home? Why didn't you call?"

"I did call, twice in fact. I left messages on your mobile before we launched off the carrier and again when I landed at Joint Base Andrews. Seems my messages didn't penetrate the subterranean depths of CIA Headquarters." Cassie quirked an eyebrow at Sam.

"I didn't turn it on when I left the building. All I was thinking about was the presidential briefing at 09:00. I just wanted food, a shower, and some sleep before I headed back to the White House." Sam noticed a frown mar Cassie's features. "What?" Sam could usually read Cassie and her moods.

The pair had met at the Naval Academy and spent four years trying to outdo one another. That was more than twenty years ago, almost thirty now. Their competition for academic supremacy and physical dominance led to a close relationship. They graduated one and two in their class. After graduation, Sam entered the Marine Corps and went to flight school in Pensacola Florida, before flying Tomcats from the decks of aircraft carriers during various conflict situations. Cassie went to the Naval War College in Newport, Rhode Island, and she held various command positions on a variety of warships stationed around the globe. Their personal relationship grew into something more when Sam was promoted to major and stationed aboard the US aircraft carrier *Enterprise,* where she commanded one of their Tomcat wings. Cassie was the chief of staff for Admiral of the Fleet and outranked Sam as a full commander.

At that time, their carrier group was stationed in the Persian Gulf to support troop action in Desert Storm. When Sam was shot down and the search and rescue helicopter crashed, Sam thought she was going to die and realized how short life was. She knew she couldn't continue to hide her feelings for Cassie. After her stay at Landstuhl Military Hospital in Germany and her rehabilitation at Walter Reed Hospital in Washington, DC, Sam invited Cassie to visit her during her next leave. They hadn't looked back since.

"I have a debrief at the Pentagon at 07:00 with Admiral Benson."

"I see…" Sam could feel Cassie's anxiety.

Cassie stood and started to pace. She ran her hands through her close-cropped hair. "The Super Hornet flight back was hell. I hadn't heard from you and assumed you were lost in some project beneath Langley." When Sam grunted, Cassie waved her comment away. "I was going to come home, rest a couple of hours, go to the briefing, and learn what was left of my career." She turned to Sam, and a few tears slipped out of her control and traced down her pale cheeks. "My career is well and truly over, I'm afraid." Her defeat was palpable. Sam struggled to get out of bed to hold her. But she couldn't get her back to cooperate.

"I'm sorry I scared you. I should've tried harder to get in touch, but everything was going so fast." Sam couldn't help herself and laughed at Cassie's unintended pun. She ignored the spasm which followed.

"Do not laugh at me." Cassie's barely controlled emotions rose as she stomped her foot.

"I'm not laughing at you, just at the pun."

Cassie tipped her head in question and then, laughed as she realized what she'd said.

"It's my fault for not turning on the phone. But with the uncertainty of the situation, I was focused on other things. Jesus, beautiful, I could've killed you." Sam's pain-laced voice choked out.

Cassie came back around the bed and cleared their dishes to the dresser. Settling beside Sam, she cuddled against her side again. "Can you tell me what you're working on? Or is my clearance not high enough?" Sam grimaced, this was a standing joke between them and often created a sore point. Although Cassie had a TOP SECRET clearance level. EYES ONLY classifications were different. In this case Cassie was involved and had taken direct action in the situation, so Sam felt comfortable sharing her project and early findings.

Sam pulled Cassie along her side and whispered, "Things are escalating in North Korea. Given the increase in new military activities I've identified across North Korea, we're headed to a confrontation. We know from the supreme leader's last address to his assembly, he explicitly stated 'he would not be ignored by South Korea or by the remainder of the world.' He went on to demand the world pay attention, and if they didn't, he would make them recognize the Democratic Republic of North Korea. And him." Both women were silent as the reality of what this meant sank in.

"Thank god, you were in the right place at the right time, beautiful."

"I had no choice, Sam. That missile was on a direct path to Tokyo. I had no way of knowing if it was a test vehicle or contained an active warhead. And if it carried a warhead, what type of weapon it contained."

"I've identified increased activity at the Punggye-ri nuclear test sites. He's enlarging and expanding his test tunnels. So, my best guess is viable nuclear warheads are a real possibility in the next few months." Sam swallowed hard. "But that's a guess."

"I'd bet my entire annual salary on your guesses, Sam. You have an amazing ability to combine a multitude of disparate facts and build a coherent picture. Then make an educated guess as to what will happen next." Cassie wrapped the word guess in air quotes.

Sam laughed and grimaced as pain lanced up her back. "I appreciate your belief in me, beautiful, but I have no idea what's next. Other than this is an overt act of defiance by the supreme leader. And tomorrow while you're at the Pentagon, I'm to educate the president about this escalating clear and present danger we now face with our southeast

Asian allies." Sam yawned sleepily. "Maybe we should both get a few hours' rest."

Cassie turned off the bedside lamps, and soon they were sleeping soundly.

5 November, 09:00 Hours Local (UTC 13:00)
Situation Room, White House
Washington, DC, United States

The morning found Sam gingerly sitting in her chair along the outer wall of the Situation Room. Her back was better, but the muscles were still tight. One wrong move and she'd be in spasm again. Sam rifled through her messenger bag and retrieved the flash drive to illustrate her presentation. This briefing was to provide the president background information about the DPRK and their military capabilities. Information to allow President Haley to create a framework for decision making. Information about critical systems, capabilities, and stockpiles. Sam hoped to also provide a window into the North Korean leader's thinking. Second guessing a despot like Pak would not be easy. No one truly knew what was going on within North Korea because of the country's sealed borders and Pak's paranoia.

The president arrived before the Joint Chiefs and nodded at Sam to begin. The lights dimmed as the first slide flashed on the monitors. A picture of a tree-lined avenue and a nondescript concrete building appeared. There were no people milling around the lushly landscaped lawns. "This is the Bio-Technical Institute in Pyongyang, North Korea." The next slide came up, showing a similar concrete building with detailed landscaping. "This is the administrative building of the Nyŏngbyŏn Nuclear Chemical Research Facility." The third slide was another concrete building. "This is the Chemical Materials Institute in Hamhŭng."

The president tilted her head and scrutinized the montage. "They all look the same."

"Exactly, they all look the same." Sam forwarded to the next slide, a topological map of North Korea. More than a hundred colored dots populated the area. "This is the sum of our geographic knowledge of the core facilities within the North Korean NBC program infrastructure. Military programs for development and testing are imbedded in civilian factories and institutes across the country in order to camouflage, conceal, and deceive. Not only from outside analysis, but from UN inspectors and the general populace. Their military command and control structures are diversified bureaucracies. No one talks to one another nor shares information, period."

"How do they advance their research if they are so divided?" The president asked a logical question.

"Their obsession for secrecy is one of the major roadblocks they must continually combat. I believe they move highly knowledgeable personnel around among their facilities and projects. These core experts hold the knowledge and share only as much as needed. Information, data, and expertise are vertically and horizontally compartmentalized, except for those few key individuals. We only learn of advancements or achievements when an event such as the missile launch occurs. Then we analyze activities, view construction in situ via satellite images, watch for movement of components by rail or road from one complex to the next, and attempt to put the puzzle pieces together. But we are in the dark without hard scientific data to support our guesses. We do not have eyes on the ground, nor can we get them.

"As I noted in my prior presentation, they need guidance, propulsion, warheads, and fuel to launch and control a missile and deliver it to a target. Currently, they possess all four critical components."

The president frowned. "What are their capabilities? Was this a one-off or do they have an arsenal for an offensive?"

"I have no way of precisely gauging their offensive capabilities, but our remote analysis indicates an escalation of military activities. We are waiting on the recovery of any missile fragments from the Sea of Japan. Then we may be able to quantify their technological capabilities."

Sam called for the next slide. A large engine was held upright within a metal frame, as a fiery plume blasted out of a circular exhaust manifold. "This photo was smuggled out of North Korea by a defector. It shows a test burn of a Hwasong-14 rocket engine. We believe this is the propulsion engine, part of the rocket system, used on the ICBM launched over the Sea of Japan. Flight distance for this system would be limited to approximately two-thousand kilometers. Should they develop a two-stage system, the range would increase to ten-thousand kilometers." A gasp went around the room and forced Sam to pause. She looked at the president. "It would be capable of reaching the west coast of Canada and the United States."

The president ignored the responses to this information and waved Sam on. "I believe North Korea is capable of producing enough fissionable material to produce six to seven nuclear warheads per year. We do not have an estimate of stockpiled inventory. We do not have a way of estimating yield of their warheads. However," she said, as another slide appeared on the central monitor showing a steep-sided valley with three visible tunnel entrances dug into the cliff, "this is the Punggye-ri Nuclear Test Site. It is located in the country's mountains approximately 370 kilometers north of Pyongyang." The next slide was a satellite image of the site area. Several train tracks, roads, and encampments dotted the image. "This is the Hwasŭng Concentration

Camp," Sam highlighted the small cluster of buildings about two kilometers west of the tunnels. "This is a penal-labor camp for political prisoners, sentenced to life at hard labor. They supplied the workforce who dug and expanded the test tunnels in the mountainside of the previous slide."

"You cannot tell me the North Koreans—"

The president was interrupted by the arrival of Admiral Benson and his entourage.

"Madam President, I'm sorry for the late arrival, but I needed to complete a critical debriefing." The admiral moved into the room. Someone followed on his heels. Sam barely contained her surprise as Cassie entered the room. "May I present Captain Cassandra Stanley, Commander of the *USS Arlington*, the guided missile cruiser that shot down the North Korean ICBM."

Cassie stepped up to the president and snapped to attention, a crisp salute followed by her greeting. "Ma'am. A pleasure."

"Captain Stanley. Although I understand your use of an untested weapons system may have been outside the scope of your orders, I appreciate your quick and successful actions. You may have averted an international crisis."

Sam watched as Cassie's cheeks blushed pink. She hated to be singled out as much as Sam did. "We did what we had to at the time, Madam President. It was a team effort. My crew deserves the accolades."

"Be that as it may, Captain, your actions saved lives and brought into focus the threats which exist on the Korean peninsula."

Admiral Benson walked over to his seat and smiled at Sam. "Carry on, Colonel, I apologize for the interruption."

"No worries, sir." Sam turned back to the president. "You were saying, ma'am."

"You're telling me the North Koreans used what amounts to slave labor to build this facility?"

"Yes, their use of prisoners in their military programs is well documented. From laborers to chemical and biological test subjects." Sam put up a series of overlapping satellite images on adjoining monitors. "From left to right, this series was taken over the same geographic spot at time intervals of four months. As you can see the amount of material piled along the Hwasŭng River is increasing exponentially in each photo. From the estimated size of the debris piles in the righthand photo, we estimate the tunnels to be approximately two to three kilometers long. Although we do not know if this is one tunnel system with three entrance/exit points or three separate tunnels, we do know they are preparing this site to test nuclear warheads." Sam returned to the rightmost slide. "If a nuclear test were to occur, we would be able to estimate weapon yield from the resultant blast and synthetic earthquake generated."

"Have they not tested nuclear warheads before?" the national security advisor asked.

Sam turned away from the slide. "Yes, sir, they have. But only in controlled experiments within the confines of laboratories in Nyŏngbyŏn." Flipping through several slides, Sam stopped at an aerial photo of a large industrial complex along a wide, rapidly flowing river. "This is the Nyŏngbyŏn Nuclear Chemical facility. Please note the small buildings, here, here, and here." Sam highlighted three demolished buildings sitting within a large retaining wall system. The area was flooded with water. Only partial roofs and failing walls were visible. "I believe this damage was caused by an enrichment test that got out of control."

The Secretary of Defense leaned toward the monitor. "Out of control?"

"The North Koreans do not have the computing capabilities to theoretically calculate the amount of radioactive material needed to reach critical mass for the development of viable warheads. Their raw fissionable material is impure. Therefore, they must experiment. In this instance, they add small amounts of fissionable material to a test vessel up to and until they reached critical mass, and a spontaneous fission reaction was initiated. If they hadn't added enough, they would have had an inert hunk of uranium or plutonium, whereas if they added too much, they could have had an out-of-control nuclear reaction."

"But this facility is within a city, on a watercourse used by the locals for fish and commerce."

"Yes, ma'am. That is how we know they had a runaway reaction. The level of nucleotides released into the river and measured kilometers out at sea as well as the airborne measurements of radioactive Cesium-137 told us they almost had a miniature Chernobyl event." Sam turned back to the image. "That is why the area is now underwater. To stop the reaction and isolate the contaminated laboratories, they built the retaining wall and pumped in river water to cover the experimental vessels, cooling the experimental pile of fissionable materials and stopping the runaway reaction."

"My god, what is being done about this? Doesn't anyone in the region want to stop this activity?" The Secretary of Defense was new to his post, and obviously he hadn't read the brief Sam had provided as introductory material. If he had, he would know the history of North Korea's neighbors and the steps they'd taken to try and stop these activities.

"All good questions, sir, but I don't have answers. If one facility is shut down due to natural disasters or unsuccessful experiments, they simply move the activities to another of the hundred or so military locations and carry on."

The president rose. "I have another meeting in a few minutes but, Colonel, I would like your assessment of Pak, the man."

"Of course, ma'am. I can provide a brief this afternoon."

The president turned to her chief of staff. "Stephanie, block out thirty minutes this evening for the colonel to go over her information with me." She turned back to Sam. "Would you be able to join me for dinner to continue this discussion?"

Sam blinked twice, taken aback by the offer. She was just an analyst, an eccentric one at that. Few in the CIA understood or appreciated her work or her for that matter. Her image analysis was done by hand. Analysts today let the computers do the evaluation, whereas Sam looked at each image herself. She was convinced a computer was only as good as the questions asked of it. Also, she knew none of her superiors would be pleased to hear she has the president's ear. But one didn't deny the commander-in-chief. "Yes, ma'am."

"Very good. And Captain Stanley," the president turned to Cassie, "I would also like to hear about the AEGIS system and your *Arlington*. Please join us?"

The president had obviously done her homework. This was well played. President Haley knew much more than she was saying. Sam saw the small quirk of the president's lips. Oh yes, she knew what she was doing.

Cassie rose from her chair. "Yes, ma'am. I am at your orders."

5 November, 20:00 Hours Local (UTC 24:00, November 6)
Residence, White House
Washington, DC, United States

A young Secret Service agent ushered Cassie and Sam into the residential wing of the White House. Shown into the China Room, the agent turned to the pair. "The president will be with you shortly." The agent moved to the hall and took up a position to the side of the partially open door.

Sam looked at Cassie and grimaced. She felt out of uniform, dressed in her customary black slacks and shirt, covered by a formal high-collared black blazer; while Cassie was resplendent in her tailored Navy service dress uniform with all the accompanying gold braid, stripes, and four rows of "fruit salad" above her left breast. It was all Sam could do to keep her hands to herself. She loved Cassie in uniform. But handprints would show on the dark wool if she weren't careful, so she clasped her hands behind her back.

"I can feel you looking." Cassie whispered at Sam's reflection in the display case holding the muted orange and gold embossed, Hermann Nast China selected by James Madison in 1814.

"Can you blame me? You look truly delicious."

"I would have to agree, Colonel." Both women jumped at the sudden appearance of President Haley. She laughed at the pair. "Sorry to startle you."

Sam saw the smirk and knew the president wasn't sorry at all. "Madam President," she said with a small bow of her head. Cassie stood rigid at attention.

"At ease, Captain, before you sprain something." Sam covered her chuckle with a hand and glanced at Cassie. A blush rose from the neck of the captain's starched white shirt to slowly cover her pale cheeks. One might believe a naval officer would carry a permanent suntan, but on modern warships, officers rarely went outside. Unlike sailing ships of old, where the officers strode the decks in all weather. Cassie was as pale as she was. Sam's was earned from her existence in the underbelly of Langley.

"Shall we head upstairs? We have a lot to discuss, and the chef tells me dinner is about to be served." The president swept from the room, towing a pair of Secret Service agents in her wake.

Once on the second floor, Sam and Cassie were led into an intimate room with an elongated mahogany table set for three. The white room with burgundy accents was dominated by a huge mirror along one wall. "Please make yourselves comfortable." The president took the chair at the head of the table and the pair settled on either side.

Once her napkin was across her lap, President Haley began speaking. "I've asked you here to discuss the events of the last weeks." She paused and seemed to consider her next words. "I want to hear your words, not those filtered by others, nor sanitized for my protection. I don't care about your bosses at the CIA, Colonel. You are my best source of true information."

In the overhead light of the crystal chandelier, the lines around the president's eyes and mouth were prominent. She appeared exhausted. "What the hell is really going on?" The president seemed startled by her use of profanity, and she reached for her glass to take a sip of water. "What are we going to do about it?" Another sip. She turned to Cassie.

"But first, Captain, if you would, please tell me about your ship and the AEGIS launch."

In a minimum of words, Cassie summarized the launch detection and subsequent AEGIS activation. She gave credit for readiness and success to her crew. "I'm just the head coach. I don't have the needed expertise, contributed from all positions on my team, to complete the complex tasks for this job."

Cassie looked at Sam and raised a burnished gold eyebrow. Sam picked up the summation. "Madam President, you know what we know. The North Koreans successfully launched a ballistic missile toward Japan using a mobile platform from the hamlet of Iwŏn. Captain Stanley was able to bring the bird down using the *Arlington's* AEGIS guided missile defense system. At this time, we are attempting to recover missile fragments from the impact area, though I don't hold out hope we'll be successful. I believe the missile was a single-stage design and had a nominal range of two thousand kilometers."

"Yes, yes. I understand all that." She fluttered her hand in dismissal of the information. "I'll ask again. What is going on in North Korea?"

"I can't answer that directly, ma'am." Sam folded her hands in her lap. "It may be a response to the wargames. It may have been a timing coincidence and just a test launch. It may have been Pak's response to South Korea increasing their troop allotment at the demilitarized zone per our request. It may be a response to current sanctions. It may be a false-flag operation to divert our attention away from another more critical operation." Sam swallowed. "Or it may be Pak had a bad day and wanted to play with his toys."

The president grunted at this last point. "I don't think Pak does anything offhanded or for fun. There is a plan here. A plan I want to know about."

"I would agree, ma'am." *In for a penny, in for a pound*, Sam thought. The president cocked her head, listening intently. Sam took this as her cue. "Very well." She paused to gather her thoughts. "At this time, I believe, and I must stress this is my assessment alone and not one held by my superiors at the CIA, the current supreme leader of the Democratic People's Republic of Korea is a psychopath." Sam sat forward in an attempt to emphasize her next statement. "Add to that, Pak's recent public statements indicated he will continue to escalate military activities in a desire to be recognized. And when you combine this with his mental instabilities, we must be careful with what we do and how we react in turn."

The president reared back, startled, her hand stalled halfway to her glass. "I see." She refocused and took up her glass. "What makes you say this, Colonel?"

"Allow me to summarize what we know about the supreme leader." The president tipped her head and Sam continued. "Pak Sung-un was born on the Eighth of January, though the year is not specific. We believe it was either 1982, '83, or '84. He is the third supreme leader of the DPRK within the Pak dynasty. He succeeded his father who died in 2011. He is head of the government, the military, all their industry, and the Worker's Party. He was educated in Swiss boarding schools under assumed names. He studied anthropology in Lyon, France. He holds a military degree from the North Korean officer college and a degree in physics from Pak Il-jong University. This gives us a clue of his innate intelligence. He is an avid fan of the NBA. He is obsessed with Michael Jordan. His idiosyncratic tendencies notwithstanding, he is the most highly educated and intelligent of the three Paks, the most knowledgeable of the West, the most cultured, the most diabolical, and the most driven to accomplish what his father and grandfather could not." Sam paused and studied her wine glass.

"And that is?" President Haley prompted Sam to continue.

"The reunification of the Korean peninsula. The world dominance of the DPRK and their totalitarian regime."

Sam's recitation was interrupted as servers brought the meal's first course in. Once alone again, she continued. "In 2014, the United Nations Human Rights Committee brought charges against Pak for the various purges, acts of torture, and execution of family members and political opponents." Sam noticed the president had not begun eating. "I'm sorry ma'am. I know this is all very disturbing."

"Nothing I haven't heard before about other world leaders. Please continue, Colonel."

"He is the middle of three children from his father's first wife and not originally thought to be a successor to the Pak dynasty. However, when his elder brother was caught trying to enter Japan on a false passport to visit Tokyo-Disney, the elder brother was dishonored, and Pak became the heir-apparent." Sam considered her next words carefully, as she took a bite of the beet and feta cheese salad, chewing carefully.

"The only firsthand information we have on Pak comes from his father's personal chef. Fujimoto reported, 'if power is to be handed over, then Sung-un is the best for it. He has superb physical gifts, is a big drinker, and never admits defeat.' Also, according to him, Sung-un smokes western cigarettes, loves Scotch whisky, and has a Mercedes Benz 600 luxury sedan. Although some of these traits are hedonistic and irrelevant, his never admitting defeat is critical to our evaluation of the man Pak is.

"The people believe Pak is the reincarnation of his grandfather, as the physical resemblance is striking. This has created a cult-like following from the people." Sam pulled a folder from her messenger bag and placed several photos on the table. "I believe he had plastic surgery as a young man while in Switzerland to modify his features."

The servers cleared the first course and replaced it with a sea bass entree. A white bean and artichoke medley with a parmesan crust accompanied the fish. Wine was poured, and again the small group was left alone.

Sam continued her summary. "His psychopathic behaviors and uncontrolled temper are well documented. These tendencies cause him to irrationally lash out." Sam paused, as she tried to choose the best way to conclude her remarks. "I believe he angers easily and is not forgiving. Therefore, one must approach any interactions with him carefully. Also, he doesn't think twice about sacrificing the wellbeing of the Korean people to achieve his goals. He is obsessed with doing what his father and grandfather were unable to—unite the Korean peninsula and drive the westerners from their shores."

The president wiped her lips and sat back. She scrutinized Sam through narrowed eyes. "What's his next move?"

Sam wasn't expecting this question. "I'm not in a position to speculate, ma'am," Sam said, falling back into her analyst persona.

"You're not at Langley now, Samantha. May I call you Samantha?" Sam nodded and the president continued. "You are here, and I need your analysis. Your best estimate of what's coming next. Your suggestions for how to defuse this situation and limit Pak's ability to further militarize his country."

Sam placed her cutlery carefully across her plate. Most of her food untouched. "As I said in our first meeting, you cannot box Pak into a corner. He is a feral dog and will always come out fighting. A military strike, however surgical, is not the correct move. This would only galvanize his fervor. Also, given their ability to camouflage and conceal military assets, we cannot take overt action and attempt to remove all the strategic targets. We wouldn't know which targets to choose. We must not allow our military superiority to blind us with the false belief of an easy victory. We're deluding ourselves if we think we can bomb away their knowledge. If we were to try and take preemptive action, we would only drive their militarization further into hiding, farther underground. And then our ability to watch and learn would stop."

The opulent room seemed to shudder at the gravity of Sam's remarks. All three women sat back as they faced this stark reality. No one spoke. Their meal was forgotten. A head appeared around a slowly opening door and the woman caught the president's eye. "Dessert, ma'am?"

"Please, Cathy, and compliments to the chef as usual." The server shook her white-haired head in dismay. She obviously didn't agree they liked the food, as the plates she removed were mostly full.

7 November, 09:00 Hours Local (UTC 24:00)
Main Meeting Hall, Mansudae Assembly Hall
Pyongyang, Democratic People's Republic of Korea

Pak Sung-un, Supreme Leader, Chairman of the Party and First Commander of the People's Military, strode onto the dais. He stood before the two thousand members of the Supreme People's Assembly as applause rained down upon him. He raised a single hand, and the applause ceased between one clap and the next. He was a short, rotund man with slicked-back black hair and small black eyes. He wore a dark tunic over black trousers. Gripping the podium with pudgy hands, he began to speak. "Members of the People's Assembly, Members of the Workers' Party, and esteemed officers of the Central Military, we achieved a great success with the launch of our first Pukkuksong-One intercontinental ballistic missile." Applause swelled in the large hall. The supreme leader raised his hand again and the applause halted. "Our missile performed flawlessly from launch through first-stage burn and exit from the atmosphere. However, prior to the separation and atmospheric reentry of the warhead, our missile was destroyed."

The room erupted in disbelief. The supreme leader held up both hands. The noise took longer to dissipate. "I know, my friends. The attack came from an unknown source owned by our archenemy. Their destruction of our missile is a direct attack on our country, on our sovereignty. A direct threat to our survival." A roar filled the hall.

Pak shouted over the tumult. "We must stop this enemy now. We must remove them from this earth. We must be victorious!" Thunderous applause erupted in the hall. Again, he raised his hands to quiet the assembly.

"Therefore, I call for the initiation of *Songun*-military first. We will build our forces and weapons to greater levels. We will achieve our ultimate goal of *juche*. We will crush the archenemy pigs who dare to deny our place in the world. Who wish to obliterate our culture. Who threaten our very existence." Pak was shouting to be heard over the deafening roar from the assembly. Sweat poured from his brow. Droplets flew in all directions as he pounded the podium. "We will focus our scientific efforts on the next Pukkuksong rocket. This one will have two stages. We will power this engine with a new fuel. We will launch it against the archenemies of our state."

The assembly was on their feet, stomping and cheering the words of their supreme leader. "To accomplish our mission and develop these harbingers of destruction, we must sacrifice. Remember the sacrifices of my grandfather and his group of guerrilla fighters in their Arduous March against overwhelming odds. When the archenemy dared violate our soil, the few fought against thousands. They fought in twenty-degree-below-zero temperatures. They fought through heavy snow. They fought while starving. The red flag carried in front of their rank never faltered." A chant began to swell. "They survived and won. They created this wonderful country—our home. The sacrifice of the few for the good of the homeland allowed our present-day advancements."

The supreme leader paused. "I call on each of you to join me in our next Arduous March." Again, the assembly roared with approval. Pak looked to his right at the empty seat of the president of the Presidium. An evil smile curled his lips as he thought of his screams of terror as the president died at the hands of his executioner. *No one stands in my way.*

"We will focus our resources on our scientists and military."

The assembly answered: "WE WILL!"

"We will limit resources to the common worker."

The assembly roared: "WE WILL!"

"We will build our infrastructure to create more weapons to protect our land."

"WE WILL!"

"We will not bend to the will of the archenemy!"

"WE WILL NOT!"

"We will not allow the archenemy to destroy our country."

The floor of the assembly hall vibrated in sympathy to the tumult: "WE WILL NOT!"

"We will triumph!"

"WE WILL TRIUMPH!"

SECTION TWO

Alarms sounded as various seismographs came to life around the room. A quick survey of the active instruments told the technician the earthquake had occurred within southeast Asia. Not an unusual location given the geology around the Ring of Fire which circled the Pacific basin. Faults associated with the multitude of plate boundaries in the area were in constant motion—grinding against one another to create a myriad of earthquakes.

Computers began to process the waves traveling around the globe, generated by the quake, as they arrived at various monitoring stations. These results would be used to determine epicenter location, focal point, depth of rupture, magnitude, and estimated damages. They would correlate geolocation versus population density for estimated loss of life. The United States Geologic Survey would estimate the potential for aftershocks.

As data continued to flow in from remote sensors, the technician called the geophysicist on duty to report the event. Within fifteen minutes, preliminary analyses filled the worldwide map display on the lab wall. A quick look at the data told the technician this quake was unique and perhaps not a natural event. He picked up another phone and placed a call to the Comprehensive Nuclear Test-Ban Treaty Organization in Vienna, Austria. He reported the occurrence of a possible underground nuclear test, details to follow.

As he concluded his call, the on-duty geophysicist entered the lab. "What've we got, Derrick?"

"Looks like an underground nuclear test somewhere on the Korean peninsula. I put the P-wave data on the main screen for you. We are still analyzing the S-waves, but they're weird. I'm triangulating the exact epicenter and depth to the focal point now."

Cynthia Brockstone dropped into her ergonomic chair and entered her login identification. Data immediately filled the screen. Derrick was correct. This was an underground explosion. The P-wave, or primary compression wave, which was created when the bomb exploded at the subsurface locus, dominated the seismogram. These initial P-waves quickly died off and were not replaced by the usual cluster of larger S-waves, or secondary shear waves expected in a natural earthquake. S-waves were created as the earth shook intensely around the subsurface rupture and the waves rolled outward to travel near the surface of the globe.

Entering commands to load data from three seismographs triangulated at strategic locales into one of her proprietary programs, Cynthia picked up a phone and placed a call to CIA Headquarters in Langley, Virginia. It was only five o'clock in the evening on the East Coast, so someone should answer straight away.

"Langley tactical analysis group," a bored voice answered.

"This is Cynthia Brockstone with the USGS Earthquake Information Center in Colorado. I need to speak to the Southeast Asian desk immediately."

"Wait, please." Silence filled the line as she waited for one of the analysts to pick up. The minutes stretched as Cynthia watched her algorithms digest the data.

The line clicked. "This is Samantha Michaels. To whom am I speaking?"

"Cynthia Brockstone here." She got right to the point. "We've detected an underground nuclear test originating from the Korean peninsula."

"Location?"

"We will have that information momentarily." The resultant data continued to fill her monitor. She clicked on one waveform and leaned closer to the screen. Her fifty-two-year-old eyes weren't as sharp as they once were.

Sam ordered, "Hold one, Doctor Brockstone."

The line went silent. Ten minutes passed but now she had an epicenter—the point on the surface directly over the underground point of detonation. 41°16'48" N, 129°5'11" E. North Korea. Next step magnitude—how large was the artificially created earthquake? With a few keystrokes she loaded the P-wave deflection plot into another program. The distance the needle traveled on the seismograph—or was deflected—measured in millimeters above or below the baseline was an indication of the amount of energy released from the blast. Another few minutes and her computer system pinged. Magnitude of 5.1 on the standardized Richter Scale. "Preliminary" blinked at her over the results box. This number would be refined over the next several days from observations of actual surface damage around the epicenter. She realized since this was North Korea, there would be no ground observations or any information released. Therefore, 5.1 was the recorded magnitude.

"Doctor Brockstone?" Sam's voice shattered the silence.

"Yes, I'm here."

"I need you in DC as soon as possible. An Air Force jet is waiting for you at Buckley Air Force Base in Aurora, Colorado. How soon can you get to the base with your data?"

Cynthia was stunned into silence by this command. And it was a command. She knew she didn't have a choice to decline.

"Doctor Brockstone?"

"Sorry, yeah, I'm here. Just never had a request like this before."

Sam's contralto voice soothed her. "I understand. But this is vital, and I cannot continue to discuss this on an unsecured comm line. Also, I need you available for a presentation to the president should that become necessary." Sam paused. "Are you certain of your initial analyses?"

This was where Cynthia felt secure—she believed in the data and her analyses. "Yes. We have just completed preliminary epicenter and magnitude calculations. The blast occurred—"

Sam interrupted. "Do not give those data over this line, Doctor." The voice demanded obedience.

Cynthia swallowed hard. "All right, I'll gather my preliminary data and head to the base. I'm across the Denver metro area from Aurora, and it will take me more than two hours in rush hour traffic."

"Very good, Doctor. A car will meet your plane at Joint Base Andrews to bring you to Langley unless the situation changes. If it does, it will take you to a different location as needed. I will see you in four hours. Travel safely."

The line went dead in her ear. Slowly Cynthia cradled the receiver and looked up from her workstation.

What she heard couldn't be correct. It was a four-hour flight, minimum, to DC from Denver, and she was two hours from the airbase. She shook her head to clear her scattered thoughts. Just focus on the data. "Derrick, please load our preliminary data as well as the raw waveforms on a flash stick. And print me a copy of the event as recorded at the Yreka Bluehorn Mine seismometer in central California. I know YBH will have the best display."

The YBH site was 1 of 321 within the International Monitoring System set up to record underground nuclear testing. Cynthia stood and opened her backpack. She checked her laptop and added all its requisite chargers and connection cords before dropping her mobile on top. "I'm on my way to DC." He handed her the stick and printout as she left the lab and headed for her car. Why couldn't the CIA wait for the report to be posted on the USGS website, like everyone else?

7 January, 15:00 Hours Local (UTC 06:00)
Private Conference Room, Mansudae Assembly Hall
Pyongyang, Democratic People's Republic of Korea

Kim Hye-su sat quietly in the corner of a cold concrete room. She had no idea why she was summoned to Assembly Hall and hustled to this windowless dungeon. She couldn't think how she had offended the leadership or her military overlords. She had work to do and wanted to get back at it.

The data from Punggye-ri was only now coming in, and she would be hard-pressed to complete her analyses since half her monitors were destroyed when one of the tunnels collapsed following the test. The workmanship was shoddy, and the tunnel lacked adequate internal support. She tried to tell her superiors this but arguing against the time-limiting demands for results was difficult. If not deadly. She swallowed hard. Perhaps, she'd gone too far? Maybe I pushed too hard in my recommendations for changes to the tunnel design? At this thought, her heart rate increased. She folded her hands on her lap to hide their trembling.

Purges had increased lately. She'd heard that several scientists, including the director of the Hŭngnam Fertilizer Complex, had disappeared. It was more difficult to receive South Korean television. And now that listening to western music was a capital offense—possessing anything from outside the country could be a fatal luxury. Have they found the receiver in my laboratory?

Before she could work herself into a deeper state of fear, the door opened, and several military leaders strode into the room. Her heart stuttered as she rose on shaky legs to bow to the three men. The next to enter the room seemed to stop her heart altogether.

Pak Sung-un took a seat at the table. "What are the results?"

All four men looked at Hye-su. She bowed to Pak and swallowed against a suddenly dry throat. "Results?" Her question came out in a squeak.

"Yes, from the test. What are the results? Are you not the lead scientist on this project?"

Finding her courage, she knew she had no choice but to answer truthfully. "I am. That is, after the departure of Doctor Kwŏn, I assumed the role of test coordinator."

"Very good, then. The results."

"I have not completed all of our preliminary analyses, Supreme Leader."

"Not completed? How is this possible? The test occurred over eight hours ago."

"Yes, the detonation occurred at 23:11 hours UTC."

Pak's face was beginning to flush red and his hands balled into white knuckled fists. "Do not repeat information I already know. I ordered the detonation. I know when it occurred. I ask for the results."

Hye-su swallowed around her fear and recited the results of the test. "The detonation was a success. We achieved complete device destruction. It produced a ground displacement of approximately five meters and a synthetic earthquake magnitude of approximately five."

"Approximately!" Pak barked. "I do not want approximately! I want results! We must report this to the world. We must show our strength. I cannot do that with approximately! What is the yield? How much destruction would this device create in a city? A city like Tokyo? Or Los Angeles?"

A shiver ran up Hye-su's spine. Of course this is what the supreme leader wants. To flex his muscles on the world stage. Taking a deep breath, Hye-su knew she couldn't avoid his questions any longer. "Approximately seven to twenty kilotons." She knew the Nagasaki explosion was twenty-one kilotons. The bomb completely destroyed the central portion of the city directly beneath the initial detonation point.

"Again, with the approximately. Are you not doing your work? Do I need to remove the distraction of your family to improve your focus?"

This was not a veiled threat, but Hye-su had no family. It appeared, Pak didn't know this. Regardless, he could make her life miserable. Isolate her from her research lab and co-workers. Take her work away. Cut off her access to international research and advancements. Deny her travel to scientific conferences. Hye-su shivered in the cold concrete room. Send her to a camp. No more prevarication. "Sixteen kilotons."

Pak gave her a long hard look, and she lowered her eyes to the floor. "Thank you, Doctor. Remove yourself from this room. A driver will return you to your laboratory."

7 January, 03:30 Hours Local (UTC 07:30)
Situation Room, White House
Washington, DC, United States

Sam watched Doctor Brockstone closely for signs she needed a break. The geophysicist had traveled halfway across the continent before spending several hours detailing her preliminary results with the CIA's cadre of analysts for southeast Asia. Now, she was in the White House Sit Room. The doctor had to be as exhausted as Sam was.

Things were escalating in North Korea. Sam felt it in her gut. They were headed for a showdown with Pak. One she hoped they could avoid with information and planning. She feared they wouldn't have enough time to determine their needed steps before Pak lashed out against the world. She wondered how one stopped a runaway freight train?

The president entered the room with her usual gaggle of followers. Everyone settled into a seat once the president sat at the head of the table. "We've got to stop meeting like this, Colonel."

Sam was the only one in the room to chuckle. "I agree, Madam President, but this is of utmost importance."

"So, I understand. Please, Colonel, let's hear it."

"At approximately seventeen-hundred hours Eastern Time, a seismic event was recorded around the world. Triangulation of the data indicates the event occurred at the North Korean nuclear test site, approximately 370 kilometers north of Pyongyang." A map of the Korean peninsula flashed up on the screen with a star over the North Korean capital and a radiation symbol over Punggye-ri. "The event was not a natural one."

President Haley dropped her hands to the table and shook her head. "I thought they were being too quiet."

"Madam President, may I introduce Doctor Cynthia Brockstone of the United States Geological Survey Earthquake Information Center in Colorado. She will give you our technical understanding of this nuclear test. Doctor Brockstone?"

The gray-haired geophysicist stood and pushed her tortoise-shelled glasses up her nose. She nodded to the communications officer, and two diagrams filled the monitors on the far wall. "Madam President, we control a net of seismometers positioned around the world to record seismic events. Once one occurs, the first question we ask is whether it was naturally occurring or artificially produced. If we determine from the data the event was artificial, we ask whether it was a nuclear explosion in violation of the 1996 Comprehensive Nuclear Test Ban treaty or something else, such as a building being demolished or a massive explosion similar to the one which occurred several years ago in Lebanon. Lastly, if we suspect it was a nuclear event, we ask whether it was generated by a fission or fusion device. Once we calculate the location of the event, the magnitude of the explosion, the shape of the ground rupture, and ultimately the potential yield of the weapon, we can determine the type of device tested."

"You can tell all this from the recorded data?"

"Yes, ma'am. Given an understanding of the earth and how pressure waves travel through it, we can determine quite a lot about the device."

Cynthia turned to the displayed diagrams. "The leftmost diagram is the seismogram from the 2011 Tōhoku earthquake which occurred in the deep offshore trench east of Japan. This 9.1 magnitude quake created vast destruction across Japan and a devastating tsunami. Please note two things—first, the initial displacement is called the pressure or

P-wave and is created by the initial release of energy when the fault ruptures. After the initial rupture, the ground heaves and produces a swarm of shear or S-waves." Cynthia highlighted a cluster of oscillating, ringing waves which occurred following the P-wave. "S-waves are usually larger in displacement and longer in duration than the initial P-wave. These S-waves travel at or near the surface and radiate outward, oriented along the direction of fault failure." Cynthia paused.

Sam noted the president was leaning forward and focused intently on the display. She flashed the geophysicist an okay sign and a nod to continue.

"The right display is the seismogram of the event we recorded yesterday. Comparing the two, one can easily see the differences. In yesterday's event, the P-wave is the most prominent feature, and there is a distinct lack of an S-wave cluster. This recording was gathered at one of the 321 active monitoring stations located around the globe dedicated to the detection of nuclear events.

"Given this first indicator of a nuclear event—the absence of S-waves—we triangulated among the various recording stations to determine the epicenter location of the event—the point on the globe's surface above the explosion. Next—"

The president interrupted her. "I understand the basics of earthquake mechanics given my home in the Bay Area."

"Of course, ma'am. I'm sorry if this is too elementary."

"Not at all, Doctor. I just wanted to clarify my understanding. Though, I am not versed in the differences between nuclear events and natural ones."

Cynthia nodded. "Given your understanding of California geology, Madam President, consider this—you are standing on the eastside of the San Andreas fault on the North American tectonic plate, looking west." President Haley nodded. "The ground on the westside of the fault, which is on the Pacific tectonic plate, would move to the north in an earthquake. The energy released by the earthquake would also be oriented in this direction." Again, the president nodded. "Now think about an explosion. The energy from this event would be omni-directional without a preferred direction—it would spread outward in all directions. We can see this difference—directional versus omnidirectional—in the recorded data.

Sam was impressed with the presentation and with the geophysicist herself. She knew how stressful it was to be in the Sit Room in front of the president. Add to that, it was three in the morning. But the doctor didn't seem phased in the least.

"The next confirming fact of a nuclear test is the depth to rupture. In this instance, the event occurred at 0.0 kilometers below the surface.

"From these data we can determine the magnitude of the explosion.

Or in this instance the ability to calculate the yield of the device. This event magnitude was 5.1, as calculated using the standardized Richter Scale, which gives us a device yield of approximately ten kilotons."

Cynthia paused, and Sam jumped in when she noted the president frowning. "Any questions, Madam President?" Sam asked.

Before the president could answer, one of the security council personnel interrupted from a side communication room. "Madam President, North Korea has just released a statement through Reuter's news services. It announced the successful test of a..." The young officer swallowed hard. "A hydrogen bomb, ma'am."

Sam stumbled back into her seat. The room exploded in a cacophony of overlapping questions and comments from those around the table. Sam watched the president settle back into her chair as a storm cloud passed over her face. Slowly the tumult died down and everyone turned to the president.

"Doctor Brockstone, you stated you could determine different weapon types from your data?" The president's voice was barely a whisper, but it filled the room. Sam strained to hear the question over the pounding of her heart.

Nodding, Cynthia answered the president. "Though nuclear physics is not my specialty, I can outline the differences in devices and how they might be recorded seismically."

When the president waved her hand, Cynthia continued. "A fission device is created by bombarding a core of a heavy element—Uranium-235 or Plutonium-239—with neutrons to initiate a chain reaction. This chain reaction in a few hundred milligrams of matter releases an explosion of energy as the heavy element's atoms divide spontaneously. This is a physical example of Einstein's $E=mc^2$ equation. In contrast, a fusion hydrogen bomb uses light elements—usually Hydrogen-1 and Hydrogen-2—and tremendous pressure and temperature to fuse the hydrogen atoms together creating a heavier atom. In most instances helium plus energy, lots of energy. Fusion reactions occur naturally within our sun, producing the stellar radiation we feel on Earth. To attain solar temperatures and pressures for a fusion reaction to initiate, the fusion device is typically encased within a fission device. The fission explosion creates the needed temperature and pressure regime to initiate the fusion reaction within the hydrogen mass."

"So..." The president paused to gather her thoughts. "The North Korean test was or was not a fusion device?"

"It was not a fusion device."

Sam watched the president's face, as her brow wrinkled in question. She asked the follow-on question. "Are you certain, Doctor?"

"The earthquake we recorded was from a fission device. The calculated yield was too low to be a fusion device. And, if it were a fusion device we would normally record a two-stage event—there would be two distinguishable P-wave clusters. The first produced by the fission explosion to create the fusion environment and then picoseconds later a second, larger cluster from the fusion explosion. Neither criterion—calculated yield nor the occurrence of two P-wave clusters—was met to classify this as a two-stage fusion weapon."

The president and Sam settled back and exhaled a sigh of relief. Though Sam wasn't sure what relief she would have over the next days. She had yet to determine where Pak was headed. What his goal truly was.

"Are you certain, Doctor?"

"Ma'am, we don't need a truthful nation to figure out the real story. Our scientific analysis—a single stage, low yield, fission nuclear explosion from within North Korea—is correct. The earth doesn't lie."

7 January, 09:30 Hours Local (UTC 13:30)
Michaels/Stanley Residence
Georgetown, Virginia
Suburb of Washington, DC, United States

"Good morning, Doctor." Cassie smiled as she pulled a tray of cinnamon rolls from the oven. "Coffee is in the carafe. Mugs are on the tray. Please help yourself."

Cynthia Brockstone rubbed her eyes and moved to the center island, pouring herself a cup. "We've not met." She said as Cassie watched the geophysicist try to straighten her clothes. They were rumpled beyond help.

"Right, I'm Cassandra Stanley, Sam's partner." Pulling off her oven mitts, she offered her hand. "You can call me Cassie. Given the early hour you got in, I was already in bed. Did you sleep well?"

"Very, all things considered. I never would have guessed my quiet life studying earthquakes for the USGS would lead to a two-hour flight across the country in a military jet or a presentation to the president at three in the morning."

Cassie grimaced. "I can relate to the flight and a bit to the presentation. Those jets are made for speed and don't offer any amenities for inflight comfort." Both women acknowledged their shared experience, as Cynthia nodded in agreement.

"When Samantha said she had a jet waiting, I assumed it was a Gulfstream, not an F-18 Super Hornet. I felt like I was dropped into a Top Gun movie."

Sam came into the kitchen. "Good morning." She gave Cassie a quick kiss on the cheek and turned to Cynthia. "My aide will arrive shortly with a selection of clothing for you, Doctor. Sorry for all the rush yesterday but time was of the essence."

"I understand. Though, some clean clothes will be appreciated. It seems my luggage missed the flight from Denver." All three women laughed.

Sam helped herself to a roll and a mug of coffee, adding a generous amount of sugar and milk to the mix. Just as she raised the cup to her lips, the front doorbell rang. "Drink your coffee milk, Ace. I'll get the door."

Voices approached as Sam's aide entered the room. Grant braced to attention and saluted Sam. "Ma'am, your requested provisions." The young woman held out a black duffle bag.

"At ease, Grant. And stop with all the military hoo-ha, you know I hate that." Cassie caught the twinkle in Grant's eyes. She realized someone else enjoyed tweaking her partner. "Allow me to introduce Doctor Cynthia Brockstone, geophysicist from Colorado."

"Doctor, this is Amelia Grant, lieutenant in Her Majesty's Royal Navy. She is on assignment to my organization and has the unfortunate task of being my aide."

Sam and Cassie watched as Cynthia slowly turned on her stool, to stare at the younger woman. "Lieutenant, a pleasure." She extended her hand.

"Amelia, ma'am, and the pleasure is mine." The usually boisterous lieutenant stuttered as she grasped the offered hand. Cassie winked up at Sam.

Sam interjected, "I hope you find what you need, Doctor. If there is anything missing, I'll send Grant back out."

A shiver ran through Cynthia, and she dropped Grant's hand as if burnt. "I'm sorry, I missed that."

"Clothes, and if you need anything else, please let me know, ma'am." Grant answered for Sam. A blush blossomed on the lieutenant's cheeks as she smiled at the older woman.

Sam started to laugh, and Cassie elbowed her in the ribs. Shaking her head no, Cassie whispered, "Do not interrupt."

"Err...right." Sam cleared her throat, which caused the other women to startle. "Why don't you get changed, Doctor. Then we'll head to Langley. Did you receive any additional information on the earthquake this morning?"

A question about her work shook the geophysicist from her fog. "Confirmation of epicenter and depth to rupture. All the recording stations outside the shadow zone have now reported in, and their data are incorporated in my analyses. Nothing has changed."

"Very good, we'll present those data to the director and his staff. I do appreciate your expertise and willingness to travel here. You did a good job last night with the president." Cynthia smiled at the compliment. "We'll get you back to Colorado as soon as we finish at Langley."

"I'm glad I could help." Cassie noticed the good doctor hadn't taken her eyes off Grant as she spoke to Sam. Cassie knew Sam was oblivious to the undertones in the room. As usual.

7 February, 13:28 Hours Local (UTC 04:28)
Chemical Materials Institute
Hamhŭng, South Hamgyŏng Province
Democratic People's Republic of Korea

White-robed scientists stood in a cluster in front of a large tank. Pak Sung-un paced around the perimeter of the stainless-steel storage vessel. It was twelve meters in diameter and twenty meters high. He clasped his hands behind his back, frowning. "Is it ready?"

The lead chemist stepped out of the group. "Well…"

Pak spun around. "Not well, Doctor. I asked a simple question. IS… IT… READY?" He enunciated each word individually.

"The separate components are ready, Supreme Leader." He swallowed. "However, we have not tried to combine the components yet."

"What are you waiting for? We need this now if we are to continue to expand our missile fleet."

"I understand, sir, but—"

"If there is a but, you do not understand. You do not understand you are the one piece delaying our efforts to achieve juche." Pak's face was reddening to a sickening puce, as he clenched his fists at his sides. The small cluster of scientists took a collective step away, leaving the lead chemist standing alone. "When will you have the combination ready?"

"Supreme Leader, we have successfully created a large batch of hydrazine, and it is stable in average environmental conditions. We have not completed the combination yet, as we do not have an adequate amount of nitric acid to determine the titrate amounts to produce a stable hypergolic compound."

"Well, get on it. Use what you have. I will acquire more. I want it no later than the sixteenth of February. We will show the world our might on that day."

Pak and his entourage swept from the storage facility. The group of scientists let out a collective breath. "Sir, we cannot determine the proper combination and have enough acid left to produce a useable quantity," one of the technicians stated.

"I know, I know." The lead scientist was quiet for a moment before she spoke again. "We will not test by titration. We will use the proportions noted in the Soviet scientists' report. If Pak wants his test by the sixteenth, we have no choice. And I will not fail in providing him with the needed amounts."

Pak was driven from the Chemical Materials Institute to the Hŭngnam Fertilizer Complex. Although the world believed it decommissioned in late 2019 due to a lack of power resources and feedstock precursors, Pak restarted the complex in secret and slowly added new staff. This included a team of highly specialized physicians and scientists. Now the complex employed nearly two thousand.

Things were coming together on all fronts. "I must keep the pressure on these scientists. They all work at their own speed without a sense of urgency. My sense of urgency. I will transfer a cadre of National Security Police here to ensure my deadlines are met. Tapping his chin, Pak's thoughts moved to the next step. Remove all distractions. If necessary, remove their families." Pak mumbled gleefully to himself.

Stepping out of his car, he met the director of the Complex. "Doctor, thank you for taking time from your projects to meet with me."

"Of course, Supreme Leader. We are pleased to have you visit again and show you our progress. We have made tremendous strides. Your suggested distribution method is proving promising." The director led Pak up a steep set of white concrete stairs and into the main facility.

16 February, 18:13 Hours Local (UTC 22:13)
Sublevel 4, CIA Headquarters
Langley, Virginia, United States

Satellite images were strewn across Sam's desk. The last pair she reviewed held interesting information. Her telephone rang, and she scrabbled for the receiver. "What?"

"Colonel, NORAD has detected an ICBM launch."

"And?"

"Data are coming in now, ma'am. Hold one." Sam slowly sat back. She scribbled a note on the margin of her yellow legal pad. "New construction—Hamhŭng. Train cars—steel vessels."

"Launch coordinates are 40°40' N by 129°12' E. Outside the coastal town of Kimkeek," the technician stumbled over the foreign name.

"Kimch'aek," Sam automatically corrected. Here we go again. "Trajectory?"

The rattle of keys was loud over the background hiss of the internal comm line. "East by southeast, just south of Hokkaido."

"Interceptors in the area?" More key rattles.

Sam tapped her fingers on the desk and waited. These were times when she wished she had a better communication system in her office. She needed Grant now but had no way to place one call on hold to initiate another. There was a tap on her door and Grant peeked around the edge. Speak of the devil. Sam waved her in.

"The director is on his way down." Sam raised an eyebrow. "I don't know." The two had worked together long enough to be able to complete each other's thoughts.

A voice sounded in her ear. "The missile has destructed. I repeat the missile is down."

"Location?"

"West of the Tsugaru Strait." Sam wrote this name down on her pad and rotated it to Grant. Her aide nodded and left the room.

"Thank you. Please deliver all the available sat images to my office immediately."

"Will do. We had three birds overhead at the time of launch."

Sam smiled an evil grin. "You're going down."

"Beg pardon, ma'am."

"Nothing. Thank you."

Five minutes later, the director of the CIA tapped on Sam's partially opened door. "Colonel, a moment please."

"Of course, Director. Please come in." Sam stood and extended her hand to the man. The current CIA director was military: a two-star Army general, retired from service just two years ago. It was unusual for military personnel to come to the CIA in a presidentially appointed position without a significant time lag between the end of their military career and their appointment. However, given the increasing tensions in the Asian theater, the president had pushed his appointment through. "What may I do for you? You usually don't find time to make the trip down here."

"I wanted to see how your analysis of Pak was coming. The president's national security advisor called me this morning requesting an update." Sam laughed. "Colonel?"

"Sorry, sir. But I find it ironic you appear at my door just as I receive word North Korea has launched another ICBM."

The director's face paled. "They what… "

"I know. What a coincidence, though I don't believe in them," Sam remarked as she slid a satellite image across her desk. "Take a look at this."

He leaned over her desk and squinted at the photo. "What am I looking at, Colonel?"

"This is an image of the Chemical Materials Institute in Hamhŭng. Of note are the rail cars waiting to be offloaded. Although most are covered, three are not. They are carrying large, steel vats or tanks on cradles. The length is approximately seventeen meters given the average length of the flatbed railcar. Although diameter is more difficult, the tanks are wider in diameter than the width of the car."

"Got it. The metal is pretty shiny."

"Good call, sir. I am guessing they are stainless steel or a similar non-corrosive metal."

"Use?"

"Hard to say. Possibly acid storage of some kind. There are fifteen on this train. If we assume the radius of the tank is four meters, with a height of twelve meters, each tank holds approximately 603,000 liters. The cumulative volume of the vessels on this train would be 9.048 million liters."

The director stood slowly. "Excuse me?"

"Nine-point-zero-four-eight-million liters. With other indications of new construction within the Institute grounds, I believe they are preparing a storage facility for a large volume of liquid reagents."

"And the ICBM?" The director sat carefully in the chair before Sam's desk.

Sam leaned back and steepled her fingers under her chin. "Self-destructed or failed just east of the main island of Japan."

The telephone rang on Sam's desk. Grant wouldn't interrupt her meeting with the director unless something critical occurred. "Excuse me, sir." He waved her to answer.

"Michaels."

"Grant here, ma'am. Call from the White House. You're needed there now."

As Sam placed the receiver back, she began to gather the sat images into a neat stack. "The president wants me in the Sit Room."

"My pager didn't go off."

Sam smirked. "Sir, my office is a Faraday cage. If your pager had gone off, something would be very wrong."

The director stood and walked out into the hall. His pager exploded with alerts as soon as he crossed the threshold. He never looked back as he ran down the hall.

16 February, 21:54 Hours Local (UTC 01:54 February 17)
Situation Room, White House
Washington, DC, United States

The president was resplendent in a plum Versace gown, accessorized with a Winston diamond choker. "What are they doing now, Admiral?"

Admiral Benson, in his mess dress uniform with white tie, was equally overdressed for their locale. "I apologize for interrupting cocktails with the British prime minister, but they've launched another ICBM, ma'am."

"Where's Samantha?"

One of the national security council techs answered, "On her way, Madam President. She's held up in traffic."

"How long?"

The tech pulled a secure smartphone out of his pocket. "Her text indicated an estimated two hours."

"Not good. Admiral?"

"On it, ma'am." The admiral entered the small self-contained communications booth in the back of the room. Several minutes later he reappeared. "Joint Base Andrews is sending a helicopter. She's pulling off at the next exit to meet it. ETA from now will be thirty minutes. The colonel asked if she gets a ticket for driving on the shoulder for half a mile, will you cover the fine?"

Despite the mood in the room, President Haley laughed. "Tell her I'll cover the fine, but she has to pay for the helicopter's fuel."

"Aye, ma'am. I'll relay that message to her." The admiral chuckled as he returned to the comm-booth.

"Very good. I'm headed back to our guests. Please let me know when she's here and ready."

Sam bent at the waist and rushed across the south lawn of the White House as the Marine helicopter rose back into the dark sky. Rotor wash blew silvered strands from her braid, as she clutched her messenger bag to her side against the turbulence.

"This way, Colonel," a Marine guard at the door saluted and stepped aside. Two Secret Service agents nodded in greeting and moved with her down the long hall to the elevator.

Entering the Sit Room, Sam sorted through her materials. Unfortunately, she didn't have time to prepare a digital presentation, so she'd have to teach the president aerial photo analysis. Or would it be Aerial Photo Analysis for Dummies? Sam laughed at the idea of calling the president a dummy.

President Haley entered, followed by Admiral Benson and a distinguished gentleman in white-tie evening wear. Sam didn't recognize him. "Samantha, I see you made it."

"Yes, Madam President. Thanks for the ride. I'd still be in traffic had the helicopter not landed in a 7-Eleven parking lot and picked me up." She smiled at the president. "And all it cost me was two Slurpees."

"Ah, no ticket then."

Sam smiled at their inside joke. "No ma'am, no ticket."

"Very good. Prime Minister, may I present Colonel Samantha Michaels, US Marine Corps, retired. Samantha, may I present Prime Minister of the United Kingdom, Lord William O'Rourke."

"Sir, an honor." Sam extended her hand to the man.

He took her hand in a firm grasp and held on. "Samantha Michaels? I believe we have someone in common, Colonel."

Sam frowned. "Sir?"

"Your aide, Lieutenant Grant." Although he pronounced it Lef-tenant, not Loo-tenant, Sam understood who he meant. He released her hand.

"You know Grant, sir?"

"Indeed. The young Grant is my niece." Sam was stunned. Although Grant had a well-honed, upper-class British accent direct from the halls of Oxford, Sam had no idea she was born into the accent as a member of the British aristocracy. Sam would get her for that. She was beginning to understand Grant's assignment to her team was about more than being an aide to a CIA analyst.

"Samantha, I've asked Lord O'Rourke down to hear your analysis of recent events with our friends in the east." She curled her lips around the word "friends" as if she'd bitten into a pickle.

"Very good, ma'am." Sam sorted her photos on the table. "Unfortunately, given the time pressures, I was not able to create a digital presentation. I'll summarize our findings as well as the ICBM launch information we have at this time. Then I will ask you to view the additional construction changes we've found through a stereoscopic viewer. I apologize for this inconvenience." Sam looked at the president in question. She nodded for her to continue.

"Approximately four hours ago, the Democratic People's Republic of Korea launched another intercontinental ballistic missile from a mobile platform near the city of Kimch'aek." The national security tech flashed a map of the Sea of Japan up on the main monitor. Sam picked up a laser pointer and highlighted the coastal area around Kimch'aek. The tech flagged the spot. "This missile's flight characteristics differ from their prior launch, in that this vehicle was propelled with a two-stage rocket engine. The flight trajectory was east by southeast. The missile left the atmosphere and traveled six hundred kilometers before self-destructing or failing. Fragments of the missile landed in the eastern Sea of Japan, just west of the main island of Honshu. We have search crews in the area to recover any pieces for analysis."

The prime minister sat forward. "Any other differences from the prior launch?"

"Yes, sir. Given the recorded flight parameters, we estimate the effective range of this missile would exceed twelve-thousand kilometers, placing the missile easily over Alaska, Canada, or the west coasts of the United States and Central America."

"How do you know the missile was a two-stage vehicle?"

Sam looked at the president before answering. Not knowing how much to say, Sam feared giving away classified information. At her nod, Sam answered. "Our satellites picked up the ignition flash of the second stage. We tracked the first stage as it fell away. We are sending assets into the central the Sea of Japan in an attempt to recover the booster rocket."

"Assets, Samantha?"

"Yes, ma'am. The *Arlington* is leaving their station-keeping position to the splash down coordinates now."

The president smiled. "I am sure Captain Stanley will find something if there is anything to find."

"There is another difference from the first launch which concerns me at this time. Sixteen February is known as The Day of the Shining Star, a holiday to commemorate the birth of Pak's father. Having a launch on this day is significant. Usually, Pak is satisfied with a military parade through Pak Il-Jong Square, but I am concerned he is using this launch to increase the fervor of his people toward an unknown goal. It represents an amazing bit of propaganda. Added to their exaggeration of the nuclear test from last month, the people of North Korea are being emotionally roused with lies."

"Last November, you didn't believe Pak had the technological means to build a two-stage launch vehicle. What's changed?" the president asked.

"We now have evidence of major construction in and around the grounds of the Chemical Materials Institute in Hamhŭng." Sam pointed to a town on the displayed map. Another icon flashed on the screen. "They have constructed several immense buildings along the railroad lines connecting Hamhŭng to manufacturing plants south of Pyongyang. Their latest shipment was fifteen large metal vats or tanks. Storage capacity is calculated at greater than nine million liters." The president was frowning. "That's approximately two-point-four-million gallons, ma'am." The president rocked back in her seat.

"Your analysis, Colonel?" Admiral Benson asked into the stunned silence.

"Let me show you the basis for my analysis, sir. Then I will answer your question."

Sam took the time to illustrate the workings of her stereoscopic viewer. She explained how to overlap the photos by 60 percent and look straight down at two identical spots—one on each photo—one's eyes would naturally try to resolve the two spots, pulling them together into one three-dimensional image. The president leaned over the photos and moved her head back and forth.

"Don't move your head, ma'am. Look straight down and relax your eyes. Try to hold the same spot on each photo with each eye."

After several minutes, the president said, "Oh, my god. That's amazing." She pulled a chair to the table before leaning over the viewer again. "What am I looking at, Samantha?"

"This photo covers a portion of Hamhŭng, the second largest city in North Korea with a population of more than 750,000. This is the industrial park known as the Chemical Materials Institute. It is purported to manufacture vinylon—a synthetic material produced to clothe the people of North Korea. The country has no access to natural materials for clothing. Hamhŭng is also the major foreign trade port for the country as well as a major industrial locus, containing oil refining, metal works, and machinery manufacturing. The Institute is located on the Sŏngch'ŏn River. You can see the train beside the first new building with the covered tanks on flatbed cars." The president nodded.

When Sam stepped back to allow the president to continue her review of the photos, Lord O'Rourke asked, "Why are the construction and the tanks significant?"

Sam looked over at Admiral Benson. He nodded for her to continue. What she was going to say was really going out on a limb. Analysts were not supposed to speculate or use a "gut feel" in their analysis, at least not until hard evidence was available to augment their theoretical framework.

"I think the North Koreans are manufacturing their rocket fuel at this new facility. They have constructed a high-volume storage facility using non-corrosive metal tanks to hold acidic chemical reagents." Sam swallowed hard. "I believe Pak is producing UDMH."

"Good gawd, really? That fuel hasn't been around since the end of World War II."

The president stood up and looked at Sam in question. She expanded on Lord O'Rourke's comment. "UDMH or unsymmetrical dimethylhydrazine is a stable organic amine used as one component of rocket fuel. When mixed with an oxidizer, such as nitric acid, the two components become hypergolic." The president's eyebrow rose. "Meaning it ignites without the need for an external flame. Therefore, the rocket engine is much simpler to construct. The fuel can be onboarded in separate tanks and stored for long periods of time within the missile's assembly. This fuel will not spontaneously ignite until the components are mixed." Sam rocked back on her heels. "I believe the large tanks are constructed of stainless steel and will be used to hold the acidic oxidizer-nitric acid."

"I don't believe that fuel has been used since the Soviets discontinued its production in favor of solid fuels in the mid-1950s."

"You are correct, sir. Most nations with rocket or missile capabilities use a solid rocket fuel for environmental stability while the missile is stored for long periods of time in a silo or on a submarine. Also, solid fuels are safer and can be transported in situ within the rocket without the risk of pre-mature detonation."

"Tell me the bad news, Samantha." President Haley sniped sarcastically.

"Madam President, I cannot confirm the production of UDMH without hard evidence that the chemical components for its production—ammonium nitrates, nitrites, and urea—exist at the production site itself. UDMH is a colorless liquid, immiscible in water. So, if any leaked into the nearby water course, it should be detectable there. The production of UDMH is all a guess on my part. If and when we recover any missile fragments or acquire water samples from the nearby river, we will have a better idea of its fuel composition."

The president moved around the table and sat in her chair as the prime minister took a turn using the stereoscopic viewer. Sam watched as he expertly scanned the photos. He pulled another set from the pile and aligned them. "How do we get this evidence?"

"Ma'am?"

"I asked how we get this evidence. We need to know what's going on. If Pak has an ability to launch a missile capable of crossing the Pacific Ocean and striking the western coasts of Canada or the United States or going even farther, we need to know. And we need to stop it."

Sam didn't know what to say. Was the president planning an attack against North Korea? There wasn't enough proof of anything, just individual puzzle pieces. "Ma'am, I'm sorry. This is speculation on my part. Unless we get hard data from within the Institute, I don't know what the construction is or what it means. We don't have enough hard evidence yet."

The prime minister stood up and turned to the president. "Madam President, we may have a way of getting those samples." He paused and tilted his head in question. "If we could speak for a moment in private?"

"Of course. This way." The pair entered the small communications booth and opaqued the windows. Sam looked at Admiral Benson and raised an eyebrow in question. He shook his head. Sam gathered her photos and placed them and her viewer back in her bag.

When the president and prime minister reentered the room, they sat. "Colonel, I will need your aide for a few weeks, if you are able to be without?"

Sam wondered where this was going but answered in the affirmative. "Of course, sir. No problem." At least no problems for the prime minister, but for Sam it made things much more difficult.

"Very good," Lord O'Rourke turned to the president. "I'll get things moving on my end. Please let me know when you have your assets in place. In the meantime, I would ask you to let me know if you are successful in recovering any missile fragments." He looked at Sam and she nodded. "Give us a few days, Colonel, and I will let you know if the North Koreans are producing the Devil's Venom."

17 February, 18:23 Hours Local (UTC 09:23)
The Sea of Japan (East Sea)
Command Deck, USS Arlington
CGN-47, Ticonderoga-class Guided Missile Cruiser

In the winter months, darkness fell early at this northern latitude. It was just past six in the evening and there was nothing to see outside the thick glass of the *Arlington's* command deck. The dark sea had merged with the cloud-filled horizon, creating a solid black wall. Cassie sat waiting as her boat traveled to the initial search coordinates. Once there, they would use visual, sonar, radar, high-resolution Li-Dar, and magnetic search methods to scour the sea for floating and near-surface fragments of the missile.

Cassie had been back from Washington for almost a month and things had been routinely boring. Her orders were to maintain a racetrack cruise pattern within the northern reaches of the Sea of Japan. She knew her boat and crew were being punished for her use of AEGIS. The weather was violent in the winter, and most days the cooks couldn't risk preparing hot food as her cruiser was tossed about on the churning sea. This limited the crew to cold food. No one aboard was happy, and depression was setting in. Now, however, they had a focus, and the crew was scrambling to prepare the various search systems.

James entered the bridge swathed in an orange neoprene suit, only his face visible within the confines of his Gumby suit. Built of highly insulating neoprene and resembling the rubber toy of the same name, the dry suit would allow the wearer to survive for an extended time in near-freezing water temperatures. Once the face shield was in place, the suit also provided flotation. Hopefully, none of these characteristics would be needed today. Cassie smiled up at her tall executive officer. "Headed out?"

"Once we reach the center point of the search area and light it up, I'll help with the visual search. We can't have anyone outside for more than forty minutes even with the suits." James staggered against the captain's command chair as the deck rolled and the cruiser plunged into the trough of a wave. A wall of water engulfed the bridge.

"Waves are in excess of twenty, James. Make sure everyone is rigged and tied down. It's one thing to look for random missile fragments and quite another to search for a man overboard." James nodded and grabbed her chair arm as the cruiser rolled in the opposite direction.

"We'll have four men at the bow and stern, all in crow's nest cages and no one out on the decks."

"Very well. Be safe." Cassie spun her chair around. "Comm, ship-wide announcement, please."

"Aye, ma'am." He turned to his board and spoke into his headset. "All hands, all hands, prepare to open the hatches. I repeat prepare to open outer hatches. Close all inner bulkhead doors." A warning siren sounded.

Cassie laid a hand on James' arm. "Be careful out there. It's well below zero. You'll ice over in a matter of minutes." She recalled how much ice built up on her helicopter traveling to the carrier in January. Her crew would be out much longer.

The tall man smiled down at her. "No worries, ma'am. We'll be safe." Another wall of water crashed over the superstructure. James chuckled. "Maybe we'll get lucky, and the pieces will just wash up onboard." The bridge crew laughed.

James disappeared down to the lower deck. Another warning siren sounded. "Hatches will unlock in thirty seconds. Prepare to open outer hatches."

"Slow to ten knots. Match the speed of the waves. Open hatches when we crest the next wave." Cassie sat back and gripped the armrests of her command chair. Timing was everything. She had to get the hatches open, the crew out and tied down, and close the hatches before the next wave crested over the bow and drowned the outer decks of her ship in a wall of dark green sea.

"Wave crest now. Open hatches. Open hatches." Huge halogen spotlights flared, and Cassie could see the bow and the cleared deck below her. Crew, in their orange suits, ran to the two forward cages on the starboard and port sides of the bow. She watched as they secured themselves within the cages. The bow fell over and dipped into the next wave trough. Television monitors showed the aft crew's movement to the two positions in the corners of the fantail. The two crewmembers stationed amidship were already tied down, as they were closest to the hatches. The next wave grew in magnitude before her and rose to the height of the cruiser's superstructure. "Forty feet!" Cassie punched a stub on her chair. "Close all hatches. Next wave will fully engulf the deck. Prepare to submerge." Fear closed her throat as she watched the oncoming wave roll over the bow and a green wall hit the command deck windows.

"The XO may be correct, ma'am. We might catch the pieces as they wash over the boat."

Cassie settled back as the deck cleared and the monitors showed all crew still safe within their cages. "We can hope, Chief. Bring up the sonar and Li-Dar. Let's give 'em some help."

Time slowed to a crawl as the crew scanned the sea around them with all available means. "Contact, I repeat, contact," Bryce reported.

"Where?" Cassie demanded of her sonar operator.

"Twenty degrees off the starboard bow, it's a large piece. Less than one-hundred meters out and closing fast. Ninety, seventy, forty, coming up now."

James acknowledged. "Nothing yet. Still scanning." The orange-clad figure moved slowly, turning more to his right. Ice was becoming a problem for the crew outside the Arlington. Patches of greenish-white sea ice were visibly coating her XO's back. "Contact! Contact!"

Cassie scanned the sea. Where was it? And then it was there, a white jagged piece. It was caught in the rolling turbulence of the next wave trough. "Booms to starboard. Prepare to scoop the fragment."

Another monitor came to life as a long, white boom arm extended from the edge of the helo-deck on the fantail and moved out over the starboard beam. The boom operator was stationed in CIC below decks and manipulating the arm remotely. Its mechanical claw opened and closed to displace the accumulated ice rime. The arm made a sudden stabbing motion and stuttered as it pushed the missile fragment under.

"Emergency stop." Cassie's voice rose over the roar of the sea.

The Arlington groaned and staggered as her turbines ground to a halt and massive propellers reversed direction. The ship rolled and began to fall sideways into the trough.

"Starboard thrusters to full." Her boat was equipped with powerful thrusters along each side of the hull to maintain station-keeping when firing the AEGIS missiles. They provided counterthrust to the launch-recoil. Now Cassie was using them to keep her boat from rolling parallel to the trough and capsizing. The bow inched around, pushed by the thrusters. The mechanical arm struggled to control the large fragment.

The boat and fragment were now side by side in the deepest portion of the trough. "Come on. Pull it in," Cassie growled. She half-rose from her seat as the fragment slowly broke free of the sea and rose in the air.

"Moving the fragment to the helo-deck," CIC reported. The arm was retracting and swinging back toward the Arlington's aft decks when the next wave broke over the boat. Not fully perpendicular to the wave, the Arlington yawed to port as tons of seawater crashed over her decks.

"All ahead flank. Turn into the wave, bow forward. Prepare to enter the wave." Cassie had seen pictures of World War II destroyers moving through heavy seas by diving into the wave and coming out the backside into the following trough rather than rise and fall along the waveform, but she had men on the deck. This maneuver would have the decks under water for an extended period while they cut through the wave. "Submerge, submerge!" The cages would protect the men from the weight of the waterwall, but how long would they be able to hold their breaths?

Taking a quick look at the helo-deck monitor, Cassie saw the fragment laying across the starboard rail—half on and half off the ship—held in place by the arm. "Get that fragment onboard now."

CIC responded, "Unable to lift the fragment. The mechanical arm is fried, ma'am. Weight of the arm should hold it in place."

The Arlington came out of the wave into the next trough. "Match speed of the wave. Prepare to climb the next wall." Cassie couldn't risk diving through another wave, especially with the fragment hanging over the side. It would act like a giant outrigger, and the drag would pull the ship to starboard.

"Status of the crew?"

The deck chief leaned over, listening as reports came in. "All have reported in. One possible broken arm... another is tangled in his rigging."

James' voice came over the onboard speakers. "Retrieve the crew. I'm headed to Crewman Andersen."

Cassie pushed her comm stub and said, "No, James. Let's get a rescue crew to him." The *Arlington* crested the next wave and fell toward the trough.

"No time. Retrieve the crew. I'll move to Andersen at the next crest."

"You heard him. At the next crest prepare to retrieve the crew. I repeat retrieve the crew."

A warning siren sounded. "Prepare to open hatches. Medical team to the port outer hatch. Open hatches in ten seconds." As the ship clawed her way up the next wave, the crewmembers outside began to move. Another siren sounded. "Hatches open, hatches open." Crewmembers scrambled, slipped, and skidded toward the hatches. Cassie's attention was on James as he moved across the iced deck toward the trapped crewman. He fell, tangled in his safety rope. He rolled forward on the pitching deck. When the ship reached the trough and leveled off, James struggled to his feet. He unhooked his safety line.

"No!" Cassie shouted.

She watched in horror as her XO scrabbled on all fours and dove toward the crow's cage. He grabbed the cage's outer framework as the *Arlington* began to climb the next wave. The change in deck inclination took his feet out from under him. Now he hung parallel to the deck as the bow rose.

"Emergency rescue crews to hatches one through four. Alert the Seals. Prepare the zodiacs. Cycle the hatches to clear any ice. No one goes out until ordered." Cassie ordered through clinched teeth.

The *Arlington* crested the next wave, and James slammed into the cage as the bow dropped into the trough. Somehow, he got the cage open and pulled himself inside. Cassie knew it would be a tight fit. The cages were intentionally made to fit one standing crewmember only. This prevented injuries if they were tossed about in a larger space. The bow heeled over and began diving into the next wave. "I've got him. Give me... few minutes... untangle safe... line." James gasped for breath.

"Next wave... climbing... slide back... hatch." Her helmsman turned to her in question.

Cassie knew his plan. "He's going to use the deck inclination to slide back to the command superstructure as we climb the next wave, bow up. Get a rescue crew out there, and space them along the forward superstructure. Tie them down. Prepare to catch the crew as they slide toward them. They'll not be roped. If we miss, they'll go overboard." She turned her chair to the comm. "Inflate the zodiacs. Standby the Seals to go in." The *Arlington* had a large hatch which opened along the underside of her fantail. If the rescue crew missed and her two crewmen went overboard, the zodiacs would pop out the stern of the boat and be in position to recover the crewmen. She hoped. "Match the wave speed. Come on. Move. Let's get this right."

Movement on one of the monitors caught Cassie's eye. The rescue team was in place. "James, on the next wave, we're ready to catch you."

A garbled "aye" was all they heard as the *Arlington* began her climb up the next wave.

It all happened in an instant. As the bow began to lift, the cage door flew open, and James' large body fell out. He landed on his back. Cassie winced. He had his arms wrapped around the crewman in a rescue hold—arms crossed over the crewman's chest, wrists clasped in a two-handed grip. The bow rose. The pair slid aft, accelerating as the bow angle increased. Rescue crew moved forward, inching their way up the tilted deck. One fell and slid aft. The other two continued on, a rope strung between them.

James continued to accelerate, sliding headfirst toward the superstructure with the crewman cradled on top of him. "Commander, the rope!" cut through the tense silence of the command deck.

Cassie thought she saw James turn his head, as his arm lashed out to grab for the red rescue line. He missed.

The pair continued to accelerate as the Arlington heaved to starboard, pushed by the wave. Their slide changed direction. They were now headed for the starboard rail. Rescue crew scrambled in and out of the monitor's view. Two more crew went down on the ice.

"Hard to port!" Cassie shouted.

Her crew responded immediately, and the 560-foot cruiser heeled over. The maneuver rolled the ship and lifted the starboard rail. James and the crewman's slide followed the deck's change in angle as the starboard beam lifted out of the sea. Within seconds, a rescue crewman dove on top of them. The three men slowed, as another tossed a bungee net. Once snugged tight, he hauled them in.

"Rescue complete. All tied down."

"Hard to starboard. Bring her into the wave."

It was too late. The next wall of water crashed over the ship and rolled her further onto her port side. "Port thrusters full. Deploy port stabilizers." Below the waterline, the stabilizers extended from the port side. Like an orca's lateral fins, the stabilizers bit into the water and slowed her roll. The *Arlington* wallowed, caught in the turbulence of the trough, weighed down by the mass of sea crashing over her. The bow went under the next wave, as the cruiser continued her port roll.

"All hands, prepare for capsize. Secure the reactors!" The command crew was already belted into their seats but crew below deck would be tossed about and injured, if not killed. Worse, the nuclear power plants could lose their cooling systems if the boat flipped over and the coolants drained away.

The inclinometer read fifty-two degrees when Cassie's ship shot out the backside of the monster wave into the next trough. "Right full rudder. Right turbine back flank. Port turbine ahead full." Cassie had to correct the roll. Her ship shuddered as the *Arlington* attempted to obey the counter move of forward and reverse simultaneously. The bow continued to come around. The next wave approached, a towering wall of green-black water.

"Port thrusters are red-lining." This came from her chief engineer deep within the engine room. "We're losing them."

Warning sirens blared as bulkheads groaned. They would slow down going up the next wave. She couldn't slow down; she had to dive into the next wave again. But what about her crew outside? *"Save the ship. The many need you now. Worry about the few crew later."* Admiral Benson's words echoed in her mind. At the time of this memory, she was battling a typhoon in the Indian Ocean aboard the USS Enterprise, and she was captain of the deck. *"Surf the waves. Don't fight it. Join it. Be one with the water."*

"All stop." The helmsman hesitated. "ALL STOP!" she shouted from her command chair. "Let the wave catch us."

The Arlington heeled over. Then the wave was upon them. But instead of diving into it, the cruiser rose, bobbing like a cork onto the wave crest. *She hovered, suspended in mid-air.*

"Ahead one-third. Maintain our position on the crest. Flow with the water, Chief."

"Err... flow," the chief replied. "Aye, ma'am."

Cassie felt her beloved cruiser right herself. Things began moving in real speed. "Retract the stabilizers."

Once the bow was aligned with the wave direction, she ordered, "Recover the crew. Medical teams, prepare to receive casualties. Stand down the Seals." Cassie glanced at the aft camera monitors. The missile fragment was still draped across the starboard rail. She could only hope it was worth the price they'd just paid.

Several hours later, Cassie was standing alone outside sickbay waiting on her chief surgeon to tell her how bad her crew's injuries were. The *Arlington* was slowly making headway toward Okinawa.

Her cruiser was damaged. How bad, they were unable to determine until they reached port or calmer waters.

A slightly built blonde stepped out of the bulkhead hatch. Her bloodied scrubs caused Cassie to swallow hard. The chief surgeon scolded her captain. "Don't ever do that again!"

Only the chief surgeon could speak this way to a captain. She was the only one who could override the captain and even rescind her command if she were deemed unfit for duty. "She was capsizing, and I had crew on the deck exposed to the swells."

"Swells? That's what you're calling twenty-meter seas? Get real, Captain. You could've lost the boat and the crew."

"But we didn't." Cassie huffed. "Now, how are they?"

"You have thirty-six injured from below deck. The most serious has severe head trauma with a depressed frontal skull fracture. I've put him in an induced coma to reduce swelling and is on life support. He needs to be airlifted to Japan now. I don't have the means to treat him further. The other injuries range from broken bones to deep soft-tissue trauma. They'll all do fine.

"As to those taking a stroll on the deck to catch the swells, one compound fracture of the left humerus. Repaired and resting comfortably. One with severe injury to the lower back—L-2 through L-4 vertebrae are fractured, though not displaced. He's in a brace and resting under sedation. One with a dislocated shoulder and fractured AC-joint. This will need surgical repair, but I can't do it while the deck is heaving. All thirteen are being treated for seawater inhalation and prevention of pneumonia. One case of severe exposure. His Gumby suit was torn in the tussle, and he is severely hypothermic. Currently, he is in a warm-water tank, being monitored for hypothermia-induced heart arrhythmias."

Cassie absorbed all this. She hated when anyone was injured or worse. And now a full 15 percent of her crew was in sickbay. "We'll call for a medivac helicopter to meet us in the morning. I won't risk trying to do a night landing on an icy deck." Cassie paused and swiped a hand over her face. "The weather report has this storm abating in the next few hours, so you should be able to attend to the shoulder. Please send me a list of names and associated injuries. I'll let USPACFLT know our status."

The young surgeon peered closely at Cassie, searching her face. "Get some rest, Captain. Regardless of how bad this all sounds, we've got it under control."

"How's James?" Cassie had been dreading this question. The surgeon didn't share names in her limited summary.

"Surprisingly well, given the circumstances. He's the one in the warm-water bath. His back looks like hamburger, and we'll need to do a wound-debridement once he's warmed up."

"Can I see him?"

"Right this way."

19 February, 10:30 Hours Local (UTC 12:30)
Sublevel 4, CIA Headquarters
Langley, Virginia, United States

Sam peered through her stereoscopic viewer at yet another pair of satellite images. The stack on her desk continued to grow. The CIA had shifted additional satellite assets over the Korean peninsula. Now a pair of high-resolution Keyhole satellites were in geosynchronous orbit. The simultaneously captured images, taken from slightly different angles, created a perfect three-dimensional pair. The images were so clear, Sam could read the license plate numbers on the trucks queued up outside the large laboratory building. "What are you moving now, Pak?" she muttered.

Picking up her office phone, Sam called the sat-imaging lab. "Michaels here. Can we redirect another pair of Keyholes over the Hŭngnam Fertilizer Complex in the next several hours? I'd like to catch some images in daylight to see if we can spot any of the trucks' cargos."

"Coordinates?"

Sam pulled her yellow pad out from under another comic book. "Thirty-nine degrees, forty-seven minutes north. One-hundred-twenty-seven degrees, thirty-seven minutes east."

"Very good, Colonel. I'll call back if we can get them shifted."

"Thanks," she said and hung up the phone. Grant had been gone for less than three days, and already Sam was feeling the weight of tasks not getting done in her absence. Her office looked like a paper bomb had exploded in it, and she would need to clear the used coffee cups out soon before something bloomed in their depths. Her stomach growled loudly. She should also head home for some food and rest soon.

A knock on her door roused her from her internal debate about food. Rest could wait until she heard if anyone found anything in the Sea of Japan. "Come."

A uniformed Air Force NCO entered. "Colonel, there is a C-5 Galaxy on final approach to Joint Base Andrews with classified cargo."

"Excuse me, Airman?"

The young man gulped. "The manifest has your name on it, ma'am. I was told to let you know. The director thought you might want to meet the plane."

She held out her hand for the paperwork. Opening the manila envelope, she pulled a single sheet out and scanned the note's content. "Very well. Thank you, Airman."

After a crisp salute the young man spun on his heels and left. The door swung closed behind him.

Sam was thrilled. A piece of the missile was recovered. Now they were getting somewhere. She picked up her phone again and dialed another number.

"Metallurgic lab, you smelt it, we melt it."

"Francis, really, this is how you answer the phone?"

"Yeah. It's pretty boring here on the mesa. The ovens are cool, and we haven't had any fun in weeks. Just waiting for our next assay assignment."

Sam laughed. She'd met Francis Douglas at the MIT student athletic facility. She was rehabbing her injured back and he was rehabbing a torn ACL which ended his professional football career. They soon became gym buddies. Francis was completing a Ph.D. in the structural analysis of metals under various stress regimes. Especially metal exposed to nuclear explosions. Sam didn't learn his specialty until later, though, when he called her out of the blue to ask a favor concerning one of his lab techs at Los Alamos National Laboratories.

"Fire up the ovens, I've got a project for you."

She could picture him rubbing his big hands together. "Whatcha got?"

"Can't say over the phone. Can you catch a flight to DC today? My package is arriving at Andrews."

"Why not forward it here? I've got all the needed equipment."

Sam hesitated. Then, said quietly, "It's too sensitive to leave Langley. Sorry, Francis, but I'll need you here."

"Ah don't know, ma'am. Ah've got a full social calendar," Francis said with a drawl, his put-on Texas accent thick. He'd played four seasons for the Houston Texans prior to his injury, but he hailed from Chicago.

"That's BS, and you know it." Sam snickered. "I promise this one will keep you in metal-heaven for a long time to come."

"If you put it like that, how can I refuse an offer from such a beautiful woman?" Sam heard keys clacking in the background. "I can be in DC by this evening. Where are you taking me for dinner?"

Sam met the C5 Galaxy cargo plane at Andrews and had her package moved to a secured storage facility on the grounds of CIA headquarters in Langley, Virginia. Once the amorphous, white, shrink-wrapped, lumpy package was safely stowed and under guard, Sam headed to Dulles airport to pick up Francis. Hopefully, he would be able to fill in some blanks for her and move her analysis of North Korean missile development forward. As she sat in her SUV in the curbside pickup lane, her secure mobile phone rang. There was no caller ID, but the identification code string displayed told her it was Cassie. "Hey, beautiful."

"Is this your standard greeting for everyone, Ace?" Cassie teased, but Sam heard tension in her voice.

"What's wrong? Are you okay?" Sam gripped the phone tighter.

Cassie exhaled a long breath. "I'm fine. My boat will be fine once she's fixed, and all but one of my crew are on the mend."

Now Sam was really worried. "Cassie, what the hell's happened?"

"I can't discuss the details, even over a secure line. Let's just say, I hope it was worth the trouble to get you your birthday present."

"Err… my birthday isn't—"

Cassie jumped in. "I know when your birthday is, and I hope you enjoy the present. It should be at Andrews soon." The light finally dawned, as Sam caught the clue.

"It's already arrived and is in safe keeping until my birthday." Sam paused. Cassie didn't sound right. "Are you really okay?"

"Yes, Ace. I'm fine." Sadness thickened Cassie's voice. "We'll be in Okinawa for several weeks while repairs are made to my boat. James is recovering, though he can't lie on his back yet."

"You said, all but one. Who's not doing well?" Cassie hated to have crew injured or worse, and this sounded like worse. Cassie ignored her question.

"Do you think you can head over here for a few days? I would love to have you close."

Now Sam knew something wasn't seriously wrong. Whatever it was, it was bad. Her worry ramped up accordingly. Cassie had lost one or more of her crew. "I'm at Dulles picking up Francis."

"What's the big lug doing for you?"

"Not important. Once I feed him and get him settled in, I'll check flights and let you know when I can be in Japan."

Cassie heaved a sigh of relief. Sam could picture her small smile. "That'll be great. I know James will love to see you. His mom is heading here from West Africa. We'll make it a party for your birthday."

"My birthday, right. I'll call you in a few hours. I can see Francis headed this way. I hope Morton's has enough beef on hand to handle his appetite." Sam swallowed and said, "Be safe, beautiful."

"Always, Ace."

20 February, 23:32 Hours Local (UTC 03:32, February 21)
Secure Storage Facility 6X, CIA Headquarters
Langley, Virginia, United States

Francis looked up at the white, lumpy package resting on two long pallets. He slowly walked around it and asked, "Can we open it? I was never good at waiting for Christmas morning."

Sam tossed him a large, machete-like knife. "Have at it."

"This is going to be so much fun. I can feel it. I've got the same butterflies in my stomach I had at the beginning of the championship game." He made a slice through the tough plastic and the shrink-wrap snapped away. His next cut was perpendicular to the first. As the plastic began to curl back, a portion of a red star against a white background appeared. Francis lowered the knife to his side and slowly turned to Sam. "What the f... is this, Sam?"

"I was hoping you would tell me. It cost the life of a seaman to recover it from the northern Sea of Japan."

"If this were a Chinese star, it would be yellow." He pointed at the red star with the knife. "North Korea?"

Sam made a buzzer-sound. "The big guy gets it in one." Francis wasn't sharing in her laughter.

"As I asked, what the f..., Sam?"

"If I remember correctly, your security clearance is TOP SECRET-EYES ONLY."

He nodded and continued hacking the shrink-wrap plastic off the package. As more was exposed, a large, curved white surface came into view. The casing was ripped and torn, creating a jagged metal edge, like the interlocking teeth of a great white shark. The "teeth" were all pointing outward. Francis placed the machete on a nearby rolling toolbox and slowly walked around the large metal fragment. "Ten meters long, four and a half meters in height, exterior surface pristine except the damaged edge. Interior metal surface marred by..." He paused to sniff the sooty coating, "a chemical explosive residue. Only viable marking, the red star of the Democratic People's Republic of Korea."

Francis stepped back and put his meaty hands on his narrow hips. He huffed and turned to Sam. "What the fuck are you doing with the external housing of a North Korean missile?"

"It's a long story, and I'll give you the background on the way to the house. In the meantime, what you need to tell me is the following: What caused the missile to fail? Mechanical failure or self-destruction? What is the metallurgic composition of the casing? What kind of fuel was used to propel the missile? Would the missile use a single or two-stage propulsion system? What was the overall size of the missile: mass, length, and diameter? What is your best estimate of its effective range to target?"

Shaking his head, Francis looked back at the hunk of metal. "I'll need more equipment than I brought with me to answer all that. Probably access to a full lab." He grinned at her. "And an open tab at

Morton's."

"Make a list. You'll have whatever you need, including an unlimited supply of beef." Sam headed toward the door of the warehouse. Francis seemed mesmerized by the deformed metal hunk. At the door, she turned. "Oh, and by the way, I need those answers yesterday."

23 February, 14:05 Hours Local (UTC 05:05)
Jigokudani Monkey Park
Yamanouchi, Nagano Prefecture, Japan

Sam leaned over a redwood railing. Steam rose all around. She was enveloped in a shroud of mist which soaked her hair and dappled her puffy, down jacket, fogging her yellow aviator glasses. Light snow was falling. It was an idyllic place, full of fantasy and mystery. Sam expected wood nymphs to peek out from around the winter-worn trees.

Cassie stood several meters away, trying to capture the antics of the local residents—the famous hot-springs-soaking snow monkeys. Sam laughed as one of the monkeys seemed to clown for the camera. Standing on a rock ledge surrounding the hot pool, he jumped into the middle of the spring, swamping his fellow bathers. The matriarch of the macaque clan grumbled a chitter at him and splashed water in his direction.

After Cassie's worrisome telephone call, Sam quickly organized travel to Okinawa, leaving Francis up to his elbows in metal analyses. He had all the toys he needed and then some. If there was something the CIA technicians couldn't supply, Francis would fly it in from Los Alamos. She didn't think he even realized she had left. He promised his results within the next week or so. Her credit card would scream with his dinner bills, but it was worth it. His results would answer a number of questions about the North Korean missile. She'd sent an encrypted email to Grant informing her of the recovered fragment and asked she relay the message to her uncle. As yet she hadn't heard back from her young aide. Sam was beginning to worry.

During her flight to Narita International Airport, she made several decisions. One, she would get Cassie away from the *Arlington*, if possible. Two, she would invite Cassie's XO, Commander James Alexander, and his mother along. And three, she would listen and provide what comfort she could.

Sam read the after-action report from the missile fragment recovery operation and knew what had happened. The most severely injured seaman did not survived his head injuries. His body would be flown back to Joint Base Andrews and receive all military honors prior to burial at Arlington National Cemetery. Cassie had wanted to accompany the body, but her boat and crew needed her more, so she stayed at Fleet Activities-Okinawa. Naval repair crews were swarming the *Arlington* to evaluate her damages and prepare a repair plan. Once approved, Cassie would be in dry dock as long as her boat was.

It was winter in Japan and Sam had the perfect plan. A trip to the Japanese Alps, some skiing, some sightseeing, some good food, but most importantly, rest. Rest for Cassie and for James. Time to heal physically and mentally. Sam could see the weariness etched in their faces. Though, neither would admit to their exhaustion. Rest and time to distance them from their ordeal were sorely needed.

"You did a good thing." A small voice rose with the mist, and Sam turned to James' Mom—Julia Alexander. She lifted an eyebrow in question. "This…," Julia waved at the monkeys, "is just what they needed."

The four were staying in a Ryokan—a traditional Japanese inn. This one sat on the edge of the park in Shibu Onsen tucked in a cluster of ancient cherry trees. The classic Japanese hostelry was run by the sixteenth generation of the founding family. The tatami-mat rooms and sparse furniture made Sam feel like she was in a doll house. She stepped carefully, trying not to damage anything or put her foot through a fragile wall. The staff served communal meals of wonderful Japanese food twice daily. The inn, built in the late eighteenth century, had developed the numerous hot springs in the area, affording their guests a restorative experience using hydrotherapy.

Sam laughed as it seemed the doctor could read minds as easily as she could read bodies. "I was just thinking the same thing. How's James' back doing?"

"It's coming along, but he's going to have some interesting scars. He said he might get a full tattoo to cover the damage once the skin heals." Sam raised an eyebrow in question. "Seems the *Arlington's* surgeon didn't get all the neoprene fragments out of his wounds. There are some orange and black spots scattered throughout the healing tissue."

The doctor's face turned serious, and she frowned up at Sam through the rising steam. "Though, it's Cassie I'm worried about. She's putting up a good front—all captain in control—but I believe it's bullshit."

The profanity stunned Sam. She'd never heard Julia swear. Sam turned back to the frolicking monkeys and lowered her voice. "I agree. She says she's fine, but she's not sleeping and she's eating only enough for fuel. Usually, you can't keep her away from food, especially when it's a new cuisine."

"Perhaps, a hike and lunch away from the other guests and out of hearing of unknowing ears? The thin-walled rooms do not allow her to relax enough to speak candidly about the experience." Julia laid a small hand on Sam's arm. "She's shaken to the core, Samantha. She lost a crew member and nearly lost her boat with all aboard. She's hiding behind her command mask, reserved and untouchable." Sam nodded.

"But she saved the boat and her crew. Those are the positives she needs to focus on." Julia's voice trailed off, and Sam just caught her whispered words. "No one can bring back the dead. Lord knows I've prayed I could."

"I'll take your suggestion. Perhaps a traditional inn wasn't such a good choice on my part. I didn't realize there wasn't any privacy. But a hike, in this beautiful area may be just the thing." She wrapped an arm around Julia's shoulder and hugged her tight. "Thank you."

"You're welcome." Julia chuckled. "I'll send my bill in the mail." Both women dissolved in a fit of giggles.

"What's got you two going?" Cassie stepped up to Sam and leaned into her side. Sam's arm automatically pulled Cassie to her. Her head fell onto Sam's broad shoulder, where she nuzzled into the soft downy surface.

"We were just discussing a hike, a picnic, and James' tattoo." Sam smiled down at her partner, and her heart stuttered with a realization. Cassie was her life.

"Tattoo? No way. James is too straitlaced."

Julia burst into another fit of giggles. "Oh, you have no idea, Cassandra." She became serious. "But unless he has another debridement, he'll have a colorful set of scars."

Cassie stiffened in Sam's grasp. "I…err…didn't know. The surgeon said he was fine and just needed some time to allow the soft tissue to heal." She stepped out of Sam's hug.

"A captain stands alone," Sam thought with regret.

"He's fine. You mustn't worry." Julia pulled Cassie close and looked her in the eyes. "All things considered, it's just a big scratch. He had worse when he fell out of his treehouse and slid down the side of a eucalyptus tree. Then, he looked like he'd dumped a motorcycle doing eighty. Every part of him was covered with 'road rash.' We had to soak him out of his sheets each morning."

"Ouch." Sam winced in sympathy.

"Indeed."

Sam slung a laden backpack onto her shoulders. "Ready?"

"Let me tighten this boot and I'm good." Cassie stood up from the low bamboo bench at the front of the Ryokan and stamped her feet, settling the new boots. "Let's not over do it today. I don't want blisters."

"Right, no blisters. I thought we'd head up the Observation Trail to the last set of hot springs. The guidebook says it's about forty minutes. We could have lunch there and afterward hike back along this abandoned road which curves through the adjoining forest." Sam held up the annotated map.

"Sounds good. Lay on, MacDuff." Cassie waved her hand toward the sign at the trailhead.

Sam knew if Cassie was quoting Shakespeare, things really weren't good at all. "I promise I won't kill you, MacBeth." Sam tried to lighten the mood, suddenly turned grave by Cassie.

"I know, Ace."

After fifteen minutes up a gentle climb into the hot springs area, Cassie seemed to realize her error and hugged Sam from behind. "I love you." Her voice whiffled into the puffy down of Sam's parka.

Sam stopped and turned within her grasp. "And I you. But I'm worried, Cassie. Worried for you." A little voice spoke sarcastically into her head. *Real smooth, Sam. You were supposed to allow her to talk.*

Cassie looked up with tears in her eyes. "I killed him, Sam."

"Oh, beautiful. No. No, you didn't. It happened—yes. He died—yes. But you saved your boat and your crew. Over three hundred lives. Due to your correct actions." Cassie buried her face in Sam's parka and sobbed. "Come on, let's sit over there." Sam pointed to a clearing within a stand of trees and led them off the trail.

Sam spread a woven mat on the snow-covered ground. Sitting, she gathered Cassie onto her lap. The stalwart captain of the US Navy's most powerful warship lost her battle for control. Sam rocked her gently as Cassie sobbed out her fears and hurt. She whispered nonsensical words of love and support. Of understanding and compassion. Only another survivor of wartime leadership with its associated grief of loss would know the depth of Cassie's pain.

Cassie's sobs lessened. Her body relaxed, and she loosened her hold on the front of Sam's parka. Slowly, the *Arlington's* captain succumbed to her grief and exhaustion. Minutes passed, and Sam realized her partner had fallen asleep. Pulling a fleece blanket from the backpack, Sam wrapped them up and settled against a tree trunk. She kissed the top of Cassie's head and exhaled a sigh of relief. This was the first step of healing. They had a way to go, but Cassie took the first step. The remaining steps they'd travel together, however long it took.

Although darkness was filling the narrow valley and a light dusting of snow now coated the pair, Sam remained motionless, holding her wounded captain against her chest. Cassie's head rested over her heart. This was a position Cassie often settled into, claiming the steady beat of Sam's heart made her feel safe.

Cassie stirred and Sam loosened her hold. Looking down, Sam's gaze was met by red-rimmed, ice-blue eyes. Smiling, she asked, "Better?"

"Yes, I think so." Cassie looked around the small clearing. "It's snowing."

"So, it is. Has been for a bit." Sam lifted the blanket and turned to the pack. "Hungry?" A low, almost inaudible rumble answered her. "I'll take that as a yes." Pulling various small containers from the insulated-pack's depths, she spread them out on the edge of their mat.

Cassie rubbed her gloved hands together. "This looks interesting. Any ideas what all this is?"

"None. I asked the innkeeper for a picnic lunch, and he provided this."

"All right. Let's see what we've got." Cassie's stomach growled again.

Sam felt her muscles relax at the warm sound. Two well-filled bento boxes released a wave of aromatic steam when Cassie pried off their lids. "Oooh, soba." She handed Sam a pair of chopsticks and one of the deep boxes. Crispy fishcake pieces floated in a light broth over a bed of noodles, garnished with parsley and scallion rings. A master of all eating utensils, Cassie easily gathered her noodles and began slurping them up. She caught Sam grinning at her. "What?"

"Nothing. You're so cute."

Cassie gave her a skeptical look and returned to her soba. The other boxes contained a meat-rich stew in a thickened broth, a steamed snow crab with a mirin-based dipping sauce, and a surprise which excited Cassie. "Oh, my god. I can't believe they prepared zenzai."

Sam looked into the last box. Small white balls floated in a crimson liquid. She raised an eyebrow, not understanding why this was a big deal.

"You're going to love these. They're mochi balls."

Sam wasn't convinced.

"Sweet rice compressed into balls and cooked in a red bean soup. They're a real treat."

"Where did you learn about all these foods?"

"One can't be stationed in Japan without trying all the local cuisine. I took a Japanese cooking class on my last shore leave before…" Cassie trailed off. A cloud passed over her face. She placed her mochi to the side and leaned back against Sam's side. Time passed, as snow continued to fall. The darkness surrounding them was complete.

Safe within the small clearing, Cassie began to speak, a whisper to the wind. "He was only nineteen. A reactor tech, third class. On his first cruise." She fell silent. Sam waited. Cassie was far away within her memories.

"Thomas Jefferson Washington. Everyone called him TJ. How could a mother tie a child to two such large, historical figures?" The quiet wrapped around them again. "He applied to reactor school to increase his rating. He wanted to be a nuclear physicist. Only now he won't. Can't. His dream is gone. Cut short."

Cassie sighed, tears tracing down her pale cheeks. "He fell from the top of the reactor core. He was trying to close the coolant drains in case we capsized. Keep the reactors safe. Keep the boat safe. Keep the crew… " Her voice bled out.

Neither spoke for a long moment until Sam finished her thought with a whispered, "Doing his job as he was trained."

"I recommended him for the Navy Medal." Cassie turned to Sam, who clearly saw the silvered moonlit trails on Cassie's cheeks. "To Admiral Benson. The recommendation, I mean. I sent it directly to the head of the Navy. The least I could do. I couldn't save him."

Sam felt hot tears run down her own chilled cheeks. How many brave women and men were lost doing their jobs? Doing their duty for their crewmates and for their country? "He lived up to his names," she said, her words seeming to echo in the stillness of the winter forest.

24 February, 12:14 Hours Local (UTC 04:14)
Wuhan Institute of Virology
Xiaohongshan, Wuchang District
Wuhan, Hubei, China

The officer on duty stood as a communication tech knocked on his door. "Yes?"

"Sir, this just arrived." He handed the officer a yellow flimsy envelope.

Ripping the envelope open, he read the message. His breath caught in his throat. Pressing a button on the telephone, he spoke into the handset. "Get me the director."

"I am sorry, sir, but the director is in the Bio-Safety Level Four lab and unavailable at this time."

"I don't care where he is. I need to speak to him now. We have a bio-hazard priority one alert from Hong Kong."

"We will notify the director. He should be available within thirty minutes."

The trembling young officer sank in his chair. "Now what?" He looked at the crumpled paper in his hand. Fear gripped his heart.

SECTION THREE

15 April, 12:26 Hours Local (UTC 03:26)
The Day of the Sun National Holiday
Pak Il-jong Square
Pyongyang, Democratic People's Republic of Korea

Kim Hye-su huddled on the upper tier of the supreme leader's reviewing stand. She tried to remain as invisible as possible among the throng of high-level government and military personnel around her. She kept her hands folded in her lap and her eyes forward as rank after rank of military brigades goose-stepped past. The morning sun flashed off their highly polished boots. Their rifles were balanced in their palms, barrels pointing to the heavens, arms extended parallel to the ground. Quite a feat of physical stamina considering how long the parade route was. All the onlookers cheered with bursts of sound when ordered over the loudspeakers.

Doctor Kim couldn't believe it when a military car arrived at her laboratory in the Nuclear Scientific Research Center in Nyŏngbyŏn to take her to the parade. She wasn't given a chance to change clothes. She only had enough time to wash her hands and grab her purse before they were off on the one-hundred-kilometer trip to the Capitol building.

Several months earlier, she received a list of design specs with accompanying environmental demands. The only instructions—build it within the limited time allotted. She had successfully miniaturized the new warhead to the demanding specifications. This warhead was unique. It was charged with Plutonium-239, and her new design was stable under all environmental conditions. It also showed promise when the warhead was stressed by extreme physical changes—tested through a range of temperatures and pressures. Most importantly, it was survivable to impact. She had no idea what its intended use was, but she delivered the new design to Pak before the deadline.

Hye-su hoped this success would allow her to get the needed travel permits to Geneva, Switzerland. There she would attend a nuclear-energy conference. Her next assignment was to revamp the design of their aging Magnox-style reactors to increase the amount of plutonium they could extract from the spent fuel rods. She hoped to also improve energy-production efficiency. This would not be as easily completed since she was being reassigned to the Kangson Enrichment Site in Ch'ŏllima, outside of the Capitol.

Being that close to Pak and his group of sycophants made Hye-su uncomfortable. Just as uncomfortable as she was now. Her dress was stained with the dirt of her machine shop. Embarrassed, a blush colored her cheeks. Something was up, but she couldn't figure out what. She wished for the quiet and freedom of the wilds around the Punggye-ri Nuclear Test Site. She only had a short trip scheduled to the site to load the next test weapons, though, so would not be enough time to rest and relax in the mountains.

The crowd cheered and Hye-su suddenly realized the videographers were pointing their cameras at her. Damn her lack of concentration. Pak Sung-un was huffing his way up the risers to her row at the top of the viewing platform. As he got closer, he signaled for her to stand. Slowly rising to her feet, the crowd roared in approval as the announcers identified a new weapon, developed by her. Then she saw it, the smaller Pukgeukseong-1, rolling by on a flatbed truck.

The cameras had zoomed in, once he reached Hye-su. He grasped her hand in a sweaty palm and shook it vigorously for the cameras. Hye-su could only force a smile and pray she would survive this day. Hye-su's hand began to sweat in the supreme leader's grasp. Her head swam as she tried desperately to remain conscious. *What did they do to my design? How is he going to use it?*

15 April, 00:24 Hours Local (UTC 04:24)
Sublevel 4, CIA Headquarters
Langley, Virginia, United States

Grant burst into Sam's office, the door bouncing off the wall.

"For the love of god, what is it?" Sam's heart pounded from the sudden intrusion. Despite the interruption, Sam was glad to have Grant back. Things were better organized, and she felt she could focus exclusively on North Korea and their next actions, leaving all the other demands to Grant.

The young lieutenant bent over and grabbed her knees. "South Korean newsfeed... parade... new weapons." She gasped between breaths.

Sam stood and rounded her desk. "Well, come on, then. Let's have a look." Long strides took her out of her office and down a flight of stairs, deeper into the depths of the Langley facility. The communications center was a dark, cavernous room filled with computer workstations aligned on a series of tiered platforms. All faced a twenty- by- fifty-foot wall of hi-resolution monitors. Entering the darkened room, Sam saw the monitors were melded into one huge screen. Ranks of troops marched by a tall viewing stand. Trucks, tanks, and armored personnel carriers rolled across the screen in precise lines. Next came the missiles, deadly-looking ICBMs on multi-wheeled launchers. Flatbed-mounted surface-to-air missile launchers moved by on trucks. Their deadly, eye-filled boxes pointed off at an angle to the heavens.

Sam watched the next missile appear. Smaller than the ICBMs, and painted a deep blue instead of white or green, they were emblazoned with the blood-red star of the DPRK. They looked evil. "What are those?" she asked in the silent room.

"Unknown, ma'am. These are new."

The feed cut from the rows of small missiles to the viewing stand. Sam watched Pak laboriously climb the risers and point to a young woman. The woman hesitated and slowly rose to her feet. She was dressed in a wrinkled, dirt-blotched gray dress, her hands clutching a worn purse in front of her. Pak thrust out a meaty paw, and the woman reluctantly grasped his hand. "Zoom in on her. Run full facial-recognition. I want to know who she is. Full dossier."

Sam wound her way through the banks of computer workstations to stand directly in front of the monitor-wall. "Capture individual screen shots of those missiles from as many angles as we have."

"Already done, ma'am."

Sam turned to the analysts in the room. "Where's this feed coming from?"

"We intercepted the broadcast of the Korean Central Broadcasting Committee by piggybacking on their analog-signal transmission. It's the same way South Korea listens in on North Korean broadcasts; except we're doing it from a geosynchronous satellite directly above Pyongyang."

"How's that possible? They aren't broadcasting into space. They use a ground-following terrestrial signal."

The analysts in the room guffawed. One young man in the front tier answered. "Several years ago, the North Korean government issued tablets to the populace. The tablets have no Wi-Fi access other than a direct link to the country's intranet, but the government allowed various apps to be developed for the tablet. The central broadcasting committee developed an app to send their broadcasts directly to all those tablets."

"And?"

"We simply loaded the app into our satellite's operating system and are receiving the signal as if the satellite were a tablet."

"Awesome," Grant whispered. Sam turned to her lieutenant. Grant shrugged. "You must admit, it is great when we can hoist them on their own petard."

Another Shakespearean quote. It seemed she was surrounded by literary snobs. "Indeed. Get me a recording of the entire parade. And find out who that woman is."

Sam left the darkened room and returned to her office. *Petard indeed. We'll be the ones hoisted if we can't figure out what Pak is planning.*

17 April, 21:24 Hours Local (UTC 12:24)
The Sea of Japan (East Sea)
Command Deck, *USS Arlington*
CGN-47, Ticonderoga-class Guided Missile Cruiser

Evening settled into night, as Commander James Alexander entered the command deck. "I have the conn," he told the ensign sitting in the captain's chair.

The young brunette rose and turned to the XO, snapping off a crisp salute. "You have the conn, sir. Seas are calm with one-meter swells. The helicopter arrived back from Okinawa approximately thirty minutes ago with mail and communiques. Comm is working through them. NOAA (National Oceanic and Atmospheric Administration) has issued a weather alert for a low-pressure system developing in the Johore Strait. The captain was informed of this alert. It doesn't look like much at this time. Weather satellite images show only a low cloud deck over the area with no indication of rotation. The fleet continues steaming north toward La Perouse Strait. No change in orders. At current speeds, we should enter the Okhotsk Sea before morning."

"Thank you, Ensign. Enjoy your dinner."

"Aye, sir."

The command deck bustled with activity as the evening watch was replaced by those assigned to the night watch. After the crew handoffs, quiet settled over the deck. James reduced the bridge lights to a low glow. Various computer monitors were spots of sharp light, but the technicians and officers soon reduced the brightness of their screens to mellow, comfortable levels.

"Your coffee, sir." The sonar operator appeared at James elbow. He gratefully took the steaming aluminum mug.

"Thank you, Bryce."

"No problem, sir. I was getting my own and figured you could use some caffeine, too."

James smiled. "A Navy ship runs on coffee."

"Without a doubt, sir." Bryce settled back at his post and replaced his earbuds and throat mic.

Hours of mundane tasks occupied the crew and James relaxed back into the comfortable warm leather. At least he was comfortable sitting now. A few months ago, he couldn't stand any pressure on his back or wear his snug uniform T-shirt.

He thought about his mom. They'd had a great holiday with Cassie and Sam, a wonderful three weeks in the mountains of northern Japan. This was the first time since leaving for the Naval Academy James had spent such an uninterrupted period with his mom. Enough time to discuss her acceptance of a new post with the National Science Foundation. Eight months stationed at the South Pole as the sole physician to the seventy or so scientists and technicians assigned to Amundsen-Scott Base. Four months of her tour would be spent in total darkness. She would be trapped at the base, high on the central Antarctic plateau at 9,306 feet, during the long, dark polar winter.

No flights would occur in or out between mid-February and late October, when temperatures averaged minus 45 degrees Celsius. Several military satellites provided scientific data transfers, broadband internet, and limited telecommunications. Some satellite calls would be available using the commercial Iridium system when weather permitted and the commercial satellites were in range. It all meant his mom would be out of communications for most of the time, save for the random email message and limited Zoom chats.

James couldn't bring himself to be upset about the situation. His mom was an adventurer. She'd traveled the world healing the sick, chasing pathogens for the WHO, vaccinating children against measles, polio, and tuberculosis. When she'd told him about this NSF opportunity, she'd called it a vacation. A time to rest and chronicle her travels. Finish the virology textbook she'd started about her experience hunting Ebola patients in West Africa. Continue her research into other hemorrhagic viruses.

He worried, nonetheless. Of course he did. That's what a son did, right? It would be hypocritical of him to keep his mom from doing her thing. She never told him not to join the Navy, not to get his helicopter wings, not to get his certification in deep-diving submersibles, nor follow in his father's footsteps aboard a Navy warship. Nope. When he saw her next, he would kiss her on the cheek and wish her well. After all, who knew where the *Arlington* would be in December.

Klaxons sounded and snapped James out of his self-reflection. "Sonar-contact. I repeat sonar-contact."

"Bryce?"

"Sonar-contact six thousand meters astern off the port flank. Moving parallel to our course at eleven knots. She just rose above the thermocline."

"Bring the crew to Alert Status Two." Klaxons sounded again around the ship. "Let's see if we have a tail. Come to heading three zero five. Maintain speed."

"Three zero five, aye." The bow dipped as the cruiser turned to port and aligned with the new heading.

"Comm, message the fleet. Send them the data. Ask for a flight of 60R Seahawks to pound the area. Let's paint this guy." He spun in his chair. "Gunny, order the LAMPS up. Drop their buoys. Do not go active, passive sweeps only. Load the torpedoes—standard spread. Prep sonic depth charges."

"Aye, sir." Gunny placed her hand over her earbud. "Helos are rolling onto the deck. They'll drop passive buoys once deployed. Tubes one through five are loading. Depth charges are online."

The Alert Status Two warning brought the captain to the bridge. Stanley entered her command deck, pulling a sweatshirt adorned with the Navy insignia over her head. "Report."

"Ma'am, we've picked up a tail. They just popped above the thermocline, and we painted them with passive sonar. I ordered a turn to northwest by west to see if they are following course. LAMPS are rolling and will be airborne in less than three minutes—passive buoys only. I've requested a flight of Seahawks from the carrier in support."

"Very good, James." He stood from her chair, and she settled in his place. "Thanks for keeping the seat warm."

The bridge crew laughed as the large leather chair swallowed their small captain. She lowered the seat, so her feet touched the deck. It had been adjusted to accommodate her XO's six-and-a-half-foot frame. "Sonar, track and course, please." The plexiglass board now had a large red X—point of first contact and initiation of their course change. The track of new course was being drawn in.

"Course is unchanged. The sub's heading remains zero-zero-five degrees. They've not flinched with our change."

"Helos are away. Fanning out to cover our beam. Buoys dropping now."

Cassie crossed her legs. None of their allies had reported any submerged activities along the fleet's course. "Sonar, type of contact?"

"Computers are chewing on it." Bryce turned to the captain. "It sounds like a diesel-electric, Skip. I haven't heard one of those since sonar school. Maybe an old Soviet Romeo or a Golf?"

"Let me know when the computers spit something out."

Cassie noticed green dots appearing on her board—drop points for the sonar buoys. They created a neat cross-pattern which would hold for a while in the calm seas. "Data return, Skip. The computer calls it a diesel-electric Project 629A Soviet Golf II class boat."

"And tell me about this antique, Mister Bryce."

Pulling a manual from beneath his workstation, Bryce flipped through the pages. "She's one hundred meters long with three diesels and three electric motors. Top speed submerged is seventeen knots. Submerged duration seventy days. Crew complement is eighty-three." Bryce looked up, pale. "She can be a ballistic missile sub, Skip. Missiles would be housed in the sail."

"She's what?" Cassie punched a stub on the arm of her command chair. "CIC paint that contact. Full sweep. Bring the buoys to active search." She released the stub. "Bring us about to zero two zero, all ahead two-thirds. Intersect her course. Comm, get a message to the fleet with Bryce's data. Request permission to force her to the surface."

"Aye, Skip."

Commander Alexander leaned over the arm of Cassie's command chair. "Who the hell owns that rust bucket?"

"A rust bucket with teeth, James. She could be on the west coast of the US in a matter of a few days. And if she had stayed away from our normal cruise patterns, we'd never have known she was there."

The petty officer of the deck swiped the plexiglass board clean as digital data filled the space. A cross-hatched grid overlaid their course information. Each buoy occupied one of the grid intersections. "Fleet admiral on the comm for you, Skip."

"Patch it through." Cassie activated her comm system and Admiral Armstrong's nasal voice filled the command deck.

"What the hell is going on, Captain? Can't you make a smooth crossing without all this nonsense?"

Cassie gripped the command chair armrests, her fingers white-knuckled. She really disliked this man. "Sir, we have a positive ident on a Project 629A Golf II class ballistic missile submarine matching our course direction to the La Perouse Strait."

"That boat was decommissioned in the 1960s, Captain and was never known to carry ballistic missiles. No one in this area would keep a boat of that age in their fleet."

Cassie looked up at James. He shrugged and scribbled a note on his tablet. NORTH KOREA?

"Sir, the DPRK is known to have a number of older Soviet submarines in their fleet, including several Golf IIs."

"And they hold their boats within the fifty-mile exclusionary zone. They don't venture out this far. Your sonar tech needs a refresher course on contact identification." Bryce inhaled sharply, and Cassie shot him a warning glance, augmented with a slash beneath her chin. He grumbled but turned back to his screen.

"I don't believe so, sir. I think this is a North Korean boat." Cassie remembered all the notes she'd read on Sam's project. She was sure she'd seen a picture of Pak touring a submarine pen which held a modified Project 629A boat. "Recent CIA reports indicate Pak has modified several of his 629As, sir."

"Just because you have an inside track to CIA analysis and you sleep with the analyst doesn't mean you know what you're talking about. Get back on course and recall your LAMPS. Fleet out!"

"That was fun," Cassie groused. "Bring us back on course, heading zero-zero-five degrees. Comm, how's your contact with the LAMPS?"

"Skip?"

"The LAMPS, how's your radio communications with the helos?"

Her comm officer looked over at her, and she raised an eyebrow. He nodded. "A bit garbled, ma'am. They're over the horizon and at the outer reaches of their patterns. Won't be back for fifteen minutes."

"Very good. We'll let them fly free until they're within visual range of the boat and you can paint them with FM-line of sight communications. Have them pick up their buoys as they fly in."

"Aye, Skip."

James leaned down. "Or you could just call them on their mobiles."

"And where would the fun be in that?" Cassie rubbed her hands together. "Let's play Battleship." Both officers turned to the plexiglass board. "Gunny, ping that bastard with all we've got. If nothing else, we'll make their ears ring for the next several hours. Then capture a file of all active sonar and sonobuoy sweeps. Once the file is recorded, send it to my office." She rose from her command chair. "You have the conn, James." The plexiglass board flared with data as sonar and sonobuoy sweeps arced out to fill the sea around the *Arlington* with acoustic waves. A hazy blob began to resolve at the intersection of the sweeps. "Gotcha."

Well into the dog watch of middle night, klaxons again rang out on the *Arlington*. "BATTLE STATIONS. ALL HANDS—BATTLE STATIONS. THIS IS NOT A DRILL." Cassie ran forward from her cabin and entered her command deck. Controlled chaos filled the space. Night watch crew gave way to day crew, and additional backup crew arrived to stand behind each station. The bridge glowed a blood red. "CIC reports a missile launch, ma'am." The young ensign hovered at the arm of her chair.

"And?"

He swallowed hard. She gave him her best command glare. "Err… two minutes ago, a… a ballistic missile exited the sea, eighty-five kilometers off our starboard flank. Possible submarine launch."

"And?"

"Missile's course was east, ma'am. Directly over Japan. I initiated battle stations not knowing the missile's intended target."

"Next time, all that information in one go, please."

"Aye, Skip."

The XO made it to the command deck, settling a Naval Academy baseball cap on his head to hide his mussed hair. Cassie swung her chair around. "Looks like it was a ballistic missile sub, and—"

"Skip, comm from the fleet. 'Bring the AEGIS online and fire if you have a solution.'"

Another set of alarms sounded. "It seems our good admiral is going to let us have some fun." Spinning her chair toward the helm she barked, "Bring us about to zero-niner-five. All ahead flank."

"Course zero-niner-five. Flank speed, aye," the helmsman answered.

"Preparing to capture trajectory, velocity, and altitude. Assigning satellites to active tracking," came the call from CIC.

Cassie continued to issue orders. "Gunny, plot the arc. We've got to be perpendicular to the missile's flight path."

The XO said, "CIC reports satellites three, four, and six are now hunting for acquisition of the target. Triangulation in thirty seconds. Missile is entering the upper atmosphere."

"All stop." The *Arlington* wallowed as she responded to the sudden change in forward speed. "Deploy port stabilizers. Prepare missiles two and four. We will fire when we have a solution."

The command deck was eerily quiet, as the computers deep within the ship analyzed all the satellite telemetry and prepared a firing solution for the AEGIS missiles. "Solution has a 20 percent chance, Skip. Computers do not recommend firing. The missile will be out of AEGIS range once it begins its downward trajectory." CIC information pierced the air.

"Maintain missile tracking. Let's give it a few minutes."

Not two minutes later CIC reported, "Skip, missile has self-destructed."

"Location?"

"Thirty miles west of Honshu."

"Stand down the missiles. Release the birds back to their original orbital paths."

"Comm, get a patch into South Korean and Japanese television. Let's see if anyone else noticed the launch."

Earlier, Cassie had sent the files on the sonar contact to Sam with a note on the ident her sonar technician had made. Now, Cassie settled back and waited. Someone had to see that missile. Even if it was a fishing boat with a smartphone.

17 April, 11:54 Hours Local (UTC 15:54)
Situation Room, White House
Washington, DC, United States

Sam watched Grant twitch her sleeves into place again. "Stop that. You look fine."

"Ma'am, there's fine and then there's fine. I won't embarrass Her Majesty's Navy in front of your president if I can help it."

"Right. Just be ready if she starts asking questions. She's not going to be pleased with what we have to tell her, and her security brats will be out for blood. We can't let them draw ours. Nor can we allow the president to make any aggressive moves which will only push Pak's buttons."

"Of course, Colonel."

"And stop being obsequious. It pisses me off."

Before Grant could reply, the president and her cadre of security advisors entered with the Joint Chiefs following behind. "Let's get to it." The president was angry. Her mouth was drawn into a thin white line, and she flattened her hands on the tabletop. Sam thought it was to keep from drawing them into fists.

Admiral Benson took his usual seat across from Sam, his face a thundercloud of anger and frustration. *Shit, this is so not good. We may not be able to control the situation anymore.*

"Ma'am, may I introduce Lieutenant Amelia Grant of the British Royal Navy." Grant stood and nodded at the president. "She participated in the recovery of water samples from the Sŏngch'ŏn River downstream from the Chemical Materials Institute in North Korea." The president's eyebrow rose as she looked Grant over. "She will present her findings in a moment as well as the metallurgical analyses from Los Alamos, which Doctor Douglas completed on the recovered missile housing."

Sam nodded to the security officer, and he displayed a map of the northern portion of the Sea of Japan. Numerous symbols adorned the area. "Four hours ago, the DPRK launched a ballistic missile from a submarine. A portion of the Pacific Fleet was in position to capture a sonar sweep of the submerged vessel. Given the analysis of the engine noise and overall size of the vessel, I believe the submarine was a modified Soviet Golf II class diesel boat. The North Koreans obtained a number of these vessels in the mid-1990s when the Soviets sold them for scrap. Pictures of Pak touring a newly constructed submarine in dry dock was released via the state-run news agency two months ago."

A picture of a large submarine on a dry dock cradle in a cavernous building flashed up. "Analysis of this image by nautical engineers at Annapolis indicates this is not a newly constructed vessel but a modified Golf II boat. The superstructure has been enlarged to carry ballistic missiles and fire them vertically from within the sail. I believe the missile fired a few hours ago was a Pukgeukseong-1." Another image appeared beside the submarine.

"What's this guy's fascination with parades?" one of the security council advisors asked.

"It's all part of the continuous propaganda campaign run by the state, sir. This parade occurred two days ago on the Day of the Sun. As we discussed previously, this national holiday celebrates the birth of Pak's grandfather." A video of the recent parade was cued up on another monitor. Sam nodded, and it began to play. After several minutes, Sam asked, "Please stop the video." Centered on the screen was a closeup image of a young woman. Dark haired, slightly built, hollowed cheeks—almost starved in appearance. The woman was dressed in dirty clothes.

The president leaned forward and scrutinized the image. "Who is that?"

"That, Madam President, is Doctor Kim Hye-su, the leading nuclear physicist in North Korea. Please continue the video." The next scenes showed Pak greeting her and shaking her hand. "I believe Doctor Kim designed the miniaturized warheads for Pak's new toys." At Sam's nod another missile on a carrier rolled into view. "This is the Pukgeukseong-1, a new, smaller, nuclear ballistic missile. Its compact warhead assembly would easily fit into the sail of a Golf II submarine. It may be fueled by their newly produced UDHM."

"And you know this how, Samantha?"

Sam turned to her aide. "Grant, if you would please?"

Grant rose from her seat and stepped up to the table. "On the night of twenty February, I, along with my team from the Royal Navy Special Boat Service, piloted a silenced zodiac up the Sŏngchŏn River. There we retrieved water samples from the nearshore environs next to the Chemical Materials Institute. Once we returned to rendezvous with *HMS Unicorn*, we took the samples to port in Japan and onward to laboratories at the MI6 Headquarters, London. As the colonel hoped, these samples contained trace amounts of monochloramine and dimethylamine, both known precursors used in the manufactory of UDMH. Other substances—hydrochloric acid and formaldehyde—were also present. These are intermediate by-products of the chemical synthesis process. Trace amounts of nitric acid were also found—this is the most common oxidizer used with UDMH to produce a hypergolic rocket fuel. These chemical results in addition to the metallurgic analyses completed on the recovered missile fragment indicate the Democratic People's Republic of Korea is manufacturing large quantities of UDMH. The colonel has identified new stainless steel; noncorrosive tanks being installed in the facility for chemical storage. Given these data, we believe North Korea is fueling their mobile launch-capable missiles as well as the newly deployed submarine-launched missiles with The Devil's Venom."

"You and your boat service team?"

"The Special Boat Service is the special forces arm of my Navy, ma'am. On par with your Navy Seals."

"I see. And you are a member of this team, Lieutenant?"

"Aye, I am the cyber tech for Team Bravo."

Sam smiled. She had only just learned the true nature of her young aide's background. A member of the British aristocracy, she denied her place in society in favor of a position at the Royal Military Academy, Sandhurst, at sixteen. She graduated second in her class at the age of nineteen—two years ahead of her classmates. Grant became only the fourth woman to pass the Special Boat Team training regime and be accepted into their ranks. She was now a decorated tech specialist for one of the United Kingdom's most highly trained covert operations group. Special Boat Service Team Bravo would probably best Seal Team Six, given they had more highly trained computer specialists embedded with each team. Sam hid her smirk behind a hand. Grant could probably hack all the tech in this room given ten minutes and a tablet.

The president's expression was inscrutable. Sam thought she was grinding her teeth as the muscles in her jaw clenched repeatedly. Moments later she spoke in a quiet voice. "That's it. I'm done being played. Admiral, your recommendations?"

Admiral Benson looked at Sam then President Haley. "The Joint Chiefs recommend an increase to Threat Level One along the demilitarized zone."

Sam winced. This was one step away from taking immediate offensive action. The admiral's recommendation made it imperative Sam ensured the president understood this escalation would force Pak to react in kind.

The admiral continued reciting his recommended next steps. "An increase in personnel deployment by another 50 percent. The deployment of our new THAAD system (Terminal High Altitude Area Defense) along the South Korean border and encircling Seoul. This will augment the newly installed Iron Dome system the South Koreans purchased from the Israelis. A cyberattack against their launch hardware and associated software systems." Grant stifled a snort.

"You have something to add, Lieutenant?" The admiral growled.

Grant stood again. "Sir, I do not believe a cyberattack will gain you access to their military operating systems. Their military systems are stand-alone and isolated from their national intranet. As to the Kwangmyong civilian intranet, access would be easy through various program backdoors." Grant paused, and Sam noticed a dusting of a blush appear on her cheeks.

"We're listening, Lieutenant." The president's words spurred her on.

"Most of their military hardware is antique. Old MS-DOS systems with software independently loaded from flash drives." Grant looked at Sam. She made a "go ahead" sign. "The Korean Computer Center is highly distributed and operates on a melded Windows XP/Linux operating system called Red Hat. There are eight regional centers within the country with satellite branches in China, Syria, Germany, and the UAE for redundancy. Their new system—called Red Star OS, is an amalgam of applications, most stolen from Apple OS and Google.

"A hack through the known backdoors in the old Windows XP

system, used in Red Hat, would be a starting point. Alternatively, Red Star Version Four has a vulnerability through the embedded browser Naenara. This application is a modified version of Mozilla Firefox. Gaining entrance there would also allow access to the tablets given to the general population." Grant took a moment. Sam thought she was weighing her next words carefully as she rocked back on her heels.

"The tablets are loaded with a stolen version of Microsoft Open Office, and this would provide another point of entry. Open Office is a piece of Swiss cheese. However, this would not gain access to their military systems. Those are highly distributed and would require hacking numerous individual workstations to get a full picture of the data stored within each. The hack attempt would be easily traceable by any of their firewall security systems."

"I see. How should we proceed?" the admiral asked.

Grant looked down. The seconds accumulated, and Sam shifted in her chair. Where the devil was she going with all this?

Grant looked up at the admiral and squared her shoulders. "I recommend embedding a Trojan Horse into a pirated movie, loaded on a flash drive, sir."

"You'd what?" Snickers rose from the tech staff in the room.

Grant didn't hesitate. "If the movie were popular enough, it would quickly gain wide distribution through their black market and be loaded on numerous tablets throughout the country. However, the ultimate goal would be getting the movie into the hands of a military technician. The technician would be prohibited from bringing his tablet into a facility, but if he had the flash drive, he might be tempted to load the movie on his workstation to view during his shift. Most of their low-level workers don't do much and are very bored. They sit for twelve hours, monitoring essentially nothing. If the technician loaded the movie and opened the video file to watch at work, you would have access into a military-level system."

"That's a lot of ifs, Lieutenant. What would we gain if your idea was successful?" The admiral appeared intrigued.

"An ability to map their military computer system, determine distribution of key computer assets, identify the software they're using, and determine operating systems in major branches of their military. Once those are known, we could identify backdoors into those systems. This would give us direct access to their military assets, strategies, and objectives."

The president's attention never wavered as Grant answered the admiral's questions. "Although I am not a computer specialist, I can see where the lieutenant is going with this. Major Dawes?"

One of the security officers operating the technology within the situation room stood. "Madam President?"

"Is what's being suggested feasible?"

"I would think so." He scratched his chin and appeared to think through Grant's recommendation. "Yes, ma'am. Although it would rely on quite a bit of serendipity."

The major was correct. This was a pipe dream at best. But perhaps it was their only option for military system access.

"As to the rest of your recommendations, Admiral. I agree. Move the additional personnel into the region. Transfer THAAD from Japan to South Korea. Protect Seoul first and then the DMZ." The president stood, bringing the room to its feet. "I'll call the South Korean president back. He called immediately after the missile launch to ask for additional support. Now I can give it." She paused. "Do we need to augment our other resources in the area?"

The head of the Army said, "We can move some troops from the Middle East to Japan and our bases in Indonesia, but I don't want the terrorists to recognize a drawdown as an opportunity for them. I'd recommend a Marine contingent from Camp Pendleton in California be moved to a staging point in the Pacific."

Admiral Benson said, "I'd turn Admiral Armstrong around. Have them continue to occupy the Sea of Japan. Perhaps, ask the South Korean president to add some nearshore coverage from their Navy."

"Very well. Make it happen, folks. I want this completed as soon as possible."

The room cleared after the president left. Sam remained seated, lost in her thoughts. Grant cleared her throat. "Colonel, I'm sorry."

Sam whipped her head up. "Sorry? For what? There's no need for sorry, Grant. You did good. Better than good, in fact. I'm impressed yet again." Sam saw the young lieutenant's blush deepen. *She's so intelligent, so eager.* "Explain to me again, why you're my aide? You should be out saving the world."

"I'm filling in the gaps, Colonel. Learning from you. You're saving the world. Trying to do it without bloodshed and loss of innocents. Using intelligence, not brute force."

SECTION FOUR

20 April, UTC 23:24
CNN WORLD NEWS ALERT:

The low-pressure system in the South China Sea is now Tropical Depression 2. Overflight has confirmed rotation around a central eye. Internal barometric pressure is falling from 985 millibars. Surface water temperatures have exceeded twenty-six degrees Celsius, and storm surge is predicted at two meters, depending on the tides. Coastal flooding and inland wind damage warnings are extended to mainland China, Hong Kong, and Taiwan. The overall storm track remains the same. The storm is moving north-northwest at twenty-two kilometers per hour. Storm advisories are issued for the western islands of Japan and South Korea. This storm should reach typhoon-levels within the next twenty hours.

20 April, 00:41 Hours Local (UTC 04:41)
Sublevel 4, CIA Headquarters
Langley, Virginia, United States

Sam's communication center rang. "Michaels."

"Don't you ever go home, Colonel?"

Sam snapped her chair upright and dropped her feet to the floor. "I could ask you the same, sir."

"Touché."

"To what do I owe the pleasure, sir?"

The admiral's sigh reached down the line, and Sam cringed. "We have an intensifying typhoon in the South China Sea, heading north-northwest at over twenty klicks per hour. The eye is forecast to pass directly over Taiwan and continue north into the East China Sea. The Tropical Typhoon Center predicts this storm to reach category five after it passes back over warm waters. If it maintains course, it will enter the Yellow Sea."

"I see." Sam was rapidly evaluating scenarios of the storm's impact on the area, especially on the Korean Peninsula. "How does this affect the presi—"

"Not on this line, Samantha. Come over to my office and bring Grant. We may need to speed up the deployment of her little project."

"On our way, sir."

The admiral laughed. "So, neither of you have gone home yet. Does the CIA pay overtime?"

"Not that I've seen in my paycheck, sir." The admiral's guffaw cut off as the line went dead.

Sam left her office and traveled up three levels to Grant's small hole-in-the-wall. The lieutenant had refused a larger work area on Sublevel 4, stating it was too far underground for her comfort. So, she had chosen a small corner of one of the unused LANDSAT imaging labs. Grant built her space by maneuvering floor-to-ceiling bookcases, loaded with thick project report folders, to enclose an eight-by-ten-foot corner. Sam knocked on the edge of one of the bookcases which defined the narrow opening. Grant jumped out of her seat, crouched, and reached to her mid-back. Holding her hands up and out, Sam eased around the edge. "Sorry, Grant. Didn't mean to startle you." She kept her hands out, palms forward until she saw the woman relax.

The young lieutenant slumped back in her chair with a swoosh of breath. "No worries, Colonel. But don't do that again. Make more noise as you enter the lab to give me fair warning." Sam realized she'd nearly had a weapon drawn on her and nodded her understanding.

"What may I do for you? I was just about to head home."

"We've been invited to the Pentagon for a weather briefing."

"Weather, ma'am?"

"There's a typhoon building in southeast Asia, headed to the Sea of Japan…"

Before Sam could finish, Grant spun around and began rapidly typing into a miniature keyboard. A small tablet, laying face-up on her desk, lit up, flashing with information.

Grant lifted the small device and thrust it at Sam. "Bloody hell. Look at this."

"What's this?"

"A real-time video feed from a weather satellite over the South China Sea. I tapped into the Meteorological Office in London and linked into one of their satellites."

"Is that legal?"

Grant shrugged. "Don't know. Might be in a gray area." She did not look repentant.

"And…"

Grant stood and took the tablet from Sam. She angled the screen to share and pointed. "This is an image of the admiral's storm. It fills the entire South China Sea basin. That would make the storm six hundred klicks across. This is more than a category five, ma'am. This is a super typhoon. It might surpass Typhoon Haiyan in size."

Sam looked at the mass of gray-white clouds on the small screen. She saw the violent rotation about an evil black eye at its center. "Where is this headed?"

Grant sat back down and clattered more keys. The image fuzzed out and reformed at a smaller scale. The large, swirling cloud mass was still present but now occupied the lower third of the screen. A dotted red line extended north-northwest from the eye across the Yellow Sea into Korea Bay. Then east, crossing the Korean Peninsula.

"Shit."

Grant grimaced. "Shite, indeed."

Sam slowly lowered the tablet to Grant's desk. "We'd better go. And bring your toys. Don't know what the admiral needs or wants."

21 April, UTC 11:11
CNN WORLD NEWS ALERT:

Typhoon Palawan is now a super typhoon. Sustained winds of 310 kilometers per hour were measured as the storm passed over the island of Taiwan. Internal barometric pressure at the eyewall is below 915 millibars and continues to fall. Storm surges of six meters have swept across Taiwan, and caused devastating flooding to the country. Taipei is expected to experience a second round of storm surges as the backside of the storm moves over the city once the eye enters the East China Sea. Typhoon-force winds and flooding have decimated coastal areas. Inland wind and rain damage warnings are issued for the cities of Hang-chou, Shanghai, and Tsingtao in mainland China. The ports of Macau and Hong Kong have sustained heavy damage. All shipping across the East China Sea is halted until further notice. The storm is traveling on a north-northwest track at fifteen kilometers per hour. Flood and high-wind warnings are extended to the western islands of Japan. Seoul, South Korea, is in direct line with the storm.

23 April, 18:24 Hours Local (UTC 09:24)
Nuclear Scientific Research Facility
Nyŏngbyŏn, North Pyongan
Democratic People's Republic of Korea

The outer bands of Typhoon Palawan were lashing the western corner of North Korea. Kim Hye-su ran through the driving rain toward the indistinct concrete edifice in the distance. Rain soaked her thin clothing, and she began to shiver violently. Food rations had been reduced again for the general populace. Even though she was in the science community and rations were larger, one couldn't maintain any body mass on a starvation diet of eight hundred calories per day.

The gigantic concrete building housing the Magnox-style reactors loomed above her head. Hye-su ran up to the side of the building and jerked a steel door open. She burst into the reception hall and slid to a stop on the polished floor. Five members of the Central Party leadership were talking to one of the facility's technical directors. All heads turned at the interruption.

"I came as soon as I could." She panted. "The road is washed out between here and Pyongyang. My driver had to detour through fields to get me here." Water sheeted off her narrow frame and formed a large puddle on the pristine floor.

"Get her some dry clothes, and maybe we can prevent a disaster."

Hye-su was led away by an elderly matron toward a dressing room off the main reception area. "I am so glad you are here, Doctor. No one knows what to do. The storm is coming, and the reactors are open to the sky." Hye-su nodded at the old woman, as she struggled to get a technician's jumpsuit over her wet body. The dull gray vinylon material was stiff and smelled of machine oil and old sweat.

"I understand, Halmeoni." Grandmother was the honorific she used for the elderly woman. Hye-su got the zipper closed and sat on a bench to pull on a pair of rubber boots. Standing again, she bowed and tried to smile, but she knew it was forced. She hugged the woman close— two women taking comfort from each, or so she hoped it would appear to the cameras scattered about the dressing room. Hye-su whispered in her ear. "Move your family to the south, Halmeoni. It will not be safe here. Get as far away from the river as you can. More than fifty kilometers. The tides and storm surge will fill this valley. Go soon, the roads are failing." She released the elder woman and tipped her head.

The elder woman looked closely at Hye-su and nodded. "I know you will be successful, Doctor." She left through a small side door.

Hye-su made her way back out to the reception area. The group of men turned. "Now we will get somewhere. What is your plan, Doctor?"

"Drop all the control rods into place. Shut down the five reactors. Close the containment doors over the reactors. The pumps will not be sufficient to protect the reactor rooms from flooding if the predicted storm surge moves up the Kuryong River. The reactor buildings will be covered at the height of the storm. We must isolate the reactors and protect the surroundings and populace."

"No," the head of the Administrative Council barked. Bong Sok-mun was new to his position, serving for less than a year. Hye-su knew he needed to make a name for himself to maintain his status.

"Sir, I beg—"

"No, no begging." He chopped his hand down violently. "We cannot stop electrical generation. Our cities need power." He scowled at Hye-su. "If we halt power generation, how will you operate the pumps?" Bong leered at her, thinking he had her boxed in a corner. "And what of your projects, Doctor? If you do not have the fuel rods from the reactors, you do not have the materials for our supreme leader's projects."

"That is true, sir. But if the research facility floods and the reactors are not isolated, the flood waters will be contaminated with radioactive material from the exposed cores. When it flows back into the river, the contamination will devastate the surrounding farmland."

Nyŏngbyŏn was situated in one of the few areas within North Korea with arable land. Potato and grain crops were grown along the river and within the delta to the west. Losing the use of these lands would cause irreparable harm to the country. Rations would be cut again. The populace would suffer irreparable harm. The country would be more dependent on China for foodstuffs. The world could sanction food and starve them.

This seemed to give Bong pause. He hesitated, before turning back to Hye-su. "Very well, Doctor. Close down the Magnox-reactors but leave the light-water reactor functioning. We will continue to provide our people with power from there. But you, Doctor, will have to find another way to supply your projects." His face twisted into a grin.

He thinks this will halt my future projects and delay meeting the imposed deadlines. Hye-su bowed to lower her face and hide her smile.

Bong had no understanding of the reactors in this facility. The reactors were linked in series. If she took one Magnox offline, all the reactors would come down. "Yes, sir. We will begin as soon as you order." As for her project, she had more than enough enriched fuel to meet her project deadlines.

"Now would be good, Doctor. The storm is coming." He spun on his heel and headed out into the rain. Of course he didn't get wet. Hye-su watched as a number of drivers with large umbrellas covered Bong and his entourage on the way to their cars. She smiled, they would not make it back to Pyongyang this night.

Hye-su hurried to the reactor control room. The Magnox reactors in this facility were unique to the world. Invented and first built in the United Kingdom in 1956, these reactors ran on natural, poorly-refined uranium—0.711% Uranium-235, 99.284% Uranium-238, and a trace of Uranium-234 (0.0055%). The uranium fuel was enclosed in a Magnox alloy cylindrical case made of magnesium and aluminum. The cases were held within a massive graphite block at the heart of each reactor. The carbon atoms within the densely packed graphite matrix acted as moderators for the nuclear chain reaction, absorbing neutrons and controlling the speed of the nuclear chain reaction so it did not run out of control. Boron control rods were also present. These could be lowered into the graphite matrix block and augment reaction control.

The major difference between Magnox reactors and those used elsewhere in the world was that the Magnox used high-pressure carbon dioxide gas to cool the core rather than water. Nuclear chain reactions produced a large amount of heat. The circulating gas carried the excess heat away, where it was captured in a heat-exchanger. This waste heat drove steam turbines to generate electrical power. The downside of this design was the inefficiency of the gas, which had a much lower heat-carrying capacity than water. Safety was another consideration all together. The United Kingdom recognized the underlying safety concerns inherent in this design—should gas pressure catastrophically fail, control of the reaction would be lost. The British halted its use of Magnox reactors in the mid-1960s.

North Korea did not care about safety issues or the low power production efficiency (<23%). They only cared about the byproduct which drove them to use this antiquated, dangerous nuclear reactor—the ability to recover and enrich Uranium-235 and Plutonium-239 from the spent fuel rods. The enriched elements which fueled the production of weapons-grade nuclear material for Pak's toys.

Hye-su couldn't do anything to protect the nearby enrichment facility or their enrichment centrifuges from the storm. She had simply ordered all radioactive materials moved into the underground, self-contained cooling ponds and the building evacuated. She hoped the enclosed ponds would withstand the pressure of the flood waters.

As she entered the control room, she scanned the banks of dials and monitors wrapped around the periphery of the large, windowless space. Each reactor had its own set of control monitors. Core temperature, gas pressure, gas temperature, boron-control rod position, turbine speed, and electrical power output were all monitored at individual workstations—one station per reactor. Paper-fed recording devices spat out printouts of the primary reactor parameters on command. Banks of alarms ringed the room above each control positions. Currently, all alarms were silent, and all warning lights were in the green.

Hye-su would begin the shutdown procedure at Reactor Five within the series chain and would work her way forward to Reactor One. Following shutdown, it was critical carbon dioxide gas pressure remained at the highest level and gas circulation rates at maximum flow. She needed to continue circulating the cooling gas until the reactor core dropped below critical temperature.

If the gas flow failed, the temperature generated within the core of the nuclear mass would remain high, creating a corrosive environment. The boron control rods would not be stable in such an environment. Without the neutron-absorbing boron control rods, the nuclear chain reaction would reinitiate and continue uncontrolled with no way to stop it.

Hye-su knew these uncontrolled reactions were now happening beneath the destroyed Chernobyl Unit 4 in Ukraine. The initial reactor explosion and subsequent fire at the nuclear facility melted the fuel rods, boron controls and the surrounding graphite matrix. This amalgam mixed with the sand used to put out the fires forming a lava-like liquid. The super-heated liquid burned through the reactor floor and spilled into basement rooms beneath the reactor core, where it cooled and hardened. An increase in neutron production had been detected recently in this hardened mass. This indicated there was enough nuclear fuel remaining to initiate fission reactions. With the basement inaccessible and no boron control rods available, the Chernobyl complex was headed to another uncontrollable nuclear accident.

Hye-su would prevent this from happening here. If she could. She began issuing orders to the men in the control center. She was ignored.

The supervisor turned and gave her a blank stare. He wasn't listening. "Do you want to sit here through a meltdown?" Hye-su was furious. They couldn't afford any delays.

"But, Doctor, we must maintain power," the supervisor argued. "We have our quotas of electricity to meet each day."

"Your quotas will not be met when the reactors are under water. Your quotas will not be met when there are no more reactors after they meltdown. Your quotas will not be met when you are not here. Your quotas will not stop the flood. This valley will be under ten meters of water within the next six hours. The road to Pyongyang is already washed out. We are all trapped here. So, we either shut down the reactors to control the situation, or we watch it all explode." When the supervisor didn't respond, Hye-su stepped into his personal space and raised her voice so everyone in the control room heard her. "Your choice. Control or meltdown?"

"Control," he said in a whisper.

"Very good."

She turned to the technician for Reactor Five. "Lower the boron control rods in groups of one hundred." She couldn't drop all sixteen hundred rods at once or she would damage the graphite matrix block. But she had to gain control of the 120-ton core. "Increase CO_2 flow to 100 percent. Monitor the temperature of the core. When the gas outflow temperature drops below 250-degrees Celsius, let me know what the gas pressure is."

The technician turned to his board and began to lower the first set of rods. Hye-su watched his actions through the first several groups. She turned to the technician for Reactor Four. "You will be next. What is the current electrical output of Reactor Four?"

"Thirteen megawatts." That was half of maximum electrical power generation. This reactor was only providing supplemental output.

"When Reactor Five has 75 percent of its rods in place. You will begin to drop the rods in Reactor Four. Do so in groups of 250 at half-lowering speed."

She turned to the technician for Reactor Three. "Please proceed as I ordered once Reactor Four has 75 percent of its rods in place." Hye-su knew she was running out of time. If she waited for each reactor to be completely shut down before starting on the next, she would never get through a safe shutdown on all five reactors before the meters-high storm surge was upon them. Regardless of what she did, they may still be doomed.

23 April, 07:16 Hours Local
BBC WORLD NEWS-South Korean Desk:

"Reports are coming in that Super Typhoon Palawan will pass directly over the North Korean city of Nyŏngbyŏn and its nuclear reactor complex. This government-built city has never been visited by outside scientists but is known to house ten-thousand residents in three housing sectors surrounding the reactor complex and associated fuel-enrichment facility. The North Korean government and its leader, Pak Sung-un, have ignored humanitarian aid offered by their neighbors.

If the North Korean reactors are damaged, contamination from airborne nuclear isotopes of iodine, strontium, and cesium is possible. The isotopic half-lives of these nucleotides are eight days, twenty-nine years, and thirty years, respectively. Health concerns from release of the isotopes are: iodine is linked to thyroid cancer, strontium can lead to leukemia. Cesium is the most dangerous. It can remain in the atmosphere and travel the farthest in the jet stream, while lasting the longest in the biosphere. This nucleotide affects the entire body, especially the liver and spleen."

With the prevailing west to east winds, nucleotide particulates ejected upward would enter the atmosphere's jet stream. Anyone within a twenty-thousand square-kilometer area downwind of the reactor site are asked to remain alert.

Japan has issued a warning to take appropriate cover should a nuclear accident occur. South Korea is preparing for a nuclear accident and planning the evacuation of urban populations nearest the DMZ, including the millions in Seoul.

23 April, 20:56 Hours Local (UTC 00:24, April 24)
Naval War Room, National Military Command Center
Pentagon
Arlington, Virginia, United States

After several non-stop days of detailed analysis, Sam and Grant were ushered into yet another underground facility at the Pentagon. The first one was several days ago when they met with Admiral Benson in a secured comm booth, about the size of a broom closet, adjacent to his office. This one was different—a large, well-lit room with four tiers of workstations horseshoed around a large monitor-filled wall. A duplicate to the imaging room at Langley. Sam quickly counted twenty-three uniformed personnel seated at various computers.

Grant whistled quietly and pointed to the side of the room. A glassed-in enclosure held a desk with a red communication unit on top. The door to the enclosure was guarded by a fully armed, body-armored Marine. The infamous red telephone—the direct line to the Kremlin in Moscow. Established to allow the US president to reach the Soviets directly should the need arise. Maintained here and not at the White House Situation Room for fear a Russian hack through the comm unit could infiltrate the president's office.

Their first meeting had been a ten-minute game of "guess the storm track" and its associated impact on allies and enemies alike within the southeast Asian region. Sam was told the THAAD deployment would be delayed due to the storm. Any troop transfers were on hold for the same reason. Sam couldn't have been happier.

She disagreed with the admiral's recommendation to deploy THAAD. This weapons system was designed to shoot down short-through-intermediate-range ballistic missiles during the descent or reentry phase of flight. THAAD missiles lacked a warhead. They were designed to deliver a kinetic strike—like a hammer blow—to the ICBM. Theoretically, this would bring the missile down without detonating the incoming missile's warhead, thereby protecting ground troops and assets. THAAD was the Army's ground-based equivalent of the Navy's AEGIS system. Sam worried about Pak's reaction to a THAAD deployment. She feared, Pak would see this as a direct, aggressive move against the DPRK and respond in kind. How that response came she couldn't determine. Yet.

The admiral and his aide entered, and the ambient noise in the room dropped to zero. "Everyone but station two-one, out." When no one immediately moved, the admiral's aide snapped at them. "Out now! Close down your station and get gone." Everyone but the armored Marine did as ordered, "Admiral, the room is yours."

"Thank you, Captain." The woman left the room on the heels of the scrambling techs. Benson nodded at the Marine. The guard pulled a keycard from his Kevlar vest and opened the door behind him. Once inside the glass enclosure, he opaqued the glass.

"Why all the cloak and dagger, sir?" Sam really had better things to do. A side trip to the Pentagon was not on her to-do list. Pak's activities across North Korea were increasing. Sam was receiving new images every hour when daylight shown down on the peninsula.

The admiral sat at one of the workstations and entered a long string of login credentials. The monitors on the wall blended into one large screen and showed a nighttime satellite image of the southern Sea of Japan and Yellow Sea. The only way Sam could locate the image was the blurred shape of the Kyushu coastline peeking through the cloud deck. The remainder of the image was smudged darkly by the heart of the giant storm.

Admiral Benson turned to Sam. "This is Typhoon Palawan. It is still moving to the north-northwest. The eye will make landfall over the Kuryong River delta in the next couple of hours. It is projected to turn east-northeast and travel across the breadth of the DPRK. Then, back out into open ocean over the central Sea of Japan. Winds in excess of three hundred kilometers per hour will clear a path across the country. If this happens, over thirty of North Korea's nuclear facilities will be impacted. Loss of life and infrastructure will be high. Flooding will be widespread. Major highways and railroads will be closed or destroyed. The storm will effectively wipe North Korea off the map." He turned to Sam and raised an eyebrow in question.

"Would you please put up a map of the Korean Peninsula with the projected storm track?" Sam asked.

Admiral Benson looked at Grant. "Can you operate the work-station?"

"Aye, sir." Grant dropped into the vacated seat and began inputting parameters to fulfill Sam's request.

Once the map was on the wall, Sam handed Grant a flash drive. "Plot the facilities listed in this file on your map."

Icons began populating the map—yellow and black radiation symbols were intermixed with canary biohazard and red ionizing radiation warning symbols.

The program stopped filling the map, and Sam turned to the Admiral. "These are the one hundred or so facilities I've identified from satellite imagery with their projected use." All three looked at the large map. "If the storm is six hundred kilometers wide, it will cover the entirety of the Korean Peninsula as well as extend over a good portion of mainland China. Storm damage will decrease away from the track of the eye."

Sam pulled a laser pointer from her bag and highlighted several facilities in and around Pyongyang. "These will be out of the main storm path and shouldn't be as heavily damaged. They should be able to salvage those. However," she pointed out two places—Nyŏngbyŏn in the southwest and Kilju to the far north of the country. "We spoke about Nyŏngbyŏn last time we met. If the storm tracks across the country, damage in the Kilju area is more worrisome. This small county is part of Hamgyong Province and contains the heart of the North

Korea's nuclear development programs. Facilities include the Hwadae-ri atomic weapons training facility. Built with Soviet assistance in 1958 it is the site for all officer and technician training. The Punggye-ri Nuclear Test Site lies in the area of Mantapsan mountain, in the northernmost part of the province. The Musudan-ri missile launch facility is here. And a new SCUD facility not listed in our database, which I identified through image analysis, is also in the storm's direct path. If any or all of these are lost or damaged, the overall impact on Pak's program of military self-sufficiency will be shutdown. His ability to attain *juche* through the use of his nuclear arsenal will be gone."

"And this means what?" Admiral Benson asked, concern lacing his usually gruff voice.

Sam looked at Grant, the answer to his question called for her speculation again. She'd already been warned about this due to her presentation to the president. "I can only give an estimate based on my analysis of activities at various military sites and Pak's state-of-mind, sir."

"Let's hear it, Samantha." Benson turned to fully face her. "I know your director is not happy with you right now, but I need answers. I'll protect you as best as I can."

Sam clasped her hands behind her back. "Very well, sir. This is my assessment and mine alone." Grant grunted. Sam ignored her. "Sir, we are headed into a perfect storm. And I don't mean Typhoon Palawan. Palawan is the spark which will light the fire and create a conflagration. If Palawan wipes out the majority of Pak's military assets, especially his nuclear capabilities, it's over. He's pushed against the wall. He's asked the North Korean people to go along with his plans, to sacrifice all for the good of military growth. News footage from the most recent parade showed him extolling the virtues of another Arduous March, just like his grandfather did during the Korean Conflict of the 1950s. Continued UN sanctions are starving the people. If we go ahead with the deployment of THAAD, in conjunction with an increase in ground troops along the DMZ and naval operations along his coast, those actions will add more fuel to an already volatile situation."

Sam scuffed her toe against the carpet. This was it. She nodded to herself and looked Admiral Benson in the eye. "His only recourse is an offensive move. He will deploy all available assets. He will utilize his stockpiled nuclear arsenal. He will move troops to the DMZ and mobilize against our forces, using those weapons ahead of a ground assault. He will send his submarine fleet to sea with their new nuclear ballistic missiles. He will attempt a preemptive strike on the west coast of the United States from the subs."

Admiral Benson paled at Sam's summary. "Are you sure?"

"As I can be, sir. Pak is mentally highly unstable. With his uncontrollable temper, no one can predict how he will react in any situation. Pak has ultimate control over the arsenals. But he will lash out. Especially, if he feels threatened or…" Sam hesitated. She was stepping away from image analysis to profiling. "Sir, I believe he feels ignored by the world and threatened by the West. This will further ignite his temper. What I don't know is when or how he will act.

"If his goal is the unification of the Korean Peninsula under his regime, Pak needs the South Korean economic infrastructure to support his ongoing militarization. In addition, if he wishes to complete his grandfather's goal—removing the US from southeast Asia—Pak will utilize any and all means available to him to accomplish this. In addition, you must remember, he is not constrained by the mores of conventional warfare or by any internationally recognized treaties."

Sam looked back at the monitor image and the blinking red storm track for Typhoon Palawan. "This storm is just the beginning." She turned back to Admiral Benson. "One thing I do know, sir. Before Pak does anything, he will close his borders to the west and north—to shut out China and Russia. He will not fight on multiple fronts. Closing the borders will be the signal something is coming. Therefore, I recommend we increase all our remote surveillance to its highest level. Pull satellite resources from other areas if needed. And commandeer the weather and new LANDSAT 11 satellites to help."

After long moments, Admiral Benson clasped Sam on the shoulder. "Thank you, Samantha. I appreciate your expertise. Who provided this information will remain between us, but I will immediately begin moving resources as you recommend." He turned to her aide. "Grant, how long will it take you to move forward with your little movie project?"

"All I need is the right movie. Sir, I would recommend one not yet released. One which has been highly advertised. Perhaps, one of the *Marvel Comic* movies or the new James Bond film. However, I'm uncertain how to obtain a pre-release copy."

"Leave that to me, Lieutenant. You'll have your movie before the end of day tomorrow."

"Once we load the flashdrives, I have access to several sources in western China who can get the bootlegged copies into North Korea within a few days." She looked at Sam. "Once the storm passes."

25 April, 21:33 Hours Local (UTC 01:31, 26 April)
Sublevel 4, CIA Headquarters
Langley, Virginia, United States

NAEWOE NEWS AGENCY ALERT:

Two days ago, Super Typhoon Palawan passed over the Korean Peninsula with devastating impact. Although not in direct line of the eye, Seoul and the remainder of South Korea sustained heavy wind and rain damage. The eye of the storm passed directly over the Democratic People's Republic of Korea where the heaviest damages and horrific flooding occurred. The storm swept away the Kuryong River delta. A fifteen-meter storm surge moved up the river's valley and inundated the area in and around Nyŏngbyŏn. No damage or casualty reports have been received from the DPRK. We have learned from our contacts at the Korean Central News Agency in Pyongyang the nuclear facilities within the valley were destroyed.

Loss of life in the area is unknown. Monitoring stations along the DMZ have not reported any nucleotides within the atmosphere. It is hoped the reactors and storage facilities were safely locked down before the storm surge arrived. The United States military has moved radiation containment and cleanup resources into the area.

Sam read the report from the South Korean News Agency. This agency was the only one with direct contacts in North Korea. She was frustrated because the area was still covered by a thick mass of clouds which hindered her image analysis. Sam picked up her telephone and dialed. "Grant, get down here."

Five minutes later her aide knocked and entered the darkened office. "Where are we on your project?" Sam asked.

"I got the digital file for the new James Bond film yesterday from Admiral Benson. I uploaded it to MI6 with instructions to hand it off to their contacts in Dandong, China. A thousand copies of the file on flash drives will be distributed from there over the next week." Sam nodded. "Now we wait."

"How will we know what's happening?" Sam was lost with this level of technology. She didn't need to know how it worked, she just needed to see the results to plan her next steps.

"I embedded a line of code in the file which will send a secured ping to me once a file is loaded and the movie opened. I plan on plotting the growth of the distribution using this."

"What about storm impact?"

Grant settled into the desk chair opposite Sam. "That's going to be a problem. All the flash drives have to move into the country. To do that, they must cross the Kuryong River valley to get to Pyongyang." The lieutenant rubbed her hands together. Sam laughed at her aide, who was acting like a kid on Christmas morning. Excitement rolled off her in waves.

"I'm hoping the black market will move the drives away from the devastation, north into Kanggye. This is one of the larger cities in North Korea." Grant pulled her little data pad out. "Population is over a quarter million." She ignored Sam's frown.

"And this is good why?"

"Number Twenty-Six General Plant."

Sam rocked back in her chair and placed her feet on the desk. Of course. It would be perfect. It was the largest underground military manufacturing facility in the DPRK.

Grant continued. "The plant employs more than twenty thousand and produces munitions. Enough munitions they export the production excess to various countries in the Middle East. This is a source of tradable international currency for Pak. The facility should have a large system of computer technology."

Sam sat up and began rooting around on her desk, sorting through stacks of satellite images. "I remember something about Number 26. It's hidden beneath another manufacturing plant, I think?"

"A tractor factory. What's interesting is the surface plant has never produced any tractors. You're probably remembering the accident from November 1991. A massive explosion in the underground munitions plant killed more than six thousand and destroyed the overlying tractor factory. Fires erupted from the crater and the explosive pressure-wave destroyed the nearby power generation station and the surrounding twenty-block area. The crater was two hundred feet deep. The underground complex was completely destroyed."

"That's right. Pak's father described the Number 26 factory as 'the mother of our military industry, our treasure.' It has a history of generational service—father to son to grandson."

Grant nodded. "That's where we'll get a hit."

"What do you hear from your sources about Nyŏngbyŏn?"

"The latest update stated only the top of the reactor containment building was above the flood water. The enrichment facility is a total loss. Most of the city was evacuated as the storm approached. Loss of life is unknown."

Sam rocked back, feet back up on her desk. She steepled her fingers under her chin, deep in thought. She tapped her lips. "I wonder. Would it be possible? Could we be so bold? If we were caught..." Her muttering continued as she played various scenarios through her mind. She dropped her feet and grabbed another pair of images out of a red folder. Placing the pair under her stereoscopic viewer, she studied the area. "Maybe, just maybe."

"Colonel?"

"Grant, get me Admiral Benson. I think we need to augment your movie project."

26 April, 11:54 Hours Local (UTC 15:54)
Oval Office, White House
Washington, DC, United States

"No, Colonel, the risks are too great. I will not agree to this."

President Haley scowled at Sam.

"I don't mean to diminish the overall risk, ma'am. I understand this is a long shot. But the potential benefits would be priceless. We wouldn't have to wait on serendipity. We'd have direct access."

Admiral Benson, who was recently promoted to Chair of the Joint Chiefs, the president, her chief of staff, her national security advisor, and the Secretary of Defense were the only other persons in the room with Sam and Grant. Sam had called the admiral and asked for a meeting at a secured location. He was already at the White House when he took her call and asked her to meet him there. Forty-five minutes and several broken traffic laws later, the pair arrived. Sam outlined her idea to the admiral. He immediately called the chief of staff and asked for fifteen minutes of the president's time.

"Madam President, I agree with Samantha. It has the potential for tremendous rewards which should outweigh the risks."

"At what costs? I can't order anyone on this suicide mission." The president shook her head. "No."

Grant stood. "You would not be ordering anyone, ma'am." President Haley swung her attention to Sam's aide. She raised an eyebrow in question. "Not if one volunteers."

"What are you saying, Lieutenant?"

Grant snapped to attention. "I volunteer. This mission has the highest probability of success. We would have direct access. I would be able to embed any number of programs within their systems."

Sam swiped a hand over her face as her plan was becoming a reality.

"I wouldn't need more than thirty minutes, ma'am."

"Sit down, Lieutenant." The president paused and closed her eyes. Sam recognized this. It was something Cassie did to shut out any distractions from hindering her thought process. When the president opened her eyes again, she pinned Sam in her gray-blue gaze. "Colonel, this is your idea. I want to hear all the ins and outs. All the imminent dangers. What resources you need? Who you would assign this to? Step by step, how would this go?"

The National Security Advisor sat forward. "Madam President, this has nightmare written all over it. If any of these assets were captured, we'd be charged with invading a sovereign nation. A provocation of war." He barked a sarcastic laugh and shook his head.

"I agree, ma'am," The Secretary of Defense added. "The United States would be seen as taking advantage of a country during a time of great humanitarian need in an effort to steal secret information and sabotage their infrastructure. We'd lose face in the international community and perhaps be subject to United Nations sanctions ourselves."

"I understand, but the colonel and lieutenant have a point. This is a once in never opportunity. I need to hear all about it before I can decide how to proceed." She paused as the security advisor's face turned puce. "If we proceed."

"Very well, ma'am, but I am registering my disagreement. I strongly recommend the US not participate in this." The Secretary of Defense stated emphatically.

The president ignored his protest. "Colonel?"

Sam stood and placed her laptop on the coffee table. "Lieutenant, if you would please." Grant rose and settled before the small computer. "Let's start with an overview of the area and proceed from there." A map of a verdant valley appeared as Grant entered commands. The president leaned forward and scrutinized the tiny screen.

"This is the Nyŏngbyŏn nuclear scientific research area along the Kuryong River. Our objective would be the roof of Reactor Building One, here." Grant pointed to one of the three large buildings. "Enter the building and proceed down to the reactor control room where computer assets would exist. Access the computers, download our trojan horse, upload their computer architecture and directories, exit the building, and move west into the hills for pickup." Grant summarized.

The president continued to scrutinize the image. "What do you anticipate as roadblocks to this plan of action?" Sam realized the president was trying to do a critical analysis—weighing pros and cons.

Grant looked at Sam. She nodded for her lieutenant to continue. "Madam President, there are three major roadblocks to this mission. First and foremost, the structural viability of the building, including the risk of nuclear contamination. Second, contact with any North Korean citizens still in the building. And lastly, the state of the computers themselves. IT does not like to get wet or be without power for extended periods."

"I see." The president turned to Sam. "Colonel, how would you address these roadblocks?"

Sam gathered her thoughts. "As far as the structural integrity, the team will be able to assess this as they approach the building. I have one sat image of the buildings after the storm passed. The containment roof was closed and above the flood waters. This implies the building is intact. The team would wear radiation warning badges and dosimeters. We don't know the state of the reactors themselves or if the North Koreans were able to shut them down."

Sam swallowed before continuing in a quiet voice. "As to contact with North Koreans, the team would have to assess this threat on a case-by-case basis. They would need a standing order to capture or kill any contacts prior to thier entry into the country."

President Haley's lips were drawn into a thin white line. Sam realized listening to the plan highlighted the immense danger involved. She turned to Grant and asked, "What about the IT issues, Lieutenant?"

"We would carry two portable power stations. This would allow us to reboot the computers. I doubt any internal power is available in the building. Each unit weighs approximately thirty kilos and would provide two hours of runtime at fifteen hundred watts and thirteen amps. I don't anticipate needing more than thirty minutes." Grant looked at the president. "This is all contingent on the computers being above the floodwater."

29 April, 22:46 Hours Local (UTC 13:46)
Yellow Sea
Command Deck, *USS Arlington*
CGN-47, Ticonderoga-class Guided Missile Cruiser

"Colonel, sit down or leave my command deck," Cassie snapped as she swung her chair around and scowled at her partner. "Harassing my comm officer will not speed up the process. When the signal comes through, you will be the first to know." The *Arlington* was alone, cruising through a fifty-kilometer oval course, seventy-five kilometers off the coast of the DPRK in Korea Bay. The remainder of the fleet was three hundred kilometers south-southeast, just northwest of Cheju Island. The *Arlington* had snuck away from the tail of the fleet and sailed north into the Yellow Sea and on to Korea Bay under the cover of darkness.

Sam looked sheepish. "Sorry." She dropped into one of the auxiliary command stations.

"It's okay, Colonel." James smiled at her as he walked past to give Cassie the latest weather satellite image. Thick cloud cover remained over the area and hopefully would continue until the *Arlington* sailed south again. An ancillary low-pressure system had developed over Korea Bay after Typhoon Palawan passed.

The quiet hum of the command deck did nothing to calm Sam's nerves. The *HMS Unicorn* ferried Grant with four members of her Special Boat Service Team Bravo and five members of Seal Team Two to the mouth of the Kuryong River. There, they exited the submarine via an underwater chamber and proceeded upriver by zodiac to Nyŏngbyŏn where they would attempt to gain access to the reactor facilities. No one knew the physical state of the facility or the risk of radioactive contamination to the ten members of Grant's team.

All had volunteered, as Grant indicated they would. The president reluctantly authorized the mission in conjunction with the British prime minister and MI6. Sam knew the risks were still off the chart, and her fears rose with each passing minute. Currently, the combined team was ten minutes late for their last scheduled check-in. Sam watched the large red digital numerals accumulate on the mission timer. *Come on, Grant. Get the lead out.*

Five more minutes passed. "Captain, I have a signal from Seal Team

Two."

Cassie nodded. "Go ahead."

"They are requesting medical assistance and evacuation from the designated extraction point."

Sam jumped up and headed off the command deck.

"Where do you think you're going, Colonel?" Cassie voice was sharp.

"The helicopter. I need to get a firsthand look at the facility. I can calibrate my image analysis with real-scale."

Sam didn't look back as she ran down the stairs and exited the superstructure onto the helipad off the fantail of the *Arlington*. A USN RAH-66 Comanche helicopter sat ready for takeoff, its rotors spinning. This stealth aircraft was never mass-produced due to engineering issues with its carbon-fiber skin, but the two prototypes were maintained for use in covert operations. The aircraft's carbon-fiber skin absorbed standard radar sweeps and made them invisible. Or so Sam hoped. She jumped up into the copilot seat, located aft and above the pilot who sat in the nose of the hornet-like craft. The well-armed Comanche would fly cover over the extraction point.

Once the Comanche was airborne, a British Westland Super Lynx helicopter would rollout and launch to pick up the team. This helicopter was not stealthy but was highly maneuverable. It would use a terrain-following flightpath to fly under the radar of the North Korean coastal stations. Again, Sam hoped this would be the case.

Pulling her flight helmet on, Sam plugged into the helicopter's comm systems and tugged her crash harness into place. The Comanche rose in a rush of rotor wash and nose-dived over the stern of the *Arlington*. "Nice to have you along, Colonel." The pilot waved at her over his shoulder. "Isn't every day I get to chauffeur a retired colonel into enemy territory."

Sam keyed her mic. "No worries, Commander. I'm not really here."

"Roger that."

Without running lights or other external markers, the helicopter disappeared into the low-hanging cloud deck. Sam couldn't see a thing. Her hand itched to take over. Having someone else fly wasn't easy for her—she hated giving up control. She watched the HUD—heads-up-display—fill with data supplied by the onboard computer. They were flying dark and silent without the aid of their onboard radar. Instead, satellite telemetry provided global positioning information to maintain their course. "Five minutes to the coast. Suzie estimates three minutes to the extraction point from there."

"Excuse me, Suzie?"

"I had to call my onboard computer something. Siri and Alexa were already taken."

Sam laughed and tried to relax. She flexed her hands and rubbed her palms on her knees. Nothing seemed to help. Her pilot must have sensed her squirming. "You can fly back, Colonel."

The computer screen flashed and filled with green-lettered text. "Satellite message, ma'am."

Sam squinted at the tiny text. "FLASH MESSAGE—ELEVEN TO PICK UP. RADIATION PROTOCOL REQUIRED"

"What the...?" Sam spoke at the same time as her pilot. "Radiation, ma'am?"

"I don't know, Commander. Can you relay the message to the *Arlington*?"

The pilot toggled a stub on his cyclic. "Message away."

"Extraction point in thirty seconds. Decreasing altitude to one hundred feet. Unless the North Koreans have some high-powered flashlights, we should be good. Lynx is one minute behind us." Sam turned her head, trying to see the British helicopter. "They're twenty feet off the deck at five o'clock."

Sam turned farther around in her seat and felt her back protest. She caught movement as a dark spot blotted out the underlying field. "I've got them. They're lower than twenty."

"I have the team." A laser painted the Comanche. Someone on the Boat and Seal team had aimed a small tracking device at their bird. The pilot banked to the left and circled above the small group. "Lynx is hovering."

"Vehicular traffic noted to the north, one mile," a calm female voice stated.

Sam felt the helicopter drop. "Commander?"

"Suzie picked up movement in the hills across the river. I'm going to take her down to river level and hover. Hopefully, we can distract them from the Lynx's extraction. Even though they won't be able to see or hear us, our rotor wash will blow up the river, creating a pretty good distraction."

"Carefully, please." Sam's heart rate picked up as the black helicopter dropped toward the dark, rapidly moving river. Yellow whitecaps curled off the top of thirty-meter-wide standing waves in the center of the broad river. Flood waters were receding back into the river's channel and out to sea.

"I don't see anything."

"Half a kilometer from the bank, moving to the east. Couple of vehicles on a road paralleling the river's course. Maybe a truck convoy."

Sam saw a flash and recognized a shielded headlamp, as a vehicle bobbed over a small rise. "I've got them. They haven't spotted us yet."

"The Lynx is taking off, ma'am. Headed back to the west. I'll hold for another minute and then fly along the opposite bank."

It happened as the Comanche dipped into a left turn toward the far bank. Something struck the left skid and scraped along the undercarriage of the helicopter's belly. Warning lights lit up the console in front of Sam. The helicopter was stalling and falling toward the churning river.

"Commander?"

The pilot fought to control the helicopter. Mechanical noise filled the cockpit, as the helicopter leapt into the air. "Must've snagged on some floating debris in the river, a tree or something. We've lost the cowling over the exhaust. "

Sam could hear the engine noise continue to increase in volume. "Commander, the trucks have turned. They're headed toward the river."

The pilot didn't respond as he kept fighting the damaged aircraft. More warning lights lit Sam's console. "Weapons fire detected. Evasive maneuvers." Suzie commanded. The pilot rolled the aircraft to starboard. This turned the belly of the craft toward the far bank.

Ping. Ping. Ping.

More warning lights flashed on, engine temperature, oil pressure, rotor synchrony. The engine screamed as the pilot increased thrust and pulled the collective up. The helicopter shot upward like an out-of-control elevator.

Ping. Ping. Glass shattered.

Wind tore through the cockpit, howling around Sam.

"Arghhhh… hit… controls… " The helicopter slewed to port. Sam realized the commander was injured. As he slumped forward, he pushed the cyclic to the left.

Sam grabbed the cyclic joystick which rose from the floor between her legs and flipped several toggles on her console to transfer control to the rear seat. Sam grabbed the collective beside the left side of her seat and pulled up to gain more altitude. As she pulled up on the collective, she turned the throttle to increase their speed.

"Oil temperature is critical. Rotor transmission temperature is at redline," Suzie, warned in her calm voice.

Sam fought the wounded craft but continued to force the helicopter higher. "Come on you. I know you can do it." She growled through gritted teeth. "Gotta get back to the coast. Over the water."

The wounded engine sputtered. "Suzie, how far to the coastline?"

"You will cross the coast in thirty seconds. Altitude is 550 feet. Airspeed is 120 knots."

"How far to the *Arlington*?" The helicopter bucked, as the commander slumped farther forward. His left arm further obstructed movement of the collective.

"Flight time six minutes."

Sam didn't know if they'd make it. "Suzie, send a message to the *Arlington*. Declare an emergency. Prepare for possible water rescue."

"Satellite uplink lost. Unable to comply."

"Send it by whatever comm system is available."

"Standard radio is available but will be detectable."

Sam continued to pull up on the collective, demanding more altitude while she twisted the throttle in her left hand to gain more speed from the wounded engine. She maintained her heading with small movements on the cyclic with her right.

"Wait to send until we're fifty miles off the coast." That would be considered international waters by most countries.

The engine hiccupped. The craft faltered.

Helicopters were not meant to fly. They were aerodynamic impossibilities. The spinning rotors, pushing down on the air, created lift and kept them in the air. Tilting the rotors to the front or back allowed the craft to maneuver fore or aft or hover. Without lift, they'd drop like a rock. If she lost the engine, the rotors would stop. If she lost the transmission, the rotors would stop.

Sam hoped if the rotors were compromised, they would continue to slowly spin down until they stopped. This was called autorotation. Sam should be able to use this to slow their fall out of the sky and maintain a heading. However, she did not want to attempt an unpowered autorotation into the sea at night if she could help it. But, the real danger was a catastrophic transmission failure, when the transmission seized and the rotors would immediately stop. The result would be comparable to an elevator falling straight down.

"Message sent."

"Helo One, Helo One. This is Mother. Please state your intentions."

Sam thumbed the comm link on the cyclic as she fought the damaged bird. "Mother, Helo One. We are thirty nautical miles and closing at 550 feet. Pilot is injured. Will need medical assistance. Engine and transmission are compromised."

"Helo One, we have you on radar. Rescue bird is in the air and on the way to you. They will follow you in."

"Roger that. Where is the Lynx?"

"Onboard. Medical teams are assessing the wounded." *Grant, if you're dead, I'm going to follow you to hell and kick your butt.*

"Airspeed is falling below 110 knots. Stall speed is 90 knots," Suzie informed calmly.

More warning lights strobed to life. The aircraft faltered again. Sam saw the darkened rescue bird just as her engine seized with a scream of failing metal. Fragments tore loose from the transmission housing above Sam's head, and the cyclic went limp in her hand.

"Mayday. Mayday. Helo One is going down."

The rescue helicopter shot past her starboard side. "Helo One, you are losing oil."

"Engine seized. Transmission failure. Attempting autorotation. We are going in."

"Roger that."

"Come on, you can do this." Sam grasped the cyclic in two hands. "Keep the nose up. Bleed off airspeed. Put the tail boom in the water first." She went through the steps for an emergency autorotation water landing. "Shut off the fuel, tightened crash harness."

The commander groaned from the front seat. "Arghhh. W—what?"

"We're going in, Commander. Prepare for a water landing." Sam pulled back on the cyclic to lift the nose. She could just make out the dark outline of the *Arlington* ahead.

Sam was losing her gained altitude rapidly. The rescue helicopter was fifteen meters off her portside. "Keep the nose up, Colonel. You're looking good. Seventy feet to the water." Their glide path would drop them in the sea less than a kilometer from the *Arlington*. Sam saw the rescue helicopter pull forward. "We're dropping the swimmers now."

The sea rose up and grabbed her crippled bird out of the air. "I'm sorry, Cassie."

29 April, 11:38 Hours Local (UTC 15:38)
Oval Office, White House
Washington, DC, United States

President Haley strode into her Oval Office. "Admiral."

Benson stood and bowed slightly to the president. "The overall mission was a success. The team entered the reactor control room, powered up the computers, and accessed a workstation." The president dropped onto one of the facing sofas, and the admiral sat on the other. They were the only two in the room. "Lieutenant Grant got a complete download before they were attacked."

"Attacked?"

"Yes, it seems one of the nuclear technicians stayed behind to monitor the reactor shutdown after the facility was abandoned. Once the storm surge covered the reactor buildings, she was exposed to significant radiation from the flooded cores. She is expected to recover."

"Admiral, attacked?"

Benson grimaced. "How a tiny North Korean woman could attack the combined commando team is unbelievable. It took guts." He shook his head in wonder.

President Haley leaned across the coffee table. "What happened, Admiral? Who's hurt? Who died? Out with it! I need details."

"I apologize, ma'am. Yes, a technician attacked the Seal and Boat team as they accessed the workstation." The admiral summarized the remaining mission report. "Let me begin again. The team safely exited the *HMS Unicorn* and proceeded by muffled zodiac up the Kuryong

River to the nuclear facility. There, they were able to access the primary reactor building roof, where they proceeded down to the control room via a partially flooded stairwell. Luckily, the control room was sealed against flooding.

"They entered through an emergency hatch above the control room blast doors, allowing only a small amount of water into the room. As Lieutenant Grant completed a system and library download, they were attacked by a single technician brandishing a length of steel pipe and a pistol. One Seal was shot in the upper arm, a flesh wound. The technician was quickly neutralized. When the extent of her radiation exposure was discovered, she was sedated and isolated in a lead-lined body bag." The president settled back onto the sofa and stared at the admiral in disbelief.

President Haley made a circular motion with her hand and whispered, "Go on."

"The team with their sedated captive exited the control room and allowed the control room to flood behind them. This drained the stairwell. They made their way back to the roof and via zodiac to the shore. They hiked five kilometers into the hills above Nyŏngbyŏn, where they rendezvoused with the British Lynx helicopter and returned to the *Arlington*."

The admiral paused to gather his thoughts. He didn't know how to share the rest. The president was going to be angry. Hell, he was angry beyond belief. He didn't know why Samantha was on the mission. His best operative for southeast Asia recklessly put herself in danger and could have been killed or worse, captured.

"And? What aren't you telling me? Who died?"

"No one died, ma'am. However, Commander Nelson and Colonel Michaels were seriously injured when their Comanche helicopter crashed into the sea."

The president sagged back into the couch. Her formidable persona shrank, and she shivered visibly. "Oh, Samantha. What've you done now?"

Before his eyes, the president pulled herself together to sit up straight, anger radiated off her person. "She was injured? What the hell was she doing on this mission? How is Captain Stanley?" Her questions were rapid-fire.

Admiral Benson ran a hand over his close-cropped gray hair and grimaced. "According to Captain Stanley's report, the colonel was the copilot on the stealth Comanche which was providing hidden cover for the Lynx during their recovery operations. She wanted to see the facility firsthand. Their helicopter was hit by debris in the river as they hovered above it. This significantly damaged the aircraft, and they lost their stealth capabilities. They took live fire from North Korean forces, which wounded the pilot. Colonel Michaels took control of the damaged craft and made it back to international waters before ditching into the sea." President Haley blanched, and Admiral Benson hurriedly continued. "Both the pilot and the colonel are alive and will recover."

Several long moments passed as the president digested this information. She swallowed hard and turned steel-eyes on Benson. "Was the mission compromised? Was anything left for the North Koreans to find and accuse us of invading their sovereign territory?"

"No, Madam President. All matériel the team took into the country is accounted for and secured, including the additional asset we picked up. The damaged Comanche was recovered before it sank. An overall success. We now have a complete map of the computer architecture used by the DPRK's military and scientific community. A complete list of their projects with status. And a nuclear operator technician."

Nodding her head in understanding, President Haley circled back to the other critical issue. "And Colonel Michaels, how badly was she injured?"

"As I said, the pilot of the Comanche was shot. He has a penetrating chest wound and is being transferred from the *Arlington* to the *Nimitz* for surgery, and from there he will be evacuated to Hawai'i. He is in stable condition and is expected to make a full recovery. The colonel's injuries are being assessed."

When the president sat forward at this news, Benson raised a hand. "Her orthopedic specialist is here at Walter Reed. He is the one who reconstructed her back after the injuries she sustained in Iraq. The *Arlington's* surgeon is afraid she loosened and displaced several Harrington rods in her back when the helicopter crash into the sea." He paused. "Or she could've injured her back smashing through the canopy and rescuing Commander Nelson."

At this news, the president shook her head in amazement. "A hero, again?"

"So, it would seem. Nelson was unconscious and trapped in the forward pilot compartment. Once Samantha successfully autorotated into the sea, the helicopter was taking on water, sinking rapidly. She climbed out of her compartment and over the top of the pilot, smashed the canopy when it wouldn't release, pulled the commander out as the aircraft was sinking, and swam him to the rescue raft 150 meters away." He gave the report in a rush, as stating the happenings aloud illustrated the true horror of the actual events. It was one thing to read it and another to speak about it.

"Is that all?" The president shook her head. "What can't she do?"

Admiral Benson had to agree, Colonel Michaels was an escape artist, but he worried one of these days her guardian angel would be on holiday and Samantha would pay the ultimate price.

"Her injuries are manageable. However, she can't escape the wrath of Captain Stanley." President Haley winced. "Seems the captain is none too happy with the colonel. The *Arlington* has been ordered to Japan. There, they will meet Samantha's orthopedic specialist for evaluation and treatment.

"They will also move the nuclear technician to the Japanese radiation therapy unit at the National Institute of Radiological Sciences in Chiba, near Tokyo. Her level of radiation exposure is so high, the *Arlington's* surgeon is worried her immune system is destroyed. She is in radiation isolation to prevent exposure to infectious pathogens and to protect the crew from nuclear contamination. Her body remains radioactive at this time. Her blood samples have been airlifted ahead to begin looking for a stem cell donor."

"Stem cells?"

"A new treatment developed for victims of the 2011 Tōhoku earthquake. Following the tsunami and subsequent inundation of the Fukushima nuclear powerplants, several workers and rescuers were exposed to high levels of energetic ionizing radiation. Two of these workers' immune systems were destroyed, and they were given an experimental treatment—stem cell replacement therapy rather than bone marrow transplant. The attending physician felt this was a faster way to replace their immune systems and jump-start their own bone marrow to initiate white blood cell production. They were successful in their treatments. If the Japanese can't find a suitable donor, the North Korean technician will receive growth factor followed by a transfusion of umbilical cord blood stem cells from a newborn."

"Do we know who this technician is? Is he conscious?"

"She…" At the president's look of confusion, Benson explained. "The nuclear technician is female. We do not have an identification as yet. She remains unconscious."

"Please let me know when they arrive in Tokyo. Keep me informed about the technician. Also, let me know how I can get a message to Captain Stanley? It seems, Admiral, Colonel Michaels' wild ride was worth the risk." He nodded. "I assume we are planning some sort of acknowledgement for these acts of heroism?"

"Of course, ma'am. Colonel Michaels will receive the Navy Cross. Seal Team Two the Navy Distinguished Service Medal. We've recommended the British follow suit with their comparable Conspicuous Gallantry Cross for members of Grant's Boat Team. All these awards would be held in secret."

He paused, waiting to capture her full attention. "Ma'am, you cannot understand the bravery this mission required. It could've gone wrong in so many ways. It almost did. We're very lucky to have gained what we did and not lose anyone in the doing."

30 April, 02:59 Hours Local (UTC 17:59, 29 April)
Yellow Sea

Sick Bay, *USS Arlington*
CGN-47, Ticonderoga-class Guided Missile Cruiser

"Is she awake?" Sam heard Cassie's voice floating through a thick fog, but she couldn't open her eyes. *Must be dreaming.*

She heard another voice next—young, female—one she didn't recognize. "Not yet. Soon, I think. We've got her on some pretty heavy meds. Pain management and antibiotics." *Not dreaming.*

"Antibiotics?" Cassie interrupted.

"The colonel swallowed half of Korea Bay, ma'am. I'm concerned about pneumonia. I don't know what nasties exist in that water." Sam could feel a heaviness in her chest.

"I'm more concerned about her back. She's got some pretty sophisticated hardware in there. With a high-impact crash, I'm not sure what damage was done. The swimmers said she contorted herself into the pilot's compartment to rescue the commander. And she had to smash her way through the helicopter's canopy to get out of the sinking bird. She saved her pilot and the aircraft, ma'am."

"I understand. Please, let me know when she's awake."

Sam heard anger in Cassie's voice, but underlying the anger she also heard fear.

"I want her awake when I kill her."

Uh, oh. I'm in for it. Maybe I'll just sleep some more.

Two hours later
Sick Bay, *USS Arlington*
CGN-47, Ticonderoga-class Guided Missile Cruiser

"Colonel?" Sam heard a soft voice and struggled to open her eyes. She blinked rapidly, grimacing against harsh white light.

"Did someone get the number of the truck that hit me?" She asked. Her words didn't sound quite right.

A female face leaned over the gurney and smiled. "There you are. We wondered when you'd join us."

"Where?" Her voice was a croak.

"Sick bay on the *Arlington*, ma'am. Do you remember what happened?"

Sam thought hard. Disjointed images rolled through her drug-filled brain like a slideshow. "Helo… dark… shot at… failure… sea."

The young medic laughed. "That's about it, I'd say. Though I'd throw in autorotation, saving the pilot, and swimming to the zodiac with said pilot. You're a hero, ma'am."

"No." She shook her head. "No hero, please." Sam felt herself fading again.

"Stay with me, ma'am, I have someone who wants to talk to you."

The face disappeared, and Cassie leaned over the gurney. Sam tried to move, reach out to touch her. But she couldn't lift her arm.

"Welcome back, Colonel."

Not good. If Cassie is using my rank, I'm in deep shit. She tried to raise her arm again to touch the beautiful face hovering above her.

"Relax. You're strapped down to a backboard. You'll stay tied down until we determine the extent of damage you did to yourself."

"Ahhh... " Sam slurred, the meds dragging her back down into the fog. She resisted the pull. Sam didn't want to leave Cassie.

"I'm not sure if I'm going to kill you or kiss you." A single tear rolled down Cassie's pale cheek.

This made Sam struggle to lift her arm to catch that tear.

"Stop, you could hurt yourself more." Cassie gently stroked a finger down her nose. Sam smiled. This is what Cassie did often. Down her nose, across her lips and then farther. But she stopped at the tip of her nose and tapped it.

"No cry." Her speech garbled to her ear. "Sorry."

Cassie shook her head. "I know you're sorry, but why do you always have to go out and be the hero?" She leaned farther over the gurney. "I mean it, Sam. I can't lose you. Not now, not ever," Cassie whispered and gave Sam a hard look. "Do you understand?"

"Yes, ma'am. Captain, sir." Sam let the darkness claim her.

17 May, 13:21 Hours Local, (UTC 17:21)
Situation Room, White House
Washington, DC, United States

Grant held the door for Sam as she maneuvered her walker through the narrow opening. The lieutenant was loaded down with several messenger bags and had a small box tucked under her arm. "I'm good, Grant. Thanks."

"You are not good, ma'am. You should be home resting, not gallivanting around Washington, DC."

"I am not gallivanting," Sam said with a growl "Neither you nor Cassie would allow me that much latitude. But today's events are a clear indication North Korea is continuing to escalate their military advances. Pak is not happy about THAAD nor the destruction of his nuclear enrichment capabilities. He's lashing out."

"Pak has waited a month to respond. He can't be too angry if he took that long. And I have strict orders from Captain Stanley to keep you under surveillance."

Sam settled carefully into a chair and pushed her walker to the wall. Her grimace of distaste at having to use the device was evident. "Is that so, Lieutenant? I'll have to have a word with the good captain about that. I do not need a babysitter."

Before Grant could argue, Admiral Benson and the National Security Advisor entered followed by a gaggle of military personnel. Sam pushed off the armrests of her seat and rose to her feet. Pain shot down her leg, and she nearly collapsed back into her chair. Grant grasped her elbow to steady her while she got her balance. *Grant might be right*, Sam thought to herself. *I may need more rest.* Her back was not as healed as she thought.

"At ease, Colonel. And sit down." The older man smiled at her and clasped her shoulder with a warm hand as she settled back. The other officers stood behind him and offered their well wishes for a speedy recovery as well as expressing their pleasure she was on the mend. Sam blushed to the roots of her silvered blonde hair.

"Thank you, sirs and ma'am." She nodded at the female Marine general who smiled warmly at her. "I appreciate your kindness."

Their greetings were interrupted as the president and the Secretary of Defense entered the room. Sam stood and came to attention, stifling a groan.

"Colonel Michaels, you're up and around, I see." President Haley smiled at Sam. Grant stifled a guffaw. "Problem, Lieutenant?"

"No, ma'am. Of course not, ma'am."

"Very good. I didn't think so." She moved to her seat at the head of the table. "Let's get this over with so the colonel can get some rest."

Sam felt another blush bloom across her face. President Haley had been in continuous communication with Cassie during the prior month and knew the status of her recovery.

"Lieutenant, if you would please," Benson said to prompt Grant.

"Of course, Admiral." Grant rose and pulled a laptop from one of the messenger bags. She placed it on a leather desk pad, opening the device. A photo of a young Asian woman seated in a viewing stand flashed on the central monitor. "This is Doctor Kim Hye-su. She is the leading nuclear scientist in the Democratic People's Republic of Korea. Or I should say she was the leading scientist."

Grant looked around the room and hesitated. She turned to Admiral Benson. "Permission to speak freely, sir?"

"Everyone in this room is cleared for this presentation, Grant, and has been read into the mission you and your team members completed last month."

"Very good, sir. As I said, Kim Hye-su was their lead scientist until last month. She was recovered from the Nyŏngbyŏn Nuclear Reactor facility by the combined Seal and Boat Team mission sent there to gain access to the North Korean military computer systems. Doctor Kim successfully shut down the five reactors and secured the enrichment plant and its stockpile of spent fuel rods prior to the storm surge which inundated the facilities during the passage of Super Typhoon Palawan. Once operations and matériel were secured, she evacuated the staff of operators and scientists. She remained behind to ensure the pumping stations maintained power."

Sam saw Grant ball her fist behind her back. The lieutenant was still deeply angry about the blatant disregard for human safety and life exhibited by Pak and his cronies.

"Pumping continued until the station's foundation was undercut by the raging currents and the building torn from its moorings. Once that happened, Doctor Kim entered the reactor rooms and manually closed the sump drains in the basement of the building. This allowed the flood waters to cover and cool the reactor cores."

President Haley interrupted her. "Manually, Lieutenant?"

"That is correct, Madam President. To close the sump drains, Doctor Kim had to manually manipulate valves beneath each of the reactor cores. This operation is normally remotely controlled, but she had no power to operate the valves. Closing the valves manually placed her in direct contact with the unshielded reactor cores. During this time, Doctor Kim was exposed to more than eighteen sieverts of radiation."

Grant swallowed hard. "Her act of bravery saved millions from a nuclear accident which would have impacted twenty thousand square kilometers."

Sam was keeping an eye on the president and when the woman's brow furrowed, she jumped in. "Sievert is the measurement of exposure to ionizing or energetic radiation. Normal background radiation produces an annual dose of two-to-four milli-sieverts for most of the population, ma'am. One sievert is estimated to increase a person's risk of developing cancer by 5.5 percent. Eighteen sieverts is an off-the-chart level of exposure. Doctor Kim's immune system was fully compromised as all her lymphocytes were destroyed." A gasp rose in the room. "Doctor Kim's brave act prevented a Chernobyl event from occurring by closing the sumps and allowing flood water in to cool the cores."

"Good god, she should be dead." The National Security Advisor was a retired physician, and Sam knew he fully understood how critically ill the scientist was.

Grant continued her summary. "She was well enough to attack our combined team, injuring one before being subdued by the other team members. Once we had her under control, our radiation warning beacons began sounding off. Doctor Kim's body was a significant source of dangerous radiation. We sedated her and isolated her in a special lead-lined body bag. With the computer download of our target information completed, we exited the facility. Doctor Kim was returned to the *Arlington* with our team and immediately began receiving radiation therapy per the US Navy protocols."

"And today, how is the doctor?" the president asked into the silent room.

"Recovering. Slowly. Currently, she is in radiation isolation at Walter Reed Hospital while her immune system recovers following the Japanese stem cell treatment. Her bone marrow is beginning to function, and her white cell counts are improving daily." Grant displayed the next image. A gaunt face covered in red lesions glowered at the camera. She had a bald head and yellow rimmed eyes. "This is Doctor Kim today."

Sam slowly rose from her chair and moved to the table. "The good news is Doctor Kim has agreed to help us. She has no family within North Korea. This, plus being presumed killed by the flood waters at the Nyŏngbyŏn facility protects her from any retaliation by Pak. With the team's successful acquisition of their computer architecture, we now have an overall understanding of their various scientific and military programs—including their successes and failures. We are hopeful adding Doctor Kim's knowledge will allow us to cut through Pak's propaganda and give you a reliable estimate of their capabilities, arsenals, and intents."

"Sit down, before you fall down, Colonel." Admiral Benson chided. Both Sam and Grant settled back down along the wall. He turned to the president. "Ma'am, we have prepared a summary for you. This contains preliminary information on the storm's impact. We've included new information on recent events in and around the Kusong Special Weapons Facility. This is another of their critical nuclear facilities."

President Haley rocked back in her chair and eyed Admiral Benson. "What do we know about actual storm damage from Typhoon Palawan? There are no estimates of loss of life or other needs for the populace. North Korea and Pak are not releasing any information and are not asking for international aid of any kind. I can't believe they don't need some."

"That is all within the summary presentation. If we may, ma'am, Colonel Michaels will give our presentation sitting down." He gave Sam a pointed glare.

Sam's cheeks heated up again. Damn, she hated showing weakness.

"Of course, Admiral. Samantha, please, let's hear how bad this really is," the president said.

"Grant, if you would." Her aide pulled Sam's secured MacBook Pro out and booted it up. A new image flashed on the screen. "This is Panghyon Airbase near Panghyŏn-dong in Kusong, Pyongan-bukto, North Korea. The image was taken prior to the storm. It is the site of Pak's most recent military development—a fully operational missile testing and launch site. Missile assembly and storage are underground in numerous bunkers with topside access by angled ramps."

Another image popped up. A row of Quonset-style, steel-roofed buildings with large rollback doors was visible. Each building was aligned along a concrete taxiway. One of the buildings had an open door. "Underground storage protected the missile arsenal from storm damage."

"Here," Grant zoomed in on the open building, as Sam continued the summary. "You can see the down-sloping ramp and the numerous tire tracks. Given the thickness of the rubber tread marks and the width of the tires used, we estimate a gross weight of twenty tons was moved up the ramp on a flatbed trailer."

President Haley sat forward and squinted at the image. "These images are amazing. The detail is exceptional."

Grant moved to the other laptop and a new image appeared on one of the inset screens. "This is a KH-12 Kennen Keyhole satellite which took these pictures, ma'am. This series of birds is the first to use electro-optic digital imaging. They provide real-time observational capabilities to an object size of fifteen centimeters. The birds can act in concert or alone. They can resolve images from an angled view or directly above an object of interest. For imaging the airfield, we used an offset angle and were thus able to measure the width and thickness of the tire marks on the ramps."

Distractedly, the president acknowledged Grant's information. "I see. Thank you, Lieutenant." She never took her eyes off the image of the bunker.

"Over the last four weeks, since the passage of Typhoon Palawan, Pak has launched four missiles using two types of mobile launchers. The missiles were moved above ground from these bunkers."

Grant placed the image of the two missiles side by side on the central monitor. The size difference was shocking. "We believe he tested three Hwasong-10 missiles—a single-stage rocket utilizing a hypergolic liquid fuel made up of UDMH with a nitrogen tetroxide oxidizer. And one test launch of a Hwasong-14 missile. This is a thirty-five-ton missile with a two-stage rocket using the same liquid fuel."

"We know North Korea sold some of the Hwasong-10 missiles to the Iranians, so we have a bit more information about it from Iranian sources. Known as the Khorramshahr in Iran, this medium range intercontinental ballistic missile has an operational flight distance of three thousand kilometers. Pak can cover most of eastern Asia and the central Pacific islands with this weapon. We believe North Korea has fifty or so of these missiles with their paired launchers."

Pointing to the larger of the two missiles, Sam continued to summarize North Korea's missile capabilities. "The Hwasong-14 is a different weapon entirely. Depending on the size of the warhead, it has an effective operational range between eight and twelve thousand kilometers, and the missile is capable of carrying up to a five hundred-kilogram warhead." The room was stunned into silence. All tasks at the secure workstations stopped.

"If they use a smaller warhead of less than 250 kilograms, the missile could deliver its payload as far as New York City or other locations on the eastern seaboard. Weight of the payload controls dictates the range. Regardless of payload size, it would reach the west coast.

"The Hwasong-14 uses a detachable launch platform over a reinforced concrete pad. According to Doctor Kim, these pads were being constructed at hidden sites across the country. Typhoon Palawan halted their construction, and she estimates most sites were destroyed by the storm. This will effectively stop all future test launches of the Hwasong-14. The one test Pak launched either self-detonated or was remotely destroyed before it reached Japan."

Sam looked at the military leaders and security council members sitting around the table. Everyone was transfixed on the image of the big missile. "Our intelligence counterparts in South Korea have evidence that Pak received twenty Rd-251 engines from the Russians in 2016. This is the two-stage rocket engines used in the fourteen. Subtracting test fires to determine fuel mixture and test launches as we saw yesterday, their arsenal should have approximately fifteen workable rocket engines remaining. We do not have an estimate of the total warheads available.

"Doctor Kim has stated the bulk of their nuclear material for warhead construction is held in two places—Kangson outside Pyongyang and Nyŏngbyŏn. We know the combined team effectively destroyed the Nyŏngbyŏn nuclear facility when they allowed flood waters to fill the reactor control room. We do not know the extent of damage to the storage vaults in the adjacent enrichment facility. Doctor Kim has indicated this site was locked down.

"My firsthand assessment of conditions at that facility as well as subsequent image analysis of the Nyŏngbyŏn enrichment building indicates the building was completely submerged at the height of the storm. Following retreat of the floodwaters, the enrichment building's roof was missing, and the interior was filled with water. Doctor Kim told us the sealed vaults were four levels below the exposed first floor, which held the enrichment-centrifuges before the storm."

"Will he continue to test these missiles?" the National Security Advisor asked softly into the silence. "He is not a party to any of the international treaties limiting the testing and launching of nuclear missiles."

Sam stood and shuffled up to the table. "At this time, storm damage is extensive across the country. Pak lost most of the country's infrastructure—highways, train systems, airports. The Nyŏngbyŏn nuclear reactor complex and enrichment facilities are a total loss. This leaves the country without their primary source of electrical power. Before the storm, less than 26 percent of the populace had power and most households were limited to two hours of power per day. The remaining power was earmarked for the military installations. Now their power is even more limited. Currently, electricity is being supplied by several hydroelectric power stations in the north of the country around Huichon. In the south, two coal-fired thermal generation stations survived the storm and are back in operation.

"Pak's source of enriched uranium and plutonium for nuclear warheads is gone. His uranium mines are flooded, and we presume beyond his engineering capabilities to recover." Sam nodded to Grant and the image changed.

A photo of a mountainous valley with a raging river in its depths filled the central monitor. More startling were the numerous adits dug into the steep slope above the river. Each adit had a torrent of water gushing from it. "These are the North Korean uranium mines." Sam watched the president nod. "Engineers from the Colorado School of Mines do not believe any are salvageable given the extensive storm damage. Therefore, Pak's future warhead production is limited to what raw uranium he has stockpiled.

"The Kangson Enrichment facility located near Pyongyang sustained damage, but its central gas centrifuge building remains intact." A nondescript concrete building flashed up next. "However, the train and highway systems into the facility are a complete loss, so the facility is isolated and cannot receive additional raw material until the rail and road systems are reconstructed. They cannot move spent fuel rods from Nyŏngbyŏn there. This also limits the amount of available weapons-grade uranium and plutonium to what is held in reserve."

Sam leaned heavily on the table. Her back was beginning to spasm. "At this time, Pak is shut down. It is unknown for how long. He has to rebuild multiple facilities and transportation avenues. He will rebuild. The only thing I do know is any more sanctions will hurt the general populace and drive them to starvation. Some of the isolated villages have depleted their food resources and the villagers are eating dirt and weeds.

"The deployment of THAAD along the DMZ is what caused him to launch his four missiles from the Panghyon Airfield complex. He is flexing his muscles. Trying to show the world North Korea cannot be stopped by anything as mundane as a super typhoon. More importantly he wants the world to know he is not afraid of the United States' superior military position in South Korea."

No one spoke. President Haley sighed explosively. "Recommendations, people?" She looked at Sam and continued. "And for god's sake, sit down, Colonel, before you fall down. My cleaning crew will be angry if they have to scrape you off the carpet."

Sam settled back into her chair. Admiral Benson spoke into the stunned silence. "Maintain our alert status along the DMZ, complete the installation of THAAD, watch the bastard with all means available." He looked at Grant. "That's your cue, Lieutenant. What's the status of your project?"

Grant reopened the first laptop and typed in several strings of code. The central monitor image fuzzed out to be replaced with an image of her desktop. One of the security techs stood. "Ma'am, she can't do that."

The president laughed. "Seems she can, and she did. I assume you are hacking my secure systems for a reason, Lieutenant?"

"Not hacking, ma'am. Just borrowing your visual display capabilities. I've cloned my laptop to your system." Grant didn't quite hide her smirk as she glared at the security tech, who dropped back into his seat with a shake of his head. When the image morphed from her desktop to a map of the Korean Peninsula, Grant highlighted several details on the map.

"This is a real-time map showing the current distribution of the James Bond movie downloads. One thousand flash sticks were snuck into the country just as Typhoon Palawan reached landfall. The small red dots are individual tablets which have downloaded the movie. Currently, the movie has been downloaded to approximately seventeen hundred tablets."

As Sam watched, new dots appeared in various locations across the map. She did say it was real time. Sam suppressed a snicker. The security tech began madly typing into his workstation.

Grant tapped a key, and large red triangles appeared. "These are the eleven military workstations with the download. Given we now possess the complete computer system architecture for their military, we can enter one of these workstations and download their current work projects, their current status, and future plans." Grant rattled more keys and a black screen with a flashing "C:/" appeared. A few more keystrokes entered a line of command code. Grant hit "Enter."

The same security tech jumped up again. "Are you live? Shit! Are you on a North Korean workstation from the Sit Room of the White House?" He turned to President Haley. "Ma'am, this is an open access point to our systems. Shut it down!" The president raised an eyebrow to Grant.

"Actually, ma'am, this is a snapshot of a virtual machine talking to the North Korean workstation. The virtual machine doesn't exist in real space or on any hardware platform. Therefore, there is nothing to trace. Your systems are still secure and locked down behind your firewalls."

President Haley looked at the clocks above the central monitor. Sam followed her gaze and noted the local time in North Korea—09:31. "You have two minutes to complete your presentation, Lieutenant. Then I want this stopped."

"This is the workstation of a nightshift technician in the Chemical

Materials Institute in the Hamhŭng-Hŭngnam area. Since the storm, the Institute has been shut down while the buildings are inspected for structural damage. This technician has been absent from work for the last several weeks."

"And the fingerprint your leaving will show up like a flare at night," The security tech barked.

"I am not leaving a fingerprint because I am not really in his machine. Again, this is a virtual machine—a ghost really—using his machine hardware to complete tasks he would complete while at work." Grant ignored the tech's skeptical snort and continued. "His current project, which we've downloaded to a secure machine in Langley, is the development of solid rocket fuel."

Sam struggled to her feet. She had to save Grant from becoming too smug. "Madam President, with Grant's tracking capabilities, I recommend we map the actual storm damage to their key military installations using the eleven workstations. This will give us an indication of how bad things really are, how Pak has decided to rebuild, and where."

President Haley reclined in her chair. She closed her eyes and hummed softly to herself. When she sat up, she had made her decision. "Very well, unless Pak does something provocative in the next few days, Lieutenant Grant, you have two weeks to gain as much information as you can from your cyberwarfare project. Then I want it shut down. I don't care how good you think you are, someone over there may find you. We all know how good at cybercrime the North Koreans are, especially after the last Bitcoin incident." President Haley waved her hand. "From those two weeks, I want to learn about storm damage, status of current military projects and the storm's impact on them, his overall military plan and timetable, and most importantly the status of Pak's Arduous March and how it is impacting the populace. With the storm damage to their agricultural resources, I agree his people are starving.

"Colonel, I expect you to continue your satellite surveillance and if you learn any new information I want it immediately." Sam nodded. "That's all." President Haley stood. "Everyone but Admiral Benson, Colonel Michaels, and Lieutenant Grant, please leave."

The security tech jumped up. He moved around the table and confronted Grant. Sam watched in amusement as he tried to manhandle her aide into giving over her computer and all its components. She let him bluster for several minutes before interrupting. "Major, the lieutenant's hardware and software are not her own. They belong to MI6 and ultimately are the property of the Queen. So, unless you want to create an international incident, I suggest you back off."

"Yes, I don't want to explain to Lord O'Rourke what happened to his equipment," the president said. The tech left the room, grumbling under his breath.

"Lieutenant?" Her aide handed the president the small box she'd carried into the room. "If you would stand again Colonel, I'll make this quick." She opened the box and removed a medal hanging from a blue and white striped ribbon. "For extraordinary heroism in the successful rescue of your injured pilot and the completion of the combined team operations, I award Colonel Samantha Michaels the United States Navy Cross." President Haley stepped up to Sam and pinned the medal to her lapel. "As per the stipulations of the secrecy act, this award will be held in secret." She stepped back and saluted Sam.

"Ma'am, err, I don't know what to say. It was a team effort. Everyone did their part above and beyond expectations."

The president moved Sam back to her seat and settled beside her. "I know, Samantha, but you saved the most critically injured and protected your team as they made their escape. You took enemy fire and protected assets which could have exposed the mission to the North Koreans."

"Thank you, ma'am."

"I have a codicil to this award, Colonel. Per a request from Captain Stanley, you are not to do this again." The president paused and gave Sam a hard look. "Do you understand?"

Sam nodded. "Aye, I understand. No more heroics."

5 June, 07:30 Hours Local (UTC 11:30)
Asian Analyst Desk, CIA Headquarters
Langley, Virginia, United States

A junior analyst was reviewing the Chinese daily morning newspapers when a small notice caught his attention. The notice was printed in the *Oriental Daily News*, one of the older Chinese-language newspapers still allowed in Hong Kong. The notice included a state order limiting gatherings to no more than five individuals indoors and ten outdoors. He digitally clipped the notice and placed it in the Asian Items of Interest folder for the chief of staff to consider including in the president's daily briefing.

Though there was no mention of a reason for the limits, the analyst still wondered what the underlying cause was. Beijing could be cracking down on the continued discontent in the region and wanting to discourage the spread of information about the negotiations with the British. It could be an attempt to control the rise of the Chinese Triad organized crime groups. Or it could be something else. He'd let the chief of staff decide.

He flipped to the next newspaper and continued reading.

SECTION FIVE

Things were suspiciously quiet in North Korea over the last five months, probably due to the need to rebuild storm-damaged infrastructure. Grant's cyberwarfare project was continuing at a pace. They had successfully entered more military workstations and mapped strategic projects and timelines. Her review of the current project status was interrupted when her comm unit buzzed. "Michaels."

"Colonel, err…Samantha. This is Cynthia Brockstone." Sam carefully sat forward, Grant's report forgotten by this unexpected call.

"Yes, Cynthia, what may I do for you this evening?"

Sam heard computer keys rattling and machinery whirring in the background. "Hold on a moment, please." The geophysicist obviously placed a hand over the receiver, as Sam heard muffled voices. "Sorry about that. Things are a bit hectic here at the moment. I wanted to let you know, we have another nuclear test in North Korea."

How could Pak do something like that given the devastation in his country? "Hold one." Sam punched a stub and relaxed a fraction when she saw the red blinking light on her comm display. Grant had recently installed an encrypted communication console in her office. "I'm back, Doctor. When did this occur?"

"Approximately ten minutes ago." Papers rustled. "We registered a 6.3 magnitude event at the same geolocation as the prior five tests. The epicenter and focal point are identical—at ground level. Therefore, this is a confirmed test. Our dedicated network which monitors for nuclear explosions, is going crazy. We've recorded at least six aftershocks within the last few minutes. At this time, I'm not sure what's happening over there."

"Your best guess, Doctor?"

Cynthia paused and Sam thought she'd hung up, but the hiss of the open secured landline continued in the background. "I do not guess, Samantha. But given the—"

A voice called for Cynthia from a distance. "Hang on, again." The receiver hit a hard surface with a thud, as Sam heard more machines come to life at the earthquake center. Sam winced at the loud sounds. As she waited, she opened a second line and called Grant. This was another new addition to their communication system Grant installed.

Moments passed before Cynthia's out of breath voice picked up. "Sorry about that. We've just recorded a 2.8 magnitude event. That's a total of ten aftershocks." Cynthia drew a deep breath. "I'm going to hypothesize here."

"Go ahead, Doctor."

Grant flew through the door. "What?" Sam waved her to a seat and hit the speaker button.

"I believe the initial 6.3 magnitude event was the test of a substantially larger nuclear device than the five prior ones North Korea has detonated, perhaps from a boosted or multistage device." Grant whistled.

"Thermonuclear? You stated such a weapon would require two stages of detonation."

"I don't believe this was thermonuclear. The overall yield is too small. The calculated weapon yield is less than sixty kilotons. I would expect a true fusion device to exceed ten-thousand kilotons based on the Bikini tests in the 1950s. But, Samantha, I am not a nuclear physicist. You need someone else to give you that answer. As I said, it could be a boosted weapon, one using tritium or another isotope of hydrogen to increase the overall yield."

Sam leaned closer to the comm speaker. "I see." Her mind was spinning with possibilities. She needed to speak with Doctor Kim. She would know about the test site and its status prior to the storm. She scribbled a note and turned the pad to Grant. Her aide nodded.

"It's possible the subsequent aftershocks are due to significant ground settling with associated landslide events around the site location. They display true earthquake characteristics of ground movement and contain the typical elongated S-wave swarms."

"Please hold, Doctor." Sam muted the call and turned to her aide. "Call the imaging room. Get me the last two hours of images over the Punggye-ri test site. I want a zero-scale sweep of the area. Have them continue the sweep for the next ten minutes with real-time downloads to the imaging room." Grant ran from the office. Sam punched the release button. "I'm back. What else do you think could have caused these aftershocks?"

"If I were a betting woman, Samantha, I would say the North Koreans just lost all their underground facilities in and around the test site. The large device destabilized the mountainside and it failed catastrophically." Cynthia paused, and Sam heard the rustle of paper. "There's another interesting thing about this test and subsequent failure of the site."

Sam couldn't believe there was more. "What?" she asked.

"Three of the four monitoring sites in the region have detected radio-nucleotides in the atmosphere. When the mountainside failed, it is possible the rocks irradiated at detonation ground zero were uncovered. These rocks could have been crushed in the landslide and released radioactive dust into the atmosphere."

"How far from Punggye-ri were these radionucleotides detected?"

"Ussuriysk, Russia; Takasaki, Japan; and Petropavlovsk on the Kamchatka Peninsula. All the sites are downwind of the North Korean site. RN20—the monitoring station in Beijing, west of the site—did not report any radionucleotides. Therefore, the dust is being pushed east, the prevailing wind direction."

Sam was stunned. "Is this a Chernobyl-scale release, Doctor?"

"No, it seems to be limited in scope. The amounts detected are not dangerous to the environs. But they are an indication of a potentially dangerous irradiation exposure at the local area around the test site," Cynthia explained.

One more asset lost. "Cynthia, thank you for letting me know quickly and for your expertise. Can you send me a summary packet with your supporting data?"

"My preliminary notes and seismograms, as well as the chemical analyses from the monitoring stations, are in your inbox now."

Sam would have to leave her office to access her digital mailbox, but she'd do that after calling Doctor Kim, Admiral Benson, and the president. "Thank you, Cynthia. Will you be available at your office over the next several hours in case I need to ask any additional questions?"

"As long as the ground keeps shaking, I'll be here. The way the seismometers are jumping, it'll be a while before I go home. And I need to brief the folks in Vienna."

Sam paused for a moment. "Please do not share any of your hypotheses, Cynthia, especially about the ground failure. Limit your information to raw data only. This is now a top-secret event until I tell you otherwise." Sam heard an audible gulp.

"I understand. But, Samantha, others around the globe are part of the International Monitoring System. They know an event occurred and can complete the same analyses from the data. I don't know how long you will be able to keep this a secret."

3 September, 13:07 Hours Local (UTC 04:07)
Main Meeting Hall, Mansudae Assembly Hall
Pyongyang, Democratic People's Republic of Korea

Pak Sung-un's blood was boiling. He slammed a fist through the plastered wall of the communication center. A message had been received from the Punggye-ri site. His planned speech to the assembly was to announce the successful test of a multistage nuclear device—a precursor for the development of a thermonuclear weapon. He also planned to provide an update on the status of the storm damage and the planned next steps to replace and repair facilities. *But now this! How could this happen? It is unacceptable.* He ground his teeth and took a deep breath.

This disaster was preventable. He had ordered the arrest of the three scientists responsible. Their families were being rounded up as well. He dropped his head and rubbed his brow as a headache pounded behind his eyes.

Losing Doctor Kim to the storm was an unrecoverable happening. Pak missed her contributions and discoveries. He knew she could not be replaced. *And now these fools have irreparably destroyed our testing site with two undetonated test devices still in their tunnels.* Had Doctor Kim not preloaded the devices to protect them from the storm, he wouldn't have had anything to test.

Pak stormed out of the communications center and headed to the Mansudae Assembly Hall. The members of the People's Assembly with those of the Workers' Party and the totality of the Central Military's high officers were waiting for him. He had to tell them something. His acting president met him at the doors. This new one would never see elevation to permanent president. *I need to eliminate this position. It's just an impediment to my goals. I must continue to consolidate my power.*

"Supreme Leader." The man bowed low. "The assembly is ready for your words and direction."

"Do not tell me what is needed! I know what to do. I am the Supreme Leader. You are no one. I could remove you forever. Now, get out of my way." He reached for the door handle and yanked the heavy door open.

The assembly rose as he strode onto the speakers' dais. He looked out over the faces—so identical, so insignificant. None of them mattered. He smirked. *Only the Republic's place in the world matters. Only my place in this country matters. Yes, only I matter!*

The faces melded into a gray tableau. He gripped the edges of the podium. "Today we detonated a multistage thermonuclear device." A roar rose from the assembly. "The device was so successful and so large it destroyed its test tunnel. For this success, we are forever indebted to Doctor Kim Hye-su for her design and production of this great weapon in defense of our country. Her efforts will safeguard our glorious land for all time. She will be remembered as a Hero of the People now and forever." Clapping filled the room.

The sound washed over him. He looked at the officers sitting in the front row. Their reactions were not as exuberant as others in the hall. Some must know what truly happened.

Pak raised a hand. "Because of this great success, we have decided to cease testing. Now we will prepare to utilize our arsenal in offense against our enemies." He again watched the officers, noting who smiled and more importantly, who did not. There sat his opposition to his planned next steps. "In conjunction with our military preparation, we will focus our efforts on agricultural reform. Expand the development of organic biopesticides and fertilizers to increase our crop yields. This is the frontline of socialism and our next steps toward *juche.* Our goal is agricultural self-reliance—*Juche Fertilizers*! We will use our renewed vigor to remove our enemies from the Korean Peninsula.

"The storm tried to crush our efforts, but we are rebuilding. Building bigger and stronger than before. We owe much to that storm. It identified the weaknesses in our infrastructure, which we will overcome and remove. It forced us to make decisions, prioritize projects. Now it has forced us to action. We will not allow any delays. We will redouble our efforts toward our goal of supremacy. We will reunite the Koreas into one great nation. We will drive the archenemy from our shores. We will be victorious!" The assembly roared with agreement.

Pak Sung-un stepped off the dais and down the steps into the well of the Mansudae Assembly Hall. He moved along the line of officers, shaking each hand, while looking in the eyes of the officers. Those against him now knew he knew. He sneered as he left the hall. *Fools! The Democratic People's Republic of Korea will be victorious. I will be victorious!*

Once out of the hall, he met his driver. "Take me to Hŭngnam by the fastest route." The supreme leader settled into the warm leather seat of his luxury Mercedes S600 sedan. "I will accelerate our projects. Overt actions are having no effect. The only recourse is to push my other projects ahead," he murmured to himself. He had a course of action. He laughed, and saw his driver cringe. He laughed harder.

3 November, 14:30 Hours Local (UTC 05:30)
Presidential Offices, The Blue House
Seoul, South Korea

President Choi sat behind his large inlaid desk, fingers steepled under his chin. He had less than a year to go in his five-year term as elected leader of the Republic of Korea. Choi wished his term would end quietly with a little golf perhaps. But no! Pak and North Korea had been a continuous irritant since his inauguration. The bastard continued rattling his sabre—and now this. A potential thermonuclear device test. Why couldn't Pak just fade away? He'd hoped the storm would wipe him off the map, but the storm hadn't slowed their militarization.

The United States promised to protect South Korea and their interests along the DMZ. He was unsure if they would do so. He didn't know if THAAD would be effective against an ICBM launched from the DMZ. A North Korean missile would only need a few minutes to reach his beloved city. Therefore, he'd purchased an additional layer of protection for Seoul from the Israelis—the newly installed Iron Dome system.

Choi needed to determine what steps he and South Korea could take to halt Pak's military aggressions. The first steppingstone to Pak's desires for dominance in Asia would be through his country. That could not happen. Pak could not gain a foothold within the Korean Peninsula. Pak could not gain access to South Korea's nuclear arsenal and other superior strategic weapons. Pak could not be allowed to utilize their industrial infrastructure.

We have the fourth largest GDP in Asia. And if our economic development continues as forecast, we will be a dominant world player by the mid-twenty-first century. But this insane despot could ruin it all. Suddenly, the how became clear in his mind—economics. He would cut off Pak's access to international currency. He would halt North Korean economic development. Put Pak back in the Dark Ages. He would institute sanctions against North Korean industry. Stop all humanitarian aid to the country.

Decision made, he called his secretary. "Ask the CEOs of Daewoo, Hyundai, Samsung, and LG to meet me here tomorrow for a breakfast meeting. Attendance is mandatory. No excuses." He released the call.

Yes, that is what we will do. Cut the bastard off at the knees. No money—no military. No subsidies—no food. No food—no workers.

First step: the Kaesŏng Industrial Park. The CEOs would not be pleased if their assembly facilities in North Korea were shut down. He knew this facility, located ten kilometers north of the DMZ, was built in collaboration between the North and the South. It allowed South Korean companies access to cheap labor and Pak Sung-un access to international currency. He had to cut off this flow of tradable monies.

25 November, 14:30 Hours Local (UTC 01:30)
Bay Motel
Stewart Island
South Island, New Zealand

Commander James Alexander sat with his feet on the railing surrounding their suite overlooking Halfmoon Bay. Warm breezes swept across the balcony, and he turned his face into the afternoon sun. This was his first leave since his time with Sam and Cassie in Japan. Although that was only ten months ago, it felt like ten years. Much had happened onboard the *Arlington*. Too much. And with Sam being injured, Cassie had been strung as tight as a piano wire until her partner's recovery was assured. Cassie was headed back to DC to be with Sam for the holidays. The *Arlington's* crew would finally get much deserved shore leave while their boat received scheduled maintenance and upgrades in dry dock.

He'd flown from the naval shipyards in Pearl Harbor, Hawai'i, to New Zealand several days before to meet his mother prior to her departure for McMurdo Base and then on to Amundsen-Scott Base at the South Pole in Antarctica. James couldn't imagine spending four months in total darkness nor surviving the deadly cold. He shivered despite the mid-summer heat. His mother would be there to take care of the station's crew and researchers. She was looking forward to a respite away from pandemics, bureaucrats, and academicians.

The sliding glass door opened behind him, and he smiled when his mother dropped her hands on his shoulders, rubbing gently. She kissed the top of his head. "What are you thinking so hard about? I could hear the wheels turning from inside."

James laughed and tilted his head back to smile at his mom. Julia Alexander was not an attractive woman by conventional standards. It was the intelligence and compassion shining from dark eyes which spoke of empathy and understanding which made her beautiful. Crinkles around her eyes deepened, as she returned his smile.

"Nothing, really." She squeezed his shoulders harder. "Oh, all right. I was thinking about the cold at the South Pole."

Julia moved around and settled in the adjacent chair, squinting into the bright sun. "I'll be fine, James. This posting is much safer than West Africa or the jungles of Myanmar or the halls of academia. No desperate gangs or local terrorists or professors competing for tenure. No warring demigods or ruthless dictators."

"I get that, and I'm glad it's so. But four months in the dark. Really, Mom, what are you thinking?"

"I'm thinking about all the things I want to do for me." She looked hopefully at James, almost beseechingly, trying to get him to understand. "This seems like the perfect environment to do just that. I've had more than two lifetimes worth of adventures. I want to write. I hope someone else might enjoy traveling along vicariously, learning something about parts of our world not scheduled on a Viking River tour."

James shook his head and looked at his mother. "I get that." She smirked at him. "No, really, I do get it. Especially after the last ten months." He ran his hand over his close-cropped head and looked out over the ruffled waters of the bay. He was the exact opposite of his mom—tall, blond, blue-eyed, built like the linebacker he was at the Naval Academy. Whereas his mom was barely five feet tall with black hair containing more silver than the last time he saw her. She had the darkest, deepest eyes he'd ever seen. Nothing like his bright blue ones. Though, anyone who saw a photo of his dad knew where his genome came from—Scandinavian Viking—tall, blond, and blue-eyed. His father was an admiral in the Danish Navy before he was killed in a terrorist bombing in central Paris. James swallowed hard at the memory.

"Has it been really bad?" Julia followed his line of sight to the blue-green waves rolling toward the small beach below their hotel. She turned back to him, and he gave her a look. She held up her hands in surrender. "I know you can't talk about a lot of things you do, but I can read. More things are being leaked from North Korea, either from sources in the south or from defectors escaping the terror Pak is raining down on his country."

James wiggled uncomfortably in his chair. "Funny you should mention rain. Super Typhoon Palawan destroyed the country for all intents and purposes. Other things, I really can't talk about. But the *Arlington* was at the fore of all our activities in the region over the last year or so." His voice trailed off. James knew his mom was very good at using her Ph.D. in psychology to get him to say more than he should. Most times he didn't even know he was volunteering information. He turned to his mom. "I am going to share one thing, though. After our trip to Japan, I know you solidified your friendship with Sam and Cassie."

She nodded, an encouraging smile tickling the corners of her mouth. "During one of our little side trips in the area, Sam was injured."

Julia sat bolt upright. "What? How badly? Is she going to be all right?" Her physician's persona sprang forward, her compassion and empathy shining brightly.

"She's going to recover. I don't know all the ins and outs of her injuries. But I do know her orthopedic specialist flew out from Walter Reed and met us in Japan. I understand he reconstructed her back for a second time." James knew his mom well. She would be focused on Sam's injuries and prescribed care. On Sam's recovery and Cassie's wellbeing. He loved her so much. Hopefully, this would divert her focus away from any specifics of how she was injured and about their activities associated with North Korea.

"What the hell happened, James?" His mother's voice demanded answers. "You can't just dump something like that on me and leave it."

"Sam's back in DC and has been for five months. She's working on some super-secret project for the president. Her back is healing, though according to Cassie not as fast as Sam would like. Cassie's headed home to spend the holidays with her while the *Arlington* undergoes her scheduled inspections, gets her reactors refueled, and has upgrades installed to various onboard systems." He dropped his feet down. "That's really all I can say." His mom didn't look convinced. "She should be all right."

"I'll see about that." She rose from her chair. "I'm calling her." She looked at her watch. It was an eighteen-hour time difference. "Good. It's morning in DC. I will have the entire story before I leave for McMurdo. As frayed as Cassie's nerves were the last time we were together, I can't believe this is going over well."

James knew his mom was right about that. Cassie was barely holding it together. When Sam had been medivac'd back to DC on a private CIA jet with her orthopedic doctor and all the medical equipment that fit on the plane, Cassie hid her fears behind her captain's mask. She was curt, unforgiving, unbending, a stickler for the rules. She drove her crew crazy. James had spent his days refereeing between various officers, non-coms, and Cassie. Nothing was right, and nothing they did was good enough. He hoped time in DC would ease her mood. And when she returned, Captain Cassandra Stanley would be back in fighting form—ready to defeat their enemy and not her crew.

20 December, 16:14 Hours Local (UTC 20:14)
Michaels/Stanley Residence
Georgetown, Virginia

United States

The aroma was the first thing Sam noticed as she entered her home. Grant was parking her SUV in the adjacent garage, but Sam couldn't navigate the stairs with her walker. *Damn the thing!* Therefore, she had to use the front door. It was a straight shot along the paver stone walkway into the house. She just needed to watch her step on the uneven surface.

The foyer glowed with candles strategically placed on various side tables. Fraser Fir garland, held in place by red plaid bows, draped down the banister from the upper floors and filled the entry with a woodland scent. This smell was overpowered by one of roasting meat, garlic, and freshly baked something. Bread perhaps, Sam couldn't be sure. Or cinnamon rolls, a whiff of clove and nutmeg was also present. She smiled at how awesome it was to have Cassie home.

"Honey, I'm home." Sam laughed at herself.

Cassie appeared from down the central hall, wiping her hands on a tea towel. "So, I see. How're you feeling, Ace?"

Sam pushed her walker toward the front closet and stood to her full six-plus foot height. Or tried to, she almost made it to a straight spine. "Better today. Changing my desk chair to the new ergonomic one really helped." She wrapped Cassie in a tight hug and kissed the top of her head. "How are you? Baking up a storm, I smell."

Cassie melted into her arms, and Sam felt her smile. "Just some sweet bread for tomorrow's breakfast and rolls for dinner tonight." Cassie pulled back far enough to look up at Sam. "When is Francis arriving?"

The pair had invited all their friends who lacked family to gather for a week of holiday celebrations. "Tonight, some time. His flight from Albuquerque was delayed, and he ended up on a puddle jumper from Santa Fe to El Paso and then flights to Atlanta and on to Dulles." Sam shook her head. "I can't believe a state capital doesn't have a major airport hub."

"I can't believe you didn't send an agency jet to pick him up." A timer dinged in the background, and Cassie turned out of their embrace. "I need to baste the prime rib. Raincheck?" She winked at Sam.

"Of course, beautiful, always." Cassie gave her partner a squeeze before releasing her to hurry down the hall. Sam hung her jacket in the closet while tucking her walker in.

Just as she entered the kitchen, Grant came in from the adjacent garage, her face clouded as she scrolled through her smartphone. A defined wrinkle creased between her eyes and marred her perfect features. Cassie smiled at the young lieutenant. "An ale or a glass of wine, Amelia?" Sam and Grant startled at the use of Grant's given name.

"Just Grant, ma'am. Only my grandmum calls me Amelia."

"Very well, Just Grant, what may I get you to drink?"

Grant settled on a bar stool across from the gas cooktop and placed her elbows on the granite counter. "Ale would be most appreciated, ma'am."

Cassie headed to the drinks fridge tucked under the sideboard counter. "If I'm to call you Grant, then you must call me Cassie. I only answer to ma'am onboard the *Arlington* or on base." She turned. "India pale ale or bitters?"

"Oh, bitters, ma'am." Cassie pulled out an Old Dairy Red Top and grabbed an opener from a drawer next to the small, glass fronted fridge. Opening the dark brown bottle, she slowly poured the brew into a chilled glass. "Thank you, ma'am…err…sorry, ma'am. I mean Cassie."

Cassie placed the glass she'd held until Grant called her by her first name in front of Grant. "Better. I know it's hard, but I just want a bit of normalcy this holiday." Grant nodded and picked up the frosted glass. "Enjoy."

"Oh, I will. It's been a long time since I've had the pleasure of one of these." The young woman toasted her hostess and took a long pull; a tan mustache left on her upper lip.

"How about me?"

Cassie turned to Sam and gave her a look. "You know where we keep all the beverages. Help yourself." Sam huffed and went about pouring a Penfolds Bin 28 Shiraz into a balloon glass. She held up the bottle to Cassie and poured another glass when she received a nod. "Thanks, Ace."

Sam settled next to her aide at the bar with a sigh. "Problems, Grant?" she asked softly.

"No, ma'am. Just a note from my uncle." She paused. "Probably nothing to worry about."

"If I can help with anything, let me know. All right?"

"Of course, Colonel."

"And you can cut the colonel crap with me, too. While we're here, it's Sam. Okay?"

"Not happening, ma'am. You are still my superior."

The landline rang, and Cassie picked up the remote receiver off the counter. "Hello." She nodded and smiled, exchanged a few more comments, and nodded again. "Grant is on her way. Shouldn't be more than thirty minutes." Cassie hung up. "Drink up, Grant. You have a guest to pick up at Dulles." Both Sam and Grant turned a quizzical look on Cassie.

"Francis isn't due until later." Sam looked at her chronograph. "It's only seven fifteen."

"I've invited another guest for the holidays. She happily accepted our invitation since she was going be alone as well. Can't let anyone spend Christmas alone. And her flight arrived early. She offered to take a cab, but I said Grant would do the honors and pick her up. Told her to watch for the SUV and flag it down."

Grant stood and made her way toward the garage. "Which airline?"

"United." With a wave Grant was gone, her bitters left forgotten on the counter.

Sam looked at Cassie, her eyebrow nearly in her hairline. "What have you done now?"

"You'll see." Cassie giggled and went back to basting the roast.

An hour and a half later, Sam heard the garage door open and went into the kitchen. Grant bustled through the door carrying a backpack and lifting a roller bag over the threshold. She asked Sam, "Where are we putting your new guest?"

Sam was still in the dark. "I guess the room next to yours on the second floor if you don't mind sharing a bath." The two guest rooms on the second floor were large but shared a mutual ensuite located between the rooms.

"No, that will do nicely. Thank you." Grant was gone out of the kitchen with her load before more questions were asked. Sam watched her head down the long hall toward the stairs in the foyer.

"Hello, Samantha." A rich, age-mellowed voice interrupted Sam's thoughts. "I appreciate the invitation as well as the chauffeur."

Sam nearly jumped out of her skin and turned to come face-to-face with Doctor Cynthia Brockstone. "Doctor…" At a wave of her hand, Sam corrected herself, "Cynthia." She recovered quickly. "Welcome. Please make yourself at home. How was your flight?"

"More comfortable than the Super Hornet I took the last time. Though I have to say, the Super Hornet's pilot had better snacks and his jokes were first-rate." Cassie entered the kitchen just as the oven timer dinged again.

"Hi, Cynthia, I'm so glad you could join us. How was the flight?" Cassie opened the oven door.

"I was just telling Samantha, the Super Hornet had better snacks and inflight entertainment."

Cassie stood up, a nylon bulb baster in her hand. "Err… what?"

Cynthia stepped around the island and drew Cassie into a warm hug. "No worries. The flight was fine. I'm always worried about weather this time of year. But I got lucky. No delays." She threw a smirk at Cassie. "And thank you for the gallant chauffeur. I wasn't expecting to see Amelia again."

"Grant doesn't have family in the States, so since we're home this year, we're supplying family to all the strays we have." Cynthia guffawed at the comment. "Not that we're implying you're a stray." Cassie tried to save herself. "If our job duties allow, we enjoy entertaining during the holidays. We have another guest arriving in the next couple of hours or so." Cassie turned to Sam. "Don't we, Ace?"

Sam nodded in a daze, mesmerized watching Cassie welcome Cynthia with ease. What was it about Cassie which always made her able to be so easygoing in a group setting? Must be something they teach in Naval command school. Sam shrugged internally, knowing she'd never figure it out. Though, her heart swelled a little and she fell a bit further in love with Cassie. *After all these years, my heart gets larger and larger. I feel like the Grinch on Christmas morning.*

Grant came back in. "Doctor Brockstone, may I get you something to drink?"

"None of that, Lieutenant. I told you, around friends I'm Cynthia."

"Yes, ma'am." A light blush rose to paint Grant's cheeks. "A drink, ma'am?"

Cynthia laughed. "That goes for ma'am as well. I haven't been called that since my last IODP cruise." Sam watched Grant blush a deeper hue of red. "And I'll have whatever you're drinking, Amelia."

Sam finally figured it out. She saw what Cassie was doing. And it had nothing to do with strays and everything to do with matchmaking. Damn, something else she'd missed. "IODP? That's a new one."

"International Ocean Discovery Program. It's the deep-sea drilling program run by the National Science Foundation. I've been invited on several cruises as the resident seismologist. Makes for a great break from waiting on earthquakes to occur."

Grant handed the doctor an Old Dairy Red Top and a chilled glass. "Oooh, something I haven't enjoyed since Cambridge."

Sam saw Grant frown. "Cambridge, ma'am? That's too bad."

"Really, how so?"

"My family all attended Oxford. I don't know how to behave around a Cambridge graduate." Grant had attended Oxford for a year to acquire a graduate degree in cybersecurity after graduating from the Royal Military Academy, Sandhurst.

"Don't worry about that. I didn't graduate from Cambridge. I taught there for several years while doing a post-doctoral project on the directional orientation of strain accumulation in layered rocks. I graduated from Cal Tech."

Grant visibly relaxed. "Next time you wish to sabbatical in the United Kingdom, please let me know. My aunt is Head of House at Saint John's College, Oxford. We'll wash that Cambridge taint off straight away."

Cynthia raised her glass. "To higher education." A clink of glasses and the four women toasted each other. The geophysicist turned to Cassie. "Anything I can do to help?"

"Not a thing. It's all under control. We're just waiting on Francis to arrive, and then we'll sit down to our meal. I apologize for the late hour."

"No worries. Remember. I'm on mountain time."

24 December, 09:25 Hours Local (UTC 13:25)
Michaels/Stanley Residence
Georgetown, Virginia
United States

The good weather was a forgotten memory. A nor'easter developed out of a low in the eastern Gulf of Mexico and swept north to slam into the Atlantic seaboard. The storm dropped temperatures and brought precipitation with it. Sam stood in the bay window, watching her guests frolic in the foot and a half of snow which fell overnight.

Currently, Cassie and Francis were sheltering behind a quickly erected snow wall while Grant and Cynthia attacked from behind trees and strategically positioned shrubbery. Neither pair lacked for ammunition, and the battle was a draw to this point. Sam saw Grant flash a hand signal to Cynthia, and she caught the returned nod and smile. *Oh, this is going to be good*, she thought. Francis and Cassie were going down.

At Grant's next signal, Cynthia leapt from behind her tree, three snowballs in her left hand and one in her right. As the incoming fire dropped over the snow wall and drew attention to her, Grant darted out and flanked the wall. Snowballs rained down from two directions, and the sheltering duo quickly surrendered. Throwing their hands up and standing only made themselves larger targets. The attacking pair continued to pummel them with snowballs. Cassie tried to hide behind Francis' bulk, but with a two-pronged attack there was nowhere out of the line of fire. Sam laughed, as she watched the end of the battle.

This holiday get-together was a terrific idea. Cassie was relaxed and had lost the haunted look in her eyes over the last several days. And although Sam would have enjoyed some private time with her, she knew this was what Cassie needed.

The front door burst open and two snow-covered yetis entered. Snowballs continued to pelt the front door after they quickly closed it. Only one projectile made it in to strike the table at the base of the stairs. Sam crossed her arms and looked fondly at her partner and best friend. "That went well." Her snide remark didn't faze them. The two were beginning to drip and now stood in growing puddles on the slate floor. "Towels?"

"Put a sock in it, Sam." Francis groused. "You didn't tell me your aide could pitch for the Nationals baseball team. She has an arm like a cannon. That girl is a menace."

"She's played cricket since she could walk, Francis. You guys missed the flanking maneuver. How's that possible, Cass?"

"Don't have eyes in the back of my head, Ace. Unlike someone I know." Cassie smirked; her cheeks reddened from the cold and snow.

All of Sam's backseat navigators swore Sam had eyes in the back of her head. She could evade an attack before radar noted any missiles fired their way. She was never caught by surprise. Except the last time. Had she not lost an engine due to mechanical failure, she would never have been shot down. Sam was so focused on flying her Tomcat on one engine, she missed the surface-to-air missile launch until the last second. Her sixth sense allowed her to evade a direct hit, but the evasive maneuver flamed out her one functioning engine, and they crashed into the Iraqi desert.

"I'm missing my sensor suites on the *Arlington*. If I had those, Grant would not have gotten the drop on us."

"Be that as it may, those guys smoked you."

Francis huffed and unzipped his parka. Snow fell on the floor around him. "I'll get her this afternoon. We have a snooker game arranged."

Sam laughed at her friend. "Someone will definitely get someone. I can't believe you arranged a snooker game with a British naval officer. Don't you know that's their game of choice? And given her birthright, she's probably had a snooker cue in her hands since she could see over the edge of the table."

"Well, shit."

"Yep, you're going down again, big guy." Sam clapped him on the shoulder and moved down the hall. "Cocoa, hot cider, or mulled wine?" she offered as she disappeared into the kitchen.

Grant and Cynthia still weren't in by the time the three had finished their hot drinks. "Where are those guys? They're missing some great drinks." Sam kept a close eye on the two since identifying Cassie's matchmaking efforts. There was something going on, how much of something, she hadn't figured out. About an hour later Grant entered the kitchen.

"Any mulled wine left?"

Sam looked up from her spot at the bar where she was reviewing her email on a laptop. "Help yourself. Cassie is going to make more when this batch is gone."

"I hope she knows how good her wine is. My mother would love to have the recipe." Grant scooped up two full mugs and headed back toward the door.

"Where are you off to?"

"The gazebo. It's snowing again, and Cynthia wanted to enjoy the brisk air for a bit longer."

"Cynthia, is it?"

Grant's cheeks reddened, and she hung her head. Looking back up, she squared her shoulders before answering. "I am enjoying her company very much. She is intelligent and has a creative and inquisitive mind. She challenges me. Few do that."

"I see. I'm glad, Grant. Enjoy your wine."

Dinner was another of Cassie's wonderful creations, a stuffed pork loin with all the trimmings. After cleaning up, Cassie had excused herself to get some sleep. She would have to be up before four to start the turkey for their Christmas dinner. Grant and Cynthia were out on a moonlit stroll through the fresh snow. Francis was licking his wounds from being trounced at snooker.

"You should've stopped me, Sam. That woman will be the death of me. I'm not sure what I can possibly do to best her at anything."

"I know what you mean. A while ago I told her she was wasting her time and talents as my aide, but she said she had much yet to learn and I was helping her fill in the gaps of her education."

"I can't imagine she has anything to learn."

Sam dropped onto the couch next to the large man. "I know. She's so intelligent, and her level of cyber skills is unbelievable. I don't think I'll have her for much longer, unfortunately. Did you know her uncle is the prime minister?"

"You've gotta be kidding. Is she related to all the powerbrokers in the UK?"

Sam stretched out her leg to take some of the pressure off her sciatic nerve. "Not everyone." Her motion must have caught Francis' eye.

"How's the back?"

"It's getting better. I'm just frustrated with how slow this recovery is going."

"It wouldn't be slow if you followed your doctors' orders and completed all your physiotherapy. All you do is sit in a chair," Grant said from behind them, prompting the couch's occupants to turn. "I'm headed for bed. I'm spent."

"Rest well, Grant." Sam noticed a twinkle in the young woman's eye, as a slight blush painted her cheeks.

"Aye, ma'am."

"Stop that. You know it irritates me."

As Grant disappeared up the stairs, she said, "Not going to happen, ma'am."

"I think I'll follow. See you in the morning. Sleep well, Sam." Francis disappeared from the room. Sam watched the flames licking the oak and apple logs in the fireplace. She reached up and turned off the lamp on the side table. What a wonderful day. Cassie was happy. She was happy. Her friends were finding happiness. Couldn't be better. Minutes later, the happy thoughts, the fire's warmth, and the room's darkness lulled her into slumber.

25 December, 13:05 Hours Local (UTC 23:05)
Pearl Harbor Naval Shipyards
Pearl Harbor, Hawai'i, United States

Commander Alexander settled behind his desk and pulled up his Zoom application. He glanced at the clock. Five minutes. Entering his meeting identification and password, James waited for his mom to connect for their scheduled Christmas get-together. Six minutes later, Julia Alexander's smiling face filled his laptop screen. "Hi, Mom. How are you?"

"I'm great, James. And you?" She flipped the fuzzy ball hanging from the end of her Santa hat back over her shoulder.

He laughed. "Not as well as you, it seems. Having a good party? Or have you had a great party?"

"Both, I think. The last punch I sampled left me a little foggy. We've been celebrating one thing or another since we arrived on station. Oh, and thanks for the gift box. I really enjoyed wearing the grass skirt at our luau dinner party last night. I was the best dressed person in attendance."

"Is there anything you need or want? I can get another box out on the next supply transport ferried from here to New Zealand and on to McMurdo."

"Not that I can think of. We're all trying to maximize the twice daily trips from McMurdo, requesting all kinds of provisions for the upcoming winter lockdown. Right now, though, the Air Force is transporting all the jet fuel we'll need to operate the generators through the winter."

James was following the US Air Force's operational reports out of McMurdo. Their system acted as a scheduling and reporting authority for each flight to and from the South Pole. It also included all the supply manifests. He had gained access via the Navy's joint-procurement program. "If you think of anything, just let me know. We probably have another six weeks before they stop the flights."

"I keep asking how everyone gets their alcohol, but no one seems to know how it gets here. It's banned on the Air Force Hercules aircraft. If these parties keep going, I'll have end-stage cirrhosis by October."

Both laughed at that. Julia was the only person James knew who could drink anyone of any size under the table. She claimed her alcohol consumption was why she never contracted any horrible tropical disease. "I highly doubt that."

"How is Sam doing? I talked to her before I left New Zealand, and she sent me her radiographs. She has quite the sophisticated hardware in there."

"She's getting better according to Cassie. They are entertaining friends in DC for the holiday. Sam has stayed off her feet and away from Langley for the last six days. Cassie said she was starting to get cabin fever. But her health is more important than her work at this point. I don't know what will happen when Cassie is onboard the *Arlington* and Sam's on her own."

"I expect she'll be back at it harder than before. How is the good captain doing?"

"I can't answer that over an unsecured line, Mom." Instead, he flashed hand signals in view of his laptop camera. As a project for his Eagle Scout badge, James had learned sign language. Julia thought this could augment the effectiveness of her medical work and took classes as well.

Julia flashed back, *Thanks. Glad to hear she's better.*

"Do you know where you're off to next?"

James flashed some more signs. "Just waiting on the upgrades. All the other repairs and restocking are complete. The crew is scheduled to return over the next two days, and once we've completed the *Arlington*'s sea trials, we'll get an assignment."

Julia turned her head to someone who said something out of camera range. "I've gotta go, kiddo. I'm sorry to cut this short. The chef has burned himself lighting a lemon drop."

James totally cracked up. "Does he still have his eyebrows?" Images of flaming alcohol filled James' inner eye.

"Don't know. I'll find out. Merry Christmas, James. I love you."

"Love you too, Mom." The screen blanked out. *A lemon drop, really?* He agreed with her prognosis. Liver disease was a real possibility.

27 December, 11:12 Hours Local (UTC 15:12)
Michaels/Stanley Residence
Georgetown, Virginia, United States

Sam stood at the base of the stairs and watched Cassie wrestle a large roller bag down the winding flight from the third floor. "I'm sorry, beautiful."

Cassie looked up puzzled. "For what, Ace?"

"That I can't help you. I feel totally useless." She scuffed her toe across the slate floor. "This was your vacation too, and all you did was wait on me and feed all of us. You made sure we had everything we could possibly want or need. You spent your entire leave in the kitchen."

"And that's a problem, why?" Cassie laughed at her partner. "I thoroughly enjoyed my time off. It was even more pleasurable to have Francis, Grant, and Cynthia here to share the holiday. And you know as well as I, cooking is my passion."

"Cooking is your passion? Really? I thought our private activities were your passion. You sure exhibited your love for them last night." Sam shrugged. "I can't cook, so I guess I have no comparator."

Cassie punched Sam in the gut. "Err…right. Let me handle the cooking, and you handle the extracurriculars. Okay?"

"'Kay. I've got the extracur—"

The searing kiss Cassie gave her swallowed the rest of her sentence. When they came up for air, Sam felt dizzy. "What were we talking about?"

"Who's responsible for what in this household."

"Right. Now I remember." Sam giggled. "It really was a fabulous break. And it was all your doing. Thank you. I know Francis had a great time, even if he couldn't find anything to beat Grant at. And if I overheard Cynthia correctly, she and Grant have a ski trip planned for Colorado in February. Your little matchmaking project appears to be moving ahead."

Cassie easily slipped into Sam's embrace. "I knew those two had chemistry. Just wanted them to spend some quality time together without the pressures of the USGS or the Royal Navy breathing down their necks. Speaking of, when are you due back?"

"Middle of next week. I have a presentation to give up in Boston, and then I will be underground in my cave. I am sure Pak hasn't slowed his activities any for the holidays. So far things are quiet, and that always makes me worry." Cassie smoothed the frown lines marring Sam's forehead. "The quiet will allow me to catch up on the latest images we've gathered over the holiday break. Hope the weather's been clear."

Cassie looked deeply into her eyes. "What else has you so worried, Ace?"

"It seems like all I'm doing is chasing my tail." Sam huffed in frustration. "I feel like Pak is always several steps ahead. He acts and I react. I know something is coming. He's going to make another move soon. I think the storm threw a spanner in his timeline and delayed his next steps. I shouldn't bitch too much, I'll take all the time I can get."

"Promise me you'll stand up and stretch every hour. You'll eat right and get lots of sleep. I'm worried about your back. I know you are, too." Sam grimaced. Leave it to Cassie to pick up on her real concern. "Remember what your doctor said. This is the last time he'll be able to patch you up. There isn't much left to glue back together."

"Grant has set up a timer in my office. It chimes every sixty minutes. I can't figure out how to shut it off. I swear she's got a hidden camera in there as well, because if I don't stand up when the timer goes off, she's in my office within five minutes." Sam smiled as she thought of all the effort Grant put into her recovery. She brought her snacks and drinks of varying flavors, watched over her work, monitored her standing and stretching, chauffeured her to and from work. And physiotherapy. A light came on. "Did you and Grant talk to my therapist?"

Cassie cuddled deeper into her embrace. "Therapist? Not sure what you're talking about."

"Oh, yes, you do. What did you and Grant do? My therapist was changed after the second visit. The new one is Attila the Hun. I can hardly walk once she's done with me."

"I want you to recover, love. Be able to participate in any and all activities you desire to the fullest." Cassie smirked at Sam, and she felt a blush heat her cheeks. "Fly a plane. Enjoy a walk in the snow without fear of falling. Ride your bike in another Gran Fondo. Whatever strikes your fancy. Grant and I both agreed your first therapist was a powderpuff and wouldn't push you hard enough. She was too awed by you to make you work."

"Thank you." Sam kissed her love again. It was warm and comfortable with just the right level of passion simmering underneath. "I want to stay here with you forever. I love you."

"Same, but my boat is ready, and I don't want James getting any delusions of grandeur that he is taking her over." Cassie turned and gathered her pack from the hall table before grasping the roller bag. They had separated so many times, making each time they were together more precious. That's what they focused on, the together times, not the separating times. "Ready, Ace?"

"As I'll ever be."

SECTION SIX

Sam returned from Boston to a two-foot stack of satellite images. She was in the middle of completing a preliminary review of the most critical locations and waiting for other images to be reprocessed using a special set of optical filters she'd designed. That was four hours ago.

Now Sam's carefully constructed analysis of North Korean military assets and Pak was in shambles, all because a fresh-faced intern from the National Security Council knocked on her door. The young man apologized for interrupting her and asked if she could possibly, in her spare time perhaps, review his analysis of a potential situation in the Democratic People's Republic of Korea. He realized how busy Sam was and how insignificant his work was in comparison, but he wanted the CIA's best North Korean expert to review his report before turning it in to his advisor. He handed her an "eyes only" red folder more than an inch thick. Sam nearly laughed out loud at how frightened he was to even speak to her.

The young man, not more than twenty-five, was tasked with preparing a mock-briefing for a president as an exercise in situational analysis. At the time, he couldn't decide what to work on and culled recent world-security situations for possible topics. Nothing sparked his interest until at dinner one evening with his fiancée, he shared how stuck he was. Their conversation flowed from his work to her studies. She held a post-doctoral position in structural biology at the Broad Institute at Harvard and M.I.T.

She was working on a CRISPR-Cas9 gene-editing project under the tutelage of Doctor Feng Zhang. One of her group's recent afternoon tea discussions concerned the moral and ethical dilemma gene-editing researchers were facing. Following the 2020 Nobel Prize in Chemistry going to Doctors Jennifer Doudna from University of California, Berkeley, and Emmanuelle Charpentier of the Max Planck Unit for the Science of Pathogens in Berlin, CRISPR had evolved from a basic science to a commercial enterprise. This was a natural evolution, as the theoretical work of RNA gene-editing in single-celled organisms expanded to multigene editing of DNA in eukaryotic cells.

That dinner conversation sparked the young man's interest, and he began looking into the threat CRISPR might pose to national security. CRISPR gene-editing technology was easy to learn, and the precursor chemical components were low cost and readily available globally. He'd found his focus and developed his thesis—*Could terrorists or enemy states utilize this biotechnology to create security threats?* The report he handed Sam was the result of his analysis. Sam thanked the young man and said she'd get back to him after she had a chance to review it.

Sam's review was done, and she was no longer laughing at the intern. She placed the folder back on her desk and carefully closed the cover. The well-researched and thoroughly documented file contained nine pieces of surprisingly contradictory yet terrifying information. What he hypothesized caused her to reevaluate her analysis of the North Korean situation, realizing she'd missed a critical component. She tilted back in her chair and regarded the offending folder warily, as if it would rear up and bite her.

The nine documents presented in support of his analysis included the following:

1. A CIA analyst summary of the last twenty years of UN inspections at various North Korean locales. The inspectors concluded, "North Korea may have or have had at one point in the past a biological weapon program." This made Sam wonder. Had she allowed the burgeoning nuclear threat from Pak's successful missile launches and underground warhead testing to overshadow other threats he may be preparing? Had she been lulled into complacency by the widespread destruction in the DPRK caused by the typhoon? How could she use her image analysis tools to find out what she'd missed?

2. The official testimony of a recent North Korean defector, interviewed by South Korean officials. The defector was a doctor working at the Hŭngnam Fertilizer Complex. He stated political prisoners from the Kyo-hwa-so Number Nine camp were live test subjects for their biological weapons program.

Granted, Sam had to take a defector's testimony with a grain of salt. Any defector had an inherent incentive to give more to get more. It seemed he was too low in the organization to be aware of what all the program pieces were or how all of Pak's biological projects fit together.

Damn it, this complicates the overall picture. This is what had Sam scared. It was easy to remotely monitor the development of Weapons of Mass Destruction (WMD). Watch construction of facilities. Monitor the manufacturing of key components. Watch those components move from one place to another. Record testing successes and failures. Follow the trails of money laundered through various mechanisms to fund purchases and programs from outside the country.

But biological weapons were different. These WMD could be

developed behind closed doors—in small labs with minimal need for supplies or equipment—at very low costs. Weaponizing and cultivating pathogens were, therefore, invisible.

Now she knew she'd missed a critical element in her analysis of Pak's next steps. Pak had well-developed agricultural programs. He had touted a huge agricultural program in support of his national policy of *juche*. He had openly purchased equipment and feedstocks from China over the last five years. The WMD risk was how this agricultural equipment—incubators, centrifuges, fermenters, and spray dryers—could serve a dual function. The same equipment used to mass produce fertilizers and pesticides could easily be converted to produce deadly pathogens for bioweapons.

3. A summary of five South Korean governmental reports and white papers prepared between 2005 and 2015. All agreed—North Korea has the viable feedstock for more than eleven active biological agents, ranging from anthrax to Bubonic plague to yellow fever. With North Korea's successful missile launches over the last months, Pak now possessed the means to weaponize them for delivery to distant targets in a minimum number of days. Most of these biological agents were lethal.

4. A 2012 US Department of Defense report which included the statement of a Pentagon official. "The DPRK bioweapons program is advanced, underestimated, and highly lethal." The Pentagon official went one step further in his analysis. "Pak is far more likely to use biological weapons than nuclear ones in an offensive manner on the Korean Peninsula given his desire to preserve South Korean infrastructure."

5. An addendum to the 2006 United Nations Security Council Resolution UNSCR-1718. This stated, "All member-states shall prevent the direct or indirect supply, sale, or transfer of items, material, equipment, goods, and/or technologies, including education, to North Korean WMD programs."

6. A clipping from a 2019 *New York Times* article. This item reported, "The North is collaborating with foreign researchers to learn biotechnical skills, collect naturally occurring samples, and build the needed machinery to grow various germs and agents."

7. A technical paper from the peer-reviewed scientific journal, *Nature*. This 2018 paper, co-authored by none other than the recent Nobel laureates, speculated on the use of CRISPR-Cas gene-editing technology for the good of humanity. But it went on to warn of the potential for misuse and the production of superbugs and biological weaponry. Sam wondered if Pak's scientists had enough technical ability to utilize this advanced technology. Could they get their hands on CRISPR precursors and equipment? Sam's heart rate accelerated. She feared they could.

8. A transcript from the Director of National Intelligence's 2018 testimony before the Joint Congressional Intelligence Committees. He

stated, "North Korea has a longstanding biological warfare capability, and their biotechnical infrastructure could support a biological weapons program. This program would be highly agile and capable of rapid response and deployment, allowing integration in a defensive or an offensive military plan." The South Koreans estimated the North Korean government has a stockpile of twenty-five hundred to five thousand tons of active biological agents—preliminarily dehydrated anthrax and bubonic plague—both deadly to the world. For example, a pound of anthrax spores released into the upper jet stream could wipe out the entire global population.

9. A 2017 overview of the Outpacing Infectious Disease Program completed by the Defense Advanced Research Projects Agency (DARPA). DARPA was formed in 1958 by President Dwight Eisenhower in response to the first Sputnik launch. He wanted to ensure the United States was never beaten in a scientific endeavor again.

Prior to the COVID-19 pandemic, DARPA's Biological Technologies unit spent nearly $300 million to develop methodologies to rapidly identify pathogens using DNA/RNA sequencing. In particular, DARPA funded a biotech startup—Moderna Therapeutics, tasking Moderna with the development of a modifiable RNA vaccine production platform for response to any biomedical threat, a technique now proven successful, given Moderna's rapid and successful development of their SARS-CoV-2 vaccine.

The entire file was an exercise in contradiction. Does Pak, or doesn't he? And if he does, how much does he have? How far along are they in development? What scientific capabilities do they have? Sam couldn't answer any of these questions, but she had resources. Doctor Kim might be able to help sort out this mess, and the epidemiologists at Fort Detrick and the scientists at DARPA could provide some background.

Now Sam's challenge was to determine ways to utilize the CIA's remote-sensing capabilities to assess a biological program threat. She might be able to use Grant's cyberwarfare project to locate these projects and focus there. Determine the level of competency Pak had reached with bioweapons. Estimate his potential biological weapons stockpiles. Determine methods of use and delivery. Determine what his next steps were. Integrate these disparate pieces of information and her understanding of Pak to determine his willingness to release biological weapons into the world. Sam began to outline the threats and responses on her yellow legal pad. At the top she wrote, HAS HE ALREADY BEGUN?

Sam was deep into her evaluation of this multipronged problem when a knock sounded on her door. "Come."

The door swung open, and Grant stuck her head around the edge.

"May I have a moment, ma'am?"

"Of course, Grant. What may I do for you?"

Grant perched on the edge of a chair and began to fidget. This was behavior Sam hadn't seen her self-assured aide ever exhibit. "I, err…"

As Grant struggled, Sam encouraged her to voice what was bothering her. "Out with it. You know I won't judge."

"I know, ma'am. It's just difficult. I don't want to leave, but at this point I don't have a choice."

"Leave? What are you talking about?" This got Sam's attention. What now? Just when she needed all of Grant's cyber expertise to look into this new potential threat.

"Remember I received a communique from my uncle over the Christmas holiday?"

Sam folded her hands on top of the thick red folder. "I do," she said slowly.

"I thought I could ignore it, but now it seems I cannot refuse his request. Certain things are coming to a head for MI6, and I am needed for one of their projects." Grant looked down.

When she wasn't forthcoming with more information, Sam prompted her. "Go on."

"That's just it. I can't tell you what I am needed for or what I'll be doing. I feel as though I am failing you. You have taught me so much. You've allowed me to fully explore and utilize my cyber skills. Not being able to tell you why I'm needed elsewhere makes me feel like I am cheating on an examination." Grant's words ran together in one rapidly expelled sentence. She fidgeted again, wringing her hands.

"Take it easy. I understand. You've left before, when you collected the UDMH samples." Sam paused to ensure her aide was listening. "You've got to realize, Grant, there are things I do and things I work on I can't share either. It's often a sticking point between Cassie and I. But it's part of the job. I understand your responsibilities and duties. You need to do what you need to do. Regardless of what it means to me or our project here. Your ultimate duty lies with the UK and the Queen." Sam watched the younger woman slowly relax back into her chair. "Will you be able to return?"

"Return?" Grant questioned with a frown.

"Come back here? To Langley?" To me and this potential global nightmare?

Grant seemed taken aback. "You would have me back? If it's possible, I mean."

"Without question. Why do you think I wouldn't want you to return?"

"I never expected you would ask."

"Don't diminish the contributions you've made on our projects, Grant. You are an invaluable member of our team. Your cyber project is still ongoing and will need your continued expertise.

Grant blushed. "Thank you, ma'am."

"Now, when are you scheduled to leave?"

Grant blushed a deeper shade before answering. "I've asked Cynthia, err…Doctor Brockstone, if she would be able to move our planned ski holiday up. If she is, I would like to leave for Colorado by next Friday. This would allow me two weeks before I need to be in southeast Asia." Grant gasped. "Bollocks, did I just say that out loud?"

Sam laughed at her aide's chagrin. "You did, but I didn't hear anything." She covered her ears in a mock gesture of not hearing. "Enjoy your ski trip." Sam sat forward and gave Grant her best command glare. "And be safe. I expect you back here once your project is completed."

Grant stood to attention and snapped off a crisp salute. "Ma'am, yes, ma'am." Grant dropped her hand. "Thank you, Colonel. I appreciate your understanding."

"And Grant, have a good time in Colorado. You deserve a break and," Sam hesitated, not wanting Grant to think she was keeping tabs on her private life, "a chance to be happy."

"Thank you, ma'am." Grant's smile nearly split her face.

Sam watched the door swing shut behind her aide. Darkness again filled her subterranean office. She contemplated the dark corners. Her life was once as solitary as Grant's until Cassie came into it and provided the light and love which warmed her heart and made her soul sing with possibilities. A thought struck and pierced her heart. What would she do without Cassie? She looked at the red folder. *And now this. I will not allow Pak to destroy something so wonderful,* Sam vowed. *For me, for Grant, for anyone!*

12 January, 09:52 Hours Local (UTC 13:52)
BioSafety Level 4 Containment Room
Infectious Disease Laboratories
US Army Medical Research Institute for Infectious Diseases
Fort Detrick
Fredrick, Maryland, United States

Backlight from the negative pressure isolation box flashed off the face shield of Doctor Deidre Williams' positive pressure laminar flow suit as she turned her head. This was the only spot of light in the Level 4 lab. Biosafety Level 4 was the highest level of biosafety precautions as set by the Center for Disease Control. Such a lab was needed to work with agents transmitted by aerosol, which could cause severe to fatal disease in humans and for which there were no available vaccines or treatments. Currently, fifteen Level 4 laboratories existed in the world.

Deidre's hands were mid-humerus deep in the isolation box's neoprene gloves, as she carefully manipulated a culture petri dish from the incubator to under the microscope within the box. Once the dish was centered, she looked up at the display monitor above the isolation box to see the magnified image. Twisting the focusing knobs a few turns, she looked back up. Centered in the monitor were several large, circular, colorless colonies of bacteria. "Not good," she said to herself.

Exchanging the petri dish for the next one in the incubator, she didn't need the microscope to see the bacterial growth on the MacConkey agar growth medium. "Shit." A colorless bacterial mat covered the entire dish. She returned the dish to the incubator and pulled her hands from the gloves. Deidre turned to her plastic-encased lab notebook. Flipping back several pages she noted the time since the samples were placed within the incubator—twenty-one hours. "This is so not good."

Two days ago, she received a call from the French Ministère des Affaires Sociales et de la Santé, also known as the Ministry of Social Affairs and Health. A patient had presented to the Hôpital Saint Joseph in Paris with a high fever, uncontrollable diarrhea, severe headaches with light sensitivity, chest pain centered behind the sternum, and a sore throat. Symptomatic treatment was initiated. The patient began having tremors which escalated to seizures and a coma. He was transferred to the Pasteur Institute and placed in infectious isolation. The samples she received were from various body fluids, including from spinal and brain taps.

Deidre hadn't expected such aggressive cellular growth. Now she was worried. Very worried.

The patient's symptoms could indicate a gram-negative enteric bacterium. Her initial guess was one of the *E. coli* strains, but the cultures weren't behaving like an *E. coli* bacterium. The intestinal bugs she knew wouldn't cause the range and severity of symptoms this patient exhibited. Deidre needed more information, and she needed it quickly. Something else was going on.

Deidre rose from her stool and disconnected the positive pressure air hoses from the sides of her suit. She left the lab through the decontamination room and double airlock. After a shower, she dressed and left for her office in the next building. Deidre came in to receive the samples and begin an evaluation at the request of Doctor René Auberguist. She met René at the Institute for Animal Health in Pirbright, United Kingdom. Each was completing a post-doctoral project on trans-species diseases—particularly those which had the potential to transmute from animal to human. Deidre held a medical degree from the University of Texas and a Ph.D. in epidemiology from Oxford University. At the time they met, René was on leave from the Pasteur Institute. He was studying potential trans-species agents which could be used for bioterrorism. Together they would get to the bottom of this.

14 January, 21:12 Hours Local (UTC 01:12, 15 January)
Studio 3-A, NBC Studios
30 Rockefeller Plaza
New York City, New York, United States

MSNBC NEWS REPORT:

Rachel Maddow frowned into the camera, her regularly scheduled evening telecast interrupted by the latest wire report. "We have late-breaking news from our Chief Foreign Correspondent, Richard Engel. He is reporting live from Paris. Richard... "

"Thank you, Rachel. I am outside the Pasteur Institute where Doctor René Auberguist gave a news conference concerning one of his patients. Three weeks ago, a trans-shipping clerk working for DHL International, the German logistics services company, became ill with a cluster of serious though seemingly unrelated symptoms. The clerk died this evening of massive organ failure in the Institute's infectious disease ward. Doctor Auberguist was unable to determine the pathogen which caused his death. The clerk had not traveled outside of Paris in over four years or outside of France in over ten. Currently, the staff is waiting on the transfer of two healthcare workers who initially treated this patient at Saint Joseph's Hospital in central Paris. Both have fallen ill with similar symptoms. The French Ministry of Health is now involved and the WHO has been alerted. Doctor Auberguist said samples from this patient were sent to another laboratory where a another specialist in trans-species diseases works.

"When asked about specifics concerning this patient and the disease, the Doctor declined to comment beyond saying the symptoms could be construed as a form of hemorrhagic fever. However, since the patient had not traveled outside Paris nor visited a zoo or other animal shelter in the last three years, this diagnosis is highly unlikely. Hemorrhagic fevers like Ebola and Lassa fevers are endemic to sub-Saharan Africa. They are caused by viruses transmitted from bats or monkeys to humans. He stressed they do not spread via aerosol—droplets dispersed in the air from coughing or sneezing. The only means of transmission is direct contact with a primary patient's bodily fluids or other materials contaminated with such. So rapid population spread is unlikely according to the doctor."

Rachel interjected. "Richard, the French aren't suggesting another global health situation, are they?" Her voice rose significantly on the last words. Everyone was living in a state of heightened awareness, given the only recently controlled SARS-CoV-2 viral outbreak, better known as the COVID-19 pandemic. Many believed the next pandemic was just around the corner.

"Not at this time, Rachel. Though I find it interesting the WHO, another laboratory, and the Ministry of Health are already involved with only one confirmed and two possible cases. Contact tracing has begun and is being managed by the Ministry of Health until experts from WHO arrive in the morning from Geneva, Switzerland."

"When will we have additional information for our viewers?"

Richard answered, "The next news conference is scheduled in eight hours. Doctor Auberguist has indicated the need to evaluate and begin treatment on the two healthcare workers."

"Thank you, Richard." The image returned to Rachel in her New York studio. "Granted, not much is known about this patient or his illness at this time. We are currently trying to reach the heads of the CDC and NIAID for further comment. We will keep you informed as more information or other experts become available."

19 January, 15:26 Hours Local (UTC 19:26)
BioSafety Level 4 Containment Room
Infectious Disease Laboratories
US Army Medical Research Institute for Infectious Diseases
Fort Detrick
Fredrick, Maryland, United States

Doctor Williams was stumped. The gram-negative strains of bacteria present in her latest batch of samples from the two health workers in Paris didn't match any enteric bacterium she had ever seen, and the bacterial growth rates were through the roof. Add a little incubator heat to the sample, and the rate of proliferation exploded. She removed her hands from the isolation box gloves and turned to her reference treatise—*The Bacteria*—edited by M.J. Pelczar, Jr. It was an old text, first compiled in 1960. Her copy was the just released, eleventh edition and contained the bacterial species discovered in the last ten years. She flipped to the section on simple bacteria.

The bacterium under her microscope was rod-shaped and nonmotile until heat was applied to the sample. Accelerated growth occurred at 22-25° Celsius in a MacConkey agar growth medium with a neutral pH of 7.0 (the pH of water). The bacterium appeared to be aerobic and degraded rapidly in an anaerobic environment. It was non-spore-forming. This was the first good thing she'd discovered about this mystery organism, as it limited the ability of the bacterium to spread easily through the air. Deidre had never seen this particular strain before. She was waiting on the results of gene sequencing and phylogenetic analysis to help identify the sample. If it had ever been identified before.

She marked her place in the treatise and moved out of the Level 4 laboratory. There was nothing else she could do until the sequencing was complete. She glanced at the large digital clock on the wall—3:45 in the afternoon. That made it late evening in Paris. René should still be at the hospital. She would call and check on his two patients. So far, they were stable and responding to symptomatic therapeutic treatment.

Entering her office, she was faced with a disaster. Texts opened at various places, hardcopy reference materials, and annotated copies of journal articles competed with various digital storage devices for space on her desk. Several partially empty coffee mugs were holding other reference books open to specific pages. Plates of partially consumed meals teetered on the edge of her bookcase. She hated the chaos and knew she would need to organize things soon if she hoped to find anything. She started in on the mess, as she waited for the next set of analyses.

Several hours later a knock on her door interrupted her organizing. Deidre placed several stacks of reference materials on the floor. "Come."

A young staff sergeant popped his head around the jamb. "Doctor Williams, I have your printouts."

"Mike, that's great. Can you summarize the highlights, please?"

Mike dropped onto one of the recently cleared chairs. "You bet. This one was really different. I've never seen this strain before."

Deidre sat forward as a spike of fear streaked down her spine. Mike was one of her best technicians, and she was pleased he did the analyses. "And?" Deidre asked, prompting the young man to continue.

"Phylogenetic analysis based on 16SrRNA sequences places this strain in the genus *Terrimonas*. I'm not sure of the species, yet. It could be *arctica* or *crocea*. Were the samples colored?"

"No, none of the culture growths exhibited any color. They are non-motile, rod-shaped, colorless bacterium."

Mike said, "In that case, I'd have to say your little bug is *Terrimonas arctica. Terrimonas crocea* is yellow, hence the name. I guess."

Deidre scrambled for her work copy of *The Bacteria*.

"Eager much?" Mike laughed and placed the printouts on her desk. "I'm headed down to the cafeteria. Do you want anything? It's after dinner time, but I know you never remember to eat."

"You're the best. Thanks. A sandwich and milk would be great."

"See you in a bit, then." He left her office whistling a quiet tune.

Now Deidre had a starting point. She opened the reference book and searched for her new bug in the treatise.

20 January, 09:26 Hours Local (UTC 13:26)
Researchers Office Building, Infectious Disease Laboratories
US Army Medical Research Institute for Infectious Diseases
Fort Detrick
Fredrick, Maryland, United States

The telephone on Deidre's desk rang, and she looked up from her iPad. She was still searching for other references to *Terrimonas arctica.* Mike was correct in his phylogenic analysis. This bug was a rare, soil-loving, cold-temperature surviving, gram-negative strain of a bacterium only recently discovered. She hadn't found any other references to this species anywhere in the literature, except for the original reference when it was discovered in Spitsbergen. She carefully placed her tablet on the desk and lifted the receiver. "Williams."

"Doctor Williams, this is Samantha Michaels at Langley."

Good gawd, Deidre thought. *What does the CIA want with me? I really don't have time for this.* "Yes, Ms. Michaels." She knew she was being abrupt. This Michaels person barely contained a huff, but she heard the small sound.

"I need some background information on CRISPR technology and knew you or one of your colleagues would be able to provide it. An intern here is completing an assignment on the use of this technique by bioterrorists."

Deidre's heart rate accelerated with this request. Why would the CIA be interested in CRISPR? And where did they learn about it in the first place? "I can supply a list of references for you but beyond that, my staff and I are focused solely on a new project." She paused to consider her next words. "May I ask why you are interested in CRISPR?"

"As I said, one of our interns is completing a theoretical project on bioterrorism. His fiancée is a research fellow in structural biology at the Broad Institute and mentioned CRISPR in conjunction with her work."

Vague, but typical of the spooks at Langley. "Let me forward a list of references. Perhaps your intern's fiancée could provide any background explanations for you." Deidre didn't want to shut this agent down, but explaining a technology like CRISPR to a non-scientist could become a time-sink she couldn't afford.

"I'd appreciate that, Doctor Williams. I know how one can get lost in a project and lose touch with everything else. I'll send you an email link for the reference list." The line went dead.

"You're welcome." Deidre heard sarcasm drip from her voice and heaved a sigh as the call was already disconnected. "That went well," she murmured to herself. She knew one didn't want to piss off the CIA, but on the other hand, she had seen colleagues disappear into their projects and struggle to escape. She didn't have the time or energy to spare.

21 January, 14:24 Hours Local (UTC 18:24)
Studio 1-A, NBC Studios
30 Rockefeller Plaza
New York City, New York, United States

NBC SPECIAL NEWS REPORT:

Lester Holt looked into the camera with a grave expression. "We now have confirmed reports of three new outbreaks of the Paris Contagion. Two in the United Kingdom—in Edinburgh, Scotland, and on the small island of St. Agnes off the Cornwall coast, and a Federal Express delivery worker in Tokyo, Japan. Medical experts are scrambling to correlate these new point infections with the three cases in Paris. The new patients are being cared for in infectious disease isolation. To date only the initial patient has died. All of the surviving patients are exhibiting similar symptoms—high fever, severe headache, chest pain, sore throat, and gastrointestinal issues. The two patients in Paris have progressed from these early onset symptoms and the beginnings of general systematic organ failure to various central nervous system issues. Overall, their physicians indicate they are stabilized and have entered a convalescence phase.

Again, we want to reiterate, these patients do not present any form of airborne infection danger. They are not contagious to the general public. It seems infection only occurs with direct patient contact. Tracking and tracing efforts have begun in the United Kingdom and in Japan. We will have more on this evolving situation during the seven o'clock news hour.

26 January, 12:30 Hours Local (UTC 09:30)
World Health Organization, Global Health Observatory
Avenue Appia 20
1211 Geneva, Switzerland

SITUATION UPDATE—PARIS CONTAGION

At the release of these preliminary findings, researchers at the WHO, in conjunction with the clinicians at the Pasteur Institute and epidemiologists from the US Army Medical Research Institute of Infectious Disease, are actively studying the samples from the seventeen patients who appear to have contracted the Paris Contagion. Symptomatic expression would indicate this is a novel infection. The contagion agent may be trans-species in origin or transmuted within a human host. Contact cross infection is demonstrated in several cases.

At this time three deaths have occurred out of the known seventeen identified cases. Patients Zero, Five, and Six died from multiple organ dysfunction syndrome due to fluid redistribution associated with hypotension, disseminated intravascular coagulation, and focal tissue necrosis. Four other patients are in end-stage organ failure and not expected to survive. Patients One and Two appear to be recovering with some central nervous system symptoms, including encephalitis, myalgia, and psychosis.

Patient Summary:
All the patients live at or above 42° north or south of the equator.
Patients live on four continents.
No common familial connections were noted between the seventeen.
Ages range from twenty to sixty-seven.
There are thirteen males and four females.
All but one of the patients work outside the home.
None traveled to sub-Saharan Africa in the last ten years.
None have contact with a hemorrhagic fever patient.
None have contact with species known to carry trans-species viruses.

None visited animal confinement establishments in the last six years.

Symptomatic Summary:
High Fever (104°F/~40°C)
Rapid-onset severe headache
Fatigue/malaise
Nausea/vomiting
General abdominal pain
Pharyngitis
Centralized chest pain
Maculopapular rash
Conjunctivitis

Although the symptoms presented indicate a hemorrhagic fever, this diagnosis seems unlikely at this time, as none of the patients have any contact or geographic associations. The only organism cultured from the patient samples is a gram-negative bacterium of suspect origin. No viruses have been discovered.

Preliminary diagnosis is unknown bacterial infection. A course of MRSA antibiotics is recommended, including beta-lactam and sulfa drugs. High morbidity of greater than 90% is expected as the infection runs its course. Unlike the recent SARS-CoV-2 viral pandemic, there is no indication of aerosol formation or aerosol transmission. Only direct contact with a patient or their bodily fluids can lead to infection spread.

Clinicians are to immediately quarantine any patients presenting with like or similar symptoms in negative pressure isolation. WHO is classifying this pathogen as a Risk Group 4 contagion. This classification requires Biosafety Level 4-equivalent containment for all researchers and the handling of all fluid and cellular samples. All health care providers, in direct contact with patients, must wear proper full-body personal-protective positive-pressure equipment.

Sam rocked back in her chair, placing her feet on the corner of her desk. Bright yellow socks with small black Batman symbols peeked out from the hem of her black trousers. After reviewing the information included in the intern's report, she had set up alerts for disease reports from the WHO and International News Services. This WHO report and the seventeen reported cases of a new and novel disease were interesting but not critical. Yet. The information did warrant another call to Doctor Williams.

2 February, 20:06 Hours Local (UTC 11:06)
Central Pacific Ocean-Sea Trials of Newly Upgraded Systems
XO Quarters, *USS Arlington*
CGN-47, Ticonderoga-class Guided Missile Cruiser

Commander Alexander tried again to reach his mother. His two prior attempts at Zoom calls were unsuccessful, and his level of concern was rising. He entered the login and password for the Amundsen-Scott Base's NASA-supported tracking and data relay satellite—TDRS4. Communication with the station was limited during the winter to this satellite system, a Department of Defense satellite, and a limited-access portal using the commercial Iridium satellite constellation. James had tried to connect using the commercial system as required for personal communications. Those were his first two failures. He'd then asked a friend at NASA for a favor—a login for their satellite system to contact his mom.

A series of clicks and snaps came through his speakers. This was the usual connection feedback, as his system called the satellite which called the base. After several long moments, a grizzly-faced man appeared and slurred, "Amundsen-Scott base. How may we help you?" James couldn't tell if it was his odd Scottish accent or if his enormous mustache hindered his speech. *Or do they all drink the winter months away?* he wondered.

"Yes, hello. I'm James Alexander. I want to speak with my mother, Doctor Alexander, if she's available, please."

"Of course, laddie. We're here to serve." James couldn't miss his mocking sneer. "How'd you get this login? This is a proprietary system. It is reserved for research communications, not calls to Mummy." The man leaned into the camera.

"Where I got it is irrelevant." James wasn't going to throw his NASA friend under the bus. He let some of his command voice out. He had learned that voice from one of the best—his commanding officer. "The last two attempts to phone my mother have been unsuccessful. Given your current weather, I didn't want to miss an opportunity. Future communications will be halted when the building low pressure system covers the polar plateau."

The man sat back abruptly. "Seems you're well informed, laddie."

"Comes with the job." James wasn't sure how much his mom had shared with her coworkers about family, so he was cautious with what he said.

"I see, I see. In the future, know that communications for personal calls are restricted to the commercial system. Most often weather over the continent disrupts that system. Be patient and try again. However, you've got us now, so I'll page Doctor Alexander and see if she's available for your call."

Minutes passed as James waited; the Zoom camera showed the interior of a large communications center. Banks of routers and modems blinked in synchrony on the far wall. The windows were illuminated with a hazy half-light. The sun in February barely rose above the horizon of the plateau. Amundsen-Scott base was nearing the four months of total darkness, when the sun never rose.

"James, are you all right?" His mother's face popped into view. She had exchanged her Santa hat for a deerstalker.

"I'm fine, Mom. Nice hat."

She smoothed down one earflap. "Yes, it came with the office. The last medical officer left it as a gift. Said you needed to be a bit of a detective to diagnosis some of the maladies which present here. I thought it rather flattering and decided to add it to my daily ensemble."

James laughed. "Glad you're having fun, Mom."

"Most definitely." His mother smiled warmly into the camera. "We're coming up on our last flight in and getting the base locked down for the polar winter. We have a bit of a weather system on its way, and everyone is rushing to get as many flights in as possible." She frowned. "Why the special call, James? I don't want you taking advantage of your connections, ones others don't have access to. It's not fair. Communications are dicey at best—you need to be patient."

"I understand, and I won't make a habit of it. But I was worried when my last two calls wouldn't connect."

Julia Alexander eyed her son skeptically. "All right. I'll buy that one time." Her voice turned serious, "What's the real reason?"

Could she read him or what? "We're headed back to our last port of call, and I wanted to connect before things locked down. It's been recommended across the Navy."

Julia sat back, frowning into the camera. James knew how intuitive she was and felt sure she would catch his meaning. He didn't want to discuss his real concerns over an open channel, though he was assured the NASA satellite was fully encrypted. She nodded once. "I understand, I've been following along since your last call." She paused. "Have things continued as before?"

"Much the same. More are involved at this point, more than one hundred at last count. Still no specifics. But I'm glad you're there and I'm here. Both places are quite secure."

"You'll be gone long?"

"The usual three months and then we'll see what happens."

Julia looked away from the camera feed and nodded. "I need to go, James, I appreciate your call. Keep me informed as things progress. If you can't get a call to connect, use the email program and address I sent in my last packet. That will always arrive with other messages once per day."

"Thanks, Mom. I will. Be safe, stay warm."

He heard his mom's laughter as the call disconnected.

5 February, 09:42 Hours Local (UTC 13:42)
Oval Office, White House
Washington, DC, United States

Doctor Deidre Williams perched nervously on the edge of the brocade sofa, holding her leather satchel in her lap. A curved door opened, and a gray head leaned around the edge. "Doctor Williams, the president is on her way down from the residence. May I get you something to drink?"

"No, I'm fine. Thank you."

"If you change your mind, just give a holler." The elderly woman had been with the president since her days as governor of California. "I'm just outside the door." She pulled the large door shut.

Deidre couldn't help but laugh. She knew this office was sound-proofed. She could yell all she wanted and not be heard. "I will. Thank you," she replied into the rarified air of this space. *She's just trying to put me at ease.*

Deidre knew that would be difficult, if not impossible, to do. Since she'd received the first samples from Paris the day before Christmas, things had accelerated at an alarming pace. Not even the early days of SARS-CoV-2 were this panicked. Currently, there were 164 confirmed cases spread across the globe. Another three thousand and seven possible cases were being sent to facilities with negative pressure isolation facilities. The world press was rousing the public into a panic as each new case was diagnosed. Luckily, they hadn't discovered her involvement, yet. And Fort Detrick was a great place to hide from the hordes of reporters looking for a scoop. She was glad she wasn't at the CDC or the NIH.

A door Deidre hadn't noticed swung open on silent hinges, and President Haley stepped into the Oval Office. Deidre stood. "Doctor Williams. Thank you for interrupting your research and agreeing to meet with me. I can only imagine how busy you are."

"Of course, Madam President." She dipped her head in acknowledgement.

The president sat in a chair before the fireplace. She leaned forward, elbows on her knees, and looked at Deidre with a cold stare. "I've read your report on the SARS-CoV-2 viral pandemic. I have to say I agree with your conclusions. I understand most at the NIH didn't want to disagree with the WHO, but you raise some compelling arguments the Chinese withheld data from WHO investigators." President Haley shook her head. "I believe, at least from a layman's perspective, with your conclusions. The COVID virus was manipulated in some way. Given your depth of insight into that pandemic, I wanted to get your take on the current situation. This all seems very different to me."

"Thank you, ma'am. The accelerated rate of mutation, high degree of aerosol-based transmissibility, disproportionate degree of symptomatic impact across patient profiles, risk-factor associations, and lethality by blood type all indicate some modification to a naturally occurring SARS virus. And you are correct, China was able to successfully sway the WHO findings." Deidre dropped her head and then looked back up. "I felt an alternate opinion was needed for consideration and to initiate scientific debate on the subject. I didn't mean to create a difficult situation for you."

The president waved her off. "Doctor, everything I do has the potential for becoming a difficult situation for one party or another. Please, continue."

"As to our current situation, you are also correct. This infection is very different." She hesitated. "However, if I may say, I don't understand why you called me here?"

"I understand the attending physician to patient zero is a friend of yours and he sent you some samples in late December."

Deidre sat back a bit. The president was very well informed.

"I don't know your conclusions from those samples. I need your knowledge and expertise. Information is vital for my understanding. For my ability to explain things to the American public that this is not something to fear."

Deidre nodded. "I'm not ready to state unequivocally there is nothing to fear. This disease is unlike any we have seen before. More importantly, we have not isolated the primary agent, yet. I do believe, however, it is a two-stage system."

"Two-stage?"

"Yes, ma'am. From patient zero I was able to identify an unusual bacterium. *Terrimonas arctica*—R9-86-T is the species designator." Deidre placed her satchel on the floor, opened it, and pulled out a blue folder. Flipping to a color-micrograph, she turned the photo toward the president. "This is *Terrimonas arctica,* a colorless, gram-negative, aerobic, nonmotile, rod-shaped bacterium. We identified the species using genetic sequencing and phylogenic analysis. It was discovered in 2014 within a sample of tundra permafrost soil. The sample was collected near the town of Ny-Ålesund, Svalbard Archipelago, Norway. It's an average, soil-loving bacterium which evolved to withstand harsh arctic conditions." Deidre turned several pages over in the folder and selected another photo which showed the bacterial mat filling a petri dish.

"One of the first things I noted was the bacterium's extreme sensitivity to heat. When culturing the samples for evaluation, the addition of incubator heat accelerated cellular growth by over 500 percent. Samples exploded into these dense, colorless bacterial mats in less than twenty-one hours." Deidre tapped the micrograph.

"The next thing I noted was the absence of any obvious threat to cross-species infection. This bacterium is not actively hunting a host. It lies dormant for centuries, frozen in the permafrost. It activates and multiplies only when a bit of melt occurs at the height of the summer months. It is not part of normal human enteric systems. It has never been isolated from any human tissue before. It isn't actively taken up by any species which eats the vegetation growing in the bacteria-contaminated arctic soils it lives in."

"What does that mean?" The president leaned forward again, her eyes bright with interest.

"Let me give you an example. Native reindeer herds eat moss growing on the tundra's permafrost soils. If this bacterium were infectious, these herds would be infected by ingesting the bacteria contained within the moss. The bacterium would be found in their gastrointestinal tracks. None is found.

"Now in contrast, the SARS-CoV-2 virus did cross species and was found in household pets, wild deer in the US, and mink in Europe." Deidre paused to be sure the president was following. "However, given the severe symptoms patients with the Paris Contagion are exhibiting, one would suspect a high degree of infectiousness. This indicates another agent is involved. Whether this bacterium is activating something genetically in patients to initiate the disease or the bacterium is carrying a hidden agent, I don't know yet."

The president sat quietly for some time, gently stroking her bottom lip with a fingertip while she gazed into the distance. Her eyes refocused on Deidre. "What do you know about Svalbard, Doctor?"

"Just what I've read. It's an oceanic archipelago situated midway between the northern tip of Norway and the North Pole, between 74 to 81 degrees, north latitude. Well within the Arctic Circle. It has a small permanent population. It's been inhabited since the late seventeenth century and it is protected under a treaty signed in 1920, giving Norway sovereign control."

"None of the local population has ever experienced anything like this disease before?"

"Not to my knowledge. Nothing is reported in any of the medical literature."

"If there was no prior disease, how did the bacterium come to be discovered?"

Deidre realized the president thought about problems sequentially, linking disparate facts together to form a linear trail. She flipped ahead several pages in her blue folder and removed a copy of the published article from the *International Journal of Systematic and Evolutionary Microbiology*. It summarized the bacterium's discovery. She handed the article to the president. "The samples were gathered by a team from Wuhan University, led by a Doctor Fang Peng."

The president rose swiftly and crossed to the Resolute desk, leaning over she punched a communication stub on the console. "Get me Samantha Michaels, Admiral Benson, and Doctor Sithens at the NIH. I need them on a conference call. Now." Her voice was hard and lacked all the warmth and natural curiosity from just moments before.

She turned to Deidre. "I need a complete list of all researchers on that sampling expedition. Can you get that?"

13 February, 10:45 Hours Local (UTC 01:45)
International Transfer Terminal
Kuala Lumpur International Airport

Seapang District, Selangor, Malaysia

Lieutenant Amelia Grant stood among the magazine displays in a bookshop along the periphery of the international transfer terminal. She carried a ratty backpack thrown over one shoulder and hid her red hair beneath a Nationals baseball cap turned backward. The shop was situated in the hub between arriving international flights and departing domestic Malay flights. The Kuala Lumpur airport—one of the largest in southeast Asia while handling more than five million passengers every few days—was busy at nine thirty on a Monday morning. She casually moved around the rack, keeping an eye on passengers entering the terminal's central hub from the various concourses. Grant knew her subject's flight had landed. Now she was waiting for him to appear so she could make contact. Five minutes later he exited a concourse and began walking across the large open space.

Grant left the magazine she was reading on a shelf and exited the book shop. "I have the subject. Moving to intercept." Two clicks in her earbud acknowledged her report, as her Boat Team members moved in.

As she neared the subject, Grant noted two women moving swiftly toward them. They appeared to be joking with each other, staggering this way and that. Grant stepped up to the small, rotund man, while strategically placing herself in front of him, her back to the approaching women.

Introducing herself, Grant said, "Mister Sung. Elizabeth here. Are you ready to see the sights?" This was the code phrase. He should have immediately replied with the answer, but his attention was drawn to the two women now standing directly behind her. Though her focus was on her subject, she felt the women moving closer. In her heightened state of awareness, she sensed their first move. Spinning around, Grant caught the first woman in the chest with a stiff-arm, sternal punch. The woman dropped to one knee. Simultaneously, she dropped her backpack off her left shoulder and swung it in a wide arc, striking the other woman in the head.

Grant stepped back to block further attacks. Before she could react, the first woman drew an aerosol container from her pocket and sprayed it at them.

"Down! Down!" Grant pivoted and took her subject to the ground in a body slam. The other woman discharged a second aerosol. Most of the spray went over their heads, but Grant felt the fine mist settle on her neck. Grant tried to cover her subject. She placed a hand over his nose and mouth, while keeping her face buried in the crook of his neck. "Close your eyes! Don't open them!" She heard feet pounding on the concrete floor along with the scrabbling of dog toenails. Officers of the Malay police had arrived. The sound of automatic weapons being leveled broke the sudden silence. She felt a hand on her shoulder. "You can get up now, Grant. We've got this." Her number two on the Special Boat Team knelt beside her.

"Don't touch. Can't… move. C… n…' t… brea… the… "

13 February, 12:41 Hours Local (UTC 03:41)
Yonhap News Agency
Jongno-gu
Seoul, Republic of Korea

BREAKING NEWS
NAEWOE PRESS ALERT:

Three hours ago, Pak Jong-nam was assassinated in the Kuala Lumpur International Airport. The estranged elder brother of North Korea's Supreme Leader Pak Sung-un was traveling under an alias when attacked. The assassination was carried out by two female agents of the North Korean Ministry of State Security. One woman was reportedly from Indonesia and the other from Vietnam. The women are in police custody awaiting charges. Khalid Abu Bakar, the inspector general of the Malaysian police, stated they are investigating the event as an international murder case. Also, of interest to the police and airport security is what substance was used.

At this time, it is suspected the women deployed a form of VX nerve agent via an aerosol application. VX—venomous agent X—was discovered in the early 1930s and is a derivative created during the production of organophosphate pesticides. VX acts by disrupting neural communication within the muscular systems of the body. Death occurs from asphyxiation due to paralysis of the diaphragm. Since the women used two aerosols, VX2 is suspected as the agent dispersed in this attack.

VX2 is a nonvolatile, two-component system which becomes deadly when the components are mixed. Because of its low volatility, VX2 remains in the environment for an extended period of time. Therefore, the airport terminal will remain closed until further notice for decontamination. VX and VX2 are banned substances under the 1993 Chemical Weapons Convention and are classified as weapons of mass destruction.

A member of the United Nations Organization for the Prohibition of Chemical Weapons stated, "This attack raises the specter of proliferation of chemical arms by North Korea. The fact a VX agent made it out of North Korea and into another country undetected is of great concern."

16 February, 09:45 Hours Local (UTC 00:45)
The Day of the Shining Star National Holiday
Pak Il-jong Square, Pyongyang
The Democratic People's Republic of Korea

Rank after rank of uniformed military personnel goose-stepped up the square from the Taedong River to the Great People's Study House. The personnel were followed by row upon row of military transports carrying the latest military achievements of Pak's war machine. Surface-to-air missiles were carried in launcher-racks on the back of jeeps. Tanks, short and medium range missiles on mobile launchers, and last the gigantic two-stage intercontinental ballistic missiles on eleven axle transports rolled past the viewing areas. A crowd of over two hundred thousand cheered for each new weapon, as it moved along the parade route. Loudspeakers blared and roused the crowd to cheer louder.

Pak Sung-un stood on an elevated stand, saluting each weapon. He was alone, his usual entourage absent. *Now it is only I who controls all this. I am in power. I am the power.* A row of guards lined the base of the platform. Members of the Ministry of State Security alternated with officers of the Supreme Guard Command. Their olive drab uniforms were accented with red insignia. The late winter sun flashed off their highly polished black, knee-high boots.

The Korean Central News Agency recorded the parade and broadcast the event across the country to televisions and personal tablets. Everyone in the nation stood while the parade occurred.

16 February, 21:55 Hours Local (UTC 01:55)
Satellite Imaging Room, CIA Headquarters
Langley, Virginia, United States

Sam sat in a soft leather chair and watched the gross flaunting of supposed military might move through the central square in North Korea's capital. They were watching in real time through the uplink to the app loaded on their Keyhole satellite. The satellite sat in geosynchronous orbit above Pyongyang, recording three-dimensional images. She had already captured still images of Pak and was cataloguing the military hardware on display. So far, the only new thing was the absence of key governmental officials. No one from Pak's cabinet, the president of the Presidium, or the chairpersons of the Supreme People's Assembly were in attendance. These heads of government had always attended significant military parades and stood with Pak on the viewing platform. Their absence was conspicuous.

"Mike, please take a couple of shots of Pak and the area surrounding the platform. We're missing a number of dignitaries." Sam studied the next row of missiles rolling by.

"I noticed that too. Seems weird. Usually there are thirty or forty officials with him. Remember the parade on the Day of the Sun? You know the one where we identified the nuclear physicist?"

"Yeah, I do."

"There had to be a hundred people in the stands with Pak that day."

Sam nodded in agreement. "That holiday is more important than this one. Maybe that's why? Pak focuses almost exclusively on his grandfather. This holiday is to commemorate his father, whom he doesn't think very highly of. Maybe no one was invited."

"Then why all the hoopla? This parade is almost twice as long, and they've really rolled out the hardware."

"You're right about that. Mike, make sure we capture as many images as possible of the missiles and launchers, especially angled shots. I'll need to calculate weight and dimensions of each," Sam ordered.

"You got it. The weather is perfect. I can read the insignia on the officers' uniforms." He showed a closeup image of one of the division leaders standing at the base of the platform.

Sam could read the patch on his shoulder and thought. *Damn, that satellite is amazing.*

Sam felt her gut tighten. Something was significant about this. Different and not in a good way. She'd need to review the images with Doctor Kim. She would be able to tell Sam what's wrong.

16 February, 12:17 Hours Local (UTC 16:17)
Situation Room, White House
Washington, DC, United States

President Haley listened to the senior members of her security council argue about what they should do in response to Pak Jong-nam's assassination. The actions of North Korea were escalating from sword-rattling to deadly actions in very public places. And now, their actions were occurring outside the borders of the country. She knew direct retaliation was a fool's errand. The United States could not and would not take preemptive actions against North Korea. She would not initiate a war. All she could do was maintain pressure on North Korea through sanctions while building an international coalition to support military action if it were needed in the future.

The South Korean president was screaming for more troops. His greatest fear was an attack on Seoul using a chemical agent. If Pak took any action, all believed he would attack the south first and from there unleash Armageddon on the world. Though if Samantha were correct, Pak's actions would be tempered by his desire to reunite the peninsula, not destroy South Korea. Destruction of the south would be counterproductive to his goal. He needed their economic and industrial infrastructure. Haley believed this was a correct conclusion given what they knew at this time.

Sam had sent over her initial analysis of this morning's military parade. She noted Pak was alone without his usual cadre of governmental officials. Doctor Kim stated this was the first time officials were not included.

Sam wouldn't guess what this meant. However, Doctor Kim did. She believed the missing officials may have opposed his plans. Therefore, Pak was isolating himself, distancing himself from his cabinet. She went on to speculate the high-ranking government officials may have been removed and sent to camps. Worst case, Doctor Kim stated Pak may have ordered those opposing his plans be killed.

This scenario frightened Sam the most. She stated if the "guardrails" erected by officials tempering Pak's actions were removed, Pak would quickly move forward on multiple fronts to accomplish his goals. Nothing was in place to slow or stop him now.

Several new missile and launcher systems were identified. Sam would have specifics for each the next day. These were different, smaller and sleeker in size and shape. She needed to review these images with a weapons specialist first. Her preliminary assessment was Pak had developed a solid-fuel propulsion system and miniaturized new weapons.

Admiral Benson's voice rose above the din. "Folks, this is an exercise in futility. If we attack North Korea with a preemptive, conventional weapons strike, we force Pak to retaliate immediately. Although, we know he has chemical and biological weapons stockpiled along the DMZ, I am unsure his first move would be chemical weapons. That attack would irreparably damage South Korea. Seoul lies just fifty kilometers from the demilitarized zone. The city has a population of nearly ten million. A release of chemical agents at the DMZ would impact Seoul and make the lands around it uninhabitable."

He paused, and President Haley felt his gaze fall on her. She understood and supported Samantha's conclusions—boxing Pak in a corner would be a mistake. "Madam President, you condemned the use of Sarin gas by the Syrians." She nodded. "Given that, we cannot provoke Pak by launching a preemptive strike. Up against the wall, we may force him to respond with a WMD attack."

She closed her eyes, as the arguments swirled around her. Again, her thoughts expanded in logical order. None of her advisors had connected Pak with the Paris Contagion. President Haley wondered, was that Pak's doing? Had he already unleashed a biological weapon on the world? Doctor Williams and Samantha both believed the DPRK did not have the technical expertise to develop a biological weapon on this scale. What if they were wrong? What if he did? What was next?

A communication technician stood from one of the workstations at the front of the room and cleared his throat. She opened her eyes and nodded at him. "Ma'am, I have President Liu on a secure line for you."

The president rose from her chair. "Thank you, Brandon. I'll take it in the booth." She paused and looked at each person seated around the table. "Ladies and gentlemen, you will have a recommendation for me when I come back." She straightened her shoulders and stood tall. "That recommendation will not include a military strike. Am I clear?" After she received several nods, she entered the communications booth and opaqued the windows.

"Mister President, how are you?"

"I am well, Madam President." He paused to draw a deep breath. "I am calling to inform you I have ordered the border of my country with North Korea closed. We are moving four divisions of elite troops to the area under the guise of a military exercise."

"I see." Her heart pounded in her ears as her blood pressure skyrocketed. "Are you planning immediate action?"

"Not at this time, but my country will not tolerate continued escalation by the North Korean leader." She heard him swallow. "Madam President, I will not tolerate anything more. Pak has now moved outside his borders. He has taken direct and deadly action against one of his citizens. If he is willing to openly assassinate his own brother, what will he do next? What is happening within his country to his own people?" The Chinese president blew out an explosive breath. "How will you respond if he takes action?"

"We have not decided on next steps."

"Neither have we, but we must be prepared."

"I agree, sir."

Amanda Haley knew this man was her most powerful opponent. He had not supported her or the United States in any actions. But now, he was reaching out a hand and suggesting collaboration. Subtly asking what she was going to do. She knew, should she take action along the DMZ, China would be involved due to geographic proximity. With this communication, he was telling her he was prepared to work together, no matter the cost, to stop Pak.

She must acknowledge this gesture. "We are currently determining our next steps. However, I can tell you I will not take preemptive action against Pak. The consequences are too grave for neighbors in the area. Consequences you would suffer first."

She hesitated. Was she willing to take the next step? Yes, she would fulfill her duties. Honor treaties. Support allies—old and new. Forge new alliances. Strive for peace and stability in the region. Even if it meant taking military action.

Amanda knew in her heart she would protect innocents if she could. Thus, there was only one answer to this situation. "Mister President, should Pak take preemptive actions against our ally, South Korea, we will take all steps and use all resources to stop him."

"All resources, madam?" The Chinese president's voice was laced with pain. Both knew what the other was saying.

"All resources, sir."

Any such action would wipe North Korea off the map if the South Koreans and Americans exercised all avenues to remove Pak as a threat.

"A moment, please, Madam President." The line went dead.

Silence thrummed in Amanda's ears. Her heart rate continued to gallop. She watched the red numerals accumulate on the timer associated with this call's recording. More than six minutes elapsed, an almost infinite amount of time, but the silence continued.

Amanda Haley had committed the military might of the United States of America in action against a sovereign nation. Now, she was asking the leader of another sovereign nation to join her.

President Liu Qishan came back on the secured line. "Madam President, should Pak act, know the People's Republic of China will stand with you to stop him."

Amanda barely contained her gasp at this news, but she knew she needed a record of this commitment, so she asked, "I have your word on that, Mister President?"

"Yes, Madam President. You have my word. China will act. We will fight at your side."

"Very well. I will speak with you again shortly."

The call ended. The weight of what she had agreed to forced her to drop into the only chair in the booth. She didn't know if she had the strength to stand. But she had to rise. Had to prepare to act. Had to prepare for the worst.

19 February, 14:04 Hours Local (UTC 18:04)
Sublevel 4, CIA Headquarters
Langley, Virginia, United States

A comm unit buzzed in the darkness. Sam scrambled for the turn-knob on her desk lamp. A click warmly illuminated the papers scattered across her desk. She answered, "Michaels."

"Samantha? Uh…it's Cynthia…uh…Cynthia Brockstone."

Sam sat up straight. Now what? Another nuclear test? Couldn't be. Her latest images showed the Punggye-ri complex deserted and the tunnel entrances lost beneath massive tallis slopes. "Cynthia, what may I do for you?"

The telephone line remained open, but the geophysicist didn't answer. "Cynthia?"

"I'm here, Samantha. This was a bad idea. Just forget I called. I'm sorry for the interruption."

"No, wait. Don't hang up. You called for a reason. What can I do? What's going on? I can hear you're upset."

Cynthia sighed heavily "It's probably nothing. Amelia said not to worry. Said she didn't know how long her assignment would take. But that was more than three weeks ago. I'm starting to worry. I know you can't tell me anything. But… err… I just need to know she's all right." It sounded like Cynthia stifled a sob. "This is going to sound weird, but I can't shake the feeling something awful has happened."

Sam was floored. Had it been that long since Grant left? She had to get out of her cave more often. She had been living down here almost continuously since Cassie went back to the *Arlington* and Grant left for parts unknown. "It's not weird. When you care about someone, have a special bond with someone, you should listen to your feelings." Sam switched gears. "Are you at home?" She had no idea what day it was.

"Yes, I've been off call for the last several days. I thought Amelia would be back by now. We agreed to a second ski trip, so I rearranged my schedule a bit."

"Okay, good. Let me make some calls, and I will get back to you." Sam paused. "Cynthia, I have to be honest with you. I may not be able to find out anything. I have some contacts, and I'll do some digging."

"Thank you, Samantha."

"You're most welcome. I'll call back as soon as I can." Sam cradled the receiver and tilted back in her chair. Who should she call first? Punching a stud on her comm unit, she called the satellite communications center.

"Colonel Michaels, what can we do for you?"

"I'll be out of the office for a while. Please route any calls to my secure mobile."

"Very good. We'll forward to your mobile."

Sam continued. "Have you noted any activity over Hamhŭng?"

"Nothing has moved around Hamhŭng in the last fourteen hours. Construction is still proceeding along the Pyongra rail line as well as the primary highway from the south. At this time, the city and factories are still isolated from the rest of the country."

"Thanks. Keep an eye on the Chemical Institute. I think Pak is preparing to send some major shipments south once the roads or rails are passable."

20 February, 14:30 Hours Local (UTC 05:30)
Presidential Offices, The Blue House
Seoul, South Korea

President Choi looked at the captains of South Korea's industrial companies. "Have we succeeded with our agreed upon plan?"

Kwon Seigun nodded. "We have, but we still need an additional four weeks to remove all the proprietary equipment and remaining inventories. Then, we can shut down the complex and mothball all the projects."

"No that will not do. We are behind as it is. Although I agree we cannot leave anything for them to utilize, we cannot risk further delay." He looked at each CEO. Several nodded in agreement, but three did not look up. "Leave the inventory and destroy the equipment in situ." This brought their heads up.

The CEO of LG immediately began to argue. "We cannot do that. We would lose an investment of hundreds of billions of won as well as risk North Korea gaining access to our intellectual property. That would give them an ability to construct the templates for the microcircuits and motherboards. No. The equipment must be removed."

Choi considered this and acknowledged the potential loss of

intellectual capital in the scheme he was suggesting. "Are you able to remove the computing and database equipment but destroy the manufacturing equipment? And if so, how long would that take?"

The CEOs looked at each other. The head of Samsung spoke. "Perhaps two weeks or so, but we would need to send additional workers from the South. I don't know how we can insert more workers and accomplish the needed destruction without drawing the interest of their governmental inspectors. The North Korean line workers would also become suspicious."

The Head of Sumitomo Heavy Industries suggested, "What if we tell them we are shutting down for annual sitewide maintenance and upgrade? That may allow us to send additional workers as well as justify demolition and equipment removal."

"That may be workable." Everyone sat back and considered this suggestion. "We do normal maintenance once a year. Would it seem unusual to move this up?" the Samsung CEO asked the group. He continued to speculate aloud. "Perhaps it would work if we state the upgrades are needed for the advertised release of the new smartphone and other projects. A need to prepare for that production."

"Excellent." President Choi clapped his hands. "Let us proceed. Begin the shutdown immediately. You have two weeks to complete all needed actions to protect intellectual property and destroy equipment. If you can accomplish this more quickly, then all the better. I will send a message to Pyongyang the Kaesŏng Industrial Complex will be closing for maintenance immediately." Choi smiled at the CEOs, thinking to himself. *I've got you now, you bastard. I'll shut down your economy one way or another.*

20 February, 6:31 Hours Local (UTC 10:31)
Michaels/Stanley Residence
Georgetown, Virginia
Suburb of Washington, DC, United States

Sam had exhausted all her contacts concerning Grant—at least the ones she felt she had the ability to call directly. It was now six thirty in the morning. She eyed the analog Mickey Mouse clock on the wall of her home office. The metronomic swish of his tail was hypnotic. Her exhaustion led to her fixation on the oscillating motion. Sam shook her head to clear her thoughts and picked up the mobile for one more call. This was her last hope without going way out of bounds or way out of her chain of command. She placed her call. He would be up at this hour.

The mobile rang once before an out-of-breath voice huffed into the receiver his name. "Benson."

"Admiral, it's Samantha Michaels."

She could hear panting. She realized she'd interrupted something. "I'm sorry, sir. I've called at a bad time. I'll speak to you once you're in your office in a few hours."

"No, Samantha. It's all right." He panted into the phone. "Give me one minute to cool down on this damn bike, and we'll talk. Now is a good time for me."

Sam sat back and listened as the admiral's breathing slowed and came under control. In the background, she could her the whir of a flywheel on a magnetic trainer slowing in synchrony with his breathing. Once the whir stopped, she heard a single grunt and then the admiral spoke. "Go ahead, Samantha."

"Are you all right, sir? I didn't know you rode a bicycle." Sam was an ardent cyclist and had competed in numerous single-day Gran Fondo events across the US and Europe. She couldn't picture the admiral on a trainer or a road bike for that matter.

"I'm fine. My wife gave me a Peloton for Christmas. Said she preferred me exercising at home rather than running around downtown Washington. Seems my aides and CID protective service agents are pleased as well. I'm in a controlled environment." He chuckled. "I think they don't want me to die of a heart attack in front of the Washington Monument. That would be bad press for the military. Better to die in private on a damned trainer."

"I doubt a heart attack is in your future, Admiral. You've always been in excellent shape. I know Cassie said she never beat you at wind sprints on the flight deck of the *Enterprise*."

"Be that as it may, these Peloton trainers could easily put down any one of our Seals in a single session. Their trainers are wicked fit. Their programs are evil. And with the other class attendees fighting for first place, my competitive spirit won't let me slack off."

"If it's that competitive, I'll have to try it. Once Attila lets me on a bike."

"Attila?"

Sam snorted. "Sorry. It's the nickname I've given my physiotherapist. Maybe she is an ex-Peloton trainer?"

"Could be. Now to what do I owe this call?"

"Err, right. I got a call asking about Grant. She's been on assignment for her uncle and MI6 for over three weeks. She's not checked in. I can't find anyone who knows anything, and believe me, I've tried to find out what's going on. My security clearance is high enough to ask about her, but no one knows anything. I don't think I'm being misled or information is being withheld. More worrisome, sir, I do believe everyone I've spoken to is as in the dark as I am."

She paused to carefully consider her next words. "I am on thin ice at Langley, sir. I'm afraid if I call the prime minister of the United Kingdom or the Foreign Secretary of MI6 directly, my superiors will have kittens."

The admiral was quiet for a few long moments. "You know either of the Brits would take your call, but you're probably correct about the kittens, Samantha. However, I don't believe your professional standing is as perilous as you think. Your last report was spot on. The president was pleased. Your summary of Pak's NBC threats was succinct and constructed a viable framework for decision-making. It contained critical information the president is using, especially now with the recent Kuala Lumpur assassination."

"The president may have appreciated the report, however, my supervisor was angry with my conclusions. He's done nothing but rant for the last month. I'm afraid I won't be having dinner at the White House again any time soon. It's a shame, really. The sea bass was excellent." Her voice trailed off.

Kuala Lumpur, why did that ring a bell? Shit, wasn't Grant headed to southeast Asia? Sam had been so busy, she didn't make the connection.

"Let me see if I can dig anything up on Grant. Are you available to come to the White House tomorrow?" The admiral's switch of topics made Sam feel a bit whiplashed "I would appreciate your expertise. I believe we will need your input on our final plan."

Sam was taken aback. Hadn't she made it clear her superiors were not pleased with her or her analyses? Was the admiral hinting the president was planning to take direct action against North Korea?

The admiral continued. "I don't care about assets on the ground or troop movements or what you think will happen next." He paused. "Samantha, I need you to give the president your evaluation of Pak and what is driving him to act out."

He must have heard her gasp because he softened his request. "You've told us about his mental health or lack thereof. You've warned us not to take overt action. You've told us about his military buildup and associated assets. You've summarized the state of the country and the suffering of the general population." He paused. "Now is the time to lay everything you know out for her, Samantha. I can't tell you anything more specific over this connection."

Her mobile and the one she called were secure and encrypted. What was he getting at?

"We need to know as much about Pak as you do. What do you think he will do? More importantly, what is driving him to do it? How can we outfox him and prevent a disaster? What do you believe? What does your gut say is going to happen next, Samantha?"

It only took Sam a second to reply, her superiors at the CIA be damned. "Of course, Admiral. I can be at the White House tomorrow." A thought occurred to her. Something which may add veracity to her presentation. "May I bring a guest, sir?"

"Samantha?"

"Sir, I understand what you are asking. However, I believe what I have to say will only be received as more ravings from a crazy person who lives in a cave. If I may bring this guest, they will have firsthand information for you and the president."

Silence. Sam pulled her mobile away from her ear and checked that the call was still connected. "Samantha, do you believe you are crazy?" Admiral Benson's voice was grave.

"Absolutely not, sir. However, my methods are considered antiquated and therefore scoffed at by all the smart young things who have the director's ear. I'm a relic of times past. I do not use any sort of computer-assistance in my analyses. I visually inspect every image before I define my conclusions. I'm methodical. I work alone. I do my analyses within the confines of a Faraday cage. I don't use accepted computer assisted technologies because I fear those technologies are too easily hacked by our enemies. Technologies my counterparts cannot do without."

She paused. "If you remember, sir, I was trained by the remaining veterans from Bletchley Park. They taught me the techniques I use today. Techniques a computer cannot reproduce. With these veterans' deaths, the methodologies they developed during World War II will be lost." Sam sighed in regret. "Methodologies no one here has any interest in learning."

Sam suddenly sat upright in her chair. "Sir, with all due respect, I do not believe any of my analyst colleagues would know how to open a stereoscopic viewer, let alone use one. They wouldn't know a train car from a flatbed truck on a satellite image without computer assistance."

Stopping abruptly, Sam knew she was putting her foot in it. She'd gone too far. "Sir, I apologize. That was totally unprofessional. I will be at the White House tomorrow, please let me know when."

She was about to disconnect the call when the admiral spoke, his voice hard. "I am truly sorry, Samantha. I had no idea about the state of affairs within your organization. The techniques you use saved many lives in the conflicts we've endured during and since that war. You do not deserve the condemnation you have received from individuals who haven't the God-given intelligence of a bilge rat. Your work is the foundation on which the president is building her strategic action plan." She heard two rough breaths. "I will be letting your superiors know, in no uncertain terms, you are an asset without compare."

"Sir, I appreciate your trust in me and the president's belief in my work. However, fewer words are better." Sam left it at that. She knew the admiral would get her message: Do not rock my boat. Do not speak with my supervisors.

"I'll see you and your guest tomorrow at ten hundred hours. Be prepared to spend the day."

"Aye, sir. Ten hundred hours."

21 February, 9:54 Hours Local (UTC 13:54)
West Wing, White House
Washington, DC, United States

"No Colonel, you may not bring a guest into the presence of the president within the West Wing of the White House. This person,"—the secret service agent looked down his nose at the slightly built Asian woman standing with Samantha outside the president's secretary's office. His bulk blocked the door to the Roosevelt Room—"is not on my approved list. And how you got this far with her is a breach of security we will be investigating immediately."

"Agent, I appreciate your adherence to protocol. However, I was given permission to bring a guest to this meeting by the Chair of the Joint Chiefs."

"Colonel, this person shall not enter the Roosevelt Room."

Sam looked at Doctor Kim Hye-su, who was hanging her head. "Perhaps, Samantha, it would be best if I wait at a designated locale until you are finished with your meeting?" the Korean scientist asked in a whisper. She never looked up from the floor.

Sam began to argue when a voice interrupted her. "Doctor, I appreciate your willingness to disarm the situation, but I am in need of your expertise and perspective." The President of the United States turned her gaze on her chief of security. "Walter, if you are so concerned, please have an agent join us. I would imagine it would need to be you, as what we are to discuss is at the 'eyes only' level, although it may not be necessary as Admiral Benson and his aide will be in attendance." The admiral's aide traveled to all meetings—armed. As did Samantha.

"Very well, ma'am. However, I will be noting this as a breach of approved security in the duty log for the West Wing."

"Do what you need to do, Walter." President Amanda Haley dismissed him with a wave of her hand. "But I need to hear what Doctor Kim has to say."

Walter barely contained an aggravated huff as he spoke quietly into his wrist mic. "I shall station a security detail outside the door, ma'am."

The president pulled open said door. She tossed over her shoulder as she entered the ornate conference room across from the Oval Office, "Whatever, Walter, but I will be reviewing our security protocols after this meeting. I suggest you prepare. Start with the part on racial profiling."

Hye-su gave Samantha a questioning glance and Sam shook her head. "Doctor, after you." Sam motioned the scientist ahead of her.

The president moved to the head of the long oval table and pulled out a chair. Sam took a seat to her right and took her briefing packet out of her messenger bag. Doctor Kim stood nervously by the door, studying the seating arrangement carefully.

"Please, Doctor. Have a seat."

Doctor Kim moved to the one next to Sam and perched on the edge. Sam looked up. "Relax. No need to be fearful here. You are among friends and allies." Sam didn't think the doctor agreed but the young woman relaxed a fraction.

Several minutes later, Admiral Benson and his aide entered through the side door. "I apologize for the delay, Madam President."

He turned his attention on Sam's guest and bowed his head formally. "Doctor Kim, it is a pleasure to make your acquaintance. I appreciate your willingness to help us understand Supreme Leader Pak and his motivations as well as share your scientific expertise."

Sam noticed Doctor Kim shiver. She stood and bowed to the admiral while still gripping her purse tightly. Sam realized she used it as a shield. "Of course, Admiral, although I do not know how I can help. I am not, err... was not a member of the Assembly or Pak's inner circle." She hesitated and looked down self-consciously. "I tried very hard to minimize my visibility. I knew when I took actions at Nyŏngbyŏn I would not survive. Our medical knowledge and level of care is... lacking. And I knew no one would search for me after the storm passed. I am very grateful for my rescue and for the medical care I continue to receive."

"Be that as it may, Doctor, we appreciate the knowledge you have shared and your insight today." The president reinforced the admiral's words. "Shall we begin?" Hye-su resumed her seat. "Samantha, please."

"Thank you, Madam President. When an analyst evaluates the strategic weapons threat level of a foreign government or terrorist organization, three components are important: nuclear, biological, and chemical assets. NBC. The level of NBC capability forms the basis for threat-level determination. However, an analyst can't stop there and must look beyond each NBC asset. Those analyses must be augmented by an evaluation of motivation. This is especially important if an asymmetric conflict situation exists."

The president looked confused. "Asymmetric conflict is not a term I've heard used by others, Samantha. This is new. Admiral?" She looked at the admiral and he dipped his head. It seemed for them, this was a novel theory.

Sam couldn't believe this hadn't been raised before. It applied to many conflict situations other than North Korea. "All right, I'll try to explain. Conventional thought suggests offensive challenges by a weaker state against a stronger opponent is highly unusual if not impossible."

President Haley nodded, as Sam continued her explanation. "The theory of asymmetric conflict is based on the assumption a weaker state, one inferior in economic and military capabilities, can only initiate a successful conflict against a much stronger state under certain conditions." Sam paused, the president appeared focused, listening intently.

Sam continued. "Twenty-four hundred years ago, Thucydides hypothesized, '... right, as the world goes, is only in question between equals in power. While the strong do what they can, the weak suffer what they must.'"

"The premise behind MAD—mutually-assured destruction—balance between equal powers?" President Haley hypothesized.

"Yes, ma'am. Given conventional thought, smaller, weaker states should *only* have limited defensive ambitions confined within the borders of their own country. They should not be able to bully stronger states into conceding any ground, force them to give up any assets, or be forced to make concessions to the weaker state.

"However, it is my belief weaker, smaller states often successfully do just that. They gain much by challenging stronger opponents." Sam paused to let her words sink in. "In most instances the leaders of the weaker states are motivated by a desire to gain a domestic political advantage—their focus is often focused on an internal benefit. An international military victory is not seen as a motivation for most."

The admiral's aide whistled softly. "My god, the Pueblo Incident."

"Correct, Captain. That was the first successful challenge of a weak North Korea acting out against the mighty United States and achieving their goals. This direct offensive challenge was followed by the loss of one of our EC-121 Warning Star surveillance aircraft which North Korea shot down; the filmed axe-beheading of two US Army officers in Panmunjom; the failed Agreed Framework treaty following continued reactor development and missile testing in 1998; and most recently, the circus-like face-to-face meetings with an American president.

"As a strong state determines next steps needed to deter or prevent a weaker state from acting out, they often focus primarily on the balance of power. They assume deterrence is based on the premise North Korea cannot attack South Korea and its ally the United States because it would be destroyed in the process. Thus, in the eyes of the stronger state, destruction is the limiting factor to the weaker state's action.

"As the stronger state, we are analyzing the problem from our position of power. However, the weaker state—in this case, North Korea—views itself from a position of political challenge. The threat therefore is not external—the US and South Korea building up their military at the DMZ. The threat is internal—from a political challenge. We, the US, can never know what is driving the weaker state's actions. We can only attempt to place ourselves within the weaker state's mind and guess what motivates them to try and determine what they will do."

Sam picked up her coffee cup, looking into its depths as she organized her thoughts. "What we must do is determine the driving force behind the weaker state's actions." She looked up and captured President Haley's gaze. "I estimate there are five variables to consider in the evaluation of the driving forces behind a weaker state's actions: political-military strategy, offensive or deterrent weapons capability, domestic power structure, support of external stronger powers, and coercive pressure from stronger opponents."

Sam replaced her cup on the saucer. "Let me illustrate these driving forces using the example of Pak's father. When he led North Korea, his domestic powerbase was not well established. Therefore, the threat of overthrow was a true risk for him. Preventing overthrow was his primary goal. He initiated many of the precursor programs in North Korea's NBC program to deflect focus away from this weakness and limit his associated personal risk. He attained more power by establishing an alliance with a stronger state—the Soviet Union. His death, the failure of the Soviet Union, and an increase in military pressure from the United States and South Korea placed North Korea at a tipping point. The country's powerbase hung in the balance until Pak Sung-un succeeded his father as supreme leader."

Hye-su took a loud breath, prompting the president to ask, "Doctor Kim?"

"I apologize for interrupting, but what Samantha says is true, though I never thought about it from this perspective." Hye-su paused, and she stiffened her spine as she sat up straight. Sam watched Hye-su fighting an internal battle.

"When I was very young, we in the orphanage were tested frequently for aptitude. If one showed promise and was chosen, one would be removed from the orphanage and sent to private schools for education outside the country. I was chosen by Pak's father and educated at the Swiss International School and then at Goethe University in Frankfurt. At the time I left the country for school, the government was very unstable, and several unsuccessful coups had occurred. The economic situation was very bad. It was made worse when the Number 26 accident occurred. I was told to learn as quickly as possible, as my education would be forfeit if Pak and his government fell."

The young scientist shrank into herself and said, "Once Pak Sung-un came to power, struggles within the government settled down, and I completed my education without threat of interruption. However, rumors abounded about Pak Sung-un. The only facts we had were when individuals disappeared. These disappearances have increased over the last several years. The most recent was the disappearance of the president of the Presidium. This occurred shortly before the typhoon struck."

Hye-su looked the president squarely in the eye. "Madam President, you must understand Pak Sung-un is seriously mentally ill. He cannot tolerate challenge from any quarter. He uses assassination and purges as a means of domestic control. He uses the threat of hard labor, exile, and execution as controls over the intelligentsia of the country. The general populace is swamped by propaganda and controlled by starvation."

Her voice dropped to a whisper. "The propaganda tells them, if they give a bit more, try a bit harder, sacrifice once again, the country will attain their rightful position in the world. Their sacrifices will be rewarded in the end." A single tear rolled down her pale cheek. "If they eat dirt for one more week, North Korea will rise triumphant."

She moved to the edge of her chair. "You must understand Madam President, the people's motivations for freedom and a full stomach are not aligned with Pak's desires. He does not care about the people. He only cares about himself. About his glory. He doesn't realize if his austerity programs continue, there will be no workers. If there are no workers, there is no productivity. At the time of the storm, people were dying from starvation and neglect. No one can survive in North Korea without food, heat, shelter, medical care, light, clothing."

"Doctor Kim, what are Pak's desires?"

The Doctor didn't hesitate. "That he is destined to build North Korea into a global military power. That he will unify the Korean Peninsula. That he is a god to be revered and respected everywhere. That he will rule the world. He is a... " Hye-su swallowed hard.

Sam understood how difficult this was for her. She was disavowing all her teachings. It took strength to overcome a lifetime of propaganda and belief modification.

Hye-su took a deep breath. She set her jaw and stated unequivocally, "He is attempting to consolidate all power within himself. I do not believe anyone can know what he will do, but I think he will go to any lengths and do anything to achieve his goals. It is rumored Pak killed his father to gain power and move toward his endgame of uniting the Korean Peninsula under his control. Madam President, I believe he did kill his father."

Sam nodded. "This was the conclusion of the CIA. However, we could never prove it. Once his father was buried, Pak began a campaign to make the people forget his father and focus on him and peripherally on his grandfather, the Hero of the Korean War."

Hye-su sat forward. "This is also a true statement. Once Pak came to power, most remembrances of his father were removed from the public. Statues were torn down, and the national holiday—The Day of the Shining Star on the sixteenth of February—was reduced in importance. The Day of the Sun—his grandfather's birthday—rose in importance. Now the week around the tenth of April is a week of celebration in honor of his grandfather." Hye-su looked down at her hands. "Forced celebration. Most uncomfortable. If he would kill his father and now his brother, he has no moral constraints against any action. I do not believe he will stop at unification. His ultimate goal is the world. All of it under his control or," she swallowed hard, "reduced to ashes. And... and I... helped him." Hye-su gasped as tears ran down her face. "He has the military weapons to do all of this."

Sam allowed Hye-Su a moment to gain control before continuing. "Pak needed to establish himself in the leader's position. We know he purged his father's supporters. This resulted in the death of over one hundred military and political leaders. If we place this in context of the five criteria for asymmetrical conflict, this action strengthened his domestic power position. Secondly, he focused nearly all the country's internal resources on militarization. This strengthened his offensive weapons position." Sam paused and looked at Admiral Benson. The admiral nodded encouragement. "Next, he reopened dialogue with Russia. This garnered support from a powerful neighbor, one which assured food and domestic products for the country."

Hye-su scoffed, interrupting Sam. "Our relationship with Russia is a sham. Neither Pak nor Russia are interested in domestic trade."

"So, what are they interested in?" The president looked at Hye-su with a small nod of encouragement.

"Russia was only interested in our natural resources—Rare Earth Elements, coal for their bases on the Kamchatka, and raw uranium. Our uranium has a high U-235 content, and it is much easier to purify than their uranium ores. However, we did not receive any domestic products from the Russians. China is the one to supply food, medical supplies, and heating oil."

Admiral Benson asked quietly, "Doctor Kim, what do you think China received in exchange for this aid?"

Doctor Kim took a few calming breaths and relaxed her clenched fingers. "Oversight to our military and development of nuclear weapons. Access to our stockpiles of chemical and biological agents. Information from our surveillance of the South Koreans and your military across the DMZ. When you deployed your TAD system—"

"THAAD," the admiral's aide corrected.

"Yes, that. When this occurred, I was working on testing in the north. We had a number of Chinese specialists with us. When they heard about this new system, the Chinese military scientists at Punggye-ri went south immediately to see your system, firsthand."

The president cleared her throat. "Please continue, Samantha."

Sam looked at her notes. Her white-knuckled fists had crinkled the pages. "The most significant thing I believe Pak did was change the country's focus from his father and grandfather's goals of domestic power consolidation to one of... " She paused. This was it. Once she stated her hypothesis, she would place herself in direct conflict with her superiors. She realized her conclusions were more important than a damned job. This was the nexus from which they could devise a plan to stop Pak.

She squared her shoulders and looked directly at the president. "Ma'am, I believe Supreme Leader Pak abandoned his predecessors' focus on internal domestic power and adopted an internationally focused fait accompli strategy. Given this and in combination with his unstable mental state, I believe he will take preemptive military actions. He doesn't care about loss of life or failure. It's about personal glory now. He will use his considerable arsenal of nuclear, biological, and chemical weapons to accomplish his desire for world domination. Pak Sung-un will do whatever it takes to force the world to respect him and to—" Sam swallowed, "—to fear him."

Sam gasped. She had voiced her conclusion in a single breath. Now it seemed there was no air left in the room to refill her lungs. All the air was displaced as her conclusion displaced it. No one spoke into the vacuum. No one moved. Everyone was frozen within the horror of the vision Sam had proposed. The other four stared at Sam, eyes wide, mouths agape.

"I don't know, René." Deidre leaned into the Zoom picture. "We've isolated the bacterium, but something else is going on. An ancient bacterium which lives in frozen soil in a state of semi-hibernation for most of its life isn't going to cause the symptoms these patients exhibit, let alone be widespread enough to infect humans. And interestingly, there are no infections on Spitsbergen or elsewhere above the arctic circle. Nor within the historical medical records in Svalbard, where this bacterium exists. Our patients may be infected with this novel bacterium, but they also have something else. That's what we're missing. That's what we need to find."

René stared back at her. He ran his fingers through his dark hair in frustration. "Panic is increasing here, as it is worldwide. We must provide an explanation soon." Deidre could hear the fear in his voice and see the lines of worry on his face. He was under as much pressure as she was. President Haley had given her an ultimatum—figure this out. Now.

"I understand. People here are starting to panic as well. The press is becoming relentless. I haven't left the base in over a week to avoid them. They're camped outside my home."

An idea struck. They needed to simplify their thinking, get away from the overwhelming load of samples and all the new patients being reported around the world. Step back from the pressures put upon them by their governments. "Let's play 'what if.'"

When René frowned, Deidre cajoled him. "Come on. It's the best way to re-sort the data we have."

This was a game they played while in England. Divide the massive datasets they were working with into smaller pieces and then reshuffle the pieces into new combinations. The dataset they had gathered on this infection was gigantic, and the number of patients was rising exponentially. Deidre had more samples to analyze than she had supplies for. Her lab assistants were working 24/7, preparing new reagents and culture media. She was almost out of room in her LEVEL 4 lockers. Her ability to store the samples safely was nearing an end. They had to figure something out and fast.

"All right, it can't hurt." René shrugged as he acquiesced. He tipped back in his chair and rubbed his eyes before he looked at the camera. "First question, take the bacterium out of the picture. What do we know?"

Interesting first question. "We have over fifteen thousand known patients, all of whom exhibit similar symptoms and disease progression."

René leaned away from the camera, placing his feet on the corner of his desk. "And?"

"And…all exhibit symptoms of an infectious fever."

René began to rock back and forth. "And?"

"And…the symptoms do not indicate a bacterial infection."

René dropped his feet to the floor and rocked forward. His face filled the screen, forcing Deidre to lean away. "Ignore the symptoms and the bacterium. Focus on the *what*."

"What…the death rate amongst the primary patients is over 90 percent. We can't ignore that."

"But?"

Deidre was lost. She couldn't figure out where he was going. "But, what?"

"But, *what*, indeed. Think about this. The first patients we had were in Paris and the surrounds. But here, we've had no new patients after the first forty or so. Now infections are occurring elsewhere around the world at about the same ratio of infections versus total population as initially occurred in France. If the new Chinese reports are true, they've had infections in Hong Kong for a while longer."

"And?" Deidre prodded. She was still missing his point.

"Let's not think about the disease, the symptoms. or the death toll."

Deidre scoffed. "How can we ignore those vital data?"

"Let's think about the commonalities amongst the patients."

Deidre tilted her head. "Let's see." She pulled the latest WHO disease update from her stack of printouts. "What do we know about the patients? Wide range of ages, predominantly male by an overwhelming percentage, 84 percent work outside the home, no common connection, travel… no, continents… all over, live where… no contact… no bats or…" Deidre's voice trailed off as her brain made the one connection they had missed. *Shit…shit…shit.* She railed silently. *That's what the president recognized or at least suspected when they'd met three weeks ago. Why didn't I recognize it?*

"Are you suggesting this is a bioweapon, René?"

This admission seemed to freeze time and halt their conversation. Both now were wrestling with the consequences of such a conclusion. "I don't have another explanation, Deidre. The bacterium you've isolated is not the agent of this disease." René hesitated. "We must find the germ agent responsible. I'm at a loss as to where to look."

Deidre was still processing the ramifications of someone releasing a bioweapon into the world. Who would do such a thing? Where was it coming from? How were they spreading the contagion? What the hell was it?

"I'm sorry René. I missed that."

"Where do we look?"

Where indeed? Deidre considered this question. "I guess we look where we haven't."

René frowned. "And where exactly would that be? We sampled all the primary fluids from patients zero through forty-three here in Paris. You have similar samples from the next five thousand."

"We're thinking about this like epidemiologists, René. Perhaps we need to think about this like forensic pathologists." She watched an eager expression light his face, pushing the clouds of doubt away. "One looking for a poison as the cause of death under mysterious circumstances. To do that, we need tissue samples from each physiological system. Samples from all the organs. Starting from skin, hair, and nails to heart and vessels, endocrine and lymph to brain and neurons. I know an autopsy was completed on patient zero, three, and four. Did you gather biopsies on one and two? They have survived but with significant neurological impairment." Deidre regarded her friend. "Let's pool samples and create a composite patient. That way we can cover all the physiological systems and do a comparison at the same time."

Rubbing his chin thoughtfully, René said, "That may just work. I'll send over the gross samples from zero's autopsy and additional biopsy samples from the other forty-two we have. That should allow you to build your composite."

"How quickly can you get them here?"

"Within the next seven hours. I have a WHO jet on standby. They're waiting on us to provide a direction. Their contact tracing isn't working. This contagion doesn't pass easily from person to person. We don't have a zero-source starting point for any of them."

"Thank heaven for that." Deidre sucked in a breath. "If this had an aerosol transmission, the entire world would be at risk. Exponential spread would be uncontrollable within days of first infection."

SECTION SEVEN

27 February, 15:10 Hours Local (UTC 6:10)
Private Office—Supreme Leader
Mansudae Assembly Hall
Pyongyang, Democratic People's Republic of Korea

Pak Sung-un screamed, "What am I seeing here, General?" He slammed his white-knuckled fists on the desk and leaned menacingly at the rigidly braced officer. "You are telling me these are games? The Chinese don't do games." He threw a stack of aerial photos at the man. They bounced off the man's chest to scatter haphazardly on the floor. "These show at least four divisions of their elite forces amassing at the border. *My* border."

Pak reached behind him and pulled a red folder from a rack on the tigerwood credenza. He threw this at the white-faced general. It ricocheted and fell open on top of the photos. "And this, a communique from that ass, Liu. He's closing my border. We will not receive anything more from China. What are you doing about that?"

"Supreme Leader, what would you have us do? Currently, our troops are concentrated along the DMZ, where you ordered them. To move enough manpower to our northwestern border to counteract this show of aggression and have a chance of stopping an incursion from China would leave the DMZ unprotected." Sweat flowed down the man's face. "We have always planned a single front campaign. I do not have enough resources to cover two fronts, sir. "

Pak again slammed his fists down again. "The People's Army is the largest in the world, General. You have more than one-point-three-million active troops and an additional five-point-six-million paramilitary personnel on reserve within the general population, available on call at a moment's notice. Well General, this is the moment. Call up all the reserve and paramilitary resources. Now. I want both borders fully protected before the end of day tomorrow."

"Sir, if we pull those reserves to the borders, we will effectively shut down our weapons manufacturing and all agricultural programs. We would draft 20 percent of our total population into military service. I do not believe this is a wise move strategically. Our country cannot survive without our industrial production. We will lose our future supply of conventional weapons. we do not have enough tactical weapons to arm the reserves. We cannot adequately protect our troops without those conventional weapons. More importantly, we will not be able to feed the people without our agricultural production."

"Our strategic arsenal is full, General. We have the weapons to deploy along both borders and in stockpiles around the country."

"Sir?"

"I am not talking about conventional weapons, General. Our troops will not face opposition once our strategic weapons are deployed."

"But Supreme Leader. How will I feed the Army if our agricultural programs stop."

"The soldiers can eat what they can forage. You will protect this country, General. You will protect me!" Pak could barely look at the sweating officer standing before his desk. He was just another impediment to his plans. *I should kill him where he stands, but I do not have time to promote a replacement. And Liu, I know he is conspiring with the Americans. I will have his country too when this is finished.*

"And for your information, while you were partying with the Chinese at the DMZ, I was rounding up your wife and children. They are my guests and shall remain with me until my orders are carried out. You are welcome to join them if you wish to argue more." He frowned at his general.

"DO I MAKE MYSELF CLEAR?" His scream reverberated off the walls of the ornate office.

"Yes, sir. I shall issue the orders to mobilize the paramilitary reserves now." The general turned on his heel and hastily left the office.

Pak fell back into his chair as the door swung shut, his anger was almost uncontrollable. He felt blood pound in his ears. His vision was tinted red at the edges. Several moments later, his aide paged him on the intercom. "WHAT?"

"Supreme Leader, we have a communication from Kaesŏng." The timid voice died away.

"What is it?" Pak demanded.

An audible gulp sounded from the small speaker. "They, err … they… the South Koreans, sir. They have closed the industrial complex, effective immediately."

Supreme Leader Pak's roar was cut off when the intercom speaker shattered against the door of his office.

1 March, 13:04 Hours Local (UTC 17:04)
Sublevel 4, CIA Headquarters
Langley, Virginia, United States

"What in the hell is Pak up to now?" The pair of images beneath her viewer showed mass mobilization of troops as well as military resources. They were moving across the Kuryong River on hastily constructed floating bridges. All headed west to the Chinese border.

Sam was working to determine the state of the Nyŏngbyŏn nuclear site. As the flood waters were receding, more devastation was exposed. Her questions about the facility were multifaceted. Could they recover the facility? If so, how long would it take to be fully operational again? What activity was occurring? Could they safely mothball the facility and protect the radioactive cores of the reactors? A knock on her door interrupted Sam's review of the latest satellite images.

"Come," she said in a loud voice, not looking up from her stereoscope.

The glare of overhead fluorescent lights flashed across the paired images, and Sam snapped her head up from the viewer. Her vision was overwhelmed. She blinked rapidly. The director of the CIA stood glaring at her from the door. "Sir?"

"How dare you go over my head and grandstand in front of the president. Your observations were not ready for a conclusion. Especially, those not vetted through the southeast Asian desk." He ran a hand over his close-cropped hair. "And who gave you permission to take a known enemy of the state into the fucking West Wing of the White House?" His voice rose in volume, but Sam sat still. "I should have you arrested on charges of treason, but all I can do is fire your ass. Your privileges are revoked as of now. The Joint Congressional Intelligence Committee is reviewing your security clearance. You will be notified when you are to appear to face their inquiry. Now get the fuck out of my building."

Sam rocked back as the director slammed back out her door. Darkness swallowed her. Sam took a deep breath, amazed how calm she was, having just been fired. "That's that, then."

She pulled her messenger bag out from under the desk and loaded her personal gear. No way would she leave her custom stereoscopic viewer behind. It was a gift from a World War II veteran analyst who developed most of the techniques she uses now. She folded it carefully and slid it into its leather cover, then into one of the inner pockets of the bag. Her latest comic book, her steel ruler, the yellow legal pad with her latest notes, and her vintage fountain pen followed, and she closed the inner flap. She pulled her pager and encrypted mobile phone from one of the outside pockets and placed them on the desk.

Standing, she looked around her cave. It had been a good run. She knew she had provided solid information to the president and Admiral Benson. That was what mattered. Not this fool. The director could go to hell for all she cared.

Sam made her way out of the building, dropping her credentials off at the turnstile on her way to the parking garage. Once out of the garage and through the entry gates to Langley, she pulled her personal mobile from its holder and punched a stored number. The call rang twice. "Admiral Benson's office. How may I help you?"

"Admiral Benson, please."

"Who is this? How did you get this number?" A gruff, though pleasing female voice asked sharply.

Ah, the admiral's aide. "Captain, I am sorry to interrupt. This is Samantha Michaels calling for Admiral Benson."

"Colonel, why are you using this number? This is reserved for the admiral's family."

Sam continued to focus on the road ahead. She knew her anger was slowly mounting, as her grip on the steering wheel tightened. If her anger fully erupted, she would lose her ability to multitask while driving. "Please, Captain, I just need a moment of his time. It's critical to our ongoing problems overseas." The admiral's aide would understand. She couldn't say more on an unsecured line.

"Very well. Hold one."

Several minutes later the admiral came on the line. "Samantha, what's going on? My aide said it's an emergency."

"Sir, I need fifteen minutes of your time as soon as possible. I cannot discuss it over this line."

"Call me back on your encrypted mobile."

"Sir, I no longer have access to encrypted communications."

"What the... ?" Admiral Benson barked into the phone. "Samantha, get your butt over here as quickly as you can." He covered the receiver and spoke to someone at his location. When he spoke on the line again, he said, "I'm sending Melissa down to meet you at the veteran's tour entrance. She'll get you through the security checkpoints to my office. What's you ETA?"

"Shouldn't be more than forty-five minutes, sir. Rush hour hasn't started yet."

"Make it fifteen and I'll pay the ticket. What the hell, Samantha?"

She ignored his question. "Fifteen it is, sir. I'm on my way." Sam thumbed off the mobile and pushed the accelerator down. The large SUV surged forward.

Seventeen minutes later she rocketed into the parking lot and scored a spot in the second row behind a minibus. As she pulled her messenger bag from the passenger seat, the admiral's aide was trotting across the lot. Sam opened the door and smiled at the young captain. "Good afternoon, Melissa. Sorry for throwing a spanner in the works. I know how tightly scheduled you have the admiral. I appreciate the time."

The captain smiled and reached into the vehicle to place a gold and blue Navy placard on the dash. "This will keep you from being ticketed and towed, once the veteran tours end in an hour or so. As to the schedule, no worries, ma'am. The admiral has cleared the next several hours for you. This way please." She motioned toward a small, discreet door to the side of the veteran's entrance.

Sam followed the captain through the Pentagon labyrinth, past four security checkpoints, and up several elevators to the Joint Chiefs' floor. They continued down the long, blue-carpeted hall to the double mahogany doors at the end. The captain knocked and swung the right door open, ushering Sam in before her. "Admiral, Colonel Michaels for you."

The admiral was on the phone, and he motioned Sam to one of the couches to the left of his desk. "Would you like something to drink or snack on, ma'am?" The captain hovered beside an inner door.

"A cola would be great. No ice."

"Roger that. I'll be back in a moment."

Sam loved this room. It contained much of the admiral's memorabilia from his years of service. Photos of ships he served on and ones he commanded. Group pictures of his flight crews. Pictures of battle fields he overflew in the conflicts he fought. Pictures of him with various dignitaries and past presidents.

A picture of his wife and their three Welsh Corgis was a new addition. The corgi pups were a gift from the British monarch. A thank you for something the admiral had done for the UK—a something that was not discussed. Sam tuned into his conversation and realized the conversation was becoming quite serious. "No, Your Grace." A pause. "I understand, sir. Yes, I will. She's here now." Another pause. "Of course, sir, as quickly as I can. Thank you, sir. We'll be in touch." The admiral carefully cradled the receiver and looked at Sam.

"Before we discuss why you are here, I have some difficult news." He cleared his throat and lifted his Naval Academy mug off its coaster, taking a long drink. "That was Lord William O'Rourke, Samantha. I called him several days ago, asking about Grant. He finally called me back." The admiral stopped and took another drink from his mug.

"Sir?"

"Grant was on a mission to recover Pak Sung-un's brother from the Kuala Lumpur International Airport. She successfully recovered Pak Jong-nam, an asset MI6 has been cultivating for many years. They hoped to use him as a mole in the upper echelons of the North Korean government."

"She was what?" Sam didn't understand where this was going. "But Sir, Pak died in the attack."

"Seems that's the public story. In actuality, the young woman identified as an American was Grant. She deflected the two-prong attack and protected the asset from the aerosol dispersed at the scene. He hit his head when she tackled him to the ground and he was knocked unconscious." Benson stopped and leaned forward, placing his mug back on its coaster. "However, in saving the asset, she took the brunt of the aerosol."

Sam's heart was racing. "The attack was VX2. How could she survive a direct application of that agent?"

"Luckily, MI6 was fully prepared. They had a medical team on site, ready for any attack or even a need to neutralize Pak Jong-nam if he tried to escape their rescue. They had the necessary decontamination resources, as well as atropine and pralidoxime available. It was a close thing. They had to decontaminate her before they could attempt resuscitation. By then she'd stopped breathing. Her diaphragm completely paralyzed. She's been on a ventilator for three weeks."

"My god. She's alive?"

"Seems so. She's recovering at her family's estate in northern Scotland. She's alert and rehabbing from the intubation under the care of a military physician who specializes in nerve agents and a cadre of respiratory therapists." He chuckled. "She's one tough gal. She's asking for you, but the powers that be in MI6 won't let her have outside communication. Not until they're done interrogating Pak Jong-nam."

Sam was stunned, lightheaded, and practically hyperventilating. She slowed her breathing and began to question the admiral further when his aide entered with a tray. Two ice cold colas in their cans and a plate of sandwiches were placed on his desk. Sam rose from the couch and took a cola, drinking deeply. "How is she really, sir? Do we know anything else?"

"Recovering, that's all Lord O'Rourke shared. But he asked that you and your geophysicist come to the UK as soon as possible."

"Sir, I don't know if that will be possible."

The admiral leaned forward and folded his hands on his desk. "Samantha, what's going on? Why the call on my personal phone? Melissa almost didn't answer since it was an unknown number. She wouldn't have except one of the corgis is at the vet and we thought that was the call."

Sam was in such a state of shock it took her a minute to switch gears. She carefully placed the soda back on the tray and gathered her thoughts. "I can't leave the country at this time. I am on call to the Joint Intelligence Committee."

"For heaven's sake, why would those pinheads want to talk to you?"

"It's about my clearance, or I should say it's about them pulling my clearance."

"Samantha, what?"

Sam folded her hands between her knees and hung her head in

defeat. "The director caught wind of our meeting at the White House and our unusual guest. He fired me and pulled my CIA credentials. He then turned me over to the committee to pull my clearance at his request."

"Who the hell leaked that confidential information?"

The inner door of the admiral's office swung open, and his aide stuck her head around the jamb. "Sir, Marines are on their way up to collect the colonel and escort her out of the building."

"Over my dead body. Melissa, hold them at the outer elevator. Ask the sentry to close down the hall. Also, I need you to arrange a Gulfstream for the colonel. She'll be traveling from here to RAF Inverness." He turned to Sam. "Where is your geophysicist?"

"She's not my geophysicist." The joke fell flat, and the admiral frowned. Sam answered, "Golden, Colorado, sir."

"Melissa, call the US Geological Survey Earthquake Information Center. Let them know Doctor Brockstone is being commandeered to my office until further notice. Send a second jet for her to," he waved his hand, "whatever airfield is closest to Golden. I don't care if its military or commercial. Samantha, give Melissa her number. Call the doctor and have her meet the jet. She needs to be prepared to spend a significant amount of time in Scotland."

Sam pulled up her contacts and rattled off the number for Cynthia Brockstone and asked, "But, sir, the committee?"

Her question didn't interrupt the stream of orders being issued. "Call Commander Issacson and get his butt up here. Tell him I need someone reinstated under 10 CODE § 688 immediately. He'll need his law books for this one. And call Senator Alberts. He needs to know Colonel Michaels has been recalled to active duty. Direct report to my department, full eyes-only clearance due to an imminent danger in southeast Asia. Make sure he knows not to tell others on the Defense Committee." He paused and looked at his aide. She stood calmly waiting. "Anything I'm missing, Melissa?"

"A uniform perhaps? And a stay for the Marines on their way up." When the admiral nodded, she continued. "I'll prepare the stay for your signature while I place the other calls." Sam noted the admiral's aide hadn't written one thing down, not even the telephone number. She just listened intently. *Interesting.*

Sam's head continued spinning. Could she really be excused from a formal inquiry and so easily conscripted back into active duty? *Seemed so.*

"Take care of the uniform for me too. That's a good thought." He turned back to Sam. "Who's the mole?"

She had considered this on her drive over and could only come up with one answer. "Walter Jackson, the president's Secret Service. I sparred with him in the West Wing about allowing Doctor Kim into the meeting. The president intervened and dressed him down in front of others."

Benson punched a stub on the multifunction communication station on his desk. A muffled voice answered. "This is Benson. I need to speak to the president. Now."

That conversation was short and to the point. The president would relieve Walter Jackson of all duties and remove his White House credentials, pending a full investigation. The admiral indicated Samantha had left the CIA at the director's request and joined his staff. He also stated, he would have a full briefing for her that evening.

While her uniform was being prepared, Sam shared her latest analysis of troop movements along both sides of the Chinese-North Korean border and her summary of the February parade where several new weapons were shown off, including the suspected small single-stage, short-range, truck-mounted missile. Most important, she summarized her findings on the developments at the Tonghae Satellite Launching Ground, known as Musudan-ri. She discovered the construction of numerous concrete launch pads around the area, and identified a number of covered flatbed tractor trailers at the facility. This, combined with the movement of matériel from the facilities in and around Hamhŭng to Musudan-ri, worried her. Pak could be developing a new weapon. She had shared her concerns about these shipments with Doctor Kim. Hye-su's assessment: the North Koreans had perfected a solid rocket fuel and were preparing to test it in a new missile—a short-range, surface-to-air weapon capable of being launched from the back of a truck.

When Sam told Admiral Benson her belief, she watched the telltale signs of his blood pressure rising, including the veins in his neck throbbing. "What the hell does that mean, Samantha?"

"Sir, I believe it means Pak is done testing and will now move to armed launches with designated targets. I shared these observations with Doctor Francis Douglas at Los Alamos. His conclusion: the North was preparing a new missile, small and perhaps truck-mounted. Based on the calculated size and thickness of the concrete pads I found, he believes it's a short-to-intermediate-range ICBM.

"Francis further speculated if Pak has developed a solid fuel, this would increase the mobility, storage longevity, and overall battlefield stability of such a missile. However, he also said that a solid fuel produces less thrust and therefore limits overall range of those missiles. With a solid fuel, he could haul these weapons to the battlefield on their mobile launchers and fire them off into China or across the DMZ. Doctor Douglas cautioned that once ignited, a solid fuel rocket cannot be halted. So, use by inexperienced troops creates an extreme safety issue; one of the weaknesses for this type of rocket. It's like lighting a Roman candle."

Admiral Benson reached for one of the sandwiches. "What do you need to complete a security briefing for the president? You'll have an uninterrupted block of time on the flight to Scotland." Sam thought for a moment and then requested the most recent satellite images over four latitude/longitude windows, an encrypted satellite telephone and laptop, and communication access to the *USS Arlington.*

An hour later, Samantha stepped out of the Chair of the Joint Chiefs Office in full field dress uniform with all the gold braid and flashes, noting her assignment to the Chair of the Joint Chief's staff. Red stripes ran down the legs of her crisp blue trousers. Rows of service ribbons filled the space above her left breast, including, at the top of the rows of small colorful ribbons, a pale blue one adorned with five silver stars, the one which caused Sam so much embarrassment. That little ribbon designated her as a recipient of the US Medal of Honor. *I am not a hero, damn it.* How many times had she thought this?

She stopped walking as a new thought struck her. Perhaps she needed to let it go. To those around her she was a hero, a role model, a commander who wouldn't leave her men behind. She would not leave anyone behind this time either. Resolve galvanized, she strode down the hall, head held high.

The messenger bag at her side bulged with the latest satellite images and all her new technology. She was back in active service, on the staff of the Chair of the Joint Chiefs, headed overseas on a need-to-know mission. Her orders: immediately complete a comprehensive briefing for the president. Get a firsthand look at how well Grant was actually doing. If she was well enough, get Grant everything she needed or wanted to catch up on their hacking project. Prepare and execute the next steps of cyberwarfare and information gathering. Let Prime Minister Lord William O'Rourke know the admiral humbly requested Grant be assigned to his office for the indefinite future. And lastly, deliver Doctor Brockstone to Grant's family estate.

A car took Sam to Joint Base Andrews where she boarded a military C37B modified Gulfstream V private jet. Her estimated time to Scotland would be just over five hours, cruising at an altitude of fifty-one thousand feet. She had five hours to complete her briefing. It was time to get to work. She set up a work area on one of the teak tables in the main cabin.

Before she departed the Pentagon, Sam called the *Arlington* and shared her situation with Cassie. Her partner's words still echoed in her mind. "Thank God. That place never deserved you. The Navy does. It's our home, Sam. I'm glad you're back. I love you."

"And I you," Sam whispered, as the sleek white and blue aircraft raced down the runway into the darkening sky.

1 March, 21:58 Hours Local (UTC 01:58, March 2)
Studio 3-A, NBC Studios
30 Rockefeller Plaza
New York City, New York, United States

MSNBC NEWS SPECIAL REPORT:

Rachel Maddow was concluding her broadcast and handing things off to Lawrence O'Donnell. His news program followed hers, and they were kidding with each other about an event at the White House the previous day when a voice spoke into her earbud, alerting her to breaking news. She sobered and spoke to the camera.

"We have breaking news. The WHO has reported the confirmation of the two hundred thousandth victim of the Paris Contagion. Exponential growth for this infection is significantly slower than the recent SARS-CoV-2 global event, but the WHO is now classifying this as a pandemic and asking nations to mobilize their medical resources. We are going to our Chief White House Correspondent, Kristen Welker. Kristen…"

"Thank you, Rachel. At this time, the president is activating the pandemic taskforce under the guidance of Doctor Alexander Watson. As you know, Doctor Watson took over as head of the NIH Division of Infectious Diseases after Doctor Anthony Fauci retired several years ago. The doctor has scheduled a news conference tomorrow morning at nine. Within the next hour, President Haley will address the nation.

"Sources at the World Health Organization are not commenting further on the specifics of this disease other than reiterating it is not transmitted via aerosols. The only method of infection is direct contact with an infected patient. Luckily, this limits the spread somewhat. However, this contagion carries a very high mortality rate. Currently, 91 percent of those infected have succumbed. Hospitals across the US are preparing isolation wards to receive patients in their areas. The president is most worried about rural areas with limited access to personal protective equipment and negative pressure isolation facilities."

Rachel asked, "Do we know anything specific about the infection. Where it comes from? How the primary patients come in contact with it?"

"Nothing is being said at this time, Rachel. We hope the president will have more information for us in her address. We do know several members of the infectious disease battalion from Fort Detrick are in the White House. This includes Doctor Deidre Williams, who arrived here this afternoon."

"Kristen, can you tell us who Doctor Williams is and why her presence is important?"

"Doctor Williams is the head of the trans-species infectious disease group at Fort Detrick. This is the Army's primary facility for infectious disease research. Doctor Williams is also the primary scientist in charge of the LEVEL 4-biosafety labs within the base."

"Thank you, Kristen. We will wait for the president's address."

3 March, 18:23 Hours Local (UTC 22:23)
Oval Office, White House
Washington, DC, United States

"I need to know what to say and what not to say to the American people. I want to give them the facts but not scare them into a panic. We have enough embedded fear left over from COVID-19. So, are you sure, Doctor Williams?" The president had entered from a side door and begun talking immediately, as she moved tiredly to one of the wingback chairs near the roaring fireplace. Time obviously was of the essence.

"As much as we can be, ma'am. We were able to construct a composite patient for virtual autopsy from tissue samples collected from the first forty-three patients in Paris. The majority of the samples were from Patient Zero, augmented with samples pooled from the rest. Using a forensic pathology approach, we identified a hidden viral pathogen within cellular samples of liver tissue, spleen tissue, brain tissue, and samples from the spinal cord. It is a grossly modified variant of a hemorrhagic virus." Deidre paused, and watched the president rub her forehead. She knew her findings were frightening to a lay person. Hell, she was scared nearly to death.

"Like Ebola?" President Haley asked. "This will be frightening for people."

"Yes, a hemorrhagic fever is not good. This one is similar to Ebola, but more survivable. A hemorrhagic virus is consistent with the gross symptomatic response we've seen in patients around the globe."

"Bottomline, Doctor. What caused this?"

"Primary hemorrhagic viruses, those endemic to sub-Saharan Africa, are of trans-species origin." Deidre paused to carefully consider her next words.

"Madam President, this virus is different." She spread her hands and tried to explain her concern. "Both the virus we isolated and the genome we mapped have been grossly modified. Modifications which allow the virus to lay dormant within the bacterial host for long periods and then become instantly viable and infectious when released from the bacterium to infect a new human host. We do not understand how the bacterium-virus combination was created. In addition to this dormancy modification, its virulence was enhanced to make infection easier. Also, its lethality was modified, resulting in worsened symptoms and increased morbidity."

"How is this possible?"

Deidre sat back and relaxed a bit. This was her area of expertise, and she easily slipped into the role of educator. "Most viruses are simple organisms enclosed within a protein shell. Consider them little inorganic packets of bad news for most organisms, if infected. Viruses are not viable alone and therefore cannot exist in isolation. Unlike eukaryotic cells with double strands of DNA, viruses have only a single strand of DNA or RNA and cannot replicate without infecting host cells and usurping that host's cellular processes. Once a virus enters a cell it uses the host's replication mechanisms and begins to produce the proteins it needs to replicate. In this virus, the single strand is RNA containing approximately nineteen thousand base letters. Quite small compared to a human's three billion."

"How can you compare something so small across generations?" the president asked.

Deidre considered this question. It was a good one. "Think of it this way, your DNA is a library, and in it is stored a record of your entire genetic history, including every infection you and your ancestors have ever had. Within your DNA are genomic segments biologists once considered junk. However, we've learned these segments are records of those ancestral infections. Little slices of time, recorded in your genetic makeup, when your ancestors' cellular DNA was attacked by a virus and your ancestor successfully overcame it. A fingerprint the virus left behind in your DNA strand. This fingerprint creates an adaptive immunity in future generations, using a naturally occurring CRISPR-Cas9 enzyme."

"What exactly is this CRISPR? I've heard others mention it."

Deidre paused to consider her explanation carefully. "CRISPR is the acronym for 'clustered regularly interspaced palindromic repeat.' Early research by the Nobel Laureates discovered them in simple bacteria and found that those bacteria use these repeating sequences as weapons against invading viruses. Think of it as a naturally occurring protein production mechanism which identifies viral invaders and prepares to attack them by using the stored immunity information."

The president nodded and sat quietly. She appeared to be trying to grasp the complexities of this new biotechnology. "I do not think I will mention CRISPR, Doctor, though I appreciate your explanation." She sighed. "To the point, what are your next steps? What hope do we have to counteract this contagion?"

"We have work to do on several fronts. First, we are adapting the CRISPR-Cas13 technologies developed during the SARS-CoV-2 pandemic to develop a viral detection tool. Second, the COVID monoclonal antibody therapy is also being modified, using antibodies from Paris Contagion survivors, to create a possible treatment for those infected. DARPA and Moderna are using the identified virus to build a new mRNA vaccine."

The president gripped the arms of her chair. "Doctor Williams—Deidre—where did this come from? You said it was modified. By whom? I need more information. One of the CIA analysts has a theory but no data to support it." When Doctor Williams didn't respond, the president prodded her more. "Is it a weapon?"

Deidre studied her hands. The president had come to the logical conclusion without her stating it explicitly. She couldn't sugarcoat it anymore, regardless of what the president's staff asked her to do.

Deidre stated unequivocally, "Yes. Someone engineered both the virus and its carrier host as a weapon."

"Who?"

"I don't know. I've torn the literature apart, including classified historical files from as far back as the OSS days and more recent reports from the CIA on bio-weaponization work from other countries. I've only found two references about an engineered hemorrhagic fever infection. This occurrence was noted in an old Soviet report from the late 1980s. Two infections, attributed to laboratory accidents, occurred at the VECTOR facility in Koltsovo, Russia. Workers were infected and subsequently died. Given this, we know the Soviets developed a viral germ agent from an original strain of some hemorrhagic virus."

President Haley spoke with conviction after she considered Deidre's comment. "No." She shook her graying, dark head emphatically. "Russia is not responsible. They have one of the largest outbreaks of the Paris Contagion. They're struggling to care for the victims. I don't believe they would willingly infect their own citizens. At least not without a treatment or antidote in their pocket."

Deidre nodded. "I would agree, ma'am. This is not from the original Soviet germ agent. In the 1980s, the Soviets could have isolated and cultured the viral agent from an original strain. They could have grown an adequate amount for storage. However, they would not have had the means to genetically reengineer the original virus. They would have had to understand base editing. This methodology wasn't invented until 2022."

President Haley tilted her head and asked, "This isn't something developed by a biohacker, is it? I read a report several years ago about some guy who claimed he designed a COVID vaccine in his garage. I think he even injected himself on YouTube."

"Possible, but not likely. Although the RNA-enzyme chemical precursors needed to modify an existing virus are available on the internet for about seventy-five dollars, and the CRISPR-Cas9 RNA gene-splicing system is easy to use, I doubt a single person in a garage would be able to create this virus. They would not have access to an original LEVEL 4 biohazard virus to begin modifications or the equipment to safely produce mass quantities of the modified germ.

"Madam President, you must remember, this is a global event. The perpetrator would also need access to a worldwide distribution system."

"How do we determine the source of the infection? And, more importantly, the potential perpetrators of this heinous act?"

"We have only one data source—the victims. We must identify commonalities: activities, travel, jobs, relationships, and species interactions. It's all about contact tracing at this point. There has to be a single point source all the victims have in common. This is not airborne. This is a person-substance-contact infection." Deidre pushed her hair from her eyes.

"We need time, ma'am. I know that is a rare commodity when dealing with a global pandemic. One good thing versus the SARS-CoV-2 pandemic, this virus exhibits very low transmissibility. So, once we identify the source of the paired agent, we can eliminate it without too many more victims. The bad thing," Deidre swallowed hard. "This virus is highly lethal. If you contract it, you have less than a 9 percent chance of survival. And if you do survive, you'll have significant lifelong neurological impairment."

"We thought we'd have time to be better prepared after the last pandemic. It was one hundred years between the Spanish flu pandemic and COVID-19."

Deidre frowned. Time was the determining factor in all her work. Nothing good was coming for humans in the future. "I wish we had time, ma'am. However, I believe we are entering an era where pandemics will occur with some frequency."

The president gaped at her.

Deidre continued her explanation. "Given mankind's encroachment on natural habitats and the loss of biodiversity across the globe, I estimate we will experience five new emerging viral diseases each year. Most will be trans-species in origin. Some will be transmissible to humans. A few could be easily weaponized using the gene-editing processes in CRISPR. Either of which—naturally-occurring or weaponized—humans will have no natural immunity to these new viruses."

The president sat in silence, a frown marring her features. Deidre could almost see the wheels turning as the president sorted the information she had shared. Earlier in the day, Deidre had spent hours with the president's senior staff, educating them about viruses in general and this one in particular so the staff could prepare a draft speech for the nation. Now, the president was mentally modifying that draft.

Deidre wished she could help. Wished she could provide the president with hard data. Real information to point her and the country in the correct direction. Save lives. But Deidre was helpless. Until they knew the source and the method of transmission and identified the origin of the bioweapon, no one could design an effective means to combat it.

22 March, 17:14 Hours Local (UTC 08:14)
USS Arlington **XO Quarters**
CGN-47, Ticonderoga-class Guided Missile Cruiser
South China Sea

Not again. James Alexander's worried thought swirled through his mind as he slapped his desktop. Communications with Amundsen-Scott base was down. For the fourth time James was unable to establish a connection with the base to speak with his mom. The first time he circumvented protocol and commandeered a NASA satellite. The second and third time, his mother had contacted him using the Iridium commercial satellite array after they'd missed their agreed time by a day, explaining the cloud cover over the polar plateau had blocked signal strength. This time he hadn't heard anything, and they were seven days past due. His worry escalated, and he thought to hell with it. James sent an encrypted email to his friend at NASA, asking for another authorization code for their satellite. Now he just had to be patient.

Tipping back in his chair, he thought about everything that happened over the last several months. The *Arlington* had done well on her sea-trials and was fully rated to reenter service. Currently, she was cruising north through the South China Sea on their way to rejoin the fleet near the Spratly Islands. Their current mission: to keep watch on the Chinese construction of artificial islands in the archipelago.

After Cassie had spoken to Samantha, she shared with him Sam's leaving the CIA, rejoining the Navy on Admiral Benson's staff, and traveling to Scotland. Though why she made the trip wasn't stated. "Need to know" security always limited their discussions about Samantha.

His desktop pinged with an incoming message. He read the text and his fear escalated. His NASA friend would be happy to give him a login code, but the satellite had lost contact with the base. Currently, they'd had no contact in the last six days. Scheduled data uplinks from the researchers were missed. The National Science Foundation had requested help from the military to reestablish comm links. So far nothing had worked.

Weather continued to deteriorate over the pole. A large low-pressure system with high winds and dense cloud cover had parked itself over the area. NASA hoped this was blocking communications. Currently, NASA had requested the Department of Defense move the orbit of one of their DSCS-3 satellites to track over the polar region. This satellite was more powerful and should be able to punch through any cloud cover to reach the base. At least, McMurdo Base remained in communication.

A second email arrived while he was reviewing the first, this one from the US Air Force. A request for evacuation had been filed from McMurdo's medical group. They needed a medical EVAC Lockheed LC-130 Hercules aircraft equipped with skis to evacuate several of the crew from McMurdo to New Zealand. The plane would need medical isolation pods as the crew had contracted the Paris Contagion. McMurdo Base was going into medical quarantine until further notice.

Whoa, boy. This is so not good. Thank heaven, Mom is completely isolated at the South Pole away from any chance of infection. That's one good thing at least. Safe, just like he felt safe here on the *Arlington*. Due to the spread of the contagion, all Navy vessels were ordered to remain at sea.

The alarm on James' watch chimed signaling he had ten minutes to get to the command deck and relieve the captain for dinner. Once on deck, he'd ask his imaging tech to tap into the NOAA satellite for the South Pole and print out a radar image of the storm. Then he would see for himself how bad the weather was. If this continued, he'd ask Captain Stanley for help. Surely, she or Samantha would have some suggestions. None of this did anything to halt his worry.

23 March, 09:09 Hours Local (UTC 08:09)
Bardowie Castle, south of Glasgow
Scottish Highlands
Ancestral Home of O'Rourke Clan

Grant sat in the sunlit breakfast room, wrapped in a tartan plaid of green and red. She was cold and had been for over a month. Nothing she did—from soaking in a hot tub to being wrapped in down-filled duvets—could increase her core temperature. Or so it felt. Her physician said it was a side effect of being on a ventilator for three weeks. Weeks lost with no memory. Her last memory was dropkicking an Asian assailant across the concrete floor of the Kuala Lumpur International Airport. Her later memories were foggy, filled with bodiless voices and blurry faces. Her head swam in a miasma of disjointed images. All she remembered clearly was the pain.

Until three weeks ago when Cynthia arrived. A smile stretched her facial muscles. She wasn't sure she'd have survived the poking and prodding from all the medical professionals or the bowing and scraping of her uncle's staff without such a welcome diversion. And when she slept in Cynthia's arms, she was warm.

Memories of three weeks ago surfaced. She had been napping in her bedroom suite when a rap on the oaken door roused her. "Come." Her croak was far from her normal voice.

The castle butler's gray head appeared around the edge of the door. "Lady Amelia, you have visitors. I've shown them to the library and offered refreshments."

"Thank you, Greaves. I'll be down in a moment." She struggled from the depths of the massive four-postered Jacobean bed. Assuming her visitors were more medical personnel, she hadn't bothered with anything more than donning her dressing gown over wrinkled pajamas. When the MI6 folks visited, she wore her uniform, but it no longer fit quite right with the weight loss she had experienced.

Making her way slowly down the curved central stairs, Grant paused at the library door to run a hand over her mussed hair. She knew it stood up in all directions.

She pushed the door open, as voices rose from within the room. One voice, the voice which haunted her dreams, was present. Grant stepped fully into the room and saw her. Time stopped.

Cynthia stood beside the stone fireplace, holding a crystal goblet of golden liquid in her right hand. She was backlit by the fire in a red glow, laughing at something, head thrown back in mirth. Cynthia turned her head at the noise of the door and promptly dropped her glass.

Another was in the room, but Grant missed the colonel standing on the other side of the fireplace. She was too captivated by Cynthia. The sound of shattering glass startled everyone. Time started forward again for Grant.

"Amelia, love, how are you feeling?" Cynthia stepped toward her, the glass forgotten.

"You're here," Amelia Grant said, not quite believing it.

Laughter filled the room again, as Cynthia and the colonel responded to her obvious observation. "Seems we are here, Grant," Sam acknowledged.

To her horror Grant watched the colonel kneel and begin picking up pieces of broken glass. "Leave that. Greaves will get it."

As if conjured from thin air, the officious British butler appeared, a tea towel over an arm and a tray with another crystal goblet in his hand. "Colonel, allow me." He placed the silver tray on the sideboard next to the drink bottles and swept the shards up with a single swipe. He turned to Cynthia. "Another, Doctor?"

Grant watched Cynthia wave her hand and absently respond, "No, thank you." She moved around the sofa and stood before her. "You've lost weight, love. How are you, really?"

"Better now." Grant thought she was dreaming. "You're here."

"I am, and I'm not leaving until all is well."

Things began to feel normal for Grant with the arrival of her heart's other half. The colonel's presence helped too. She began to feel everything was going to be all right.

Since then, things were improving daily. Grant's thoughts were interrupted as the breakfast room door opened and the colonel entered. Her cheeks were flushed pink, and sweat streaked down her temples. "How was your run, ma'am? Your back is well-healed?"

Sam laughed. "Grant you've gotta stop calling me, ma'am. We're here as your guests. No need for military formality."

"Not going to happen, colonel." Grant smiled at her boss. "Breakfast? I can call for something else if the selection is lacking."

"I'm good. I'm afraid I'll weigh as much as Francis if I keep eating the way I have over the last few weeks."

"I believe that is Greaves' objective, ma'am. He thinks all of us could stand to add a few stone."

Sam grinned. "Be that as it may, I won't fit into my new uniform if I continue." Regardless of potential weight gain, Sam filled a plate from the spread laid out on the buffet. "Shall we go through any new hits you've had on the movie front?"

"I reviewed the program last night. We've had another thousand or so civilian downloads and eight more uploads on military workstations, but none were in locations of interest. I was hoping we'd get something within the Tonghae Satellite Launching facility. It may be too far from the western border to receive any of the flash drives. I'd like to learn more about those new missiles Pak paraded out in February."

Sam put her plate down on a linen placemat and filled a crystal goblet with orange juice from the pitcher in the center. Sitting and unfolding her napkin on her lap, Sam agreed. "I would also, but it may be too much to hope for."

Grant watched her take a few bites of perfect scrambled eggs and place her fork down. Sam looked thoughtful, as she asked, "Would it be possible to enter a workstation we can access and have it remotely link to another at a different location in say, Tonghae?"

"Interesting question." Grant pushed her half-empty plate away. "I wonder... " She stood and walked over to the corner of the room to pull the cord hanging there.

Within seconds, a footman arrived. "Ma'am?"

Sam laughed and Grant felt her cheeks flush. "Would you get my laptop from the library, please? And ask Doctor Brockstone if she would like breakfast this morning or just coffee?"

"Of course, ma'am." The footman bowed out of the room.

Grant watched Sam hide another chuckle behind her napkin. "Touché, Colonel. I've tried to get them to stop for years, and I can't. British aristocratic propriety and all keeps them in line. I admit I understand how you feel." Grant paused. "But military protocol will not allow me to stop either."

"Well said. Any news from your uncle or the Foreign Secretary?"

"Nothing for a few days. They're continuing Pak Jong-nam's interrogation. He has some basic knowledge of the country's science programs, but they are all related to agricultural improvements. His service in the military seems wholly ceremonial. He was never embedded within a unit or saw any active service."

Sam sat back. "Neither was Pak. But Jong-nam should still have some idea what his brother is planning. Even if it's a broad idea of direction."

The footman returned carrying Grant's computer case. "Your Ladyship, Doctor Brockstone will be here shortly. She is finishing an email."

"Thank you, Harold."

Grant pulled out her gunmetal gray laptop and opened it on the corner of the dining table. "Let's see if we can get a workstation to do as we want." A rapid string of keystrokes, a huff, and then another string. "Ah, better."

"Is it safe to be doing all this over a Wi-Fi system in your uncle's home?"

"Considering I installed the security systems in the house, as well as, the encrypted, satellite-based server system, I'd say we're safe. After all, the prime minister must maintain secure communications with the palace as well as Number Ten when he is in residence here."

"Okay, then."

Grant continued to study the lines of code scrolling down her screen. Her breakfast plate and mug of tea sat forgotten at her elbow. The eerie gray glow from the screen competed with the watery sunlight streaming in the windows. "Doable. Not very elegant, but definitely doable." Grant looked at Sam, as she continued to enjoy her breakfast. "I believe we can accomplish your request, ma'am. What would you like to know about Tonghae?"

23 March, 09:34 Hours Local (UTC 20:34, March 22)
Amundsen-Scott Base
South Pole, Central Antarctic Plateau

Julia Alexander was in deep trouble, and so was everyone on the station. She had three technicians and one crewmember down with what appeared to be the Paris Contagion. From the limited information she received from news updates contained in their daily email downloads, the symptoms matched. Plus, one of the technicians managed communications and the infected crewman was the chief maintenance tech for their generators. Key roles others were hard-pressed to fill.

How these men contracted the virus here—in isolation—at the South Pole—she didn't know. No one had been to the station since the last flight arrived with the final shipment of jet fuel and other supplies for the overwintering crew. That was five weeks ago. She had equipment to manage negative pressure isolation and care for these patients in the short term, but if she didn't figure something out soon, things would go south rapidly. She laughed at her own macabre humor. She was as far south as anyone could go.

When the first technician began showing symptoms, Julia isolated the man and began treatment with the antiviral drug Ribavirin. She also initiated supportive hospital therapy—balancing the patient's fluids and electrolytes, and maintaining oxygen levels and blood pressure. Currently, she was attempting to devise a method to replace lost blood and clotting factors, using the synthetic blood substitute she had stored at the station. Then she would prepare a schedule for blood draws from the healthy crew. Several were O-negative—universal donors.

Treatment for any complicating infections or organ system issues would have to be dealt with on a case-by-case basis. Steven Coshair was the first to fall ill and the most critical. He was the head of logistics and maintained the station's supply depot. The second patient was the maintenance chief. The third, Coshair's coworker in logistics. And finally, the communications technician.

"How are you doing, Dr. Julia?" The head of station popped around the door into her office in sick bay.

"Maintaining as best as I can, Jason. Everyone is stable so far, but I am worried about Coshair. There are indications he is headed for massive organ system failure. I've got dialysis equipment for primary care, but he's going to need interventions more advanced than I can provide here. Any chance we can get an emergency evacuation?"

Jason pulled his ponytail over his shoulder, twirling the end around his finger. She'd been around him long enough to know he did this when he was worried. "Not with this weather and not if we can't reestablish a satellite uplink for communications. No one has been able to realign our dish to the new orbital track of the satellite."

"Aren't the satellites in geosynchronous orbit over our station?"

He dropped into one of her desk chairs and swiveled around to face Julia. "Usually, but the NASA bird is close to being decommissioned, and its orbit is a bit erratic. To establish and maintain a lock, we need to manually tweak the dish during communications, and only the communication tech is able to do so. We'll keep trying, but I think we need something else."

24 March, 02:21 Hours Local (UTC 01:21)
Library, Bardowie Castle, south of Glasgow
Scottish Highlands
Ancestral Home of O'Rourke Clan

Rain pelted the floor-to-ceiling windows in the darkened library. Wind tore around the ramparts of the castle and echoed eerily. Sam was hunched over her laptop, intent on the data streaming across the backlit screen. Grant had successfully tapped into a workstation at the Tonghae Satellite Launching Ground facility via another location. Now Sam was trying to understand what they'd found—a spreadsheet or some sort of catalogue of military projects. Although her spoken Korean was excellent, reading the Hangul characters was something else. Without lifting her head from the screen she called, "Grant?"

A mumbled "what…" rose from the blanket-shrouded bundle reclining on the leather sofa.

"Do you have access to a Korean language translation program?"

A tousled head popped up. "Written or oral?" Grant's voice was a croak, her breathing ragged as she swallowed to clear her throat. She was supposed to sleep with a C-PAP mask. Her diaphragm was still partially paralyzed, and the breathing equipment provided positive pressure which prevented upper respiratory collapse. If she didn't breathe deeply enough during sleep, her blood oxygen saturations fell to a dangerous level.

Sam looked up when she heard her gasping. This was a breathing technique Grant learned to rapidly increase her blood oxygen saturation without hyperventilating.

A grumbled complaint cut through Grant's harsh breathing, as a second head appeared. "Samantha, give it a rest. It's after two in the morning." Cynthia Brockstone's complaint was ignored by Grant and Sam.

"Do you have something?"

Sam shrugged. "Perhaps. But I'm not sure I'm reading this correctly."

Grant untangled herself from the blankets. She placed a kiss on Cynthia's cheek. "Be right back. Keep the blankets warm for me?"

"Always, Love." Sam smiled at the tender scene. The two had cemented their relationship and were now attached at the hip most of the day and night.

Grant rounded the table where Sam was working and opened a second laptop. "Give me a minute, and I'll see what I can find." Her fingers flew over the keyboard, creating a cacophony of clicks and taps. She stopped and reviewed what was on her screen. "This should do. Send me the file, and I'll run it through this app."

Sam frowned. "And how do I do that?"

Grant laughed and pulled Sam's laptop over. "Like this." She entered a string of code. Sam watched as her file collapsed and reappeared on the other machine. A few more keystrokes and it disappeared again.

"Ahhh… Grant?"

"Patience. It's still there, just being converted by the translation app."

Sam didn't want to ask where this little app came from. Grant seemed to have backdoors into many of her government's computer systems. From weather satellites to the sailing orders of Her Majesty's fleets, Grant could find anything at a moment's notice. No, Sam decided, she really didn't want to know.

Time passed slowly before a blinking icon appeared. Grant hit "Enter." A printer came to life under the library table and began spitting out sheets of printed English text. "All righty then, let's see what we have." Grant pulled the pages out and tapped them into a neat stack. She began skimming the list, handing each page to Sam in order. The list was lengthy, and pages were still printing as Sam reviewed the first several.

This printout contained a massive amount of information in spreadsheet form. Everything from a construction schedule for the replacement of storm-damaged barracks and sanitary facilities to schedules for drying grain on unused concrete launch pads to feed base personnel to—Sam's heart leapt into her throat, a launch schedule in support of troop movements along the Chinese border and… shit… the targeting coordinates for missile strikes across Asia and the middle Pacific.

The information she needed to determine Pak's next steps was here. Schedules of troop movements; shipment dates; procurement invoices; transfer authorizations for warheads, fuel, and rocket engines; and transfers from other facilities to Tonghae. Matériel lists, multiple personnel rosters, and a date—fifteen April—the Day of the Sun, were also mentioned.

Her heart rose into her throat, Pak would visit the Tonghae facility on that day.

Sam dropped the pages and grabbed her ever-present messenger bag. Digging in its depths, she retrieved her encrypted sat phone. She punched in a string of numbers and listened as the device acquired a satellite and rang. "Admiral Benson's office."

"Melissa, it's Samantha Michaels. Does he have a moment? I think we've found something important."

"Hold one." The line filled with static.

Admiral Benson picked up. "Samantha, what've you got?"

"Sir, Grant was able to link one workstation to another and query the Tonghae facility's logistics and planning schedules. After running the list of projects through a written language translation program, we've learned when Pak will act next as well as what he will do."

Admiral Benson's voice held disbelief. "I can't believe strategic plans would be stored in a single, low-level workstation."

Sam placed the sat phone on speaker and raised an eyebrow to Grant. "Would you repeat your statement, sir?"

"There is no way a military as paranoid as North Korea would place all that information on a single workstation. What's going on?"

"Grant here, sir. I was able to tap the commanding officer's personal computer. Seems the man is OCD or something. All the projects going on at the Tonghae Satellite Launching Ground facility are organized within a single file. We must write Microsoft and thank them for the backdoor into their Office suite. I got in via EXCEL." Sam elbowed Grant in the ribs and frowned. Grant just smirked at her.

They heard a huffed guffaw. "Samantha, what does all this mean? Don't answer that. When you have it sorted, I'll need a summary and a detailed brief for the president ASAP."

Sam looked at the antique Julien Béliard mantel clock. It read three sixteen in the morning. "Sir, we can have a brief ready for you within the next few hours. The printer is still spitting out sheets from the file we accessed. I believe Pak will move across the DMZ and into China on fifteen April, following a barrage of missile attacks. A launch of short to intermediate-range weapons from Tonghae against various Asian targets prior to his troop's advance. Perhaps as a diversion. I don't know what the warheads will contain, but the file contains shipment schedules for chemical and low-level nuclear weapons. We'll need to be prepared for anything from his NBC arsenal. We have a bit over twenty-one days, sir." Sam paused for breath.

"Good work, Samantha. You, too, Grant. I'm calling the president directly. I don't want the spooks hearing about this from those security council toadies. When you have anything else, call me back." Sam heard him mumble before coming back on the line. "Hold one."

The gold-embossed mantel clock chimed the half hour, then the three-quarter hour, then four o'clock. Grant looked at Sam and raised an eyebrow. "Do you still have a connection?"

Sam looked at the handset. "Seems so." She turned it so Grant could see the blinking "connected" indicator.

"Samantha?" Admiral Benson's voice was subdued.

"Here, sir."

"We've got a real pickle. I just received word twenty-nine ships across all our oceans have reported they have victims of the Paris Contagion."

Grant gasped, and Cynthia raised her head above the couch. "What?" She rose and joined them.

"How's that possible? I thought all ships were ordered to stay at sea and avoid coming into port."

"They were and they did. But sickbays across the fleets are reporting the same symptoms and severity of illness. I need to focus on this, Samantha. Therefore, you need to complete your briefing and provide it to the president over a secure video link. Give her everything. Don't sugarcoat anything. And, Samantha, give her your best estimate of Pak's next steps. All of them."

"Yes, sir. Of course, sir."

The line went silent again. When the admiral returned, his voice was serious. "Samantha, I need one more thing. I am going to ask the president to speak to you privately. After your briefing, I want you to present your best recommendations as to what our response should be." Sam inhaled sharply. "I know this is something you are uncomfortable with, but I need you to act as though you are me. An advisor and counselor. Not an analyst."

When Sam didn't respond the admiral prompted her. "Do you understand, Colonel?" The use of her rank made it an order.

Sam swallowed her discomfort. "Aye, sir."

"The president needs a clear path forward. This is proof North Korea, and more specifically Pak, presents a clear and present danger to our allies and to the United States of America."

He paused and she heard him mumble something away from the handset. "The president needs to be focused when she meets with her security council and intelligence advisors. If she has a logical framework derived from all we've learned and a recommended course of action, she will be decisive and make the best decisions. And those come from being the most informed. And Samantha, remember she trusts you."

Sam shivered, worried she could be wrong in so many ways.

Sam almost missed the admiral's next words. "I don't want her cadre of advisors muddying the waters. They're all too politically motivated to do what is right. I especially do not want the CIA computer analyst wonks screwing this up. None of them could find their butts with two hands and a sat image."

"I… er…" Sam stiffened to attention. "Yes, sir. I understand, Admiral. Grant and I will provide a recommended course of action using our analysis of the information we have."

"Very good. I'm counting on you, Colonel. You're not at the CIA anymore. You're on my staff. Therefore, you are speaking for the Navy and the greater military. You're my voice in all this."

Shit. No pressure. "I understand, sir." Grant poked her in the side and pointed to a pad with a scribbled note. "One more thing, sir. How do we keep MI6 and the PM in the loop? I know you requested Grant be assigned to your staff, but we're using UK resources to gather these data."

"Good point. I'll call Lord O'Rourke tonight and let him know what we're planning. Once you speak with the president, send a copy of your brief to him. I'll let him know he can share it with MI6."

"Thank you, sir. We'll be ready within the next few hours. I'll call Melissa and let her know when to schedule President Haley."

The call disconnected and Sam slumped into a chair. "Grant, how's the program coming?"

"Almost done, Colonel. Once the translation is complete, I'm going to organize the various project line items chronologically. That should allow us to group related project components, and we can plot their movement on a national map. Maybe see patterns, areas of focus, get the big picture out of all the clutter. Determine Pak's next steps."

"Sounds good." Sam's brain kept coming back to the one thing which frightened her most. The Paris Contagion was onboard Navy vessels. Was Cassie safe?

24 March, 21:14 Hours Local (UTC 20:14 23 March)
Amundsen-Scott Base
South Pole, Central Antarctic Plateau

The readouts were erratic. Coshair's heart rate was all over the place. Currently, Julia had a drip of Indocin, a non-steroidal anti-inflammatory, going to manage his fever. His blood pressure had cratered from the high fever and rampant infection, and his heart had sped up to compensate for the drop. Now he was in reflex sinus tachycardia. If she couldn't control his heart rate, he was headed toward cardiac arrest.

His overall condition continued to deteriorate at a rapid rate, and without adequate system support, he'd be dead within the next six to eight hours. How someone at the South Pole contracted a hemorrhagic fever was beyond her, and her tracing and tracking resources were limited. If more patients presented, she might be able to do some adequate tracing. If she had time while treating the increasing number of severely ill patients. She was rapidly running out of supplies to isolate and treat them.

Julia paged Jason. "Yes, Doctor J?" Julia growled. She hated the nickname, but everyone had picked it up. She knew it was a dig about her height or lack thereof.

"Jason, we're headed for a crisis. I need a communication outlet to Fort Detrick or the NIH or CDC now. I can't wait any longer. We're going to lose Coshair soon."

"Would an email blast labeled 'urgent' work? Is there anyone you know who would respond to you?"

Julia thought for a moment. "My son is aboard a Navy ship in the Pacific. I could try him. And I have a contact at Fort Detrick. Doctor

Williams and I worked together during the last Ebola crisis in Mali."

"Fuck, is this Ebola?" Jason's voice rose two octaves in panic. Panic wasn't something one could afford in an isolated, self-contained habitat.

"No, Jason. Calm down. This isn't Ebola. We're okay as long as we continue to isolate the patients. I've got the supplies to manage for now. But I need to speak to someone immediately. And I'm going to need additional specialized equipment."

"You about gave me a heart attack. We could all die if it was Ebola." Julia cursed the sensationalist news organizations around the world. Hadn't everyone learned the basic science of infection, isolation, and treatment with the COVID mess?

"We're not going to die. This isn't an airborne pathogen. The base and the personnel are safe." At least for now, she prayed. "I've got to get more supplies soon, though. And if we can get Coshair out, we need to do that. The other three I can manage. They're holding their own."

Julia heard Jason's chair creak. He'd put his feet up on his desk. Good, she'd distracted him away from his rising panic. "No way we can risk a landing and takeoff in this weather, Julia, but an overflight and drop might be possible. We can light up the base and turn on the old VHF-localizer beacon for the aircraft to follow. Do you have a list of supplies? You could include it in your email messages."

"I'll do that. Good thought."

"Get your email messages ready, and we will commandeer an Iridium satellite on their next pass in…," she heard a thud as his feet hit the floor and papers rustled, "two hours. I'll hold the regular daily dispatch of messages. We'll send only yours if we can punch through the cloud cover."

"Thanks, Jason. I'll prepare the messages now."

To: (Cmdr James Alexander) j.alexander@navy.mil
From: alexanderj@nsf.gov
Subject: FLASH FLASH FLASH

Medical emergency at Amundsen Scott Base. Paris Contagion suspected. Need immediate contact with NIH and CDC. Four patients, one critical. Need medical drop and immediate evacuation. Weather critical. Comms down. Needs attached. Send reply via Iridium. Mom

Julia copied and pasted the same FLASH message to Deidre Williams at Fort Detrick, the CDC director, the Executive Scientist in Charge at the WHO, the NSF, and McMurdo Base. Someone had to respond. She crossed her fingers.

25 March, 03:26 Hours Local (UTC 07:26)
Researchers Office Building, Infectious Disease Laboratories
US Army Medical Research Institute for Infectious   Diseases
Fort Detrick
Fredrick, Maryland, United States

A spring ice storm had devastated the east coast. Telephone and power lines were down across the DC area. Luckily, since Fort Detrick housed LEVEL 4 containment labs, they had emergency backup power. Currently, Doctor Williams' lab and office were running off generators, but she didn't have telephone or mobile service. Email was her only mode of communication. An incoming notification sounded on her iPad, startling Deidre awake. "What the… ?"

She nearly fell out of her chair, as she rocked forward and tried to find the device buried somewhere on her desk. She'd set up the alert to wake her when a technician pinged her from the LEVEL 4 lab or René tried to reach her for a Zoom meeting.

The iPad had a new message notification flashing on the home screen. A thumb print and a tap opened her email app. Messages began to fill her inbox, but the one marked FLASH rose to the top of the list. It was the one which prompted the alert.

Who did she know at the National Science Foundation? Her iPad was spam and phishing protected and encrypted, not easily hacked or compromised. She opened the message and quickly read it. "Oh, god."

She dumped the email to her printer, grabbed the hardcopy, and ran from her office. Two floors up, Deidre knocked on General Talley's door. "Come."

Deidre opened the door and stepped into the austere office space. General Talley occupied the space normally assigned to a personal assistant. Talley had no use for an intermediary and preferred firsthand contact with his staff. His command style was warm, open, and welcoming. Educated at Columbia Medical School and a veteran of several major conflicts around the world, George Talley was an encyclopedia of medical knowledge. Deidre liked the older, white-haired man very much.

"Sir, sorry to disturb, especially at three in the morning, but I have an emergency I don't know how to handle."

"No worries, Deidre. Let's see what you have. Something to do with the Contagion?"

She handed him the printed copy. "Not directly, sir. Though if this information is correct, we've been thrown another curve ball by this virus."

He frowned at her and read the message. It was short and to the point. "Who's this Alexander J? And is this a National Science Foundation address?"

"Doctor Julia Alexander."

"The Ebola specialist? What the devil is she doing at the South Pole?"

"Yes, and I don't know, sir."

He rose from his desk and exited the small office, grabbing his overcoat from the back of the door. "Come on, then. We'll need to get to the comm center to handle this."

The pair slipped and slid across the quadrangle between the researcher office building and the central communication center located in the command bunker a quarter mile away. Neither bothered to take their cars, as it'd take longer to scrape off the inch-and-a-half of ice on the windshield than to walk across the campus.

Once at the bunker, the sentry saluted the general and opened the metal door. Or tried to. It took a strategically placed kick and a strike with his rifle butt to break the ice rime. "Sorry, sir. Rough weather, sir."

"No worries, Corporal. I appreciate the effort. I recommend you head inside for a cocoa." Everyone on base knew the general's drink of choice was hot cocoa. "You'll be the next one we need to chip ice off of if you continue to stay outside."

"Yes, sir. Thank you, sir." He saluted smartly and held the door for the two physicians.

Once inside they made their way down the gently sloping ramp. Built just after World War II, this was one of several underground facilities constructed to safely house government officials in case of a nuclear attack on Washington, DC. Deidre forcibly swallowed her claustrophobia as they continued deeper. At a nondescript door, Talley pushed the lever-handle down and entered a dimly lit space. Banks of modems, routers, encrypted computers, and video displays flashed, as technicians spoke quietly into small mics hanging from their ears. "General, to what do we owe the visit?" one of the officers asked, coming to attention.

"Need a link up to DARPA and the White House, if you would, Clint."

The young man nodded and directed the two to a comm booth. "Which one first, sir?"

The general looked at the bank of clocks on the wall, 03:41. "Let's try DARPA first and then the White House."

"Very well, sir. I'll have a hook up in a few minutes. Which department are we searching for?"

"Andy Ratcliffe at SafeGenes, please."

"Very well, sir, ma'am." He tipped his head. "Make yourself at home. May I get either of you a cocoa?"

Deidre held back a chuckle. In this weather, she welcomed a cup. With the steaming mug held in both hands, Deidre absorbed the comforting warmth and the tantalizing aroma of chocolate.

"Nothing better than a good cup of cocoa," the general said.

"Sir, we have Doctor Ratcliffe for you." A young technician called from across the room.

"Thank you, son." He turned to Deidre. "Shall we?" He held the booth door open and motioned her inside. Punching the speaker button on the console, the general spoke. "Andy, how are you? I see you don't sleep any more than we do these days."

Laughter filled the small, soundproofed booth. "Not when a pandemic is rearing its ugly head. What can I do for you, George?"

"Doctor Williams is here with me. She just received a disturbing email from an associate at Amundsen-Scott Base in Antarctica. Seems the Contagion has cropped up there as well. They're in need of medical help."

"The South Pole. Damn, isn't it winter there now?"

Deidre interjected. "Hi Andy, Deidre here, and yes, it's winter there now. You remember Julia Alexander from our Ebola mission in Central Africa?"

"Of course, no one could forget Julia. What the hell is she doing at the South Pole?"

26 March, 17:34 Hours Local (UTC 08:34)
USS Arlington
CGN-47, Ticonderoga-class Guided Missile Cruiser
South China Sea

Cassie paced the hall outside of sick bay. Things had become a total cluster over the last hours. She had six crew in medical isolation. When the first suspected case was diagnosed, Cassie informed the crew what was happening. Panic set in. Some wanted to head to port immediately. Others wanted the sick removed from the ship by any means, including dumping them over the side. Still others wanted to abandon ship.

Her chief surgeon implemented strict quarantine by department. Non-vital parts of the ship were closed. After the sixth case was reported, Doctor Aronoff ordered the water supplies purged and the desalination plants activated to produce a fresh supply. All waste systems were flushed and decontaminated. The ship went into total lockdown. Luckily, unlike on nuclear submarines, the crew each had their own bunks—no hot bunking on the *Arlington*. But crew did shared quarters. Those bunking with the six sick crew were isolated and being monitored for symptoms by medical personnel.

The fleet was distributing needed negative pressure isolation pods and additional personal protective equipment. Hopefully, they had enough to go around. Compared to other ships, they had the lowest number of patients. So far. Her mind raced, as she tried to figure out what else she could do to protect her crew.

Doctor Aronoff appeared at the entrance to sick bay. When Cassie moved forward, the doctor lifted a hand. "Stop. Hold there. Maintain distance." More than six feet separated them, but Cassie could see the lines of exhaustion and worry marring her young surgeon's face behind her positive pressure face shield. A small pump hummed at the doctor's waist.

"How bad is it, Tabitha?"

"Not as bad as some of the other ships. Because we carry nuclear weapons and utilize nuclear power plants, I have an adequate supply of negative isolation pods." She dropped her head and scuffed her blue shoe-covered toe across the deck plating. "Three aren't going to make it, ma'am. My staff and I have done all we can. They've received all the WHO prescribed treatments, but I can't stop their cascade organ failure." She raised a tear-stained face. Cassie's heart clenched.

"Who?"

"Daniels, Reilly, and Patterson."

Cassie couldn't believe it. Three of her new crew. Fresh from basic training. She had only met them once when they came onboard in Hawai'i. "How?" She swallowed hard, as her throat threatened to close. "Did they bring it onboard with them?"

"No, I don't believe this came onboard with any crewman. The incubation time is only a few days, and if someone were contagious in Hawai'i, it would have shown up weeks ago. We've been at sea for over two months. The virus had to come from something they came in contact with. Something that's on the ship."

Cassie gasped.

"I know it's scary as hell. Not knowing what or where or how. But it's transmitted by touch with an infected person, by bodily fluids, or via their personal items."

"Tabitha, I have to run this ship. I can't do that alone. I need a base level of crew in four shifts—24/7. How do we protect the remaining crew? How do we find the source of the virus? Can't you give me anything?"

"I've started my own limited contact tracing. From that I know the following: three are old hands. Two of those left the ship in Hawai'i and went home to the west coast of California. One stayed behind to supervise computer upgrades to our systems. Three are newbies."

Tabitha blew her blonde bangs off her forehead, and her face shield fogged. Frustration was evident in her stiff posture. "I have two IT specialists, both of whom bunk together. My guess is one gave it to the other by direct contact. Their symptom onset is three days apart. I have one maintenance technician, one reactor technician, an ensign who's a propulsion engineer, and a mail clerk. The mail clerk is my patient zero; and the propulsion engineer is the last. All but the first three had no contact with any of the others."

Cassie threw up her hands. "What a fucking mess." She knew she couldn't lose it in front of her chief surgeon, but this was a disaster. She felt out of control. How could something so small cripple her mighty warship? *Come on Cassie, get your head in the game, quit reacting and start analyzing*, she thought to herself.

Chewing her bottom lip, the captain of the *Arlington* suggested, "Let's take a different tack here. As you said, we've been at sea for months. But this had to come from somewhere. Somewhere on this ship. If you don't think this came onboard with the crew in Hawai'i, what happened in the weeks or days prior to the first patient presenting with symptoms? Can we expand our trace? Focus away from the patients but onto activities? Activities of the patients as well as the ship at large?"

A spark flashed in Tabitha's tired, pale gray eyes. "Not patient but activity?" she mumbled. "Not patient... ?" The young doctor spun on her heel and shouted, "Garrent, get me the ship's logs for the last three weeks. Download them to my workstation."

The sick bay hatch swung closed in Cassie's face. "All right, we have a course and heading." She climbed the stairs to the command deck. "I think I'll have a look as well. There's a key here. I can feel it."

26 March, 12:19 Hours Local (UTC 11:19)
Library, Bardowie Castle, south of Glasgow
Scottish Highlands
Ancestral Home of O'Rourke Clan

Sam tugged the sleeves of her white shirt down. The castle staff was doing their laundry and had provided a freshly ironed shirt for her next video conference with the president. They'd gone a bit heavy on the starch. She could feel the edges of the collar abrading her neck with each breath. This conference would include Admiral Benson and the Secretary of Defense. Lord O'Rourke had arrived at the castle a few hours ago after he received her brief. He wanted firsthand access to Grant and the data.

Since their first successful data acquisition within the Tonghae commander's computer, Grant had gone on a hunting trip, bouncing from one workstation to another with the hope of finding more information. They were using the base commander's email address book to pick targets for her search. At last count, Grant had accessed forty-six workstations across North Korea. Doctor Kim had provided an additional seven email addresses for her peer scientists. So far, nothing new had popped up. Perhaps their first hit would be their only success.

When Sam spoke to President Haley a day and a half ago, she had presented a detailed list of scientific projects with timelines, matériel requirements, and locations of activities. From this she recommended a course of action. As Admiral Benson ordered, this recommendation was specific and included step-by-step instructions on how to disrupt Pak's possible plans.

The recommendations included targeting key depots and bases of operation with drone strikes; seek and destroy objectives for North Korean Navy vessels; an all-out physical attack and cyberattack on his computer infrastructure: military and civilian; the location of key personnel and an analysis of their potential willingness to aid in thwarting Pak—this was provided by Kim Hye-su; and a detailed plan of recommended humanitarian aid to uplift the country once Pak was stopped. It seemed from her conversations with the admiral, the president was proceeding with most of her recommendations.

This video conference had only one objective, to create a detailed step-by-step plan to remove Pak's WMD, his computer installations, his ability to produce more WMD and their precursors, and remove Pak himself. All with steps to stabilize the headless government. Neither Grant nor Sam had even considered the action to remove Pak, as they scoured the North Korean workstations for military information to refine their strike-targeting recommendations. They needed to be as precise as possible to limit collateral damage to civilians at or near some of the military targets.

But last night at dinner, Cynthia Brockstone had asked a critical question. "Have you gotten any useful information from Pak Jong-nam? After all, Grant nearly gave her life to recover this supposed asset." The snark wasn't lost on either Sam or Grant. Her question however, sparked an all-night session of "What if?" which included the PM. Their plan sounded simple. They knew where Pak was going to be. Tonghae was on the coast with easy access for a Seal and or Special Boat team. Could they go in and grab Pak? Yes, it sounded simple, but the difficult part was how to stabilize a leaderless country.

Grant entered the library at a run, moving faster than Sam had seen her move in the last month. Her uniform was impeccable, a sharp contrast to her red face and disheveled hair. The young aide bent at the waist and grabbed her knees. She stood slowly. "More informa... tion. His... fault. All... his."

"What're you going on about, Grant? We have ten minutes until the video conference. We have to focus here." Sam said, admonishing Grant she continued gasping for breath. "Sit down before you fall down." She pushed one of the chairs over to her.

Cynthia ran into the library. "Did she tell you? That rat bastard!"

The PM arrived, his dress shirt collar open with his sleeves rolled to the elbow. An Eton tie was draped around his neck. "Samantha, they've found something. We have information on the Paris Contagion."

"Err... what?" Sam stared at the man. She was so immersed in operational planning this information threw her thinking for a loop.

Grant finally had her breathing under control. "I was able to access a workstation at the Hŭngnam Fertilizer Complex, using an email address from Doctor Kim." The young lieutenant dropped into the proffered chair. "She's responsible… "

Sam interrupted her. "For what? Get to the point."

"The North Koreans built the Paris Contagion into a weapon and released it on the world."

27 March, 03:43 Hours Local (UTC 14:43, March 26)
Amundsen-Scott Base
South Pole, Central Antarctic Plateau

Jason downloaded the email packet from the Iridium satellite and began decrypting the compressed message. "Looks like only one, Dr. J. But it's a big one."

"And? Who's it from?"

"Give me a minute." After a bit, Jason leaned toward the screen, a wrinkle between his bushy eyebrows. "That's weird. It's asking for a password to complete the decryption process." He looked up at Julia. "We don't password protect things from the Iridium system."

Julia paced behind him. Another of her patients was entering end-stage organ failure. If she couldn't get help soon, she'd lose him too. "Can't you just open the file?"

"Not without the password." Jason continued to peck away at the keyboard. "Where was your last scientific mission?"

Spinning around, she stared at the man. "What the… scientific mission? Jason, what are you talking about?"

He pushed his chair away from the console and pointed at the screen. A question in purple letters flashed on a background screen of bright pink. "Bamako in southern Mali."

He typed "Bamako" and hit enter. Another purple-lettered question appeared. "Location of your son's tree house?"

"What is this? Twenty questions?"

Jason chuckled. "Someone really wants to be sure it's you. I guess."

"Eucalyptus tree," she answered. He typed.

The screen blacked out to be replaced by a spinning blue globe. A winking icon flashed in the upper left corner. "I guess we go here." Jason tapped the icon.

Again, the screen dissolved to be replaced by a video chat window divided into three sections. One marked DARPA, one FT DETRICK, and one *USS ARLINGTON*.

"What the hell?" Jason questioned. "We can't video conference over Iridium. it doesn't carry enough bandwidth. Hang on." He rattled a few keys and stared dumbfounded at the text scrolling across the screen. "It looks like they switched satellites when the uplink loaded. I don't recognize this address or this satellite system."

The DARPA globe dissolved, and the image of a woman appeared.

"Fuck." A dark eyebrow rose. "Shit, can she hear me?" The base commander turned to Julia.

"Seems so, Jason. Way to present a professional image for the NSF." Julia pushed him out of the way and pulled another chair up. "I apologize for my coworker, Madam President."

"Not like I haven't heard it before, Doctor Alexander. Our other meeting participants should be along soon. I'm here with Doctor Ratcliffe," A burnished gold head of curly hair popped up over the president's shoulder and Andy gave a small wave.

"Hiya, Andy. How're things?"

"Could be better, but we're making progress on this end. We'll be sending you some special toys—" He was cut off as the other screens filled with faces.

The president interjected, "Are we all here?" A round of affirmatives answered. "Good, let's get started. Doctor Alexander, I believe you know Doctors Williams and Talley as well as Doctor Ratcliffe."

"Yes, ma'am."

"Very good, I need to introduce our other participants, Doctor Tabitha Aronoff, Chief Surgeon, and Captain Cassandra Stanley aboard the *USS Arlington*."

Julia dipped her head in acknowledgement. "I know Captain Stanley. It's a pleasure to meet Doctor Aronoff." She smiled at the young physician. "Thank you for caring for James." A nod acknowledged her gratitude.

"Good, let's get to it. Captain, please."

Cassie slid into the center of her camera feed and smiled at Julia and the others. "Julia, I am so glad to see you. James sends his best. He's running the boat while Tabitha and I work on our project." Cassie winked at her. Julia's heart leapt to hear James was well. "I'm going to turn this over to Doctor Aronoff and allow the medical professionals a chance to hash this out. Doctor."

The chief surgeon's face filled the screen. "Eight days ago, the first of my crew began showing symptoms of the Paris Contagion. Following this initial case, another five also presented with varying symptoms. The *Arlington* is lucky. We've had no new cases after the initial six, and only two are in critical condition. Captain Stanley and I were discussing needs and next steps for their care when the captain made an interesting observation, an observation which radically changed the tack of my tracking and tracing efforts."

All the heads in the video windows moved closer to their screens, the physicians anxious to hear her discovery. "She stated we had been at sea with no contact from the outside prior to the first case. Therefore, the Contagion had to have come from somewhere on the boat. If not from person-to-person spread nor an original patient zero, then where? This question initiated an analysis of activities for the patients as well as events on the *Arlington*. After cross-checking personnel roster assignments with three weeks of the ship's logs, we have found the source of the Contagion." A gasp rose from the speakers, and Julia sat up straight.

"What a novel concept. It's contact with a thing not a person," Andy Ratcliffe mused, extrapolating from Tabitha's initial comments.

"That's correct, Doctor." Tabitha frowned into the screen. "It seems it was on the mail."

A cacophony of words spilled over the video link as everyone spoke at once. The president broke in above the fray. "People, quiet. One at a time, or we'll never get anywhere."

"Doctor Williams, your thoughts? Questions?" the president prompted.

Deidre asked, "Doctor Aronoff, what are you saying? It can't be in the mail. This virus is very fragile. It wouldn't survive in an aerobic environment for more than a few hours without a host."

"I didn't say it was in the mail. I said it was on the mail. I'm not sure how it's surviving or what it needs to survive, but we found evidence of open mail in each of the patient's quarters. Four days before patient zero presented, we received a large mail drop. All but one of the patients received packages from home. Each package contained a variety of items from food stuffs to new mobile phones to mp3 players and movie discs as well as other personal items. The wrappings from each of the five packages, including the internal packaging material, were found in the recycling bins of their quarters. We've collected all the mail received in the last mail drop and have them under quarantine."

Deidre interrupted. "Doctor Aronoff, you stated you have six patients, but only five had direct contact with their mail."

"That's correct. The two IT specialists share quarters. I believe one got it from their package and the other contracted it directly from the first by personal contact. This is the only patient-to-patient contact infection I am reporting. I don't have the lab or equipment to go further with this. I have no way to evaluate the packages or their contents aboard ship."

Doctors Talley and Williams excitedly spoke at the same time. "We need those packages."

"And samples of body fluids and tissue from your patients," Williams said.

"Already on the way to DC. I hermetically sealed everything in bio-bags and sent them via Super Hornet to Fort Detrick a few hours ago. You should get them soon."

"Very good, Doctor. This is the first positive step toward understanding this disease that we've had so far. Anything else to add?" President Haley led the discussion with a firm hand.

"Nothing from the *Arlington*, ma'am. I could use some help with treatment suggestions, though. My patient zero is in critical and failing condition."

Julia's mind was racing. *On the mail…on the mail…on the mail. Oh, shit.* "Ma'am, patient zero here was my head of logistics. He handles the distribution and organization of all materials for the crew and base." Julia drew a deep breath. "He died yesterday of massive organ failure. My third patient, also a logistics tech, is failing fast."

"We need anything he touched or opened, Julia," Deidre stated.

Jason broke in. "Not going to happen. We're isolated here. With the current weather, we cannot get a plane in or out."

Andy Ratcliffe interrupted. "We're working on that, sir. I asked our group over in propulsion to have a go at getting something on the ground and out again."

"Err… okay. Thanks." Jason sat back. "You've got some powerful friends, Dr. J," he mumbled.

"Doctor Ratcliffe, I believe you also have something to recommend for treatment."

"Yes, ma'am. When SARS-CoV-2 struck, DARPA initiated a number of projects focused on the treatment of viral infections which cause cytokine storms and cascade organ failure. One of the projects was successful. It was the design and production of a filtering system. The filter removes the viral load from the blood stream of a critically ill patient, allowing the compromised immune system to recover. I would like to try this on your patients.

"However, it requires a hemodialysis setup and a surgeon capable of placing a jugular venous catheter for blood removal and a pulmonary-arterial catheter for blood return. These patients don't have enough time for an arteriovenous fistula or graft to heal prior to starting dialysis. So, the catheter method is required. The needed filters have been sent to the *Nimitz* for distribution to the Pacific fleet."

"Andy, how do I get them? One of my patients is critical and others are failing. I have the needed hemodialysis equipment, and I can place the catheters with our medic's help."

Andy Ratcliffe smiled at Julia over the video link. "As I said, we're working on that. I didn't know if you had the dialysis equipment, so I held off sending them your way. We'll get them off to New Zealand as soon as we're off this call."

"Very good. I am pleased, people. Let's make this work. I want a report back as soon as Doctors Aronoff and Alexander have treated their patients. If this works, we can begin mass-producing the filters and make them available globally. Also, I want a way to get material in and out of the Amundsen-Scott base now," the president ordered. "When will that be ready, Doctor?"

"In the next hour I'll have a way to get to the South Pole, ma'am," Andy stated with a firm voice.

"Get this done, people. I have another meeting, but I need results now. We need a plan to find and stop this." The president disappeared from the DARPA video screen.

"Thank you, everyone," Julia said. "I feel better now. Andy, I'll wait to hear how you're going to get materials to me."

"I'm on it, Julia. I should have something within the hour. Keep this link open."

Julia looked at Jason, who nodded. "Will do, Andy. And thanks, again."

The DARPA physician winked at her. "South Pole is easier than southern Mali. At least the penguins aren't armed with surface-to-air missiles."

26 March, 12:32 Hours Local (UTC 16:32)
Situation Room, White House
Washington, DC, United States

President Haley rushed into the nearly empty room. Although her motorcade had raced across the DC area from DARPA headquarters back to the White House, she was running late for this video conference. "Brandon, do you have the hookup complete?"

"Aye, ma'am. You're live to Bardowie Castle via an encrypted satellite. Just hit this button to activate the conference." He pointed to one of several comm studs on the console in the center of the table.

"Thank you, Brandon. Now, everyone out. I need the room."

"Ma'am, you'll need information and expertise. We need to be here."

The president turned on her National Security Advisor. "No, Harvey, I don't need you here. I have all the information and expertise I will need to decide on a plan. You will have my decision on action steps and orders. Now, out. All of you."

The security technicians began closing down their workstations and filing out of the secure room.

"Madam President, this is highly unusual. You cannot make these decisions in a vacuum. You need—"

She spun toward the CIA director. "I don't like to repeat myself, but I will since you obviously did not hear me the first time. I have all the information I need to make an informed decision. I do not need any information from your organization, sir."

"You do need my information." The director's eyes flashed.

The president pulled out her chair and gracefully sat. "Very well. If

I need your information so critically, tell me: what is the missile complement currently being prepped at the Tonghae facility?" The man frowned at the question. The president pressed on. "What is the makeup of the last warhead shipment to arrive at the North Korean launch site? What are the current troop estimates amassing along the Chinese-North Korean border and the associated strategic weapons allotment being shipped there?"

The director hesitated, then puffed out his chest in a show of dominance. "Where are you getting your information? No one should have that information outside the individuals in this room and at Langley."

"I asked you very specific questions, sir. If you cannot answer, then you do not have critical information. Therefore, you have nothing I need. Your presence is redundant. I have that information and can answer those questions. I will develop the next steps in our action plan to stop this maniac. To do so, I will utilize resources outside of your organization, resources which have the information I need to make the best decisions for the United States of America. Now, get out of my Sit Room."

The CIA director lost it. "It's that bitch, Michaels. She's a rogue, ma'am, and not to be trusted." His voice rose with each word until he was shouting. "Her techniques are antiquated, and her sources are enemies of the state."

President Amanda Haley placed her hands flat on the walnut table and pushed herself up slowly. She turned to the red-faced man. "Sir, you are relieved of your position and duties. Your security clearances are stripped as of now." She nodded to the Marine sentry. Her voice was a whisper, but it lashed the spluttering man. "You did not recognize the resource you had within your organization. Your action to remove this resource jeopardized the security of this nation. You are not fit for duty." A small nod accompanied her rebuke.

The Marine sergeant placed a hand on the ex-director's shoulder. "This way, sir. You no longer have the clearance to be within this room or on White House grounds. My men will show you to the gate." The sentry turned the man forcefully and marched him from the room.

She noticed her National Security Advisor. He stood white-faced just inside the door. "Do you want to be next, Harvey?"

"No, ma'am."

"Then I suggest you remove yourself and head back to your office at the DOD. I won't need you anymore today."

Once the room was clear, Amanda Haley sat back down and rested her elbows on the table, head cradled in her hands. She blew out a frustrated breath and rubbed a tired hand across her face. She was exhausted. Not a good state to be in when making world-impacting decisions. But sleep was a luxury she would not have for some time. If she ever slept again.

Now this. If the ex-CIA director spoke to the press, her decision process would be called into question. She had to hope he knew the risk to national security if he spoke out of turn.

Lifting a crystal tumbler off a leather coaster, she took a small sip of water. Major world powers were amassing their military assets against a country who shouldn't have the ability to provoke such action. This was a nightmare of epic proportion. *How the hell did we get to this point?* she wondered. *And how do I get us out of this mouse trap without loss of life?*

She punched the comm stud, and the wall monitor filled with the face of the one resource she trusted. "Samantha, shall we begin?"

26 March, 17:47 Hours Local (UTC 16:47)
Library, Bardowie Castle, south of Glasgow
Scottish Highlands
Ancestral Home of O'Rourke Clan

A request for the video link flashed on the large monitor. Sam punched the accept call icon and smiled when the face of President Amanda Haley appeared. She seemed a bit frazzled, but Sam could relate. Especially, given the intensity of their last days. "Good afternoon, ma'am."

"Samantha, shall we begin? I apologize for being late, but I needed to hear from the *Arlington* and Doctor Alexander at the South Pole firsthand. Seems the *Arlington*'s surgeon may have discovered the possible infection method for the Paris Contagion."

Sam smiled at this news. "As to that, I believe we may have found the source."

"Repeat, please. You've found the source?"

"May have, ma'am. Seems Grant got lucky again. An email address supplied by Doctor Kim belonged to a Doctor Ri. She's a bio-specialist physician at the Hŭngnam Fertilizer Complex in Hamhŭng." Sam looked down at her notes. "It appears Doctor Ri is the designer and producer of a modified germ agent. She utilized CRISPR technology North Korea received within a humanitarian aid program at the height of the COVID-19 pandemic."

The president's faced hardened. "Samantha, are you telling me North Korea bastardized a gift and made a bioweapon?"

"Yes ma'am, it seems so."

"Samantha, this is a nightmare come to life." President Haley was angry, very angry. She ground her teeth and spit out the next word. "How?"

"Doctor Ri's workstation contained the original technical specifications for a CRISPR program designed to aid in the production of monoclonal antibody therapy to fight COVID-19. The technical instructions, various chemical precursors, and the program itself came with the aid package. Doctor Ri took that CRISPR program, along with the needed biochemical precursors, and modified a virus to create a germ agent. The detailed modification steps are documented on her workstation."

The president's anger morphed into disbelief. She sighed. "What can we do?"

"I'm sending these data over to Doctor Williams at Fort Detrick. Hopefully, she will be able to determine what the original virus was and perhaps design a vaccine or treatment protocol." Sam paused for a moment to organize her thoughts. She was out of her depth with the medical implications of this bioweapon. "Also included in the data is information about a bacterial host. It appears one of their microbiologists accompanied a Chinese research team to Svalbard and participated in the discovery of a bacterium with unique characteristics. The microbiologist returned to North Korea with samples of this cold-weather bacterium. Doctor Ri then modified it. She increased its durability and infected it with the viral germ agent. Unfortunately, we didn't find any information about how they are releasing the agent into the world."

"Samantha, this is an attack against the population of the world. Pak is truly mad." President Haley deflated with the news, and she shrank into her chair. "How can we possibly stop this?" The video microphones barely picked up her whispered words.

Sam drew a deep breath and squared her shoulders. "Now we know the possible origin and we have the ability to identify the virus, the doctors can work their magic and figure out the rest." The president seemed lost in thought and Sam paused.

After another deep breath, she continued. "Ma'am, as to stopping Pak, we've developed a detailed plan for just such action. It is militarily aggressive. It will stop him and destroy the bulk of his strategic and tactical arsenals as well as curtail his ability to manufacture more." This statement brought the president's head up. "With the information about the origin of the Paris Contagion, I believe our allies in the region will agree to it."

"Very well. I trust you and Grant, Samantha. Let's review your recommendations. Shall I ask Admiral Benson in?"

Sam turned to Lord O'Rourke and raised an eyebrow. She didn't want to include the Chair of the US Joint Chiefs without giving the prime minister a chance to do the same.

He nodded and said, "That's probably a good idea. Once we've reviewed the recommendations with your president and the admiral, we will link in the head of our Navy for the development of action steps to accomplish our goals."

"Thank you, sir." Sam turned back to the camera. "Bringing Admiral Benson on is a good idea, Madam President."

"I agree. He's on his way to the Situation Room. Once he arrives, we can review your plan. Also, please send your findings on the Paris Contagion to Doctor Ratcliffe at DARPA-SafeGenes. He's working with Williams now."

"Of course." Sam nodded to Grant, and the young woman's fingers flew over her keyboard. Grant gave Sam the okay sign. "The package is on the way to Doctor Ratcliffe, ma'am."

"Very good." The president stepped away from her monitor. The screen filled with an image of the White House on a blue background.

When the president returned to the video conference, Admiral Benson was sitting beside her. "Sir." Sam tipped her head in salute.

"Samantha, I understand you've found more interesting information about Pak."

"We have, sir. Grant was able to infiltrate a secure workstation of a bio-specialist and retrieve information about the possible construction of the Paris Contagion germ agent."

"Yes, yes. The president filled me in. Tell Grant well done."

Grant looked over Sam's shoulder and smiled at the admiral. "Thank you, sir. I appreciate it."

The president asked, "Is Lord O'Rourke on the line with us?"

"Here, Madam President." The prime minister settled into the chair next to Sam. Grant reached around Sam and punched a key on the secure workstation. The screen split into two images, one for Sam and one for her uncle. "If we could begin, the colonel's plan is complex and contains multiple moving pieces. If approved, we will need to get assets in place in short order to meet such a tight timetable."

"I understand. Samantha?" the president prompted.

"As His Grace stated, our action plan has multiple interwoven layers, which are all timed to commence on fourteen April. It is critical we are in position to act in the twelve hours before 09:00 on fifteen April.

"As you know, that date is the Day of the Sun, a national holiday in the DPRK. 09:00 is the standard time for their military parade to begin. A military parade of this magnitude requires detailed coordination among all the branches of the military. However, we did not find a parade schedule in any of the workstations we reviewed. This tells us there is not one scheduled this year." The president tilted her head in question. "There were, however, a number of detailed schedules concerning the movement of troops and matériel. Given these factors, we believe Pak will use this day to begin his campaign and move against the combined South Korean/United States forces along the DMZ. Concurrently, he will move his reserve paramilitary troops against China along his western border.

"With his timetable in hand, our recommendations are multitiered, multinational, and synchronized." Grant tapped a few keys and a list of recommended action steps appeared on Sam's portion of the split screen. "This list shows the needed high-level steps for each military category. First: complete shutdown of his computer capabilities and countrywide networks. Second: disabling of his regular Army troops and conventional tactical armaments along the DMZ. Third: finding and destroying his submarine fleet, especially, his seven Golf II boats with their nuclear arsenals. Fourth, in conjunction with the Chinese special forces, disable the reserve and paramilitary troops and their embedded strategic weapons along the western border. Fifth: remove all the centers of science and technology located across the country. Last, the destruction of his multiple production facilities for military hardware with their associated stores.

In all of these actions we hope to minimize impact on the civilian population. Given this is a national holiday, most individuals should be at home and not at work, adding distance from our targets."

The president sat forward and asked, "Samantha, you said multinational. If our focus is stopping Pak, how can it impact others besides regional allies?"

"We have mutual support and protection agreements with our long-term, established allies in South Korea and Japan. I am unsure how far we can push our new alliance with the Chinese."

The president interrupted. "President Liu and I have an agreement of mutual support at this time. We both agree… " Her voice trailed off. She looked down. When she looked back into the camera, her voice could crave stone. "We both agree, we will use all means to stop Pak."

Lord O'Rourke was the first to recover from this news. "Madam President, you realize what you are saying, correct?"

"Yes, sir, I do. Both the United States of America and the People's Republic of China will utilize all our military capabilities to neutralize Supreme Leader Pak. I plan on calling President Liu as soon as we finish this meeting. We will need contacts within his forces amassed on the western front to coordinate any steps you recommend."

Lord O'Rourke appeared gobsmacked. Sam broke in. "I believe our allies old and… err… new… " Sam stuttered before picking up her train of thought, "…will agree to take action against North Korea." She realized what this meant.

The United States of America was allying with China, a first since the Second World War. But this is what Pak was forcing the world to do. Alliances were forming for peace, regardless of history or conflicting ideology. The theory of asymmetric conflict was playing out in reality—a weak, insignificant state was forcing the world's superpowers to ally in an effort to stop him.

"However, to your question, ma'am, a critical action step is the need to eliminate satellite computer facilities outside North Korea. Pak's Korean Computer Center has branches in China, Syria, Germany, and the UAE. Taking actions against those centers will require informing the host nations of our plans to remove facilities on their sovereign soil. I'm not overly worried about Germany or the UAE, as we have excellent relationships with both nations. If you are comfortable with our new Chinese alliance, then actions in Beijing should be doable with some warning. It's Syria which concerns me. I fully expect Syria to forewarn Pak if we share our plans for destroying his computer facility in that country."

"I agree we shouldn't have any issues with the Germans. The UAE will take a bit of diplomatic finesse. However, the Paris Contagion has hit them hard, and sharing where this came from should help. Syria is a true problem," President Haley said.

Lord O'Rourke spoke up. "Madam President, allow the United Kingdom to handle Syria. We have a large contingent in-country, monitoring ongoing peace efforts following the fall of al-Assad. We should be able to infiltrate and take down the computer facility easily." Sam noticed Grant smiling with agreement. Sam thought she was mentally designing another job for the Special Boat Service teams.

When the president nodded, Grant replaced the images of Sam and her uncle with a map of the DPRK. The map was annotated with colored lines and locales. "Given Pak's previous threats and confirmation from Doctor Kim, we believe he will begin his assault using strategic weapons—nuclear or chemical—along the Chinese border. He doesn't really care what happens to the Chinese or their lands, so the use of strategic WMD in advance of troop attacks is logical.

"He will follow up with conventional weapon attacks across the DMZ. In contrast to China, here he will want to protect and preserve the bulk of South Korean arable land, infrastructure, and populace to facilitate his goal of reunification.

"We do not believe he will utilize biological weapons on either front, as the incubation period is too long to support an immediate advance of his military. In addition, his reservist troops along the western front are not inoculated as thoroughly as those along the DMZ. They would be vulnerable to any distributed germ agents."

"That makes sense, Samantha," Admiral Benson stated. "What are the current troop numbers at each front?"

"Along the western front with China, Pak has amassed his paramilitary and reserve units, with a force strength of two million and growing. They are drawing troops from within the general population. This force is supported by a minimal arsenal of conventional weapons—artillery, mechanized infantry trucks, and armored vehicles, including tanks. Most of these assets have been pulled from their fixed defenses along the DMZ and moved west. The troops as well as the military hardware appear poorly organized and scattered haphazardly along the rear of the front lines. These movements have been confirmed visually."

Sam pointed out several locales on the map. "These are concrete bunkers and launch pads being hastily prepared for the scheduled shipment of strategic weapons due from various depots across the country, all headed for the western front. Most are truck-mounted, short and intermediate-range missiles capable of carrying nuclear or chemical warheads. Currently, these are moving along the one highway and two rail lines rapidly rebuilt after Typhoon Palawan. Doctor Kim has identified these as routes he would use. She also told us about other stockpile locations in addition to those we found by remote means."

Sam paused to take a sip of water before she continued. "Our latest estimate of troop strength along the DMZ is 1.3 million soldiers. Seventy percent are currently located at or near the border. The remainder are in holding areas around Pyongyang. These units are tagged to defend the capital should the need arise. This force is supported by an interlaced web of fixed long-range heavy artillery, antiaircraft artillery, and surface-to-air launchers—some of their SAMs are capable of carrying nuclear warheads. The troops at the DMZ are supported by a large number of medium-to-heavy artillery and over 8,500 tanks and armored vehicles." Sam highlighted the base and unit locations on the annotated map.

"Their Air Force has limited capabilities. Aircraft are aged out and the embedded equipment is technically deficient. They suffer from gross pilot inexperience. Our forces should be able to remove these assets with preemptive strikes." Sam said.

"Naval forces are stationed along both coastlines." Sam nodded to Grant, and a map of the southern Korean peninsula replaced the list of action steps. "I am most concerned with identifying the location of their Golf II submarines. These represent the greatest threat to our Asian allies and the remainder of the globe. Though their submarine fleet is estimated at seventy or so, only the seven Golfs have been retrofitted to launch ICBMs. Their refit pens are located here, here, and here." She pointed to three coastal towns. "Their successful launch of an ICBM from a Golf II confirms their capabilities to do so at will. These assets could easily slip away from the Korean Peninsula and attack Japan, the United States, or other Pacific countries, using nuclear weapons. Finding and neutralizing these boats are critical components of our plan's initial steps."

Admiral Benson leaned away from his screen. "Samantha, hold on a moment, please." When he refaced the camera, he had a paper copy of her map in hand. "Are you suggesting a naval blockade of the country? That would be a difficult thing to do without support from Japan and South Korea."

Sam nodded. "I agree, Admiral. For that reason, we recommend utilizing the information in the Tonghae CO's workstation. The base commander had a complete list of the nuclear warhead transfer orders for the Pukgeukseong-1 missiles allocated to the submarines. We believe we can now locate them easily and disable or destroy them in their pens."

"Interesting," President Haley commented. "You believe he has pulled all those submarines in to load the missiles?"

"I believe he has, ma'am. We've noted several moving at the surface into their harbors at night, headed to their enclosed docking facilities." Sam swallowed hard before voicing her conclusions. "Pak is preparing for a major offensive on all fronts."

She began to summarize their recommendations. "Grant was able to plot the locations as well as the requested armaments for all forces by using the information in the Tonghae spreadsheet. This allowed us to place assets geographically and plot movements of their support needs across the country."

"Excellent job, Samantha. Grant, without your little movie project and sojourn to Nyŏngbyŏn, we wouldn't be as prepared as we will be. Well done, both of you," Admiral Benson praised. "I expect we can begin detailed planning and asset allocation from these data."

The admiral turned to focus on Lord O'Rourke. "Your thoughts, Prime Minister? Will you be able to mobilize British assets in support of our efforts?"

Lord O'Rourke rubbed a finger over his chin and nodded into the camera feed. "Admiral, the United Kingdom is prepared to offer any and all needed naval personnel and assets." The admiral smiled.

"With one caveat. We will not land British personnel in either South or North Korea, especially along the western front. Our relations with the Chinese are not as good as yours. We are still trying to negotiate a resolution for the Hong Kong troubles. I do not think the Chinese would be pleased to see our troops in the line of battle." He leaned forward. "Our naval assets are another thing entirely. I recommend utilizing our attack hunter-killer submarines as needed in the coastal blockade and removal of surface assets as well as destruction of their Golf fleet."

"Thank you, William. I appreciate the assets as well as the clarification of your country's position. We are grateful for your assistance." The president nodded to Sam. "Anything else, Colonel?"

"One last thing, ma'am. We, that is Grant and I, feel Pak needs to be neutralized." Sam saw the president frown and heard Admiral

Benson draw a breath. "Conflicts will continue, and risks will remain if he continues in power. The people will still face untold misery." Sam looked at Grant and she nodded encouragement. "He must be removed from power. The North Korean people need a chance for freedom and growth. Their country is in ruins from the storm, and the populace are slowly starving to death. Our recommended military actions will cause further harm to the country's infrastructure. An interim government should be put in place, perhaps under the auspices of the United Nations.

"If the Tonghae data are correct, and I believe they are, Pak will be at the coastal facility for two days and one night. This gives us a location, a timeframe, and an opportunity to act."

President Haley paled and shrank away from her camera. "We don't see any other—" Sam tried to explain before she was interrupted.

"Samantha, thank you for your detailed recommendations. Please send the framework to both of us immediately. I, with Admiral Benson's help and the needed resources from within our government and military, will move forward. I ask you and Grant be available to answer questions as they arise. Also, Grant will need to continue monitoring her cyber links for new information or changes in the North Korean schedules and plans."

The president stopped and drew a long breath. "Your work will stop a madman from destroying a good portion of the world. As to removing Pak, please send your recommendations directly to Admiral Benson but not to the White House. I will take them into consideration. Again, excellent work, both of you." The president stepped away from the camera feed.

Admiral Benson filled the silence. "You heard her Samantha, get those plans over here ASAP."

"They should already be in your secure server, sir. I did not attach the final recommendation, but I can send that over now." Sam was stunned by the abrupt departure of her president. She glanced at Lord O'Rourke. He seemed as shocked as she was.

"Do not include your final recommendation—we will hold that as 'ears only.' Now I order the two of you to take the rest of the day and night off. We can't risk losing our best analysts to fatigue or illness as things develop. Also, Prime Minister, please send along a list of available naval resources in the area which we can incorporate into the plan."

Lord O'Rourke said, "It's posted with Samantha's file, Admiral."

"Aye, sir," Sam and Grant replied in unison. The admiral's connection winked out.

Grant raised a questioning brow.

"I don't know." Sam shook her head. Her shoulders slumped as an imagined weight settled on them.

The realization of what their plan meant to the United States and the world was nearly unbearable. She doubted she'd be able to rest. Their abstract scenario formed from analysis just became reality. This wasn't a game anymore. The United States and her allies would attack North Korea. If that wasn't terrible enough, she had recommended the removal of the sovereign leader of a foreign nation. The implication of her recommendation—assassination.

28 March, 02:32 Hours Local (UTC 06:32)
Drone Control Room, Propulsion Laboratory
Defense Advanced Research Projects Agency—DARPA
N. Randolph Street, Sub-Level 5
Arlington, Virginia, United States

"Do we have contact yet?"

The pilot never took his eyes off his heads-up display, his hand steady on the joystick. "Not yet, Doctor Andy. Should be near enough to spot the base within the next sixty seconds. We're getting intermittent signals from their VHF-localizer beacon." Andy couldn't see anything but darkness on the screen before the young airman.

A disembodied voice from McMurdo Flight Control crackled over a speaker. "Polar Drone One, you've passed south of 88 degrees. VHF glide path capture in two minutes. Autopilot is disabled. GPS positioning is disabled. Come left three degrees." The pilot tweaked the joystick. "Prepare for Polar Heading and Track reversal. Ignore all compass readings. VHF-glide path capture in one minute. Prepare to reduce altitude. Base altitude is 2.835 thousand meters true. Barometric pressure 946 millibars, set altimeter. Winds are 37 knots, with gusts to 49. Strong gale conditions. Possible blowing snow at ground level. Temperature is minus 45 degrees Celsius. Wind chill on the surface is minus 104 degrees Celsius. You have five minutes on the ground before engine restart is compromised.

"You have the beacon. On glide path. Descend and maintain three thousand meters. Below glide path. Correct altitude." The pilot pulled back a fraction. "On glide path. Descend and maintain twenty-nine hundred meters." The air controller's voice was steady.

Although the young pilot appeared calm, Andy noticed a trickle of sweat trailing down the young man's temple. "You should have the base in sight. Once you have the runway, you are cleared to land." Andy squinted at the black screen. Nothing. He watched the altimeter slowly tick down below twenty-nine hundred meters.

"I have the base. Thank you, Control." A few hazy spots of brightness appeared on the screen.

"Base has you in sight, Polar Drone One. Good flying, Jackson. Crew will meet you at the hub. Recommend maintain engine revolutions. No more than five minutes."

"Five minutes, roger."

Now the screen was awash in white light as high-intensity halogen lamps flooded the landing zone. The drone continued its descent. Two lines of strobing white lights appeared. The drone was centered exactly between them. The lines began to waver as the young pilot fought the winds to remain aligned with the runway. The screen jumped once and then again. "Touchdown, I repeat Polar Drone One is on the ice. Taxiing to the hub."

Seconds after the drone halted at the hub, figures swarmed out of the darkness and the camera jostled. "They're pulling the hatches open. Hope they're not frozen shut. It's wicked cold there."

Doctor Andy and Jackson were in a temperature-controlled room over fourteen thousand kilometers away in Virginia. "Well done, son."

"Not over yet, Doctor Andy." The young man smiled a lopsided grin up at him. "We still have to switch the cargos, taxi out, and take off. Then, be scooped up by Mother One. Lots to do."

Andy knew this was true. But even if they couldn't take off or crashed in the process, DARPA still got the virus filters to Julia at the South Pole. She would be able to save lives now. They were processing the packaging samples from the *Arlington* and reanalyzing the tracking information for patients around the world using Doctor Aronoff's idea about the mail being contaminated. It was just a matter of time before they had the source.

Doctor Williams had discovered the resilient bacterial host, *Terrimonas arctica*. The germ agent was identified. They knew it was a highly modified hemorrhagic fever.

"One step at a time, Andy," the doctor said to himself. "Source, method of transmission, and how it was produced. Time. It's always about time in the hunt for answers." Andy felt like he hadn't stopped since SARS-CoV-2.

"Polar Drone One, Control."

"Go ahead, Control."

"They have the cargos transferred. Should be buttoning up now." The camera image jarred as the ground crew slammed the cargo doors closed. "Hold one, Polar Drone. Cargo door three is iced over." The crew began pounding on the cargo door. The image jerked back and forth as the aircraft was jostled.

"Engine Two is beginning to run rough, Control. I'm seeing fluctuating oil pressure. Will need to leave soon, or I'll lose the engine and we'll be stuck."

"Roger that. Forwarding information on to ground crew."

The camera continued to swing erratically as they tried to slam the cargo hatch closed. Then, one final slam. "I'm all green on the hatches, Control."

"Roger that. Ground crew is headed back into the hub. Clear to taxi in fifteen seconds." The young pilot revved the engines and pivoted the drone around 180 degrees. "Winds are three-six with gusts to five-five knots. Polar Drone One, you are cleared for taxi and take off at pilot's discretion."

Jackson pushed the throttles forward and the drone bounced toward the ice strip. Once centered between the line of strobing white lights, Jackson accelerated down the runway and rotated the craft into the black sky. "Polar Drone One is airborne and headed to rendezvous with Mother One."

"Mother has you on their radar, Polar One. Safe flight."

Jackson huffed out a long sigh and relaxed back into his seat. "We're almost home, Doctor Andy. Once we're scooped up, Mother will fly us to New Zealand."

"Great. I'll let New Zealand Health Services know we're on our way. They'll be there to transfer the cargo safely to the F-18 Super Hornet for ferrying back to Fort Detrick." Andy clasped the young man on the shoulder. "You did very well, son. Great job."

"No worries, sir."

Warning lights flashed on the console and alarms rang out. All hell broke loose.

"Shit." The pilot flipped several switches and fought the joystick. "We're losing Engine 2. Oil pressure is falling. My guess is we were on the ground too long and the oil began to freeze in the reservoir. Now, we don't have enough to circulate efficiently and cool the engine." He flipped a toggle on his joystick. "Mother One, Mother One. Polar Drone One has lost engine two. I repeat we've lost an engine. We will not make it to pick-up coordinates on one engine." He reached across the console and flipped several pages in a laminated ringed binder. Jackson ran a finger down a list of latitude-longitude coordinates. "Request pickup at Rendezvous Three. Repeat need pickup at Rendezvous Three."

"Polar Drone One, Control. Activate loxodrome. Repeat, activate loxodrome." Jackson flipped more switches and turned off his heads-up display.

Andy watched the attitude indicator tip twenty degrees as the pilot released the joystick. An autopilot program took over flight control. "Err... shouldn't you be flying?"

Jackson snorted. "I am flying, just with the help of the computer. We're flying a rhumb line away from the pole. I can't fly it accurately enough without compass headings, and I don't have a compass heading when all orientations read north at this latitude."

The drone maintained a banked attitude of twenty degrees. Andy watched as the degrees of arc slowly decreased on the attitude indicator.

Jackson pulled a pencil out of his flight suit pocket and took a piece of paper off the pad at his elbow. He drew a circle and placed a dot near the bottom of the southern hemisphere. "This is the globe of the Earth, and this is the South Pole." He pointed to the circle and dot and drew an arcing line away from the dot. It spiraled outward as it moved farther away from the polar dot. "Once we arc away from the pole and cross north of the eighty-eighth south latitude, we can reinitiate our GPS and heads-up display."

Ah, a great circle route, Andy thought. "Got it."

"The loxodrome software package developed by NASA considers our position relative to the pole and to the end point we want to arrive at. In this case, Rendezvous Three—the spot where Mother One will pick us up."

"Polar Drone One, climb and maintain thirty-two hundred meters."

"Roger, climbing to three-two hundred meters." Jackson turned a dial on his autopilot, inputting the new altitude.

"Maintain altitude. Once loxodrome is complete and Polar Drone One is in level flight, recapture and maintain heading zero-one-zero true. Mother One will meet you there."

Jackson sat forward and gently placed his hand on the joystick. Andy felt his body physically leaning with the little drone as it arced away from the pole. Andy straightened up and chuckled. "Sir?"

"Sorry, Jackson. Just felt myself tilting in sympathy with the drone's altitude."

"No worries, sir. It is a common thing. We have to fight doing the same. If we tilt our heads or lean one way or the other, we can fly off course, even with the HUD. Also, you can become spatially disoriented by tilting your head as you look at the display, especially in IFR conditions. Straight neck. Eyes forward. Fly true."

The young drone pilot shrugged. "And today, I don't feel like explaining why I planted a five-million-dollar UAV into the ice because I got lost in the dark. Kinda looks bad on the record, don't you know?"

They flew the loxodrome for another ten minutes before McMurdo Flight Control broke the silence. "Polar Drone One, you should have Mother at your eleven o'clock."

Jackson leaned toward the screen. "I have Mother." He tweaked his joystick to align his approach with the rear of the aircraft.

"Mother is dropping the ramp. Prepare to shut down engines on their command. McMurdo Flight Control out."

Jackson flew toward the rear of the giant C-130J Super Hercules aircraft. Andy could see two rows of strobing lights on the descending ramp opening from the rear of the aircraft.

"Ramp descending, Polar Drone One." Mother One stated.

"I have the beacons," the young pilot confirmed.

"Ten seconds to engine shutdown," Mother reported the time to intercept.

Jackson placed his hand on the throttles, as the drone began to waver in the prop wash of the four large turbo engines on Mother One. He kept the tiny craft centered between the strobing lights.

The camera feed bounced. "Shut down. Shut down."

Jackson pulled the throttles back and toggled off the engines. "Polar Drone One is onboard. Turning for home."

"Well done, son. Excellent job." Andy clapped the young pilot's shoulder.

28 March, 03:31 Hours Local (UTC 07:31)
Oval Office, White House
Washington, DC, United States

The president sat at the Resolute Desk and prepared to initiate the call to President Liu. A cup of Earl Grey tea, laced with honey and milk, steamed at her elbow. Per her chef, the honey was added to supplement her limited food intake.

Who could eat, knowing what she did? She was exhausted. The last fifteen hours were a blur, but plans on all fronts were moving forward. The samples from the *Arlington* were being evaluated. She was waiting on word from Doctors Williams and Talley. DARPA had successfully landed a drone at Amundsen-Scott Base, in a blizzard no less, and delivered the new filters to Doctor Alexander. Samples from the base were on their way back to Fort Detrick.

Hopefully, Doctor Aronoff was correct—the germ agent was somehow embedded in the mail. This was a fact she couldn't release yet. Panic would ensue, and people would begin destroying the mail. The large package carriers would be financially ruined. No, she'd hold that information secure for now. Once they had a source, a systematic search for more of the contaminated items could be initiated. She knew this plan would lead to more lives lost, something her heart bled for, but she couldn't lose sight of the bigger picture. Pak must be stopped.

Samantha and young Grant had made tremendous progress, and their recommendations for military action were strong. Admiral Benson with his team of planners at the Pentagon were fleshing out the recommendations into actionable steps as well as the integration of needed assets from South Korea, Japan, and the United Kingdom. He would sequester these planners within his office suites until the plan was implemented. They could not afford any leaks whatsoever. She would get the needed contacts from President Liu to integrate his military into the admiral's staff for action planning. Then it was in the admiral's hands.

So many parts and pieces. All moving independently, yet so

dependent on one another for critical timing. She picked up her cup and took a sip of the hot, sweet liquid. Warmth filled her. but her soul continued to shiver.

Amanda Haley's mind kept cycling back to Samantha's final recommendation. How could it not? Would she order the capture and assassination of the sovereign leader of another country? Could she? How could she not? Everyone agreed the man was a psychopath. He would destroy the world, or a good portion, if allowed to continue. This madman controlled an arsenal of WMD in all forms. He'd already released a bioweapon of devastating lethality. He'd demonstrated his control over and willingness to use nuclear weapons.

Samantha was convinced he also controlled an unmeasurable stockpile of chemical and biological weapons. A sliver of ice slid down Amanda's spine again. She replaced her cup on its saucer. It would take so little of some agents to kill off the world. His biological weapons seemed limited, but if it were anthrax or another trans-species virus plague? Then what?

The outer door swung open, and her secretary peeked around the jamb. "Three minutes, ma'am."

"Thank you." Her secretary smiled and pulled the soundproofed door closed.

She took another sip of tea, allowing the warmth to push away some of the icy fear which threatened to overwhelm her. The large comm center on her desk buzzed, and she picked up the receiver. "Madam President, I have President Liu for you on a secured line."

"Thank you, Brandon. Put the call, please." The line buzzed as the two encryption devices talked to each other through the secure US satellite.

"President Liu, thank you for speaking with me." She paused. "I believe we are ready to discuss specifics. But first how are your doctors doing with the Paris Contagion?"

A short bark of rueful laughter shot down the line. "Not well, I'm afraid. The first infections went undetected in Hong Kong. Now, the spread seems limited geographically. Beijing and Shanghai have been most hard-hit. Our doctors are coping as best they can, and we are releasing medical supplies as needed. There are no reported cases in rural and western China."

"We have several of our epidemiologists working on a new theory. I hope to have more information soon. And you will be my first call once I know more."

"I would be grateful, Madam President."

The Chinese president switched gears. "Concerning military planning, I must say I am amazed at the speed your analysts prepared a course of action. It has been only a few weeks."

"We have both been busy. I understand your four divisions are in place and waiting for orders?"

"Touché, Madam President." The slightly built, gray-haired Chinese man smirked into the camera. "You are correct. They are ready. What are we to do to remove this madman?"

Amanda sat upright and nearly dropped the handset. Did Liu know about the recommendation to eliminate Pak? What are his analysts saying? Where is he getting his information? Does he have assets in North Korea? Does he have assets here or in the UK?

Stop this now, a voice shouted in her head. *You're being paranoid. That's why you and the admiral decided to leave Samantha and Grant in Scotland, safe and protected from foreign agents. Away from any potential preying eyes and ears. No one knows where they are. Let this be, Amanda.*

"We are ready as well, sir. If you would share the names of your staff, I will forward this information to Admiral Benson and his cadre of planners. They will be in direct contact and can jointly prepare the coordinated operation."

"I will supply the names once we complete our discussion." The Chinese president tilted his head and regarded Amanda. "I need to ask again, Madam President. Are you willing and able to complete the task before us? We cannot start something of this magnitude without a willingness to see it to completion."

Amanda carefully considered his question and what it all meant for the United States of America.

Decision made. Resolve filled her. She leaned toward the video picture. "Yes, I am committed to this action and to its completion. In addition, the United States will protect the health and safety of the North Korean populace as much as possible. Our plan takes their welfare into account both with timing and targeting."

"I understand. Given the sparsity of population along our mutual border and our desire to not invade the country proper, we can abide by that principle as well. More importantly, Madam President, the People's Republic of China has no desire to occupy the Democratic People's Republic of Korea nor to take over the country. But what are your thoughts on what happens after we complete this task before us?"

"That is an interesting question, sir, and one which has kept me up most nights. As you may know, I am bound by law to present military actions to Congress. Under the stipulations of the War Powers Resolution, I must notify them of preemptive strikes. I will time my presentation to the commencement of our joint actions. Simultaneously, I will have our ambassador to the United Nations present a statement of action to the Security Council. I hope to have all our allies sign this statement before it is presented."

"China will sign such a resolution, Madam President."

Liu's body language remained relaxed. However, she knew her next words would be confrontational. "Following this Security Council effort, I will recommend a humanitarian action plan to the entire United Nations Assembly. Rebuilding North Korea is not something either of our countries wants to do alone. Nor should we. This is an instance where the all countries must participate. After all, Pak represents a clear and present danger to the world."

Amanda felt her energy flag. "Further, we must find a way to allow the North Korean populace to take part in their country's restoration. They must be willing to participate with us. We cannot dictate how they do this. The world can provide the monetary support along with needed materials to feed, clothe, medically care for, and rebuild; as I am sure there is much pent-up need, not only from Palawan, but from decades of militarization."

She paused to carefully consider her next words. China was not a democracy and did not embrace democratic thought. "My hope for them, Mister President, is North Korean citizens will gain individual liberties while embracing societal responsibilities."

Liu Qishan's voice was a whisper when he next spoke. "Madam President... Amanda," President Haley realized this was now a personal conversation. "I believe we want the same thing. We will walk this road together. You and I. the Peoples Republic of China and the United States of America. We are on the same path."

28 March, 09:34 Hours Local (UTC 08:34)
Library, Bardowie Castle, south of Glasgow
Scottish Highlands
Ancestral Home of O'Rourke Clan

Lord William O'Rourke returned to the castle early in the morning. The UK military leaders authorized the commitment of military naval assets and personnel. They selected key staff to send to the US to work with Admiral Benson's planning team. Now he was waiting on the call from President Haley to confirm their commitment. He wanted to hear what she'd learned from President Liu. He felt strongly about not committing United Kingdom ground forces to any of the actions but needed to know if the Chinese were going to insert any major naval forces.

The secured communication unit buzzed, and he picked up the handset. "Madam President."

"Good morning, Your Grace."

"And to you."

"Your presentation with your military and intelligence leaders went well?"

"It did. I have authorization for all the steps we discussed. The planning staff under Miranda McNally will be departing for DC within the next hour or so."

"That is good news." Lord O'Rourke heard the president draw a deep breath.

"I had an illuminating discussion with President Liu. He agrees with our plans and will commit staff to preparing our joint effort."

The British prime minister heaved a sigh of relief. "That's stellar news. I am still concerned about a confrontation between our forces, but if both countries have the same desire to minimize that happening, so much the better."

"True." The president paused and the secured line went silent for a moment. "In addition, Liu stated Pak must be dealt with."

That hit home. "Did he now?"

"Yes, and moreover, he agreed neither of our countries wish to takeover or occupy North Korea. In fact, Liu stated he was not planning on crossing the western border of North Korea at all. Further, he agreed to commit resources to rebuild the country. As to Pak, there was an implicit commitment to do what was needed to remove him, but I am unsure what the Chinese definition of 'remove' is."

"Indeed." O'Rourke's mind raced. He was too familiar with Chinese inuendo and deception. "Knowing the Chinese, I would recommend caution. They may see this as an opportunity for another country to do their dirty work. This portion of the plan should remain secret between our countries. If Liu stated he did not wish to invade the country, his forces will be a good distance away from Pak's supposed locale on fifteen April and the commencement of our operations. Unless the Chinese are also planning a covert action to remove him, we may be able to proceed without interference."

William O'Rourke paused and thought about what he must say. He decided to be upfront. "Madam President, the United Kingdom is willing to provide resources to a covert action to capture and detain Supreme Leader Pak. We will not however participate in his execution or assassination. This is an action too far and the United Kingdom will not be party to."

He lifted his water and took a sip against his suddenly dry throat. "Our military leaders, with the foreign secretary and MI6, agree permanently removing him would create an unfillable void and destabilize the country at its time of greatest need. Therefore, once captured, we recommend presenting him to the International Court of Justice in The Hague to stand trial for crimes against humanity. We believe this is a solution which would garner international support, producing a public, non-partial judgment outside the borders of North Korea." He sighed and leaned back in his chair. "Especially when the origin of the Paris Contagion is revealed."

"I see," the president stated softly.

He pressed on. "I believe the court's actions and highlighting his crimes would teach the North Korean populace of his evil and debunk his propaganda. Educate them about the characteristics needed of an appropriate leader. And show the remaining Pak family members the world will not stand for a repeat of Pak's actions. We believe the country needs to heal from within."

Both leaders paused to consider his words. "Thank you, sir. I appreciate the position you and your country is taking." She sighed. "And, I do believe you have given me the solution to a problem which has haunted me." The president of the United States stated unequivocally, "Let us capture and detain the man. And utilize the International Courts to bring justice to North Korea and the world."

30 March, 07:47 Hours Local (UTC 11:47)
BioSafety Level 4 Containment Room
Infectious Disease Laboratories
US Army Medical Research Institute for Infectious Diseases
Fort Detrick
Fredrick, Maryland, United States

Deidre Williams frowned while she studied the virus under the scanning microscope in the negative pressure isolation box. She had successfully isolated the germ agent from the lymph nodes, liver, and spleen tissues of Patient Zero. All the sampled cells were infected by the virus. The small, single-celled organism had infiltrated and co-opted the reproductive mechanisms of these cells to produce the proteins it needed to proliferate. The viral particles were filovirid— filamentous particles which appeared in the shape of a shepherd's crook, a "U" or a "6." Some were coiled or toroidal, and others branched.

After sending non-vital, irradiated samples to the other Level 4-lab for Mike to provide genomic classification, she waited for his analysis of the bioengineered germ agent impatiently. With his results as the starting point, she would try to reverse-engineer the genome back to its original composition. Concurrently, George Talley and Andy Ratcliffe were analyzing all the package materials recovered from the patients aboard the *Arlington* and those returned from Amundsen-Scott Base. So far, they had found nothing. Deidre's level of frustration was escalating with each passing hour.

The pager on her belt chimed, and she removed her hands from the isolation box's neoprene gloves to punch the accept button. "Yes."

"I've got your starting point, Doctor Williams." Mike's voice was muffled through the positive pressure hood she was wearing.

"Can you give me a half an hour to get back to my office? I need to decontaminate."

"Will do. I'll see you in your office. Sandwiches are on me."

Deidre laughed as Mike disconnected. She proceeded out of the Bio-Safety Level 4 lab. He was always trying to feed her. That was a good thing, she guessed. She couldn't remember her last meal. Her stomach growled with agreement.

After a shower and a change of clothes, Deidre headed back to her office. She arrived to find Mike setting out plates and glasses on a cleared desk. "Ahh, Mike, I didn't need you to clean up my office."

"No worries, ma'am. All the stacks are undisturbed, just relocated." He indicated the carefully lined up piles along one wall near the door.

Both researchers laughed. Deidre said, "Let's eat while you fill me in on your findings."

To the side of their plates, Mike arranged a series of electron micrographs, genomic maps, and a pencil-sketched cartoon of a spiky snake. The drawing appeared to have a head and a tail.

"Okay, Mike, I give. What's with the Toon?"

"Not a Toon, ma'am." He pointed to the drawing "That is the structural representation of your virus."

Deidre sat and reached for her fork. "Really?"

"Really. Your virus is made up of seven viral proteins and a non-segmented negative-sense RNA strand nucleocapsid encapsulated within an envelope which appears to be derived from proteins within the bacterial host. In this instance the *Terrimonas arctica* bacterium. It has approximately nineteen thousand bases in the single RNA strand. It's the spikes that are important." Mike took a large bite of his roast beef sandwich and chewed.

Deidre was fascinated. Mike had characterized this germ agent and went on to develop a structural analysis and hypothesize about its functionality. "How are the spikes significant?"

"Kinda like they are in SARS-CoV-2. The spike proteins facilitate cell fusion and entry. In this germ, the spike protein is a filovirus-glycoprotein."

Deidre dropped her fork; chicken salad scattered across her desk. "Shit. Ebola."

Mike shook his head. "Similar but different. This viral filament is smaller in diameter, less than eighty nanometers. If I were to guess, I would pick one of the hemorrhagic fevers. Not Ebola. Maybe Marburg. But that one is so rare, I don't know how anyone would get their hands on the primary stock."

Deidre pushed her plate away. Food no longer held its appeal. "Why Marburg?" Mike was onto something. He was the one technician who reviewed all the samples as they came into her lab. He had amazing recall and noticed differences in structural cell appearances. This allowed him to easily compare new samples with ones he'd seen before.

"The size and abundance of crooked filovirid-particles over other shapes and the appearance of the glycoprotein spike." He tapped one of the micrographs. "If one were to change this protein, make it spikier, it would enhance its ability to grab on to a potential host cell. The germ would have a higher degree of infectiousness. It could slice the eucaryote cell membrane more easily. But slides I've seen of incubated Marburg viral mats contain all the viral shapes. Statistically, each shape occurs equally, about 33 percent of the total. In these samples, more than 80 percent are the crooked shape. That is weird. Could that change another disease response? Like lethality?" He gobbled another bite of his sandwich.

"Possibly, quite possibly." Deidre's answer was distracted. Was this Marburg virus? She reached for one of her virology reference books and flipped to the Marburg virus entry. After a quick review, she looked up at her young technician. "Mike, you are a genius! I'd like a complete genomic map of the nineteen thousand bases. Can you do that?"

"Yeah." Mike placed his sandwich down. "But it's going to take some time. That's a lot of chemistry, and we don't have much bulk sample. What if we try RNA sequencing, followed by high-efficiency RT-PCR?"

"Like the COVID rapid test?"

"Just. We have some rapid test kits around here somewhere. We could sequence and then RT-PCR and look for mRNA. If the messenger RNA is found, we could type that to the ones found in the Marburg viral glycoprotein spikes."

Deidre jumped up and grabbed the micrographs and Mike's cartoon snake. "I'm going to see Doctor Talley. You're going to sequence our little germ down to the last base. All nineteen thousand, Mike. Including any mRNA you can gather from RT-PCR. And quickly."

She jerked her office door open. "I'd bet my lunch it's Marburg." Deidre didn't share her knowledge about Doctor Ri and the North Koreans. That information was need-to-know only. She was stumped as to how Ri obtained the old Soviet germ agent cultured from an original Marburg virus. Or, how she figured out how to modify it using CRISPR?

2 April, 23:38 Hours Local (UTC 03:38 3 April)
Oval Office, White House
Washington, DC, United States

The clock on the mantle struck the half hour as the president entered her office. She buzzed the Sit Room. "Brandon, I need a secure teleconference between the *USS Arlington,* Bardowie Castle, the Pasteur Institute, DARPA, and Fort Detrick as soon as you can, please."

"Of course, ma'am. Give me five minutes, and I'll have all the links established. Do we need the Pentagon?"

The president smiled, realizing he didn't ever miss a beat. She really needed to get Brandon out of the Sit Room, off the national security staff, and onto her own staff. He thought ahead and anticipated next steps. She appreciated that, especially in stressful times.

"No, but thank you for thinking ahead. Admiral Benson should be here within the next ten minutes."

"Very good, ma'am. I'll signal when the links are coordinated."

Amanda Haley sat in the ergonomic chair behind the large desk. Tonight, the chair did not relieve the pain in her shoulders or upper back. She felt her headache intensify.

Nevertheless, plans were coming together. Resources were being gathered. Allies were cooperating. And time was not the enemy it was just a few days ago. She had minimal concerns about the military plan. She had absolute faith in Admiral Benson and his staff, and in Samantha and young Grant. They had it handled.

But the news from Doctor Williams was a true shock. How were they going to manage this new information within the context of the global pandemic crisis? The news would create worldwide panic.

And then there was Pak.

A knock on her door pulled her from her morose thoughts. "Come." The door opened and her secretary looked in. "Don't you ever go home?" Both women laughed at the president's absurd question.

"Not until you're in bed, ma'am, and even then, I sometimes stay if things are brewing. Now, I'm here to tell you Admiral Benson just entered the east gate. He'll be here in five minutes."

"Thank you."

"Of course. May I get you anything? I understand you skipped dinner this evening."

The president was caught out and felt a blush bloom on her cheeks. "You got me, Beatrice, but make a note, please, I need to talk to the Secret Service. Seems my staff is conspiring against me."

"Not against, ma'am. We're all concerned about you and your health. Not eating is a bad thing. I'll have the chef send something down for you and the admiral. I'm sure he is as bad at missing meals as you are." The door closed behind the elderly woman.

The admiral and his aide arrived at the same time as the cart with their mandatory, late-night meal. The steward set out the place settings and uncovered dishes of a hearty beef stew with fresh bread and a fruit compote for dessert. "Seems we've been caught, Admiral. Our staffs' think we are not eating right."

Benson huffed but his aide barely swallowed her guffaw. "I see I am correct. Please, both of you, help yourselves. I will initiate the teleconference once we're settled."

The three filled their plates and took seats around the Resolute Desk, straw placemats covered the oaken top. "Can we eat and listen at the same time?"

"Of course, ma'am. We're used to eating with a rolling deck beneath us. This is a luxury." The admiral chuckled with his aide.

"Very well." President Haley punched a stub on her communication center. "Brandon, please open the conference."

"You're live in ten seconds. Please let me know if there are any comm issues." The speaker snapped and clicked as the various remote callers were allowed onto the secure link. "All good, ma'am."

"Very well. I have linked us together to hear firsthand what Doctors Williams and Auberguist have discovered about the Paris Contagion. Please hold any questions until their presentation is complete. Also, Doctor Ratcliffe, I would appreciate it if you would send a copy of this discussion off to Doctor Alexander at Amundsen-Scott. She needs to be kept in the loop as well."

"Of course, Madam President."

"Doctor Williams?"

A throat cleared over the connection, and Doctor Williams began her introduction. "Yesterday, I received the structural and genomic identification of the viral germ agent which causes the Paris Contagion. During a discussion with my technician, he made some interesting observations and supplemented these with a sketch of our virus." She held up a hand-drawn cartoon. "It is a crooked rod-shaped organism covered in recombinant spike proteins. In essence, a spiky snake. He noted the spike proteins and correlated them to those he observed in the SARS-CoV-2 virus."

"But this doesn't behave like SARS-CoV-2," Doctor Aronoff stated.

"I agree. These are completely different diseases. Mike was simply noting that structurally each virus utilizes spike proteins." Papers shuffled and Deidre Williams continued. "My technician further postulated we may be able to use a variant of the rapid COVID test to look for a messenger RNA. If we recover mRNA, we can sequence it and compare it to other filovirid particles. Try and get a match without sequencing all nineteen thousand bases in this virus."

The president noted Admiral Benson was sitting on the edge of his seat, obviously wanting to hear the results and willing Doctor Williams to get to the point. His Navy was so hard-hit anything with potential to end this disaster would be welcome.

Doctor Williams continued. "He also compared the general viral shape to other filovirid viral particles from other known hemorrhagic fevers. His discovery—this looks like a Marburg virus. And I agree. We are dealing with a highly modified Marburg hemorrhagic fever virus, one which has been edited for lethality and infectiousness."

When several of the doctors spoke at once, the president broke in. "Quiet, everyone. Let's ask questions, one at a time. Doctor Aronoff?"

"I suppose this information helps, but if I recall my epidemiology, Marburg, like Ebola, has no known cure or vaccine. We are left with the DARPA filtering system to remove viral load from the bloodstream and continue symptomatic treatment."

Andy Ratcliffe responded. "That's correct, but now I have a starting point, I may be able to build a vaccine fairly quickly using the Moderna mRNA platform."

"What else have you learned? Doctor Auberguist?" the president asked to wrangle the doctors back in line.

"A point of history, I suppose," René Auberguist said. "Marburg was first noted in medical records in 1967, when a group of German workers were exposed to necropsied samples from African green monkeys. They were harvesting kidney cells for medical research. That initial outbreak had thirty-one cases—twenty-five primary and six secondary infections. Seven of the infected died of the virus. Since then, several cases have been documented in Sub-Saharan Africa.

"The ones which concern me most are the record of infections at the VECTOR facility in the old Soviet Union in 1988 and 1990. These were the result of laboratory accidents. Both patients died. Obviously, the Soviets were attempting to develop a hemorrhagic fever germ agent for a biological weapon."

This information caused a collective breath to ripple across the connection from all quarters. The president spoke over the noise. "Doctor Williams, we spoke about VECTOR. You indicated you did not believe this came from there. Are you changing your mind?"

"No, ma'am. As we discussed, during the late 1980s, the Soviets would not have had the technology to modify their viral agent and create the Paris Contagion germ. They simply would have cultured enough for experimentation and stockpiled the rest."

"Thank you, Doctor. What else have you learned that is significant for our discussion?"

"Modifications are noted in the spike proteins. These changes would increase the infectiousness of the virus. Also, my technician noted a change in the statistical occurrence of crooked-shaped viral rods versus other shapes. The crooked shape makes up 80 percent of the total viral population in our samples. In an unmodified sample of the Marburg virus, each of the three shapes occurs in equal amounts. I believe this predominance of one shape increases the lethality of the germ in this bioweapon. We are currently sequencing the entire genome from the samples we have. However, this will take time to complete."

"Very well, thank you. Samantha or Grant, have you learned any more on Doctor Ri?"

"Grant here, ma'am. We have not. Our focus has been on the planning and execution of next steps. However, I can easily reenter Ri's workstation and continue to dig for more information. If the researchers could supply some keywords, it would be helpful with focusing my search."

Deidre Williams answered Grant's question. "I would look for any references to the Marburg virus, its taxonomic classification of Mononegavirales Filoviridae Marburgvirus *Marburg Marburgvirus,* any notes about measles, mumps, or rabies, and any other hemorrhagic fever, especially Ebola, which is in the same genus. Then I guess, locations: Svalbard or Spitsbergen, Koltsovo and VECTOR."

"Thank you, Doctor. That helps." They all heard keys begin to clatter over the conference link. The president raised an eyebrow at Benson.

"Grant is obviously already on it," the admiral answered softly.

"How are we coming with a source? Although I can't tell the American public to dump all their mail, we need to share some of this information."

Andy Ratcliffe piped up. "We are narrowing our analyses. There is nothing in the boxes, cardboard, or filler materials. We are now focusing on the other packaging materials, including the tape. We are chemically separating the adhesives from the cellulose acetate backer, and I'm guessing we'll find the bug there. Either inorganic capsules containing the virus or the *Terrimonas arctica* bacterium with the virus inside."

"Why there?" Doctor Aronoff asked.

"The Marburg viral particle is very fragile and would easily die outside a host in an aerobic environment if it were on the cardboard or within the filler. As Doctors Deidre and René noted, *Terrimonas arctica* bacterium was the first germ discovered in Patient Zero and the others around the world. This bacterium lives in permafrost soils above the arctic circle and does not move into mammalian species. It would be an excellent host for a fragile viral germ since it's hearty and can lie dormant for indefinite periods of time. The other thing I want to explore is the origin of all the packages we've recovered. If they all came from the same place, we might have a source before we isolate the mechanism of infection."

Doctor Aronoff said, "We did that here on the *Arlington.* The packages were from various companies—Apple, Samsung, LG, John Deere, Ingalls Industries, and Sumitomo Heavy Industries. We didn't find a correlation."

Melissa, the admiral's aide, spoke up. "Interesting. Some are South Korean companies, easily among the top fifteen in Asia." She paused.

Sam's frantic voice cut in. "The industrial zone. Grant."

"On it. One moment." Everyone heard more keys rattling and

silence before Grant began reading. "'Located ten kilometers north of the DMZ, the Kaesŏng Industrial Zone was closed for annual maintenance and upgrade per an announcement by Samsung on 1 October. All the North Korean workers were released.' There's no information about reopening or future plans. And nothing since from any of the other companies."

"With the complex's closure, Pak lost another contact with the outside world when those companies ceased operations in the Industrial Zone, ma'am." Sam elaborated. "If that is the source of the contaminated materials, it was a limited supply and is now halted."

"Let's go with this theory, but the South Pole doesn't receive mail during the polar winter." Andy wondered aloud.

The president took charge. "Does anyone have any other questions for the doctors?" No one spoke up. "Very well. I appreciate all the hard work and innovative thinking, people. Let's wrap this up. I will expect updates as more information becomes known. Especially, you Andy. If you find the source, please let me know as soon as you have something."

"Of course, ma'am. And I will send this information on to Julia immediately after we finish."

"Deidre and René, thank you for all your efforts. And Deidre, make sure your technician knows how much I appreciate his out of the box thinking."

George Talley answered for Deidre. "Madam President, that young man is headed for a promotion and a commendation of the highest order."

"I'll sign that when it's ready, George," the president agreed.

Admiral Benson concurred. "As will I, Doctor Talley. Send it through to my office when it's ready. We need to acknowledge and reward that kind of initiative."

"Thank you, Admiral. Consider it on the way."

Everyone dropped out of the conference call, leaving the three in the Oval Office. "Well, I am… " the president paused, "I guess I don't know what I am besides amazed and overwhelmed." She looked down at her now cold beef stew and winced. She knew her chef would give her what for. She knew there wasn't any time left. "Next steps, Admiral?"

"Planning is proceeding on course. We'll have everything in place within the next five days. British and American naval forces are rendezvousing off the western Japanese islands now. Samantha is continuing her detailed satellite image analysis and will have locations for the seven Golf II boats in the next day. Ground forces are preparing for a missile attack across the DMZ. THAAD is fully operational and will protect those troops as well as Seoul. We are preparing detailed plans for the combined special ops team to enter Tonghae and proceed to procure the package."

The president interrupted. "President Choi does not feel as confident as you are, Admiral. He is convinced THAAD will fail and Seoul will be badly damaged. The populace will be attacked with chemical and nuclear weapons."

"That's not going to happen, ma'am." Melissa chimed in.

"How can you be sure, Captain?" She leveled a frown at the young woman.

Melissa smiled thinly. "Pak doesn't want to destroy infrastructure in the south. This desire will limit his use of missiles along the DMZ. Also, we believe the colonel has identified all of those short and intermediate-range launch sites. Our drones will disable and destroy them during the night of 14 April to early morning of 15 April, as we concurrently strike Tonghae. We will remove any longer-range missile threats there. Colonel Michaels has identified more than 271 sites for the drones. This includes mobile targets still being deployed along the western front and threatening the Chinese troops across that border. Movement of matériel has followed the timetable recovered from Grant's cyber activities precisely. Not one variance has been noted."

"I'm glad you are so confident, Captain, but I do not believe in certainties when it comes to a psychopathic dictator. I believe he will have an ace up his proverbial sleeve and throw us a curve ball." The three chuckled. "I apologize for the mixed metaphor, but I cannot risk certainty in this situation. Something will happen we don't expect."

4 April, 09:30 Hours Local (UTC 1:30)
Presidential Offices, The Blue House
Seoul, South Korea

The telephone on President Choi's desk rang, and he slowly reached for the receiver. This was not going to be a good conversation. He knew from his ambassador in Washington the president of the United States was angry. Oh well, too bad. So was he. The US was not doing enough to protect his country.

With the Chinese amassing forces in the west, war was coming. It would move across his country and destroy everything. Nothing would be left to rebuild. He was sure of that.

"Good evening, Madam President."

Amanda Haley's rich voice traveled through the connection. "And good morning to you, sir."

"How may South Korea be of help today?"

He heard her chuckle. "I think that question needs to be turned around."

"Perhaps, but I understand things are moving ahead, and we will soon know our sentence."

"Don't be fatalistic, Mister President. I know the difficult position you and your country are in, but I do not wish to discuss those plans. Today, I am calling for another reason."

As she paused, his shirt collar was suddenly too tight. *Now what?*

"I need to know why you closed the Kaesŏng Industrial Complex in North Korea. I understand from company press releases the closure was to allow upgrades and maintenance."

Choi was shocked. They'd mothballed the complex in October. That was almost six months ago. "Yes, Madam President. It was a difficult decision to make, but we felt it was the best way to remove a source of tradable currency from North Korea. We... I had hoped this would slow Pak's militarization."

"Be that as it may, Mister President, you may have done more than that. Do you know how Pak was using the companies within the complex?"

"As I said, it was to halt access to western currency. The North Korean workers' wages were taken by the state and used by Pak."

"True and removing this specific monetary source may have slowed his military buildup some. But I'm talking about the North using the companies. Do you know about North Korean biological weapons?"

"Biological weapons? Of course, we have always suspected he controlled a large cache of such weapons but nothing in Kaesŏng. The plants were inspected frequently using sniffers and trained dogs to detect such things."

"Mister President, it appears your decision to close the complex has saved many lives."

"Lives?" President Choi felt whiplashed by her words.

"Yes, sir. We have discovered the source of the Paris Contagion." He rocked back in his chair. His country was devastated by this pandemic. No amount of isolation, shut down, or tracing could stem the tide of the disease.

"Madam President, please, I beg you. Get to your point." He felt his anger rise. "My country has suffered much from this deadly pandemic. We have been unable to determine the cause and source. If you have a source, you must share this with me... " He backtracked. "With the world."

President Haley said, "Sir, we only learned the suspected source thirty-six hours ago and are attempting to determine the method of infection. The reason for the call is to ask you to send your South Korean company representatives back into Kaesŏng and gather samples of packaging and shipping materials left in the complex."

"Are you saying my companies are the source of this pandemic? How dare you." He was nearly shouting, his blood pressure rising to dangerous levels. He stood and slammed a hand on his desk. Papers scattered.

"Mister President. Please. Calm down. No, I am not accusing you, or your companies, or your country. Sir, I believe Pak used your companies as a distribution point, embedding the Paris Contagion in the packaging materials."

Choi felt his anger drain away as suddenly as it had risen, and he sagged into his chair. "What?"

"To confirm our working hypothesis, we need samples of the boxes, filler, cardboard inserts, envelopes, and packaging materials. Can you recover these materials from Kaesŏng and have them sent to the United States?" She softened her voice. "Are you able to do this for your country? For the world?"

Choi Myung-yong couldn't speak. He was crushed by this information. How could that bastard use his country like this? What was the world going to do? South Korea would be blamed and punished. He couldn't comprehend the magnitude of this disaster.

His voice quivered when he said, "I am unable to answer this immediately. I would need to discuss such a need with the company CEOs and garner their help. However, I do not know if we will be allowed back in, given the military buildup of the last months. Pak may see it as a way to infiltrate his country."

"I understand the position you are in. I am not accusing South Korean companies or your country of complicity. No, in fact Mister President, I am praising you for an action which may have saved lives. By closing the complex when you did, we believe you shut off the viral source. That action prevented additional germ agents from being spread across the world. I must insist. You cannot tell the companies *why* you need these material samples. Do you understand?"

Did he understand? "Yes, Madam President." He modified his tone. "I understand what you are asking, but I do not know how to do that. I cannot order representatives from our companies to do something. And reentering North Korea at this time would be very dangerous for them."

"We need those materials as soon as possible, sir. If you are unable, I will find another way." Her voice hardened again, and he realized how important this request was.

The line was quiet as he thought. The president didn't interrupt. He would send his special forces team in under the guise of Samsung representatives. This company was the driving force at Kaesŏng. Pak would allow them in if told they were preparing for a reopening. Yes, that is what he would do. "I will handle this. Either I will recover the materials in the next few days, or I will call back and tell you I am unable to get into the complex. Will this suffice?"

"Yes, Mister President. I thank you. The world will thank you. You will save lives."

Yes, he thought. Save lives. But what of his country? Will his country survive the next days to be thanked?

6 April, 09:11 Hours Local (UTC 08:11)
Library, Bardowie Castle, south of Glasgow
Scottish Highlands
Ancestral Home of O'Rourke Clan

"We've got it, ma'am." Grant's words interrupted Sam's review of another set of satellite images from the western front. Doctor Kim had sent Sam a drawing of the launch pad design for the short-to-intermediate-range solid-fuel rockets. Its unique horseshoe shape with a pit dug in the middle of the shoe was easy to spot with satellite reconnaissance. So far, she'd found fifty-four being hastily prepared. The North Korean crews were making no attempt to hide the construction.

"Got what, Lieutenant?" Sam looked up from her stereoscopic viewer.

Grant waved a stack of printouts as she plopped down in the chair beside Sam. This is the most active Grant had been since Sam arrived. Her cheeks were pink and her breathing easier. The young woman was improving daily. Their cyber projects switched Grant's focus from her recovery to something challenging, something needed, something useful. "Ri traveled to Koltsovo for a six-month internship after she completed medical school in Switzerland. It was an exchange of sorts. One Soviet doctor went to the Hŭngnam Fertilizer Complex, and she went to VECTOR."

"Okay. And that tells us what?"

"Ri had opportunity and probable motive to steal from the Soviets." Grant shrugged dramatically. "I doubt the Soviets would just give her samples of the Marburg virus. She had to take them."

Sam rocked back. "True. However, there's something else to consider. How could she move a Level-Four biohazard agent out of the Soviet Union through numerous international airports back to North Korea?"

"Ah, this is where it gets interesting. She didn't fly as far as we can tell."

"Didn't… how'd she get back? It's a long way from the Ural Mountains to North Korea."

"Not if you take the Trans-Siberian Railroad." Grant smirked smugly.

Grant could be insufferable. Sam quirked an eyebrow and the young lieutenant grimaced. "Really, she took the train?"

"Seems so. Ri has a picture of a really weird bulbous building as her screensaver. Cynthia figured out it was a photo of Biotechno Park in Koltsovo. We dug deeper. Found notes on her internship and a travel log of photos across eastern Soviet Union. She's got snaps of her tickets and everything."

This set off alarms bells for Sam. Were they going too deeply into these workstations? What fingerprints were they leaving? Their entry had to leave a trace of some sort. "I need you to stop digging through the computers, Grant. We're so close to starting Operation Razor's Edge, we can't risk being found now."

Grant looked like Sam had slapped her. "I'm careful, ma'am. We're not leaving a trace."

"I know how good you are, but you recall what President Haley said?"

Grant looked puzzled.

"She very clearly stated, 'We all know how good at cybercrime the North Koreans are, especially after the last Bitcoin incident.' They're in planning mode too. Getting ready for 15 April. This creates a heightened sense of urgency for them. Given enough time, Grant, North Korea will find you. So shut it down. I can't believe we'll find anything else useful at this late date."

"I understand. But I want to keep the movie bot running. It may be useful in the future."

"Fine." Sam waved her hand. "But only that. Let's not push our luck any further." Sam picked up her satellite phone to call Admiral Benson about the link to Koltsovo.

6 April, 18:30 Hours Local (UTC 09:30)
The Sea of Japan (East Sea)
USPACFLT with the Japanese Fleet
Captain's Mess, *USS Arlington*
CGN-47, Ticonderoga-class Guided Missile Cruiser

The steward entered and filled glasses at the beautifully set table. Her senior officers were expected for dinner with the captain. It was the first time since the Paris Contagion blew up they could take the time to get together. The DARPA filters had proven to be a godsend, and her sick crew were on the mend. Though all the sick would be transferred from the *Arlington* to Walter Reed, Doctor Aronoff felt each would recover. Cassie adjusted a fork at one of the five places as she waited. This would also be her opportunity to outline the *Arlington's* upcoming role in Operation Razor's Edge.

Cassie's XO ducked through the hatch and came to attention. He snapped off a perfect salute. Cassie laughed but returned his salute. "Really, this is what we've come to?"

"No. Just wanted to acknowledge the commander of this wonderful boat. I am pleased she is back. Crew and captain are functioning at optimal levels."

Cassie's eyebrow rose at his comment. "Really, and we weren't before? Trying to tell me something, James?"

He hesitated for a moment before he realized she was teasing him. He grinned. "Err… right. Not at all, ma'am."

"I see, let's—" The rest of her comment was interrupted by the arrival of her other officers.

The meal was wonderful, and now, everyone was relaxing over coffee and chocolate cake. They had a good discussion about the upcoming operation and the role the *Arlington* was assigned. Cassie was to command the combined United States cruiser and Japanese VTOL-carrier and British submarine fleets for Operation Razor's Edge.

She raised her glass. "I want to acknowledge the amazing job Doctor Aronoff did. The impact of this deadly situation was minimized due to her actions."

Everyone toasted Doctor Aronoff, and she blushed to the roots of her pale hair. "It was a team effort, ma'am. The medical staff went above and beyond. Adapted as the situation evolved. All our patients got optimal care. And the staff provided it without one break in protocol. None of my staff contracted the contagion."

"Yes, Doctor, but you directed the band and got it done. You saved lives. Well done." The others nodded in agreement.

"Be that as it may, ma'am, I hope the folks at DARPA and Fort Detrick find the source. I feel certain our hypothesis about the mail is a good one." This comment led to a discussion of how the officers and crew pulled together to stem the tide of this virus. They'd all saved lives.

"You said hypothesis. Do we know anything else about the source besides the packages the crew received? I've wondered if any of our onboard supplies were contaminated as well. I have three techs sick. That's a lot from one department and 50 percent of our total patients. Our maintenance supplies might be another point source besides the mail," Steven Carlson, the ship's chief engineer, stated.

Cassie said, "We've sent our data on. Now, it's in the hands of the experts."

"Oh, my god!" James Alexander sat up so suddenly, he nearly dropped his coffee cup.

"What is it, Commander? Are you all right?" He waved away the Doctor's question.

"Ma'am," he said as he turned to Cassie, "I have the complete list of everything transported to Amundsen-Scott Base." He looked at Doctor Aronoff. "Would that help the researchers? I was using the operations reports out of McMurdo to track my mom. Their system acted like a scheduling and reporting authority for each flight to and from the South Pole. It includes all the supply manifests."

Doctor Aronoff jumped up. "May we be excused, please? I need to send these data off to DARPA." The young surgeon moved toward the mess hatch with the *Arlington's* XO hot on her heels. "Doctor Andy can sort those manifests. See if they need to warn the base about quarantining other supplies."

Cassie waved them on. She turned to the other two. "Finish your cake, or my steward will have my hide for wasting her dessert."

7 April, 17:23 Hours Local (UTC 04:23)
Amundsen-Scott Base
South Pole, Central Antarctic Plateau

"Julia," Andy Ratcliffe said, "I think that's all we have on potential sources. With these new data from the supply manifests your son gave us, I recommend you quarantine anything sourced from a Korean company, if not everything in the inventory."

Julia winced. They couldn't quarantine everything.

He went on, asking, "How are your patients doing?"

"Holding their own. We lost Coshair." Julia's heart clenched. She had done all she could for the young head of logistics before the viral filters arrived, but it had been too late. His organ failure was too advanced. "The others are improving. I plan on a second round of filtration for two of them." She smiled to herself. It was so good to talk to a peer about this overwhelming situation. Being the only physician was difficult. No wonder the last doctor left the deerstalker for the next one in this position. Being so alone and without a sounding board made it difficult to be sure of a diagnosis or treatment plan.

"That's fine. It sure can't hurt. Do you have enough blood and plasma to replace the volume damaged by hemodialysis?"

"I've plenty. We're lucky to have several O-negative folks here. I don't have to rely solely on synthetic substitutes." Julia thought about how the seventy-three healthy staff had pulled together. No one panicked. Everyone was helping out and doing whatever was necessary to keep the base functioning. "Any ideas about method? I can't shake the thought it has something to do with materials from logistics and supply. Two of my patients were in that department. It's weird the other three from the logistics department are okay so far."

"We're working that out. There's nothing in the packaging materials so far. I'm waiting on the results from our analysis of the tape used on boxes packed in the Kaesŏng Industrial Complex. The South Koreans have sent several cases of tape for our work. Our guess is the germ agent is there."

Julia rubbed her forehead. *Tape, why did that sound familiar?* Something was niggling at her brain. Something someone said about Coshair. "Let me know as soon as you have something, Andy. We need supplies from the base inventory. I can't quarantine it all or we'll freeze to death while we starve in the dark. And I for one do not want that to happen. James would kill me." They both laughed.

Her brain continued to itch. What was bothering her? Tape. It had to do with tape. Suddenly, it felt as though a lightning bolt shot through her. "How could I miss that?"

"What's wrong, Julia?" Andy leaned into the camera.

"I think you're right. It's in the tape, Andy. One of the logistics techs was bitching about Coshair at dinner, a day or two before he got sick. The tech was mad about always having to pick up after Coshair. Seems he pulled the tape off the boxes as he opened them. The tech couldn't understand why he didn't slice the tape like everyone else. Slicing, left the tape on the box." Julia swallowed hard. "Andy, the second tech to get sick was the one picking up after Coshair. He directly touched all the tape torn off the boxes."

"Julia, call your techs and ask them how they open their boxes."

She was already standing before Andy finished his request. "Hold on, Andy. I'll be right back. I need to go over to inventory control."

Less than ten minutes later, she was back, panting from running from one end of the base to the other. "That's it. All the techs agreed. They open the boxes by slicing the tape with their belt knives. Coshair was always leaving his knife somewhere and didn't have it most of the time. Then he would open the boxes by pulling the tape off and throwing the discarded tape on the floor. One of Dickerson's duties was keeping the inventory depot cleaned up. He would have handled all the discarded tape." She continued to breath hard.

"I think you're on to something. If we find the germ agent in the tape, we'll have the method of infection. Julia you may have solved it." Andy's excitement poured through the Zoom link.

Julia Alexander shook her head. "No, Andy, I didn't do anything. Just talked to a colleague about a difficult case. More heads are better than one. I'll quarantine the Korean items and make sure the techs slice the boxes open if we need something from one of those."

"Be that as it may, you're on to something. I wonder how pulling the tape is different than cutting the tape." Andy's whispered question was lost as Julia closed their Zoom call.

14 April, 06:00 Hours Local (UTC 21:00, April 13)
The Sea of Japan (East Sea)
USPACFLT with the Japanese Fleet
Captain's Cabin, *USS Arlington*
CGN-47, Ticonderoga-class Guided Missile Cruiser

It was 06:00 on the fourteenth of April aboard the *Arlington*. The crew was securing the boat for battle stations. Operation Razor's Edge would begin in eighteen hours. Cassie sat on the edge of her bunk and watched Sam pace across the blue carpet of her cabin. "You're going to wear a groove in the deck, Sam."

Sam paused and gave her a look. "So many things can go wrong, Cass. There are too many dependent parts. If one of them gets delayed or fails, it will impact all the others. It's like a house of cards. Pull one and the whole structure comes tumbling down."

"I know, Ace. But you've done your best. An amazing job given the timeframe and number of resources required in the integration. Operation Razor's Edge is a solid plan. Believe in it. Believe in yourself." Cassie stood and took Sam into her arms. She smiled up at her. "Unexpected things will happen. We'll adapt to those as we go. You know it's one of the strengths of the US military. We don't wait for commands from on high. We know what we're supposed to do, what the ultimate goal is, and we execute. If we need to make changes as the plan unfolds, we do."

Sam relaxed, and Cassie gave her a squeeze. "I know, but I still worry." She looked at her chronograph and grimaced. "It's almost time for the attacks on the satellite computing centers in Europe and the Mideast to commence."

"Why don't you head down to CIC and be there for the first reports?"

"Sounds good. I'll see you on the bridge once we hear from the centers in Germany, the UAE and Syria."

"Ping Grant and have her meet you there. I'm sure she's as anxious as you are."

Sam laughed sardonically as she left the captain's cabin. "I doubt that. Her belief in all things technical will overcome her worries."

SECTION EIGHT

"BATTLE STATIONS. ALL HANDS—BATTLE STATIONS. THIS IS NOT A DRILL." Klaxons sounded as Cassie slid into her command chair. Once the klaxons fell silent, she punched a comm stud.

"All hands, this is the captain. In ten minutes, we will begin Operation Razor's Edge. We have practiced. We are ready. First task for the *Arlington*—blockade the Port of Sinp'o. Two North Korean Golf II submarines are in their pens in the Mayang-do base. We will fire on the pens, catching them at home and destroying them there. If the North Korean submarines try to escape, we will take them out with all means available to us." Cassie paused and lowered her voice. "Believe in your training. Believe in each other. Believe in the *Arlington*." She released the stud.

She turned her chair. "Bring us to three zero five. All ahead full. Put us between Mayang-do Island and Sinp'o. Prepare to launch the LAMPS. Drop all sonobuoys. Bring the sonic depth charges up. Load the torpedoes. No one gets by us tonight."

The crew scrambled to do her bidding. Data began to fill the plexiglass navigation board. Cassie looked up at the clock. James stepped up next to her. "Five minutes, ma'am." She nodded absently.

As the *Arlington* prepared to blockade the submarine base, over two hundred drones were launching from bases in South Korea and Japan, headed to strategic targets across North Korea. Their primary mission— cripple the in-country computing centers. A second wave would target the known WMD-arsenals. A third and fourth flight would follow to remove North Korean military industrial complexes. They hoped to blind Pak as they declawed him.

USPACFLT command was distributed. This allowed each tactical group to focus on specific tasks within the complex, multifaceted Operation Razor's Edge. The *Nimitz* and her escorts were 250 miles south-southeast of the *Arlington* in the Sea of Japan. Super Hornets were launching from the *Nimitz* and F-15 Strike Eagles from airbases in South

Korea and Japan. All headed for embedded troop and artillery emplacements north of the DMZ. Six attack hunter-killer submarines from the United Kingdom were strategically placed along the coast, waiting to stop any surface naval movement. Their orders, remove all naval craft they encounter. The Chinese were simultaneously launching a heavy artillery bombardment into western North Korea. Chinese special forces in conjunction with US Navy Seal Team Two were moving to destroy the computing center in Beijing.

"LAMPS are away. Sonobuoys dropping. We'll be active in thirty seconds," Bryce reported from his sonar station.

"Very good. James, what does the satellite image tell us from the subbase?"

He handed her a copy of the image and pointed at a couple of bright spots. "The subs are home. Heat signatures indicate their powerplants are spun up, probably preparing to go to sea. The images Colonel Michaels shared yesterday showed munitions still being offloaded from trucks outside the pens. New images from six minutes ago show crew moving about the exterior of the building. The pen doors were still closed at that time."

"Bring up the TLAMS. Targets one and two will be in the pens. Let's catch them unaware." TLAMS were the Arlington's Tomahawk missiles. These subsonic cruise missiles were launched vertically from armored box launchers within the foredeck of the cruiser. Internal inertial guidance GPS directed the flight. Satellite imaging aided in target acquisition. Bomblets carried twenty-four canisters within each missile and could be concentrated on one target or sent to separate targets as needed.

"Tomahawks One through Six are online." The young firing officer flipped the covers off her Tomahawk controls. Her voice was hard and steady.

"Skip, transmission from the *HMS Unicorn*. They have acquired surface targets leaving the Port of Hŭngnam. Will fire on them once they clear the harbor," her comm tech reported.

"Thank you." Cassie looked at the board again. "Chief, any civilian shipping traffic in the area?" None was noted on the petty officer's navigation board, but Cassie wanted to be sure she wasn't missing any.

The CPO stood beside the large board and tilted his head, listening to information coming up from CIC. "All clear, Skip. We have no surface traffic."

Cassie saw James focus on the board as the sonobuoys came active and digital data began to fill the plexiglass board. "No subsurface traffic noted," he said after a few seconds, allowing the data to solidify.

"All stop. Deploy the port stabilizers. Fire missiles one and three on my mark."

The *Arlington* heaved to and settled in the calm waters. Cassie looked at the counter again. At five seconds to midnight, she began her countdown. "Five, four, three, two, one, and FIRE!"

The brilliant flash of burning JP-10 jet fuel exploded across the deck of the *Arlington* as two missiles erupted from their pressurized launchers. The command deck windows opaqued to preserve the crew's night vision.

The firing officer began to give the status of the missile deployment. "Missiles away. Wings are deployed. Air scoops are open. The turbofans are engaged." Several seconds passed. "Missiles have acquired their targets. Birds are autonomous and flying true. Impact in fifty seconds."

"We have SAM-launch. I repeat, radar has projectiles in the air," CIC reported. Cassie wasn't worried about this. At 550 miles per hour, her missiles were difficult to nearly impossible to shoot down.

However, if the North Korean ground crews were that alert and detected her Tomahawks, the US and her allies may be in for a bigger fight than anyone planned for. "Send a message to the *Nimitz*. Our birds are being fired upon. North Korean ground crews are alert and active."

"Aye, Skip."

James placed a hand over his ear. Cassie raised an eyebrow. "The *Unicorn* has launched torpedoes at two Najin Class Frigates running for open ocean. One direct hit. Boat is burning. Turning to reengage the second."

The firing officer gave an update on the Tomahawks. "Ten seconds to target. Trajectory is turning down to impact zone." Cassie leaned forward, willing the birds home. "Impact. We have impact."

Thirty seconds later, CIC provided an action report. "Direct hits. Satellite images show both buildings burning with secondary explosions."

"Retract the stabilizers and come to course zero-nine-zero. All ahead full. What are the satellites telling us about the frigates?"

"Second frigate is burning. First is listing to starboard. Survivors are in deployed rafts. *Unicorn* is proceeding to coordinates off Tonghae." James reported.

The *Arlington* swung to the east and leapt forward. Sam entered the bridge as the deck dipped into the course change. Cassie turned her chair toward Bryce, her sonar operator. "What have we got?"

"Other than the big boom from the Tomahawks, nothing is moving. All quiet below the surface, Skip," he reported.

"Let the LAMPS sweep for five more minutes, then return home. Pick up their buoys as they fly in."

She turned her chair around to the auxiliary station Sam was seated at. "Colonel, any word from the other fronts?"

"Nothing yet from ground forces. We have reports all the remote computing centers have been eliminated. We're waiting on word from the first drone sorties and confirmation the in-country computing centers are down." Cassie heard the relief in Sam's voice. She smiled and turned back to her navigation board.

Alarms sounded. "Nuclear detonation detected. NORAD has confirmed the detonation of multiple nuclear devices."

15 April, 00:13 Hours Local (UTC 15:13, April 14)
Command Bunker, Ground Tracking Facility
Tonghae Satellite Launching Ground
North Hamgyong Province
Democratic People's Republic of Korea

Supreme Leader Pak could barely control his rage. He beat the map table with his fists. "What is going on? Why aren't my orders going out to the commanders along the DMZ?"

The young communications officer bowed deeply. "Sir, we've lost all communications. We have no connection to our surveillance or communications satellites. Our computer network is down. We have no way to contact the DMZ at this time."

Pak swung around and slapped the officer across the face. "No, that is not possible. It is your incompetence and that of your staff keeping me from communicating. I want this fixed now." His shout echoed off the hardened concrete walls of the bunker.

If he couldn't issue orders on an ongoing basis in response to the attacks against his country, only the pre-issued primary orders for Phase One of Operation Dragon's Roar would be in effect.

14 April, 11:17 Hours Local (UTC 15:17)
Situation Room, White House
Washington, DC, United States

High-definition monitors on the wall at the far end of the room were all tuned to different battlefront images. As reports came in from the various hotspots, the satellite images changed to illustrate the new information. The main screen showed the satellite image of destruction at the Mayang-do submarine base. Admiral Benson leaned toward his aide. "Looks like the *Arlington* eliminated the first two boats, Captain." Melissa nodded, her gaze transfixed by the changing images. They were waiting for the news the other five submarines were destroyed. Things were progressing according to plan.

A major stood up at the front of the room. "Admiral, NORAD reports our Keyhole satellites have detected nuclear detonations." Everyone in the room turned to him.

Benson felt his heart stutter. He swallowed hard. "Where?"

"Along the western front. It appears twelve missiles were launched at the Chinese. Their missile defense system destroyed all but four. Those detonated fifty-five kilometers south of Baishan behind their troop deployment. The Chinese are implementing nuclear containment processes." A map of the western front filled the central monitor with the four impact zones highlighted by small yellow and black radiation symbols.

"What do we know about this area?"

Melissa spoke up, reading from her tablet. "Baishan is an industrial city with an area population of 1.2 million people, and four hundred thousand live within the confines of the city proper."

"All right. I need a list of resources we can send from the DMZ to support the Chinese troops." The admiral was interrupted by one of the comm techs.

"Sir, I have President Liu on the comm for the president."

Benson rose from his seat and moved into the secure communications booth. "Major, prepare to transfer the call to the Beast. I'm calling the president now."

14 April, 11:18 Hours Local (UTC 15:18)
The Beast—armored limousine, Presidential Motorcade
Washington, DC, United States

The secure line rang in the armored Cadillac, and the president's chief of staff answered. "Yes?" She listened. "One moment please." She held the receiver out to the president. "It's Admiral Benson, ma'am."

"Admiral, I am nearly at the Capitol."

"I understand, ma'am, but NORAD has reported four nuclear detonations along the western front. President Liu is on the line for you."

She felt light-headed and struggled to get some air into her lungs. Her chief of staff put a hand on her arm. "What?"

Shaking her head to clear her thoughts, she said, "Put the call through, Admiral." She turned to her new chief of security. "Felicity, I need you to stop the motorcade and get everyone out while I take this call." No one moved. "Now! We don't have time to waste."

"This is not a secure area, ma'am. It could be an attempt on your life."

"I don't think an unplanned call indicates a threat. Now, stop the vehicle." The president's voice was hard, and her security chief flinched. The chief spoke into her wrist mic. The car rolled to a stop. "You too, Stephanie. Please, get out."

Amanda Haley took several deep breaths and pressed the accept call button on the secure comm console. "Mister President, I've heard the latest. I'm so sorry. My god, how could he deploy nuclear weapons? What can I do for you? What do you need? What do your citizens need?"

"Madam President, the strike did not catch us unprepared. Our troops were ready for such an event. Most of the rural population was moved across the Liao River away from the conflict area. Luckily, none of the impacts were in populated or developed areas. Preliminary reports indicate the devices were very low yield. Less than ten kilotons each. We are moving containment resources into the area now." He hesitated.

Amanda bit her tongue to keep from interrupting his thoughts. "At this time, Madam President, the situation is in hand. It is decided we will not retaliate at this time. However, should Pak utilize nuclear weapons against populated or urban areas, we will respond in kind."

The Chinese were being prudent in their use of force. President Liu was warning her what would cause them to take action. As an ally should. "Mister President—Qishan—my heart goes out to you and your people. We can have additional containment resources to you in less than an hour. They are stockpiled along the DMZ. Please do not hesitate to ask. I will inform my commanders in South Korea to begin preparing these supplies."

"Thank you, Madam President. I will be in touch as needs arise." She heard him exhale loudly. "This attack reinforces our need to act against Pak as we discussed earlier. The battle was not even joined, and he utilized nonconventional weapons against another country. He must be eliminated."

"Plans to do just that are in place. We will know in the next six hours if they are successful. I will speak with you then." Amanda Haley's voice softened. "Again, the offer still stands, Qishan. We will provide any aid you need. You simply need to ask, and it is yours."

"Thank you. I believe the path we walk just became more challenging. However, there is nothing our two countries cannot accomplish when we are united. We will speak again soon." The line went dead.

A single tear rolled down the president's cheek.

14 April, 11:30 Hours Local (15:30 UTC)
Chamber of the House of Representatives
United States Capitol, Washington, DC, United States

The Chamber was filled to capacity. The balcony crammed with various press corps members. The Sergeant of Arms of the House of Representatives opened the rear door and called the members to order with his introduction. "Madam Speaker, the president of the United States of America."

The members of Congress rose and turned as President Amanda Haley walked down the center aisle to the speaker's dais. Her dark, gray-streaked hair was pulled back in an austere French twist. Her black suit over a black blouse matched the thundercloud marring her face. She stepped onto the dais.

Turning to the room at large she began. "Mister Vice President, Madam Speaker, esteemed members of the United States Congress. We are facing a national emergency. An overt attack has been launched against the United States of America and the world. The pandemic the world is fighting is the result of a bioweapon released by North Korean Leader Pak Sung-un." Gasps rolled around the immense chamber. The president continued, her voice hard. "I am here this morning to inform you, pursuant to the consultation requirements of the 1973 War Powers

Resolution, that a half an hour ago the United States military began actions of force against the Democratic People's Republic of Korea." The chamber exploded with noise. The president raised her hands.

When the members did not respond, the speaker of the house struck the gavel forcefully and shouted into the microphone. "Quiet! I will have quiet in the chamber." Slowly silence fell.

"Less than fifteen minutes ago, Pak Sung-un, the Supreme Leader of the DPRK launched twelve nuclear missiles against our Chinese allies along the western front. Four of the missiles successfully detonated behind Chinese lines." Again, the chamber exploded in shouts.

The president raised her hands for quiet before she continued. "No action has occurred at the DMZ. Our troops will attack across the DMZ if," she stressed the word "if," "Pak makes a deliberate show of aggression against South Korea. At this time, our drone forces are surgically removing strategic cyber targets and military assets across his country. The US Navy is hunting and destroying his fleet of nuclear missile submarines. Our allies in the British Navy are eliminating his surface fleet of three frigates, two of which have already been destroyed by one of their attack hunter-killer submarines. The remaining North Korean naval assets—one frigate and thirteen corvettes—will be hunted and destroyed in port or at sea by the British."

She paused to take a sip of water from the glass beneath the podium. Amanda needed to give the members of Congress time to absorb this information before she continued. They must listen and understand what she had to say next. The chamber was silent. Shock had settled over the assembled members of Congress. The press corps was equally stunned, but their cameras continued to roll. "Pak's computer capabilities have been eliminated within North Korea and around the globe at remote centers in Germany, the UAE, Syria, and China.

"We will continue our combined actions until all of Supreme Leader Pak's abilities to deploy his weapons of mass destruction are destroyed. We will eliminate his ability to produce new weapons." Another pause. She needed the members of Congress to *hear* what she said next.

"Our scientists and physicians at the US Army Medical Research Institute of Infectious Diseases in Fort Detrick and at DARPA have determined Pak's medical specialists at the Chemical Materials Institute in the Hamhŭng-Hŭngnam area designed and deployed the germ agent known as the Paris Contagion. North Korean doctors bastardized a humanitarian gift and created this bioweapon."

Amanda Haley looked out over the faces of the elected representatives of the United States. They were pale. Some had slumped back down into their seats. "Our medical experts are working to determine the source and transmission method for the pathogen. The Paris Contagion is a deadly virus. A virus Pak deliberately released on the world in an attempt to achieve his personal goal of world domination. We are hopeful, we will be able to defeat this threat soon.

"Our allied troops will be successful. They will destroy the North Korean military. They will remove Pak's weapons of mass destruction. They will eliminate his nuclear, biological, and chemical stockpiles. Once these actions are complete, we will *not* occupy the country."

She emphasized her point by leaning forward. Her grip on the podium tightened. "With our allies, we will provide the needed humanitarian aid and monetary support to rebuild the country. We will provide the general populace with the resources to feed, clothe, and care for themselves. Medical aid will be provided for those ill or injured. We, with our allies, have agreed we will give the North Korean people the freedom to determine their own destiny. We will aid in their efforts to rebuild a government and their country. The world will stand together in this effort." Her face was a mask of determination.

"The Joint Chiefs and I will continue to provide this body with real-time updates on the current state of affairs within the conflict zone. In addition, our medical experts are working on the next steps to stop the Paris Contagion." She turned and nodded to the vice president and house speaker. "Thank you."

She moved down the stairs and back up the center aisle. No one reached out to her. No one spoke to her. Amanda Haley owned the decisions she made. Decisions which sent the United States of America to war. She walked alone. This was her path.

15 April, 01:07 Hours Local (16:07 UTC, April 14)
Off the Coast of the Democratic People's Republic of Korea
Command Deck, *USS Arlington*
CGN-47, Ticonderoga-class Guided Missile Cruiser

"Reports are coming in. China has engaged North Korean ground forces along the western front. Satellite surveillance indicates heavy artillery is hammering the North Korean rearguard. The Chinese have advanced but are not crossing the Yalu River." CIC reported.

"That's all part of the plan," Sam stated from her auxiliary console position. "China will not invade North Korean soil. They will hold at the river and continue to utilize long-distance weaponry."

"Response to the nuclear attack?" Cassie asked.

Sam had considered this scenario for the last few days. What would the United States or the Chinese or the Japanese do if strategic weapons of mass destruction were deployed? "No retaliation." That drew a gasp from several command crew. "All indications are the weapons were very low yield and deployed in areas of little to no population." She sorted several of the images she'd brought from CIC. "We won't know about damage until dawn when the satellites can capture what the Chinese are doing to cleanup."

"Message from the *Chaffee*, Skip."

"Go ahead." Cassie swung her chair back around to face forward.

There was nothing they could do except execute their orders. She felt a chill run down her spine. This was going to get ugly before it was over. The North Koreans fought without the mores of conventional warfare. No, she realized, not the North Koreans. Pak. He lacked ethics and human morals.

"*Chaffee* reports four of the five pens destroyed at Ch'aho submarine base. Fifth pen was empty. Repeat, fifth pen empty."

Sam jumped up and turned toward the stairs. "I'll be in CIC. I need to hijack a Keyhole and hunt that missing boat. Heat signatures confirmed they were all in their pens yesterday."

Stop thinking bad thoughts, Cassie. Don't jinx this.

"Message to the *Chaffee*: 'Lay down a buoy net in the harbor. Uplink them to the satellites for data dispersal to the fleet. Utilize a standard search pattern in the harbor with all available acoustic means. Boat known to be in pen as of yesterday. May be lying doggo on the bottom.'"

The *Arlington* continued to cruise north-northeast. Things on the command deck were quiet as the boat sailed seventy-five miles out from the North Korean coast. Their next task was to protect the Boat and Seal team's mission into Tonghae. Cassie tried to relax into her leather chair. The plan would take on a life of its own as strike and counterstrike played out.

Sam burst on to the command deck. "I have the boat. As of two hours ago, it was cruising north by northeast along the coast, within the fifty-mile exclusion zone. It submerged less than twenty minutes ago off the coast of Iwŏn." Cassie realized this was where it all started. How ironic.

Cassie reviewed the navigation board. All her fleet members were noted in green. "Message to *HMS Queen Elizabeth*. 'Launch your LAMPS. Full spread of sonobuoys. We're searching for a submerged Korean asset. Last known location… '" Cassie turned to Sam. "Colonel?"

"40.3242°N, 128.6507°E."

"Embed those coordinates and send the message." She turned to her firing officer. "Prepare to launch the LAMPS. Full sweep. Bryce, go active. Let's fill the water with noise, people."

Data began filling the navigation board, and the chief petty officer added additional non-digital information as it became available. The *Arlington* was receiving telemetry from the various sonobuoy spreads via satellite.

"Change the scale on the board, Chief. I need to see one hundred miles of the coastline. Message to the *Chaffee*. 'Discontinue your search. Retrieve your buoys. Move south to Hŭngnam and prepare for Stage 3.'"

Data continued to update the navigation board, and Cassie relaxed a fraction. James appeared at her elbow, a steaming mocha latte in his hand. "This will help. Take a minute to breathe," he said in a whisper, as he handed off the cup to her.

"Thanks." The aroma of warm chocolate tickled her nose, and she smiled tightly at her XO.

"Message from *Queen Elizabeth:* 'Nothing on sonar. Continuing to sweep north along the coast toward Tanch'ŏn. Moving LAMPS buoys to expand the search.'"

Cassie nodded and continued to sip her warm drink. Buoy-markers winked out on the board, as others took their place in a tight grid parallel to the coast.

"Contact! Contact! Unidentified aircraft bearing one niner zero. Flight of five." Five red blips lit the board southwest of the *Arlington*, headed directly for their current position. Her AN/SPY-6 radar system was the best in the fleet and had picked them up. No one could sneak up on her.

"Positive ident on the aircraft." Cassie didn't want to shoot down friendlies in the cluttered airspace over the combat zone.

"Aircraft are not displaying standard ident codes. No response to hail."

"Very well. Bring up the Mark 26's. Load with RIM-66s. Man the deck guns. Let's get these guys before they close in." Alarms sounded throughout the boat. Missile launchers rose from the foredeck. This railgun system was controlled by a single crewman in CIC. Several different projectile types could be selected and fired at a rate of two missiles per nine seconds.

"*Queen Elizabeth* has contact. I repeat *Queen Elizabeth* has a subsurface contact."

"Positive ident on the incoming flight. Five MiG-29. Flight will be in range in less than five minutes. They have gone supersonic." James moved to the radar operator's console to reconfirm the ident on the MiGs. He nodded to Cassie.

"MARK 26, fire when you have a solution. Do not let them get into cannon range."

"CIC reports 26 is hot and tracking."

"Message to *Queen Elizabeth:* 'Identify and destroy. Positive ident required. We have subsurface assets in the area.'"

"Contact. Contact." Bryce's voice rose. Cassie spun toward her sonar operator. "I have a subsurface contact bearing one-one-zero. Course is one-six-five true. Range is twenty thousand. Depth is one hundred feet. They are steaming away from our position."

"Come to course one-eight-zero. All ahead flank."

The *Arlington* spun around on a dime and dug her bow into the waves as she accelerated. Her twin turbines bit into the ocean as they spun up to maximum speed. "Prepare the depth charges." The windows of the command deck darkened as a RIM-66 leapt off its rails and filled the night sky with fire. "Distance to MiGs?"

Cassie was fighting on two fronts, one in the air above and one beneath the sea. She kept the three-dimensional spatial images of the two engagements in her head, as her warship and crew responded to her orders. "MiGs are now in a stern chase. They will be on top of us in less than three minutes. RIM-1 impact in ten seconds."

Bryce spoke into the scrum of information flying around the command deck. "We will be over the contact in one minute. Preparing to drop the charges. Depth now one…two…zero feet."

"One…two…zero feet, aye." The firing officer acknowledged the information, as she input it into the depth charges.

A bright flash lit up the sky off the fantail of Cassie's boat. "RIM-1 has detonated. Splash two MiGs. Three are continuing on. Two minutes to cannon range." Another flash lit the foredeck and then another.

"Keep the windows dark. Bring the deck guns to bear as needed. Dump radar tracking to the gunners."

"We are over the target. Matching speed and course." Bryce stated.

"Come to course one-six-five. Reduce speed to fifteen knots." The *Arlington* wallowed as she slowed and turned to track over the submarine. "Fire depth charges. Sonar, report any compressive air loss."

If a depth charge scored a hit, they would fracture the submarine's hull, and internal atmosphere or compressed air from the ballast tanks would be catastrophically released. The deck pulsed beneath Cassie's feet as the *Arlington* pumped depth charges off her midship launchers.

"We have 30 charges in the water," the firing officer reported. "Falling to one…two…zero feet."

Two more RIMs leapt off the forward launcher.

"All ahead two-thirds. Let's get ahead of him and drop a full spread of depth charges. Distance to MiGs?"

The boat surged forward. "MiGs are one minute out and closing," CIC reported.

Her comm tech interrupted. "Message from the *Nimitz*. 'The main fleet is under attack. Two flights of hypersonic cruise missiles have penetrated the air defense net and are closing on the carrier. Flight operations are halted.'"

Admiral Benson's deep voice whispered in her ear. *Use your resources, Cassandra. You don't have to do everything yourself.*

"Colonel, take over satellite surveillance of the fleet, including aircraft tracking."

"Aye, Skip." Sam left the command deck for CIC.

"Do we have an update from the Hummers? They should've spotted incoming missiles and responded." The E-2 Hawkeyes were also known as Hummers due to the unique sound their turboprop-engines made. These aerial surveillance aircraft kept a constant radar net above the carrier group. Or they should have. Something was seriously wrong.

"Splash three MiGs." The excited voice of CIC sang across the bridge.

"Well done. Stand down the MARK 26. Continue manning the deck guns. Load torpedoes. Bryce, what have we got?"

"First spread. No sound. Contact is maintaining course, depth, and speed. Second spread is… " His voice trailed off and Cassie moved to the edge of her chair. "Hit! I have air. Contact is blowing tanks. Target is surfacing."

"Come about, course three-five-zero," Cassie said. "All ahead one-third. Let's get this bastard on the surface." Six-thousand feet off the starboard bow, a North Korean submarine shot out of the ocean like a breaching whale. "Fire tubes one and three. Get the MARK 32s in the water."

"Tracking is online. Torpedoes away," her firing officer said immediately.

The comm officer's shrill voice interrupted. "Message from the *Fitzgerald*, Skip."

Cassie turned to the young man. The *Fitzgerald* was one of the carrier group frigates. "And—"

"Ma'am, the *Nimitz*, she's hit. The island is fully engulfed in flame. They took a missile. Flight deck is down. No report on casualties."

The command deck of the *Arlington* was stunned into silence. How could this happen? Cassie's mind went blank.

14 April, 12:20 Hours Local (16:20 UTC)
Situation Room, White House
Washington, DC, United States

The atmosphere in the Situation Room was tense. Reports were being monitored from all fronts as each part of Operation Razor's Edge unfolded. Images were constantly changing on the high-definition monitors. President Haley, having returned from the Capitol, sat at the head of the table. She watched as her military commanders carried out their orders and Operation Razor's Edge sliced across the Korean Peninsula.

The nuclear attack was the only preemptive move the North Koreans had made thus far. Now, everyone was waiting for the next one. Admiral Benson had ordered THAAD activated at the DMZ and around Seoul. The South Korean Air Force had a full squadron of F-15 Strike Eagles covering the city. This aerial lid was rotated every thirty minutes to keep the pilots fresh. No ground troops had yet engaged. Nothing had moved across the DMZ.

"Admiral, report from the fleet." The major manning the comms system stood and turned to the Chair of the Joint Chiefs. "Sir, the *Nimitz* took a direct missile hit. The island is destroyed. Below deck-CIC reports the command deck is gone." The young man swallowed hard. "Admiral Armstrong is dead, as are the CAG and the captain of the ship."

President Haley couldn't believe what he said. "What? What island? Admiral?" she asked into the stunned silence.

Admiral Benson ignored the president. "Get me Captain Stanley on the *Arlington*." No one moved. "Now!" The comm tech for outgoing orders entered commands into her console.

The chirps and clicks of an encrypted satellite connecting filled the room. "*Arlington*."

"This is Washington Command. I need to speak to Captain Stanley."

President Haley admired how calm and in control the admiral sounded.

"Hold one. We have torpedoes in the water." They put the admiral on hold. The president couldn't believe it.

Admiral Benson sat back in his chair and waited. As the president huffed, he said, "They are in an active combat situation, Madam President. I cannot interrupt the captain of the boat until she can divert her attention to me. And an island is the name of the superstructure on an aircraft carrier."

"I see. Thank you," she answered.

"Pull up the *Arlington's* tactical display, back one minute," the admiral's aide ordered. The Situation Room had the ability to piggyback on the displays from any of the primary warships in the Navy. "Back one minute" meant they rewind to action one minute prior to the current time. An image of the *Arlington's* navigation board filled the main display. President Haley couldn't make out hide nor hair of the cluttered image.

"My god, she's fighting on two levels." The head of the Navy spoke, as icons appeared and disappeared from the board in rapid succession. Two blue lines streaked across the display toward a red icon to the right and forward of the central point which denoted the *Arlington's* position. "Splash one boat," he whispered.

The president watched as the two blue lines converged on the red icon, and it winked out. This was real time in all the definitions of the word.

Several minutes passed. "This is Captain Stanley. To whom am I speaking?"

"Captain, Admiral Benson here. I need you to transfer command of the *Arlington* to Commander Alexander and move over to the *Nimitz's* carrier group."

"Sir, the carrier is hit. Damage unknown. Casualties unknown."

"Captain, the admiral, the CAG, and the captain of the ship are dead." They heard gasps in the background. "Damage reports are still coming in. Flight operations are being transferred to Japan, and inflight refueling resources are taking off from Okinawa. They will meet the wings in the air. I need someone in command of the task group. I need someone I can count on to continue Operation Razor's Edge. That someone is *you*. Do you understand, Admiral?"

Silence. The pause could have been the satellite uplink time delay, but President Haley didn't think so. She thought Captain, now Admiral Stanley, was too shocked to speak. Nothing like a field promotion while you're fighting in your own ship. "Aye, I am on my way, sir. I can't stay on the *Arlington* and interrupt her mission or dilute her resources. I need to be within the carrier group."

Those in the Sit Room watched the *Arlington*'s navigation board waver, and a new image appeared. Admiral Stanley had refocused her radar systems on the fleet to visualize ships within the task group. "I will transfer the flag to the… to the *Princeton* until I can ascertain the extent of damage to the *Nimitz*. If she's seaworthy, I will move over to her."

"We will keep you in the loop as damage reports continue to come in. Though, I expect you will be listening in as well. Good Luck, Admiral."

15 April, 02:41 Hours Local (UTC 17:41, 14 April 14)
The Sea of Japan (East Sea)
USPACFLT
Command Deck, *USS Princeton*
CGN-59, Ticonderoga-class Guided Missile Cruiser

"Admiral on the bridge." Everyone stood as Rear Admiral Cassandra Stanley strode onto the command deck.

"At ease." She turned to Captain Michael Harston and saluted. "Permission to come aboard, Captain?"

"Aye, ma'am. Welcome. I wish it were under better circumstances." He stood from his command chair.

Cassie nodded at the younger man. He was a plebe at the academy when she was a fourth-year cadet. Although she hadn't followed his career, she knew he was a solid officer. "As do I, Captain. Status on the *Nimitz*?" She had overflown the damaged aircraft carrier on her way to the *Princeton*. Even in the dark, the injured ship didn't look good. The island was badly damaged with the top third missing and the remainder a twisted wreck. Fire billowed from the below deck hangers, as flames tore through the fully fueled aircraft stored there.

"They're fighting fires below deck now. It is a compartment-by-compartment battle. The magazines are locked down and should be safe from the fires. They've lost their ability to launch and recover aircraft. Both catapults are down. The fantail was damaged from the second missile strike, as was the aircraft capture system."

"Second missile? Where are they coming from? How did they penetrate their aerial lid?"

Captain Harston grimaced. "We never saw them coming. A flight of hypersonic cruise missiles came in at sea level, barely above the wave crests. No one saw them until they popped up inside the defensive zone and drove into the *Nimitz*." He braced to attention. "It is my fault, ma'am. Our AN/SPY-6 was having resolution issues, and I took the system down to change the boards. I did not cover my quarter while the repair was being made. I assumed the Hawkeyes would be enough coverage."

He was prepared to be dressed down. She didn't have the time or resources to discipline a captain. Besides, the radar coverage around the carrier group was multilayered. Taking his coverage out would not have created a blind spot. Something else occurred to allow those missiles in.

Missiles they didn't know the North Koreans possessed.

"Be that as it may, Captain, we are still in the middle of a complex operation. The overall situation is volatile. If the *Nimitz* can't fight or protect herself, I'll set my flag here." The admiral saw Captain Harston relax a fraction.

"We cannot be distracted by past decisions. Post-action reports will deal with those made during combat. We must look forward. The next steps are most important." Cassie paused. The young captain released a sigh. Good. She needed everyone focused. "Any indication whether the missiles contained nuclear or chemical warheads?"

"N—no," he stuttered. "I don't think so."

"Check on that, please. Anything is possible at this point. And Captain, I want to know where those missiles came from. Then we are going to remove that threat from the board. They will not be firing additional cruise missiles at the fleet. Understood?"

"Aye, ma'am."

"May I use your day cabin to send some messages?" He nodded and she turned away from the command deck. She said, "I will need an open comm link to the White House."

Captain Harston turned to his comm officer. "Make it happen, Victoria." His voice was strong, commanding.

Cassie spun on her heel and left the deck. What a cluster. She'd had only three minutes to see Sam in her day cabin before she'd left for the *Princeton*.

"Congratulations, beautiful." Cassie had felt a blush heat her face. "I knew you'd make admiral when we were at the academy." Sam's smile was warm but subdued. This should be a cause for celebration."

"But not this way, Ace. Never over dead bodies." Both had taken a silent moment to remember those gone. Cassie had never liked Admiral Armstrong, but she would never wish the man ill.

Cassie shook the memory away. It was time to focus on the here and now. Figure out where those damned missiles came from. Sam hadn't said anything about hypersonic cruise missiles in any of her briefings. Cassie couldn't believe her partner would miss something like that.

Such was the fluidity of warfare. *Don't underestimate your opponent, ever.*

Cassie collapsed into the desk chair and punched a comm stud on the console. "Admiral?"

"The White House, please."

15 April, 03:00 Hours Local (UTC 18:00, 14 April)
The Sea of Japan (East Sea)
British Royal Navy
***HMS Unicorn* Attack Hunter-Killer Submarine**
Off the coast of the Tonghae Satellite Launch Facility

Dawn was two hours away but no one on the submerged submarine could see the sky. Once the *Unicorn* had dispatched the two frigates, they proceeded north-northeast to their current location. "All stop. Come to periscope depth. Prepare to release the team." The *Unicorn* was specially equipped with a dry chamber on its forward deck. This allowed commando units to enter and exit the vessel while it was submerged.

"Periscope depth, aye." The submarine shuddered, as it rose to the ordered depth.

Another slight shudder rippled through the craft, as the dry chamber was flooded. "Team has exited the chamber."

Captain Gordon nodded. "Communication to the *Arlington*. 'Team is away.' Maintain station-keeping. Now, we wait."

US Navy Seal Team Six in conjunction with British Special Boat Team Bravo were headed onshore to capture and detain Supreme Leader Pak. Keyhole satellites had noted his arrival and movement around the facility. Most importantly, satellite coverage allowed them to determine which building he entered at eight o'clock the previous evening. He had been seen outside since. What worried Captain Gordon was all the military activity continuing around the base. Transports and fuel trucks were in constant motion around the facility. He didn't know how the team would make it in or out without being seen. And Lieutenant Grant wasn't with them. She was their Boat Team's lucky charm. Although she volunteered for this mission, she could not pass the physical. Her lungs were still too weak.

Twenty minutes later an officer reported, "Sir, we have a ping. The team has made it to shore and is proceeding to the target."

Gordon leaned over his digital map table which displayed the latest satellite images of the base. "Send another message to the *Arlington*. 'Step one complete.'"

Before his order could be carried out, a message came in. "Sir, message from the *Arlington*, Commander Alexander reporting. '*Nimitz* is out of action. Admiral Stanley now taskforce commander aboard the *Princeton*. Proceed as planned. Maintain contact.'"

"Good gawd, what the hell's going on? Get me a satellite link to the *Queen Elizabeth*. Request a situational update."

Minutes slowly accumulated on the commandos' mission timer. The team was several minutes from their next scheduled update. Gordon went over to his sonar operator's booth. "Anything?"

"Nothing, sir. All's quiet." The young sailor looked up at his commanding officer. "Maybe too quiet."

15 April, 06:13 Hours Local (UTC 21:13, 14 April)
Command Bunker, Ground Tracking Facility
Tonghae Satellite Launching Ground
North Hamgyong Province
Democratic People's Republic of Korea

Supreme Leader Pak was awakened from a sound sleep by his driver six hours ago to learn his country was under attack on multiple fronts. Computer technicians were unable to link to any computer resources or communicate with his field commanders. He had shot one of the technicians in the head when the man had the audacity to suggest he try to use the shortwave radio system the base maintained.

Pak didn't need an antiquated communication system when his military had the best computer network. After fifteen long minutes of delays and black screens being the only response on his computer systems, he ordered the shortwave system be brought up. He needed to contact someone, anyone, who could take orders and launch a counterattack. After trying multiple frequencies, the radio operator finally received an answer from the western front.

"Sir, I have the western front. The radio operator is calling his commander."

"Finally." Pak placed the headphones provided to him over his ears. All he heard was static.

"Commander Yang here. We are waiting on orders. We've had no communication."

Pak screamed over the poor connection. "This is the Supreme Commander of the People's Army. You will launch your missiles into China immediately."

More static filled his ears, and he pressed the muffs harder against his head. "Are we still connected?"

"Yes, sir. I have a strong signal." The young man, a boy really, quaked in his chair.

"That order requires authentication to execute."

The supreme leader turned to his driver and snapped his fingers. The man produced a black leather case. "What is today's code?"

A plastic-coated card was removed from the case and handed to Pak. He read into the microphone. "OSCAR-TANGO-ROMEO-ONE-ONE-THREE-ALPHA-SIERRA."

"The code is valid. Launch is authenticated. Orders will be distributed to the launch vehicles. Warheads to be loaded?"

Now it was Pak who paused. Even though he lacked empathy for fellow humans as well as the moral fiber to make sane decisions, the man faltered. A moment later, his anger exploded again, and he shouted, "Nuclear." That order was his fait accompli. It sealed his destiny and that of his country.

News was slowly trickling in over the shortwave radio from visual sightings around the country and from a scattering of isolated posts, limited to a few areas. Pak had no communication with his forces along the DMZ. Nothing was happening because his authoritarian leadership style kept his commanders from acting independently. They would wait on his orders. Orders he could not give without communications.

The enemy naval forces had destroyed all his nuclear-missile submarines. Air attacks had reduced military and industrial sites across the country to flaming ruins. His computing centers around the world were out of communication, and his in-country military computer network remained down. The only successes were the nuclear hits on China and the destruction of the archenemy's aircraft carrier.

What else could he do? Thoughts rolled through his mind. Then he knew what he had to do. The missiles were fueled and ready to launch. Six harbingers of destruction aimed at the archenemy and their allies. He would see them strike in all their glory.

"Commander, prepare to launch your missiles." Pak faced the base commander.

"Sir?"

"The missiles sitting on your launch pads. You will fire the Hwasong-14 missiles against their assigned targets."

The commander of the Tonghae Satellite Launching Facility blanched. "But sir, that is twelve missiles. We would release unimaginable destruction on those targets with the warheads loaded."

Pak's face flushed an unhealthy red, and he pulled his sidearm from its holster for the second time.

"YOU WILL LAUNCH THE MISSILES!"

15 April, 06:25 Hours Local (UTC 21:25, 14 April)
CIC, *USS Arlington*
CGN-47, Ticonderoga-class Guided Missile Cruiser
Steaming north to Kimch'aek

"Colonel, we have activity in Tonghae," Grant reported from her workstation in CIC.

Sam looked up from reviewing the satellite images captured over the spot where the *Arlington* torpedoed the last submarine. Debris surrounded the sinking boat. The diesel fuel spill was on fire.

"What activity?" She looked at the operations timer. The special ops team should be well along in their mission, but they had not received an update from the *Unicorn*.

"Satellites show liquid fuel venting from six of the launch sites," Grant stated flatly. "They're getting ready to launch their missiles."

"Shit. Get me Admiral Benson, and send a message to Seoul and the Japanese. They need to go active on their THAAD systems. Let the Chinese know what we think is going on. Beijing is within the target zone."

A few minutes later, Sam was on a satellite call with Admiral Benson. "That's all we have, sir. Six missiles are being fueled, and launches are imminent. Targets are unknown, but anything within a twenty-five hundred-to-six-thousand kilometer window is possible. Warheads are unknown, but matériel has been moved from known nuclear depots to Tonghae over the last two weeks. Warheads could be up to five-hundred kilos."

Sam listened anxiously as the admiral relayed orders to various places around the eastern Pacific. "Samantha, what is your location relative to Tonghae?"

"We are steaming north-northeast, preparing to rendezvous with the *Unicorn* to pick up the team and their package."

"And the status of your AEGIS system?" the admiral asked.

Sam leaned over and looked at another workstation screen. "In standby, but all the lights are green."

"I am going to order Commander Alexander to the optimal coordinates to intercept any launches from Tonghae. Get that position calculated."

"Aye, sir." He responded before the call disconnected.

Sam pulled her compass and ruler from her messenger bag. On a regional navigation chart, she drew six track lines fanning out from the coastal facility. She drew arcs of decreasing curvature parallel to the coast. The arcs intersected each of the track lines. The third arc bisected each track line with enough separation to allow the *Arlington* to fire AEGIS missiles from a central point—three to the south and three to the north. She threw her pen down on the small desk and grabbed the map.

She ordered, "Grant, I need you to keep an eye on the launch site. Commandeer a Keyhole-11, and move it to geosynchronous orbit directly above the facility. Eyes down, use infrared to monitor the missiles. They need a thirty-minute preparation time to load the liquid oxidizer in the tanks."

Sam ran to the stairs and climbed up to the command deck.

Commander James Alexander turned toward Sam and said, "I have the orders, Colonel. Do you have our position?"

Sam handed her drawing to James. "It's the best I can do without satellite coordination. This point," she tapped the map, "will allow the *Arlington* to be equidistant between the six launches, regardless of their ultimate targets."

"Very well. Ensign, calculate this location." He handed Sam's drawing to his navigator. "Helm, come to course zero-two-five, all ahead full. We will correct our position as we near the final location."

"Aye, Skip," the *Arlington*'s helmsman answered. James startled. Being called Skipper for the first time was a shock to his system. He knew it was an indication of respect. The crew had accepted him as their leader.

Without missing a beat, James continued to issue orders. "CIC, bring AEGIS online." He looked at the navigation board. "Commandeer birds one, four, and eight. Move them over the firing position. Once in position, we'll refine our location. Load all six tubes, standard kinetic strike." He looked at Sam, and she nodded. No need to add additional nuclear contamination to the sea.

"AEGIS is online. Satellites are moving into position," the chief petty officer said, repeating the information coming from CIC.

"Time to launch?" Commander Alexander asked.

"Not more than fifteen minutes. No known destination," Grant answered from the CIC.

"Aye, no known destination," Sam repeated.

The comm officer spoke up. "Sir, we have reports from South Korea and Japan. Their THAAD systems are active, and they are commandeering birds to cover their countries. IRON DOME is 100 percent operational over Seoul to catch any low-level SCUD or cruise missiles."

James sat forward. "Let's get them before they get that far. What do you say, people?"

A chorus of "Aye, sir" rang out.

"We are at the optimal location, sir," the navigator stated ten minutes later.

"Thrusters as needed. Deploy all stabilizers. Maintain station-keeping."

"Satellites are tracking. AEGIS missiles are loaded and green. Waiting on the launch." Came the information from the weapon's officer.

Nine minutes later, Grant called from CIC. "Launch detection. Launch detection. Six birds away." Her upper-class British voice cut through the silent command deck. "One misfire. Another rose from its launch vehicle and exploded immediately. It fell back to the ground."

The firing officer spoke over Grant. "Satellites have acquired the missiles and are tracking. Computers are calculating a solution."

"Missiles have entered the upper atmosphere. Boost phase is complete. Second stage is ignited. Missiles are in suborbital flight," Grant informed the command deck.

"We have a solution. Preparing to fire AEGIS." The weapon's officer flipped the plastic cover up and placed her hand over the ignition button. "Missiles will be overhead in one minute."

"Give me ten seconds," James ordered.

"Ten seconds, aye."

Sam clasped her hands behind her back to hide their shaking. "Ten seconds in five, four, three, two, one, ten seconds." Sam heard James counting backward under his breath.

"Fire AEGIS." The fires of hell exploded over the ship as the six missiles leapt from their launch tubes.

"Missiles away."

The *Arlington* shuddered to her keel as six AEGIS SM-3s blasted from their silos in a staggered launch pattern. "AN/SPY-6 is tracking on all missiles. Flying true." The navigation board lit up with six new blue tracks, heading toward the angry red dots.

"Reload AEGIS." James leaned toward Sam. "We usually try to aim two AEGIS to one ICBM, but I can only fire six missiles at a time. Fingers crossed." Sam lifted her right hand, showing her crossed fingers.

"Skip, message from the Japanese." James nodded to the comm officer. "They are moving four Kongo destroyers to catch our misses." The Kongo destroyers were equipped with the Japanese version of the AEGIS system.

"Good to have backup. But let's not give them a chance."

The firing officer broke in. "Missiles are tracking."

At the moment of intersection, two of the four red dots winked out of existence, disappearing from the navigation board. Two of his six AEGIS missiles continued on. "Self-destruct on birds three and six." James ordered. "Estimated target on the remaining missiles?"

"Tokyo and somewhere in the Pacific. Most probable target for the other missile is Guam in Micronesia," Grant answered from CIC. She was on top of the computer calculations, giving her highest probability solutions from the missiles flight characteristics.

"Splash last two missiles. Kongo has successfully intercepted," she reported as the last two red arcs vanished.

A cheer went up on the command deck. "Quiet, people. Comm, compliments to our Japanese friends. Retract the stabilizers. All ahead two-thirds. Bring us about to rendezvous with the *Unicorn*. Helm, come to course two-eight-five. We still have work to do."

15 April, 06:37 Hours Local (UTC 21:37, 14 April)
Command Bunker, Ground Tracking Facility
Tonghae Satellite Launching Ground
North Hamgyong Province
Democratic People's Republic of Korea

Supreme Leader Pak watched in horror as the green blips representing his four missiles disappeared off the radar screen. "Where are they? What happened?" Their only remote-sensing resources were low-resolution, truck-mounted radar systems.

"Missiles must have been neutralized by an anti-missile system." The sensor tech cringed before continuing. "Our remote sensing systems are still offline due to computer failure."

Pak's face contorted in anger. "Prepare the next set of missiles."

"We are unable to comply, sir. The two missile failures destroyed our launch capabilities. We cannot fuel any more missiles. The area is contaminated with nuclear material."

Pak couldn't believe it. He controlled an immense arsenal of WMD weapons. He had successfully designed and built six different ICBM systems. He had developed the Devil's Venom and a solid fuel. He had a stockpile of NBC warheads. He had control of a suite of medical bioweapons. But now, now, he was deaf and blind. Stuck here in the north of his country. Unable to act. Unable to fight. Unable to retaliate.

Then he realized, the radio. He must solidify his position as supreme leader. He must appear in control. If his country was overrun, he must rouse the people to fight and resist the invaders. "Prepare the radio. I will speak to the people." This should buy him time. The people will protect him.

He turned to his aide. "Get the car ready. We are going to my retreat in the mountains." This was his grandfather's stronghold during the Korean Conflict. It was located in the far northwest of the country.

"Sir?"

"Set up the radio so I may speak to my people. Broadcast to the country. Now, Commander."

Five minutes later, Pak sat before the microphone and spoke to the North Korean people, hoping the airwaves carried his message.

"Months ago, I asked you to sacrifice in support of our plans to achieve *juche*. Sacrifice to allow our military to grow and reign supreme. I asked you to undertake an Arduous March, just as my grandfather did. I know this required you forego food and heat. To work longer hours. To sacrifice more." He stifled a sob.

"I must report, all of your sacrifices have been for naught. We have failed in our goal of *juche* and reunification. I have failed you and our country." Another sob-like sound.

"I am sorry. Our people placed trust, as high as the sky and as deep as the sea, in me. I have failed to live up to your trust." The supreme leader swallowed another sob.

The men in the command bunker did not see a tear. Pak's face was hard, and his eyes remained cold.

He continued. "Our people have always believed in the party. Believed in me. I am grateful for all of your sacrifices and humbly bow to you in gratitude." He paused dramatically. "I have failed where my grandfather succeeded. I can not remove our enemies from our home. And now our archenemies are again at our doorstep. I alone cannot protect us from their invasion. So, I must ask. I must beg, we band together to push the invaders back. Hold our borders. Protect our homeland. Because of this failure, I will depart from leadership and leave the country to the assembly so they may select a new leader. One who will achieve our goals." Another sob. "I have failed. I am sorry," he whispered into the microphone. He nodded to the operator and the transmission ended.

Pak rose and turned on the Tonghae commander. "Fix your launch capabilities and fire off the remainder of your missiles to their assigned targets as soon as you can." He strode from the bunker, his aide rushing to open the steel door.

14 April, 18:07 Hours Local (UTC 22:07)
Situation Room, White House
Washington, DC, United States

President Amanda Haley sat forward and squinted at the low-light green images moving against the blackness of night. "Boat Team Bravo, what is your position?" a disembodied voice asked.

A whispered, subvocal response came back from a throat microphone. "We are at the pickup point. Waiting on the package to emerge from the bunker."

As the British lieutenant commander moved his head, the president could see the surrounding area, swept in by his helmet cam. The images were real time. A sudden flare of light flooded the image, and the camera went blank.

"We have missile launch. I repeat missile launch." The Boat Team Bravo commander reported.

The screen remained dark. Admiral Benson's aide leaned toward the president. "Ma'am, the burning contrail from the missiles overwhelmed the night vision cameras. Once darkness reestablishes, we can open the cameras again." She nodded at the captain.

A few minutes later, the monitor filled with an eerie green-on-black image. "Camera feed reestablished." Again the young British officer swept the area as he moved his head from one side to the other.

"Movement. I repeat, we have movement." The image zeroed in on the door to the bunker, and a square of light flooded the camera.

"We have preliminary identification on the package."

President Haley watched as two shadowed figures exited the bunker and the door slid closed behind them. Once the door closed, the figures appeared as fuzzy green objects moving right to left across the open yard. Six black images rose up from behind walls and stacked pallets of supplies, to surround the pair. The smaller figure was dropped silently to the ground. The rounder figure was grabbed and immediately subdued. Something was thrown over his head.

The figure was dragged behind a retaining wall. The hood was removed from his head, and a light shown on his face. "Package identity is confirmed," a voice called out from the dark. As the "package" began to struggle, a hand came up and slapped a piece of silver-gray duct tape over his mouth.

"Concur—identity is confirmed. Secure the package for transport. Return to the *Unicorn*."

"Aye, securing the package." A silver needle flashed on the monitor image. It was inserted into the neck of the package. The hood was replaced as the body slumped between two Boat Team members.

"Returning to rendezvous. Request pickup in one-five minutes."

The president sagged back into her seat, overwhelmed by what she witnessed. Admiral Benson turned to her. "Success, Madam President. No casualties. No missing equipment. You have your package."

6 May, 08:30 Hours Local (UTC 12:30)
Rose Garden, White House
Washington, DC, United States

Sam fidgeted in the uncomfortable white folding chair, as she looked out over the mass of dignitaries, ambassadors, members of Congress, and the ever-present press corps. The sun shone down on the gathering. They were waiting for the President of the United States to appear.

Two Marine guards opened the double doors, and Amanda Haley stepped out. Following her were President Liu Qishan, President Choi Myung-yong, and the prime ministers of the United Kingdom and Japan. Admirals Benson and Stanley, followed by Doctors Williams, Ratcliffe, and Talley came out of the door next, to form a half-circle behind the world leaders.

President Haley stepped up to the podium. "Distinguished guests, I am pleased to stand before you with our allies, military representatives, and physicians to share the success of our joint effort to neutralize a global threat.

"Pak Sung-Un, Supreme Leader of the Democratic People's Republic of Korea, released a deadly pathogen on the world in a heinous act of bioterrorism. He utilized nuclear weapons in a direct attack against China, an ally of the United States of America. These are the worst crimes against humanity this world has ever seen." She paused. "It could have been so much worse.

"We would not have been successful with stopping these worldwide threats, stopping this man, without global cooperation. We live in a global community. We were successful because the world united." She paused. "Together, we fought and won.

"Our physicians applied technologies developed to combat the COVID-19 pandemic to identify, contain, and stop the Paris Contagion. Pandemics know no borders. Therefore, a threat against one affects us all.

"Using time-tested methods, our intelligence experts identified the weapons of mass destruction Pak created. Methods developed during

World War II. Methods just as applicable today as they were then. These methods were augmented with state-of-the-art cybertechnology which identified, penetrated, and destroyed North Korea's military computer assets. Without these forewarnings, we would not have been forearmed. We would not have been prepared to intercept Pak's assault before it began. We would have failed to stop Pak Sung-Un as he unleashed Armageddon on the world."

The president looked out over the gathering. "Currently, Pak Sung-un is in custody and awaiting trial before the International Court of Justice in The Hague, Netherlands. He will be tried for crimes against his people. Crimes against humanity. Crimes against our world. We thank the members of the combined special forces team who captured him as he tried to escape to destinations unknown.

"Pak's actions have brought together allies of old and forged new alliances which made all our countries stronger and the world a safer place."

The crowd sat stunned, silenced by the magnitude of all which occurred over the last weeks. Sam was at the fore of the action, ever since she first received the satellite images of the Punggye-ri nuclear test site eighteen months ago. Months that felt like a lifetime to Sam.

"Our success is not without great losses, however. Women and men who fought to protect the world from this dictator gave their lives in this effort. Our global community lost more than three hundred thousand souls to the Paris Contagion, a bioweapon we have now identified and quarantined thanks to the expertise and ongoing efforts of the physicians with me today.

"Admiral Armstrong, Commander of the United States Pacific Fleet, died when his boat—the *USS Nimitz*—was attacked. Captain of the *Nimitz,* Jonathan Riker, and Commander Daniel Aitika, Commander Air Group, died with him. Another 114 sailors, aboard that mighty ship, gave their lives during the initial attack or while fighting the resultant fire. Their valiant efforts saved their great ship. She will sail again.

"Our Chinese allies lost 326 soldiers and civilians in the nuclear missile attack launched by Pak Sung-un. More may follow, as the long-term effects of ionizing radiation exposure manifests in future generations. The world is here to help our Chinese allies recover from this attack. Japan is sending radiation specialists to aid in the management of those injured. We are sending decontamination supplies to the area.

"An untold number of North Korean citizens have died at the hands of this dictator or from starvation and disease due to his militarization. Mothers… fathers… sons… daughters… entire families lost due to the actions of this tyrant."

President Haley paused to allow the attendees as well as the world's population remember those lost to this madman.

"No one stood alone in this fight. We stood together. And together we succeeded. Our world united is a world safe for all."

President Haley turned the dais over to Presidents Liu and then Choi. They reiterated and reinforced the president's comments. As the remarks concluded, Sam stood with Grant beside her and applauded along with the crowd. Her eyes never left Cassie. The new admiral stood at parade rest beside the Chair of the Joint Chiefs. The single gold star on her blue sleeve winked in the morning sunlight. Sam's heart swelled with pride and love.

8 May, 05:13 Hours Local (UTC 09:13)
Michaels/Stanley Residence
Georgetown, Virginia
Suburb of Washington, DC, United States

Dawn's first rays peeked through the curtains and nailed Sam in the eye. She squinted at the clock, reading the time. It was 5:13, too early to get up. Rolling away from the window, her arm fell on empty space. Cassie was missing. Unusual for the difficult-to-awaken sailor. Sam got up and stretched her back. No one in the bathroom. She listened for noise elsewhere in the house. Nothing but birdsong. Leaving their bedroom, Sam stopped at the head of the curved staircase to listen. Still nothing. She walked down the stairs. "Hmmm... coffee and sweet bread. Yum." The aroma filled the lower floor.

Rounding the newel post, Sam moved stealthily down the hall toward the kitchen. She hoped to catch her partner by surprise, but the surprise was on her. There in her kitchen sat the Chair of the Joint Chiefs. He wore a tattered Nationals baseball team jersey over blue US Navy shorts.

"Sir?" He turned on the stool and raised a mug in salute. She looked down at her sleep shorts and tee shirt; glad she had put the garments on.

"Samantha, I understand congratulations are in order."

A fiery blush heated Sam's cheeks. "I, ah... err..." She found her voice. "Yes, sir. Thank you, sir."

"Enough of that. You outrank me now."

Her blush deepened and she felt her cheeks flame.

"That is, if you are going to take the offered position. I really fought to keep you on my staff."

"The president was most persuasive, sir." President Haley had offered Sam the position of Deputy Director of National Security, reporting directly to the president—a senior White House staff position.

The admiral chuckled just as the patio door slid open and Cassie entered. She leaned down. "I don't know, sir. She doesn't seem interested in taking a... Oh. Morning, Ace." Cassie smiled as her head popped up.

Sam was totally confused. Admiral Benson was in their kitchen before 06:00 drinking coffee and eating sweet bread. Her partner had been up and outside on some unknown errand. Something grabbed her ankle. "What the…?" Sam kicked out.

"Good grief, Samantha, take it easy on the little one. She's only nine weeks old and just flew across the Atlantic in the backseat of a British Wildcat attack jet."

A small black, tan, and white Corgi plopped down on her round bottom and gave Sam the best puppy grin ever. "Hey, little one." Sam bent down. "What's your name?"

"Yap, yap," the dog responded.

"Interesting, though I think we can do better than that." She scooped the puppy up and turned to the admiral. "Sir?"

"A gift, Samantha, from the Queen for services rendered. Her Majesty felt you and Cassandra needed a companion. You should be honored. The Queen is very protective of her pups and doesn't gift them lightly."

Sam nodded in agreement but knew the problems she and Cassie would face with this gift. "I am honored, sir. This is a very kind gesture, but neither of our jobs allow for much time at home. Who's going to keep her company?" She fluffed the little dog's ears and got another puppy grin as a reward. "Cassie will be at sea, and I'll be at the White House."

"I think you'll both be closer to home than that. Since you turned down my staff position, I had to find someone to fill it. I traded up—an admiral and a young lieutenant commander for a colonel. Win-win for both of us, I'd say." The puppy yapped in agreement, causing the three humans to laugh.

"A lieutenant commander?"

"Yes. Grant got a promotion from the admiralty and is also joining my staff as my cyberwarfare officer."

"Be careful, sir," Sam said in warning. "She'll hack NORAD or one of your seven naval fleets and take command." The admiral nodded in agreement.

Sam continued. "Seems you have it all figured out. I guess the only thing I need is an address to send a thank you note."

Cassie piped up. "Admiral, did you get the invitation to our BBQ picnic for the day after tomorrow? Are you planning on attending?"

The admiral stood and walked around the island to place his mug in the sink. "Wouldn't miss it for the world, Cassandra. I was planning on bringing our three pups as well." He patted the little dog in Sam's arms on the head. "Give her someone to play with."

Sam smiled, as she cuddled the pup. "That'll be great, sir. Grant and Doctor Brockstone will be here by then too. We are hoping Francis can make it from New Mexico as well."

"Very good. We will make a day of it." He moved down the hall and out the front door to his car.

An hour later, Sam relaxed back on the couch. The puppy was asleep on her chest, and Cassie was cuddled along her side. "That was unexpected. Are you sure you don't want to go back to sea, beautiful?"

"I'm sure, Ace. I'll miss the *Arlington,* but an admiral can't command a cruiser. I don't want a task group, and I can't command a carrier because I'm not a naval aviator. I'm not a high enough grade to command one of the fleets." Cassie paused. "Yet." This wouldn't be her last promotion. "This was the perfect posting." Cassie smiled at Sam. "Besides, I think it's time we spend time together. Been a hell of an eighteen months."

Sam thought back on all that had happened. All they had accomplished. She silently thanked any of the gods listening everyone they knew was safe and well.

James received permanent command of the *Arlington.* Doctor Julia was due back from Antarctica in a few months and would take a position at DARPA to work with Doctor Ratcliffe, tasked with studying the bacterium-virus pairing used in the Paris Contagion.

The tape was where the germ-pair resided. The contaminated tape was used on packages shipped from the Kaesŏng Industrial Complex until it was shut down by the South Koreans. She and Doctor Andy had figured out the virus was released from its bacterial host when heat was applied to the adhesive in the tape and the *Terrimonas arctica* bacterium blossomed to life. The needed heat was from mechanical energy generated as tape was ripped off a box. This was enough to cause an immediate response in the dormant bacterium.

The North Korean scientists had calculated the friction created by ripping the tape off a package was concentrated along the boundary between the cellulose acetate backer and the adhesive. And, this small burst of high frictional heat was enough to energize the bacterium. The victims were then infected by touch. People worldwide were cautioned to cut open all packages from Kaesŏng Industrial Complex companies until further notice.

As the designer of the Paris Contagion, Doctor Ri was on the most wanted list after 15 April. The South Koreans searched for her, but records indicated she died from her own virus due to an accidental exposure in her lab. A body was never recovered.

Once the fighting had stopped and they had Pak in custody, President Haley used Grant's movie app to send a blast-message to the North Korean people via their tablets.

The message was recorded by Kim Hye-su. She acknowledged Leader Pak's message to the people and contradicted all he said. She told them real help was on the way. She told them their dreams of a full belly would be a reality. She told them to not believe her words but to believe the supplies being ferried to the Kaesŏng facility and distributed throughout the country. She asked they report the whereabouts of any members of the assembly attempting to hide. Doctor Kim apologized for what her science produced, but emphasized they must not fear today or the future because the world would hold Pak accountable.

Pak Sung-un was awaiting trial in The Hague. Prisoners released from the various camps across North Korea were being treated for malnutrition, as well as physical and psychological torture. Those who were well enough and desired to do so would testify against him. Doctor Kim Hye-su had returned home and was leading the efforts to find and disable all the weapons and matériel stockpiles not destroyed in the drone strike. Hye-su was becoming a nationally recognized advocate for liberation and growth toward a new tomorrow for North Korea.

Sam thought she'd be a great leader for the country, but she had demurred, stating she didn't want to be in the spotlight. Sam thought this was the reason she'd make the perfect candidate.

The British were considering releasing Pak Jong-nam back to North Korea. They thought he might be a possible new leader, but they weren't sure of his true allegiances. Until the North Koreans rounded up the remaining members of the Pak family, all the assembly members, military leaders, and corrupt scientists, the Brits would continue to hold him in the UK.

Change was happening everywhere in North Korea. Humanitarian aid was pouring in from around the globe. Everything from food to construction materials, from medicine to doctors. The DMZ was being converted from a minefield to an open border. South Korea was spearheading the organization and distribution of materials through the Kaesŏng Industrial Complex. Koreans were now able to move freely between the two countries. Families were being reunited after decades of separation.

Although President Choi feared a flood of refugees from the north, that hadn't happened. People wanted to stay in their homes and continue to rebuild their country. It would be a long road, one fraught with hazards. However, the world was united in making this a success. Not one of the US allies had entered the country. This wasn't an occupation. This was rebirth for the North Korean citizens. The United Nations and its affiliated organizations were coordinating the uplift of North Korea.

Sam stroked the puppy, who sighed in her sleep. Cassie was softly whiffling against her side. Sam smiled at the ceiling. All seemed right in the world.

10 May, 13:23 Hours Local (UTC 17:23)
Michaels/Stanley Residence
Georgetown, Virginia
Suburb of Washington, DC, United States

Standing on the deck, Sam surveyed their backyard. The aroma of smoking meats rose from the two grills on either side of the patio doors. Four Welsh corgi pups chased each other in circles around the middle of the yard, easily weaving in and out of her guests' legs. The young male, Halsey, with his twin, Nimitz, had a stuffed mallard duck in their jaws and were playing keep away with the other two. Elizabeth, Admiral

Benson's third corgi, was hot on their heels. Sam smiled as Maggie Gee, their new pup, leapt over Francis' feet and landed on Halsey, tearing the mallard away. Cassie named their pup after the first female Chinese American World War II aviator. This brave woman ferried bombers to and from the European theater.

Sam went back into the kitchen to finish filling bowls with all the side dishes for the buffet. The front doorbell rang, and she headed down the hall. They weren't expecting any other guests, so it was probably the neighbors complaining about the noise. Opening the front door, two dark-suited men confronted Sam. "May I help you?"

"Colonel Michaels?"

"Yes." Sam repeated her question. "May I help you?"

The two men pushed past her and continued down the hall toward the kitchen. "Hey, wait up. What's this all about?" She found one looking out the patio door and the other speaking into a wrist mic.

"All clear. Pull around and park in front. Keep the street cordoned off at each end of the block."

Felicity Stephenson strode into the kitchen. "Ma'am, it's a pleasure to see you again." She tipped her head to Sam.

"Ah, right." Sam considered the smartly dressed Secret Service agent. "May I ask what this is all about?"

"Of course, ma'am. One moment, please." Felicity tipped her head, as she listened to something being spoken into her ear. "Arrival in thirty. All units, report in."

Sam finally caught a clue and headed back out on the deck. "Cass?" Sam waved to her partner. Cassie jogged over to the stairs. "You may want to get up here. We are about to have another guest."

Before Cassie could question Sam, President Amanda Haley stepped through the patio door.

"Samantha." She smiled warmly and held out her hand. Sam shook the president's hand as Cassie joined them on the deck. The president said, "Admiral, it's a pleasure. I appreciate the invitation." A smile graced Sam's face as the other guests scattered around the yard saw who had arrived. "Shall we? I would like to meet all your friends."

The afternoon continued at a leisurely pace. After all the food was consumed and the tiki torches were lit to ward off the darkening evening, everyone found a place to settle. As expected, conversation circled around to Operation Razor's Edge and the status of various loose ends. All the parts and pieces were dissected again. The president left after thanking everyone for their contributions to a successful operation.

Other guests took their leave and soon only Sam, Cassie, Grant, and Cynthia were left. "Why is it, when it's time to clean up, everyone beats a hasty retreat?" Sam asked. The evening was sliding into night as stars came out. She relaxed back into the chaise lounge, staring up at the twinkling sky. Cassie sat between her legs, cuddling Maggie under a fuzzy throw blanket. Grant was snuggled with Cynthia on the nearby sofa.

"I don't know, Ace. At least we used paper plates. That'll make the cleanup easier."

The four were quiet and settled back to enjoy a relaxing moment. "Have you heard from Doctor Kim?" Cynthia asked.

Sam had a call to Hye-su at the top if her to-do list for Monday. "Not recently. Though all the reports I've seen indicate the country is well on the way to rebuilding. Elections are planned within the next nine months."

"Cynthia, how are plans for your classes coming along?" Cassie asked. Cynthia was taking a teaching position at the Naval Academy. Her class: Geohazards and Their Impact on National Security. She and Grant had purchased a bayfront home in Eaton's Landing, near Annapolis on the shore of Chesapeake Bay. Grant was shipping her sloop from the UK and hoped to teach Cynthia to sail.

"Well, I think. We'll see how the cadets take to studying events which can't be predicted or timed or forecast on a hard schedule. Geohazards are not like the weather. We really don't have any good mechanism for precisely timing most events."

Sam was puzzled by this statement. "So how do you work with these types of events?" Her work at the CIA was based on analyzing remotely recorded events. Gathering hard facts. She was much more accustomed to… she cringed. Guessing. She acknowledged her guessing was based in those facts, but in her heart Sam knew even with all their remote sensing technology, cyberwarfare expertise, and the knowledge gained from these techniques, no one knew what any country, despot, tyrant, or terrorist; armed with weapons of mass destruction, was going to do or when. They were fooling themselves if they believed otherwise.

Then, she realized something else. Something about herself. She couldn't work alone anymore. It took a team to unravel the motives and actions of the world's crazy. She smiled at the members of her team surrounding her on this warm spring evening, knowing she couldn't have done it without them.

"Statistical approximations for the most part. We look at indirect indicators and define a statistical range of most likely time to occur—could be hours, days, or even years." Sam's eyebrow began to climb upward. "Take the forecast for the next big earthquake in the Pacific Northwest. Our model of timing is based on several imprecise datasets. First, a paleobotanist used tree rings preserved in submerged sequoia trees to approximate the frequency of these nine-plus magnitude events. We added these tree-ring data to the recorded folklore of the local indigenous tribes. Their records of titanic earthshaking give an approximate frequency of recurrence at every three to four hundred years. Currently, this event is past due."

Grant spoke up. "Why would the Navy be interested in a terrestrial event like that?"

"Because of the danger to the major submarine base in the Seattle area. The tsunami created by a 9+ magnitude event would impact the entire Pacific basin. All near-shore bases would be at risk as well as all the ships in port," Cynthia answered, sitting up and dropping her feet to the deck. "The same goes for onshore events."

"Such as?" Sam's curiosity was piqued.

"Here's another example. Take Paektu Mountain in the northern ranges of the Korean Peninsula." This got Sam's full attention. "Over the last few months, we, I mean the USGS, have recorded a series of low-frequency harmonic earthquakes beneath this huge stratovolcano. The Pacific Northwest Seismic Network just posted an eruption alert last week."

Sam's voice grew hard. Anything associated with the Korean Peninsula was critical to know. "And this means what?"

Cynthia hesitated. "This is what I mean about prediction. It could mean something or nothing. I was going to use it in one of my first classes. These same low-frequency harmonic quakes were recorded beneath Mount St. Helens before it erupted in 1980. They routinely occur beneath Kīlauea before an eruption in Hawai'i. If these are recorded, we correlate the occurrence of the low-frequency quakes to possible eruption. We think the earthquakes are created as molten rock moves upward to fill the magma chamber beneath the volcano. Near surface magma would be available to fuel an eruption."

Sam pressed harder. "And...?"

"Paektu Mountain is a stratovolcano, similar to the ones in the Cascade Range of Oregon and Washington. The volcano last erupted in 946. It was one of the most violent eruptions noted in the last five thousand years of human records. When the top of the mountain blew off, ash covered most of the Pacific Region and moved as far east as Greenland. We've found the ash in ice cores there. Enough ash was released into the upper atmosphere that the Earth's temperatures reduced, and crops failed around the globe as noted in regional records. It is one of the geologic events which contributed to the extension of the Dark Ages. The eruption was so violent, city documents in Kyoto, Japan, one thousand kilometers away, recorded the sound of the eruption."

"When?" Sam moved out from beneath Cassie and Maggie.

"That's the problem, Samantha. I can't tell you when. It could be hours, days, weeks, or never. We don't have any monitoring equipment on the mountain which could help with further analysis."

Sam moved toward the house. "Can you get the needed equipment sent to Korea?"

"Of course. It's available in Hawai'i and at various spots on the west coast."

"Get it organized and let me know when you need transportation resources." She stopped at the patio door and turned. "I am calling the president and Doctor Kim."

"But, Samantha, we don't have enough data to determine next steps."

"No, Doctor, what we don't have is time." Sam shook her head. She'd missed the development of North Korean hypersonic cruise missiles, and the *Nimitz* nearly sank with a large loss of life. She wouldn't miss anything again. If she could help it. *The world can't catch a break.*

THE END

AFTERWORD

The characters and storyline in *The Paris Contagion* are fictitious. However, the development, testing, and launching of WMDs (including nuclear, biological, and chemical weapons and warheads) by North Korea are real and have occurred over the last seven years. Actions taken by the current Supreme Leader, including the assassination of his brother in Kuala Lumpur.

The technology and medical information about pandemics are factual. Fort Detrick and DARPA exist and continue to protect us from medical threats. The information about staffing, logistics, and medical capabilities at Amundsen-Scott Base Antarctica are factual.

The author has taken liberties by rearranging the chronology of the real events within North Korea to support the plot of this adventure as well as create a possible viral threat scenario.

The author also took liberties with the names and specifications of the Ticonderoga-class guided missile cruisers. Twenty-seven of these craft were built and commissioned by the US Navy. None were nuclear-powered. The first was CG-47, the *USS Ticonderoga*, which was decommissioned in 2004. The remainder are being decommissioned at this time and will be replaced by the new Flight III Arleigh Burke destroyers. The AEGIS missile systems will continue to be launched from the Arleigh Burke class destroyers. The real *USS Arlington* (LPD-24) is a San Antonio class amphibious transport and continues to proudly serve today. This boat is the third craft to be named after Arlington, Virginia, and was commissioned following the 9/11 attack on the Pentagon.

As the manuscript was in final edits, the world lost Queen Elizabeth II. Without doubt, the Queen will be sorely missed as we struggle to improve the planet for all. Though the monarch of the United Kingdom is not named in this book, actions intimate Queen Elizabeth was still ruling the Commonwealth. The author did not change any of these references in honor of her amazing life and contributions. Our world is a better place due to her leadership and guiding hand.

ABOUT THE AUTHOR

CA grew up amidst the verdant fields of midwestern farm country. From the age of four, she spent summers on an island in Ontario, Canada, and winters among frozen fields. Her grandfather imparted his love for the natural world. CA earned degrees in geology and tectonics. She worked for an international petroleum company for many years and traveled the globe. Now she lives in the Rocky Mountains. Revised editions of the first three books in her Nexus Series will be released by Spectrum Books-London throughout 2026. The fourth Nexus book, *Quantum Time,* will be released by Spectrum January 2027. Book 2 in her geopolitical thriller series, *Deflection*, will be released in 2026. CA tries to balance her passion for long-distance cycling with her love of writing.

ACKNOWLEDGMENTS

The author's heart is her readers. You keep the author energized and motivated. I thank all the readers who embrace the *Nexus Series.* Each and every review is appreciated. This book is not from the *Nexus Series.* I hope you enjoy this new real-life adventure.

The staff at Farallon Group for the hard work in releasing this new edition of *The Paris Contagion.* Thank you for believing in me and this new journey.

Beta-readers Edith and Michaela, thank you for reading the manuscript in its early form and for your European perspective.

Mariann, friend and beta-reader extraordinaire. Thank you for your attention to detail and the time you invested for discussion.

Rachel, graphic designer, you provide a new and heart-stopping picture of the book's premise and a tease to read more.

GLOSSARY

This glossary is provided as a reference for the abbreviations used throughout the story.

ABMD/AEGIS—AEGIS Ballistic Missile Defense System, ship-borne missile defense system

AD—Assistant Director

AN-SPY6—Air and missile defense radar, active electronically scanned array system

CAG—Commander Air Group, Leader of all flight operations on an aircraft carrier

CDC—Centers for Disease Control and Prevention, national public health agency of the USA

CIA—Central Intelligence Agency, foreign intelligence service US government

CIC—Combat Information Center

CO2—Carbon dioxide

COMM—Communication, or communication officer

CPO—Chief Petty Officer, US Navy

CRISPR—Clustered Regularly Interspaced Short Palindromic Repeats, gene editing technique

DARPA—Defense Advanced Research Projects Agency, Research for DOD, US government

DMZ—Demilitarized Zone - border between two factions, e.g. 38th Parallel, Korean Peninsula

DNA—Deoxyribonucleic acid, double helix molecule used by organisms in reproduction

DOD—Department of Defense, US government

DRPK—Democratic People's Republic of Korea (aka North Korea)

ETA—Estimated time of arrival

FM—1933 radio broadcasting system using frequency modulation

GDP—Gross Domestic Product, an economic indicator of a nation's financial viability

GPS—Global positioning system, satellite-based global location system

IAEA—International Atomic Energy Agency, Vienna Austria

ICBM—Intercontinental Ballistic Missile

IRON DOME—An Israeli designed missile defense system used to protect Tel Aviv

IT—Information technology

LAMPS—Light airborne multipurpose system, helicopter-carry

submarine detection system
Li-DAR—Laser detecting and ranging system
MAD—Mutual Assured Destruction, doctrine of military strategy
mRNA—Messenger Ribonucleic Acid, single-stranded RNA molecule
MiG—Russian Mikoyan Aircraft Corporation or any of their fighter aircraft
NASA—National Aeronautics and Space Administration, USA
NBC—Nuclear, biological and chemical weapons
NIAID—National Institute of Allergy and Infectious Disease, Bethesda Maryland, USA
NIH—National Institute of Health, Bethesda, Maryland, USA
NOAA—National Oceanic and Atmospheric Agency - weather analysis for US government
NSF—National Science Foundation, USA
NORAD—North American Aerospace Defense Command, under Cheyenne Mt CO, USA
ORION—Lockheed WP P3 aircraft, used for storm surveillance and weather flights
OS—Operating system
P-wave—Primary or pressure wave recorded in earthquake events
PA—Personal Assistant
RNA—Ribonucleic acid, molecule used by organisms to regulate the expression of genes
RIM-66—Mid-range surface to air missile developed as an anti-ship missile for US Navy
S-wave—Secondary or shear wave recorded in earthquake events
SAM—Surface-to-Air missile
SARS-CoV-2—Severe Acute Respiratory Syndrome, coronavirus 2 – Covid-19 agent
SCUD—Soviet-designed tactical ballistic missile
THAAD—Terminal High Altitude Aerial Defense, land-based system of AEGIS
TLAMS—Tomahawk Land-Attack Missile, long-range subsonic cruise missile
UAV—Unmanned Aerial Vehicle or drone
UDMH—unsymmetrical dimethylhydrazine, a liquid hypergolic rocket fuel
UN—United Nations, headquartered in New York City, New York, USA
USGS—United States Geological Survey
USN—United States Navy
USPACFLT—United States Pacific Fleet - 1 of 7 US naval fleets stationed around the globe
UTC/GMT—Coordinated Universal Time (ZULU), replaced

Greenwich Mean Time in 1967

VECTOR—State Research Center of Virology and Biotechnology, Koltsovo, Russia

VHF—Very high frequency radio transmission system

VTOL—Vertical takeoff and landing aircraft

VX or VX2—Organophosphorus nerve agent developed from pesticide production

WHO—World Health Organization, Geneva, Switzerland

WMD—Weapon of Mass Destruction

YBH—Yreka Blue Horn Mine, CA, seismic monitoring station for underground nuclear tests

XO—Executive officer on naval vessels, second in command of the boat